Free Joe

Free Joe

Stories by
JOEL CHANDLER HARRIS
Selected and introduced by
JOHN TUMLIN

THE BEEHIVE PRESS
Savannah · Georgia

Contents

Introduction

THE MAN who gave the world Uncle Remus has never been so widely known as the character he created. Even at the height of his literary career, the name Joel Chandler Harris was almost synonymous with Uncle Remus. Neither name, in fact, seemed to apply to the shy Georgian known to his friends and his fellow journalists as Joe Harris.

Joe Harris's answer to fame was to court obscurity. He seldom traveled outside his home state, and he managed, by dogged determination, to live out his entire life without making a single public speech. Of all the places on the planet, he vastly preferred to spend his time on Snap-Bean Farm, his West End acreage in Atlanta, a home he dubbed the Sign of the Wren's Nest after two of the tiny birds took up residence in the Harris mailbox.

"An Accidental Author," the title Harris chose for his literary autobiography,[1] perhaps best sums up the man's attitude toward his own career. Certainly plain Joe Harris could hardly have anticipated the widespread recognition that came to him during his lifetime. Such an expectation was inconceivable for a boy from Eatonton, Georgia.

In December 1848, when Harris was born, events were converging to shape the political and literary movements of the second half of the century. The Mexican War had just ended, bringing vast new territories into the possession of the United States. The controversy over the status, free or slave, of these territories had put a growing strain along the political faultline between North and South.

American literature, long dominated by European conventions, was beginning to find its own voice. *The Deerslayer*, last of James Fenimore Cooper's Leatherstocking Tales, had been published seven years earlier. America's literary lion, sixty-five-year-old Washington Irving, in semi-retirement at his New York estate, was still writing profusely. Sailor-turned-author Herman Melville had just finished his third novel, *Mardi*, which marked the beginning of the intensely creative period that would produce *Moby-Dick*. Nathaniel Hawthorne, working temporarily as surveyor of the port of Salem, was already a successful short story writer, but the publication of *The Scarlet Letter* was still two years away. An erratic journalist named Walt Whitman had not yet published any poetry of note; and a fourteen-year-old boy named Samuel Clemens, employed in a Hannibal, Missouri, print shop, had heard many times the riverboat leadman's cry which he would one day make famous.

For Eatonton and its citizens, however, corn and cotton were of more immediate importance. For thirteen years this placid seat of agricultural Putnam County was hometown to freckle-faced, redheaded Joe Harris. Living with his mother, whom his father had deserted when the boy was an infant, Harris grew up with few restraints on his natural ebullience. Shy and inclined to stutter in the presence of strangers, crowds or girls, he was nevertheless a mischievous ringleader of the juvenile practical jokers of the town.

But by his fourteenth year, the boy had grown restless. Perhaps the cause was the war, which had broken out the previous spring; perhaps it was the fact that he himself had small chance of education higher than that he had already received at the academy for boys in Eatonton. Whatever the reason, he wrote a letter of application to Joseph Addison Turner, lawyer, owner of Turnwold Plantation and editor-publisher of *The Countryman*. By spring of 1862, Harris was working as printer's devil on Turner's country newspaper.

Harris's application to Turner was the first important move of his life. Not only did it introduce him to journalism, a profession he was to follow for nearly forty years, but it brought him into intimate daily contact with plantation life. Turnwold showed him the good and the bad aspects of that life and provided him with both the setting and some of the tales for the Uncle Remus books.

Perhaps equally influential at this stage was the plantation's owner. In his autobiographical novel *On the Plantation*, Harris wrote of his first employer, "The editor was a very original writer, and his editorials in The Countryman were quoted in all the papers in the Confederacy, but he was happiest when engaged in a political controversy. . . . Instead of clipping from his exchanges, the editor sent to the offices three books from which extracts could be selected. These books were *Lacon*, Percy's *Anecdotes*, and Rochefoucauld's *Maxims*."[2]

Shortly after coming to work for Turner, Harris began, surreptitiously at first, to contribute humorous pieces to *The Countryman* over the signature "The Countryman's Devil."[3] Soon, however, the editor was serving as literary tutor to the boy, and Harris's own signature appeared on articles and a number of highly romantic poems. Turner also encouraged the young compositor to further his education with books from the well-stocked library at Turnwold.

Harris remained on the staff of *The Countryman* throughout the war. Near the end, Turnwold was occupied briefly by Federal troops. In November 1864, Harris, not quite sixteen, watched a contingent of them sloughing their way south through the mud and hurling taunts and friendly insults at the thin, awkward, redheaded boy who sat on the fence by the road.[4]

The coming of the Federal military authority brought an end to *The Countryman*. Turner suspended publication in the summer of 1865, resumed it again for a few months in 1866, then finally abandoned it.[5]

Harris returned to Eatonton for a short time, but soon accepted a job as typesetter on the Macon *Daily Telegraph*, where the staff promptly nicknamed him "Pink Top."[6] Although Harris's first articles for the *Telegraph* were merely promotional "puffs," he soon graduated to reviewing books and magazines.[7]

But Turner's encouragement had primed the young journalist's literary ambitions. In late 1866 he resigned from the *Telegraph* and went to New Orleans to become private secretary to William Evelyn, editor of the *Crescent Monthly*, a newly established literary magazine. This sojourn lasted only a few months, during which the *Crescent* published no articles with Harris's signature.[8]

Shortly after his return to Georgia in the spring of 1867, Harris joined the staff of the little weekly *Monroe Advertiser* of Forsyth, Georgia. Though he spent three years with the *Advertiser*, he was apparently still dissatisfied with journalism as a literary outlet; for his correspondence during this period with James Wood Davidson, editor of *The Living Writers of The South*, indicates that he hoped to publish an anthology of Southern poets, a project which he never finished.[9] Without his being aware of it, however, his journalistic career was moving him slowly toward literary eminence.

Humorous paragraphs, usually written on minor items of local or national news, were popular in newspapers at the time. A veteran of *The Countryman*, which had as its motto "Brevity is the soul of wit," Harris was particularly good at this kind of writing. As exchange papers began to reprint clippings from the *Advertiser*, Harris's name became known to other editors. Partly as a result of these reprints, the Savannah *Morning News* late in 1870 offered him a position as associate editor.

In Savannah, in addition to his other duties, Harris continued to write humorous paragraphs, now in his own column, at first titled "State Affairs," then "Affairs in Georgia." As did other newspapermen, Harris frequently chose as his target his fellow journalists: "The editor of the Atlanta Constitution asserts he is the owner of four hundred acres of wild land in Florida. An editor that can't tame four hundred acres of land in one season ought to sell it."[10]

As other papers continued to reprint his work, Harris's reputation as a humorist grew among both editors and readers throughout the state. On April 23, 1873, the *Atlanta Constitution*, in a comic biographical sketch of Harris, prefaced the exaggerations with an expression of genuine admiration for the man who had "made his paper—the Savannah News—noted for the sparkle of its Georgia column."[11]

Just a few days before the *Constitution* article appeared, another important event occurred in Harris's life—his marriage to Esther LaRose, an eighteen-year-old Catholic girl of French Canadian descent. Harris had met her while he was a boarder at the Florida House in Savannah, where she lived with her parents. This pretty, rather delicate-looking young woman seemed to fill a need in the other, hidden side of Harris's nature, the side that revealed itself in his stutter, his shyness before crowds and his fear of strangers.

Harris's departure from Savannah was as involuntary as his departure from Turnwold. An epidemic of yellow fever broke out in the late summer of 1876. Fearing for the safety of his wife and their two sons, Julian and Lucien, the young editor took his family north to Atlanta.

According to one account, Harris, upon his arrival from Savannah, signed the register at the Kimball Hotel, "J. C. Harris, one wife, two bowlegged children, and a bilious nurse."[12] The *Constitution*, on September 14, carried an announcement of the arrival in much the same terms, a tribute to Harris somewhat marred by the fact that it referred to Julian and Lucien as his "two daughters."[13]

The Joe Harris who had gone to Savannah a thin gawky youth of twenty-one came to Atlanta the heavyset family man whom the nation and later the world would come to know as Joel Chandler Harris. Still inclined to be sensitive and shy in person, he had established his reputation and ability as a journalist in the eyes of his peers.

In need of temporary work to support his family, Harris joined the staff of the *Constitution* in October. As his stay in Atlanta became permanent, so did his association with the newspaper; and in November both he and Henry W. Grady became associate editors under Evan P. Howell, editor-in-chief. Harris already had a column much like the one he had written for the *News*. Called "Roundabout in Georgia," it shared the third page of the four-page daily with advertisements for real estate, whiskey, quack nostrums, coffin-makers and sundry professional services.

Harris's position with the *Constitution* established him firmly in Atlanta and provided sufficient income for his growing family. With the arrival of his mother in early 1877 and with the move, in the late summer of 1881, to the house in West End, life settled into a comfortable routine. Harris left each morning by mule-drawn streetcar for the *Constitution* offices, where he worked from nine to noon. After lunch and a short nap at home, he returned to the offices for a few hours' work. In the evenings he wrote his stories, either in his bedroom or by the sitting room fireplace.[14] It was a comfortable routine for Joe Harris, the journalist in Atlanta, but Joel Chandler Harris, the American author, was making himself heard around the country.

Harris had begun to write dialect sketches for the *Constitution* when he first joined the staff. Uncle Remus made his appearance shortly thereafter as a humble philosopher commenting on the current Atlanta scene. But not until July 20, 1879, on the editorial page, under the heading "Negro Folk Lore," did "The Story of Mr. Rabbit and Mr. Fox," the first of the tales, appear.[15]

The Uncle Remus tales, which continued intermittently in the *Constitution*, were an immediate success with both readers and editors. The influential *New York Evening Post* and other newspapers all over the country began to reprint them. For the first time Harris was reaching a national audience.

In December 1880, less than eighteen months after the first tale appeared, D. Appleton and Company issued *Uncle Remus: His Songs and His Sayings*, containing thirty-four tales, some of which were being published for the first time. In addition to the tales, the little book also included nine songs; twenty-one sketches, somewhat revised from their first appearance in the newspaper; and a series of such "Plantation Proverbs" as "Ole man Know-All died las' year" and "Troubles is seasonin'. 'Simmons ain't good twel dey 'er fros'-bit."

If the reception of the Uncle Remus stories by newspapers around the country had surprised their modest author, the aftermath of the book must have astonished him. He was deluged with letters, not only from all parts of the United States, but from other parts of the world. Many wrote simply to express their appreciation; others sent tales of a similar nature which they themselves had heard. But the letters which caused Harris the most acute embarrassment began arriving even before the publication of the book—letters from such eminent ethnologists as John Wesley Powell, explorer of the Grand Canyon. These learned men proclaimed Harris an expert on the folklore of the American Negro and bombarded him with questions which neither he nor anyone else could answer. Like it or not, Joe Harris, the "cornfield journalist" as he was fond of calling himself, was a national celebrity and a folklorist of established reputation.

Uncle Remus also brought Harris to the attention of Mark Twain, who had by this time settled in Hartford, Connecticut. Shortly after the publication of the first book of tales, Twain initiated a correspondence with Harris which culminated in plans for a potentially lucrative joint lecture tour. Although the idea of appearing before the public terrified Harris, the prospect of earning enough money to "drop this grinding newspaper business and write some books I have in mind" appealed strongly to him.[16] He agreed to meet Twain and George Washington Cable in New Orleans in May 1882; but the trip, during which Harris proved too shy to read his stories even to a roomful of children, convinced both Harris and Twain that the prospective tour was a pipe dream.

One of the reasons for Harris's desire to drop the newspaper "grind" for a more formal literary career was that magazines such as *Century* and *The Critic* had begun to print his new series of Uncle Remus tales. Although he grew interested in folklore, Harris never considered these tales to be literature in the sense that he understood the word. His goal was still the "serious literature" he mentioned in his letter to Twain.

The Uncle Remus tales had taught Harris that his own early experiences in the Middle Georgia communities—in Eatonton before the war, at Turnwold, and in Forsyth and Macon during the Reconstruction—were rich sources of material. Snatching time from his newspaper work, he began to work on pieces of short fiction. The first of these "serious" stories, "Mingo," was printed in *Harper's Magazine* near the end of 1882. *Mingo and Other Sketches in Black and White*, a collection of four stories, was published in 1884.

The 1880's firmly established Harris's literary reputation. He found himself in written communication not only with Mark Twain, but with other noted authors, including Rudyard Kipling, with whom he shared some thoughts on folklore. His firmest friendship, however, was with the Hoosier poet James Whitcomb Riley. Harris and Riley carried on a warm personal correspondence for nearly twenty years before they finally met in 1900.

Harris's new-found fame also brought him a great deal of attention from fellow journalists—some of it unwelcome. The inveterate practical joker Eugene Field wrote several bogus biographical sketches in which he described Harris as a self-made millionaire-philanthropist born under humble circumstances in the wilds of Africa. Field's victim never took offense at such jokes, but he was painfully sensitive to them, especially when some members of the public believed Field's concoctions.

Although Harris had become a recognized literary figure, he himself was never comfortable with his reputation. He spoke, half-jesting, of the "other fellow" within him who was responsible for his literary works: "He is a creature hard to understand, but, so far as I can understand him, he is a very sour surly fellow until I give him an opportunity to guide my pen in subjects congenial to him; whereas I am, as you know, jolly, goodnatured, and entirely harmless."[17]

This contrast between the inner man and the outer expressed itself in many ways, but it is perhaps most strikingly evident in the questionnaire he filled out for *The Critic*. His favorite book he listed as Oliver Goldsmith's sentimental *The Vicar of Wakefield*, but his favorite play was Shakespeare's unrelieved tragedy, *King Lear*.[18]

As his reputation brought greater pressures for public appearance, Harris's life seemed to grow more sequestered. He continued his newspaper work through the last decade of the century, but his attention centered more and more around his home and his literary work. In good weather, accompanied by his ever-present black felt hat and an enameled cuspidor, he did his writing on the west end of his front porch.

Despite the demands of his professional writing, Harris also found time to keep in close touch with his expanding family. Although three of his children had died in infancy, his surviving offspring now numbered six, the youngest, Joel Chandler Harris, Jr., having been born in 1888. The first grandchild, Lucien's son Stewart, arrived in 1896.

The 1890's were the period of Harris's greatest literary output. In addition to several volumes of stories for children, he produced another lengthy collection of Uncle Remus tales, two novels and three volumes of short stories.

During this period Harris also discovered his ideal illustrator—Arthur Burdette Frost. Frost and Harris had met in 1886, and the work of the two men was united in 1892 with the publication of *Uncle Remus and His Friends*. The fifteenth anniversary edition of *Uncle Remus: His Songs and His Sayings* was dedicated to Frost, whose illustrations replaced those of Frederick S. Church and J. H. Moser. Thereafter Frost remained Harris's favorite and favored illustrator.

Late in 1900, still chafing to devote his writing energies exclusively to literary pursuits, Harris completed an agreement with McClure Phillips Company for a fixed annual salary in exchange for his literary output during the term of the contract. In the same year, Harris submitted his resignation to the *Constitution* and retired to Snap-Bean Farm and his writing.

The following years should have been the happiest and most productive of Harris's life. He was in his early fifties; he had an assured income; and his stories were known all over the world. In 1902, President Theodore Roosevelt, a long-time admirer, singled out Harris's stories for their contribution toward reuniting the country; and in 1907 the author was invited to dine at the White House.

Nevertheless, illness and tragedy dogged him throughout these last years. The winter after his resignation from the *Constitution*, he was ill with a severe case of grippe; and during the spring of the following year he contracted septicemia. Harris never recovered full strength after these illnesses; and although he continued to write steadily, he decided in 1903 not to renew his annual-salary contract with McClure Phillips Company because the obligation to produce a certain quantity of writing had become burdensome.[19]

These years also marked the deaths of two of Harris's grandchildren, Charles and Pierre, both sons of Julian. The impact of this tragedy, coming almost immediately after the death of Esther's mother, Mrs. LaRose, caused the family to draw together even more. Julian, who was then night editor of the *Constitution*, decided to resign his position in order to be with his wife, Julia.[20] Indirectly, this decision gave rise to Harris's last major literary project.

At Julian's urging, Harris undertook in 1905 to realize his long-delayed dream of editing a Southern literary magazine. The Sunny South Publishing Company was soon founded by Joel Chandler Harris, Julian LaRose Harris and Roby Anderson, vice-president and business manager of the *Constitution*. The two younger partners persuaded the somewhat reluctant elder Harris to call the new publication *Uncle Remus's Magazine* in order to capitalize on the name of the character, who by this time far overshadowed his creator. Finally, in July 1907, after many problems and delays, the first issue of the new magazine appeared.

Despite the unpromising appearance of the first issue and the publication's difficulty in consistently obtaining contributions from good writers, *Uncle*

Remus's Magazine improved and even began to prosper. Among its contributors were Harris's old friend James Whitcomb Riley, the illustrator J. M. Conde, and staff member Don Marquis, later the creator of Archy and Mehitabel. Harris himself, in addition to serving as editor, wrote essays and stories for his new charge. Under the name Anne McFarland, supposedly a Georgian living in England, he also contributed views and reviews of writers and books.

But the strain of founding the new magazine had broken Harris's already fragile health. During the spring of 1908, his energy began to wane. When the condition was diagnosed as cirrhosis of the liver, Harris consented to surgery, but the operation produced only a brief rally. Shortly thereafter he asked for and received baptism in the Catholic faith, a step he had been considering for more than ten years.[21] A few days later, on July 3, 1908, in the early evening, he died peacefully at the Sign of the Wren's Nest.

ALTHOUGH Joel Chandler Harris will always be best known as the creator of Uncle Remus, he also created a fairly sizable body of what he considered "serious" literature. Had Uncle Remus never appeared on the printed page, some of these other stories might well have been sufficient to earn Harris a place in American literary history as a local colorist with strong artistic leanings toward the school of Naturalism.

Certainly Harris set forth an ambitious literary credo in "Literature in the South," written as he was venturing into "serious" fiction. In this essay, he noted, "The very spice and flavor of all literature—the very marrow and essence of all literary art—is its localism. No literary artist can lack for materials in this section. They are here all around him, untouched, undeveloped and undisturbed; unique and original; as new as the world; as old as life; as fair as flowers; as beautiful as the dreams of genius. But they must be mined."[22]

From his own mining of these materials, Harris produced stories uniquely Georgian, presenting the people and the ways of his native state to the nation in magazines with wide circulation. But when he wrote, he was careful to distinguish between the flavor of what he called localism, or "provinciality,"[23] and the killing taint of sectionalism.

The dangers of sectionalism are his major concern in "Literature in the

South." He believed that "literature in America must be truly American in its broadest sense" and that the failure to recognize this fact had "smothered literary effort in the South for generations."

Harris's essay further details exactly what this sectionalism was. And as Mark Twain did, he reserved his most withering remarks for the pretentious romanticism fostered by that sectionalism:

In short we have gushed until the general effect of so much gush has reacted upon us. We are asked to support southern newspapers because they are representative of southern literature, and we are asked to buy books for the same reason. Our poets are all southern poets and our novelists—such as we have—are all southern novelists. Does a publisher fill a paper full of trash from the composition books of romantic school-girls? We must all applaud and buy for the benefit of southern literature. Does Miss Sweetie Wildwood get together a lot of sickening doggerel? The newspapers must gush over the gush, not only for the purpose of building up southern literature, but because Miss Sweetie is a daughter of Colonel Wildwood. What is the result? Why simply this, that the stuff we are in the habit of calling southern literature is not only a burlesque upon true literary art, but a humiliation and a disgrace to the people whose culture it is supposed to represent.

In raising this standard, Harris had declared his intention of creating a literature that was truly Georgian and therefore "necessarily American." Within the limits of his abilities, he adhered to this basic doctrine throughout his career. His best stories show the validity of his principles, and even his poorer ones evince a peculiar integrity.

True to his belief in "localism," Harris drew upon the region and period with which he was most familiar. But while his stories almost never venture outside the boundaries of his home state, he wrote with a national audience in mind. Thus he was able to combine the sensitivity of a native Georgian with the broader awareness of an American.

Although he was not primarily a historian, Harris did write a history of Georgia, and he was acutely conscious of the impact of the war and its aftermath upon life in the South. He himself had only a brief brush with the actual war, when Union troops occupied Turnwold Plantation. His sensitivity to the change can be attributed to the fact that he observed only the secondary effects, those which altered the day-to-day lives of Georgia's people.

Certainly the effects were profound. The plantation, with very few exceptions, disappeared altogether. The freeing of the slaves wiped out a large capital investment in human flesh, and economic depression gripped the whole South. Much of the land had sustained severe ecological damage, either from poor management or from the ravages of war. Some plantations were split up and sold; others fell into the hands of their former overseers. The sharecropping system, which came to replace slavery, reduced many whites and blacks to virtual serfdom. Although the agrarian life continued important, Georgia was, within a few years after Reconstruction, well on its way to industrialization, a movement strongly promoted by Harris's fellow *Constitution* editor Henry W. Grady.

Harris lived most of his adult life in Atlanta, the thriving center of this new life. In many ways he helped to foster the cosmopolitan atmosphere necessary to such enterprise. Still, he seems to have distrusted the values of the new age, and he was never its chronicler. Instead, his Georgia tales deal with the times before, during, and just after the war.

Harris's determination to be more than a "southern" writer prevented him from pandering to local popular taste and thus becoming just another apologist. True, the expected tributes to the old South are here—the pleasant, slow-paced life on the antebellum plantation, the proud old family ruined by the war, the stereotype of a faintly ridiculous black legislator of Reconstruction days, the staunch aristocratic defender of the defenseless black, and the ex-slaves who remain faithful to their former masters. But mixed with these features are disturbingly antithetical elements—the strange power that the slave Balaam seems to have over his young master, the apparently conscience-driven fear engendered in the white community by the fugitive Blue Dave, the sometimes regal fury of Aunt Minervy Ann.

The reason for this mixture seems to be the conflicting emotions aroused in Harris by slavery. On the one hand, he clung to memories of the harmonious life at Turnwold, where slaves were humanely treated; on the other, he was beset by a conscience which rejected the traffic in human beings and its attendant evils. It was perhaps this ambivalence which led to "Daddy Jake, the Runaway," certainly not his best story, but still a unique *tour de force* which shows both sides of Harris's attitude toward slavery.

Probably only Harris, who had spread, however temporarily, the native literature of Georgia across a large part of the world, could have had this story accepted in the South. The framework is a simple sentimental children's tale, one which might have come right out of his Mr. Thimblefinger books. A lovable elderly slave runs away after striking back at a cruel overseer. The master's two children follow, a tearful reunion takes place, and Daddy Jake returns to the plantation. There is even an animal tale told in dialect by a fugitive slave named Crazy Sue. Seldom has the basic framework of a story been better designed to appeal to the widest popular audience in the South.

Within this framework, however, Harris hangs elements so inappropriate to a sentimental children's story that many white parents must have censored it. But to censor it, they must first have read it, and what they read must have disturbed even the least sensitive of them.

For here the kindly plantation owner's slaves privately discuss his blindness to the abuses which slaves of other owners suffer. Here the faithful blacks keep from the whites the secret of a fugitive slave colony in the canebrake. And here is the story, likely to give any child nightmares, of the starving of Crazy Sue's babies by her callous owner.

Harris's awareness of this grim, often brutal side of slavery counter-balanced his fond memories of Turnwold and its owner, J. A. Turner. While he loved the close community and leisurely agrarian way of life made possible by slavery, Harris had no love for the peculiar institution itself. He welcomed emancipation and felt that many of the difficulties that followed could be attributed to the ungrounded fears of white citizens. In his semi-autobiographical novel *Gabriel Tolliver,* his young hero watches the aim-lessly moving bands of the newly freed, a daily sight in the months immedi-ately following the war:

He thought that the restless and uneasy movements of the negroes were perfectly natural. They had suddenly come to the knowledge that they were free, and they were testing the nature and limits of their freedom. They desired to find out its length and its breadth. So much was clear to Gabriel but it was not clear to his elders. And what a pity that it was not! How many mistakes would have been avoided! What a dreadful tangle and turmoil would have been prevented if these grown children could have been judged from Gabriel's point of view![24]

The strength of Harris's writing, however, lies not in his views on race relations and historical causes but in his ability to create characters and to dramatize. Further, he sought in his local material those human universals of which true literature is made.

Harris's stories are replete with such fully realized individuals as Major Perdue, Uncle Billy Sanders, and African Jack, but his two strongest char-acterizations are those of Uncle Remus and Aunt Minervy Ann, both superb raconteurs. In fact, it was probably the author's admiration of narrative ability which led him to spend so much time upon portraits of these story-tellers.

Uncle Remus himself is so strongly identified with the familiar role of the teller of animal tales that it may be difficult to keep in mind that Harris wrote of him in other contexts. Reading "A Story of the War" may help redress the balance. The old man's recollection of his ax-bearing confrontation with two Union soldiers adds a dimension not readily apparent in his sessions with the little boy.

In Aunt Minervy Ann, Harris suggests the undefeatable dignity of African royalty. The granddaughter of an African prince, her strength gives a regal bearing to otherwise humble acts. Further, of all Harris's other characters, none comes closer to the narrative power of Uncle Remus than does Aunt Minervy Ann. Listening with awed attention to her story of "How Aunt Minervy Ann Frailed the Gossett Boys," the narrator of *The Chronicles of Aunt Minervy Ann* remarks:

Once more Aunt Minervy Ann brought the whole scene mysteriously before me. Her eyes gleamed ferociously, her body swayed, and her outstretched arm trembled with the emotion she had resummoned from the past. We were on the spot. The red hill-side, the hedges of Cherokee roses, Major Perdue grim and erect, Sam Gossett struggling to his feet, John Henry wiping his beaten face, Rube astounded at the unwonted violence of a negro woman, the buggy swerved to one side by the horse searching for grass—all these things came into view and slowly faded away.

What Harris admired in Aunt Minervy Ann's storytelling was that for which he himself strove—the resummoning of the past through dramatic action and vivid detail. Despite a strong streak of sentimentality which mars even his best work, he was able to objectify his material in strong dramatic scenes. The balancing effect of this talent is particularly evident in "The Colonel's 'Nigger Dog.' " Only Harris's ability to dramatize the ending, to keep the Colonel in character and to reveal his feelings only through dialogue and keenly observed detail, prevents the story from degenerating into bathos.

Though his fiction is undeniably Georgian, Harris went beyond pure local storytelling. Even in stories which appear to be completely sectional, his theme is usually broader than it first seems. In a casual reading, "Blue Dave" is merely an apology for slavery, the story of a fugitive black who returns, under bettered conditions, to bondage. If Harris conveniently ignores the possibility of flight to the North, he nevertheless centers his attention on a man's need to live among his fellows rather than apart. Blue Dave's triumph is that he returns to the society of men. And if he returns as a slave, he has still chosen his own master; the validity of his grievance remains unquestioned.

The theme of human isolation is strong in Harris's best stories. It constitutes the best evidence that his dogged optimism may have hidden a deeply entrenched pessimism verging on despair. It is as though at some time in his life he had opened a door and caught a brief glimpse of inhuman cold and dark. Although he closed that door almost immediately, the seal had been broken and the cold seeped in around the edges and found its way into his writing.

In "Free Joe and the Rest of the World," a story which many consider his best, this isolation is examined. For his main character, Harris chose perhaps the most outcast of all human beings, the free Negro in the antebellum South, a man who, as Leroi Jones puts it, could never be anything but an "ex-slave".[25] Looked upon with suspicion by most whites, Joe is bound to stay where he is because his wife is still a slave. His condition is ameliorated only by the Staleys, sympathetic and helpful poor whites.

In "Free Joe," the main character is not only a naturalistic facsimile of a freed slave of limited intelligence, but a kind of Everyman, "a black atom, drifting hither and thither without an owner, blown about by the winds of circumstance. . . ." Against the unfeeling cosmos in which Free Joe is adrift, Harris posits human charity in its broadest sense. But despite the meagre and somewhat eccentric charity of the Staleys, the general distrust of Free Joe by the citizens of Hillsborough and the vindictive cruelty of Calderwood, owner of Joe's wife, bring the story to a tragic conclusion.

The dominance of the tragic element and the scarcity of charity in "Free Joe" are not typical of Harris's Georgia tales, however. In general, his townspeople of Middle Georgia are generous and humane. The most consistent repository of the charity which Harris seems to have valued so highly is his black characters, a fact which prevents many of them from attaining the stature of Uncle Remus and Aunt Minervy Ann. One exception is Qua, a character based upon a half-legendary African prince who was brought as a slave to Georgia and who took part in the American Revolution. It was perhaps Qua's cheerfully murderous disposition which caused Harris to abandon *Qua: A Romance of the Revolution*, the novel which he began around the year 1900.[26]

Besides his gift for creating characters, his ability to dramatize, and the universality of some of his themes, Harris's short stories also reveal an astonishing range. Not only was he capable of writing sentimental children's stories; he could write "Where's Duncan?," an uncharacteristic horror tale which presages, in its limited point of view and its atmosphere of tragically inevitable violence, the works of William Faulkner.

Wisely, however, Harris usually avoided extremes and worked within the narrower band defined by the Uncle Remus stories at one end and "Free Joe" at the other. Within this range his writing flourished. Although he shared some of the prejudices of his time and his region, he was also determined and energetic enough to avoid the uncritical sloth of sectionalism and postwar bitterness. As a local writer dealing with the materials offered by his home state, he showed himself a competent and sympathetic author of truly American fiction.

NOTES

1. "An Accidental Author," *Lippincott's Monthly Magazine*, 37 (April 1886), 417–420.

2. *On the Plantation: A Story of a Georgia Boy's Adventures during the War* (1892; rpt. New York: D. Appleton and Company, 1926), p. 22.

3. *On the Plantation*, p. 48.

4. *On the Plantation*, pp. 227–229.

5. Paul M. Cousins, *Joel Chandler Harris: A Biography* (Baton Rouge: Louisiana State Univ. Press, 1968), p. 60.

6. Julia Collier Harris, *The Life and Letters of Joel Chandler Harris* (Boston: Houghton, Mifflin Company, 1918), p. 57.

7. Cousins, p. 72.

8. Cousins, pp. 74–75.

9. Thomas H. English, "Joel Chandler Harris's Earliest Literary Project," *Emory University Quarterly*, 2 (October 1946), 176–185.

10. As quoted in *The Life and Letters*, p. 96.

11. "An Illustrated Biographical Sketch of One of Georgia's Funny Men," *Atlanta Constitution*, 23 April 1873, p. 3, col. 1.

12. *The Life and Letters*, p. 128.

13. "Town Topics," *Atlanta Constitution*, 14 September 1876, p. 4, col. 2.

14. *The Life and Letters*, pp. 175–177.

15. "Negro Folklore: The Story of Mr. Rabbit and Mr. Fox as Told by Uncle Remus," *Atlanta Constitution*, 20 July 1879, p. 2, col. 4.

16. Joel Chandler Harris to Mark Twain, as quoted in *The Life and Letters*, pp. 170–171.

17. Joel Chandler Harris to Mildred Harris, as quoted in *The Life and Letters*, p. 385.

18. As reproduced in *The Life and Letters*, facing p. 568.

19. *The Life and Letters*, p. 483.

20. *The Life and Letters*, p. 518.

21. *The Life and Letters*, p. 581.

22. *Atlanta Constitution*, 30 November 1879, p. 2, cols. 2–3.

23. Joel Chandler Harris, "Provinciality in Literature—A Defense of Boston," *Atlanta Constitution*, 29 January 1880, p. 2, cols. 2–3.

24. *Gabriel Tolliver: A Story of Reconstruction* (New York: McClure, Phillips and Company, 1902), p. 114.

25. *Blues People: Negro Music in White America* (New York: William Morrow and Company, 1963), p. 4.

26. Thomas H. English, Introduction, *Qua: A Romance of the Revolution* (Atlanta: Emory University, 1948), p. 6. The conjecture about Harris's motives for abandoning *Qua* is my own; Professor English suggests that Harris simply "grew tired of a task that was uncongenial to him" (p. 11).

Free Joe

Where's Duncan?

Now, DO YOU KNOW you young people are mighty queer? Somebody has told you that he heard old man Isaiah Winchell a-gabbling about old times, and here you come fishing for what you call a story. Why, bless your soul, man, it is no story at all, just a happening, as my wife used to say. If you want me to tell what there is of it, there must be some understanding about it. You know what ought to be put in print and what ought to be left out. I would know myself, I reckon, if I stopped to think it all over; but there's the trouble. When I get started, I just rattle along like a runaway horse. I'm all motion and no sense, and there's no stopping me until I run over a stump or up against a fence. And if I tried to write it out, it would be pretty much the same. When I take a pen in my hand my mind takes all sorts of uncertain flights, like a pigeon with a hawk after it.

As to the affair you were speaking of, there's not much to tell, but it has pestered me at times when I ought to have been in my bed and sound asleep. I have told it a thousand times, and the rest of the Winchells have told it, thinking it was a very good thing to have in the family. It has been exaggerated, too; but if I can carry the facts to your ear just as they are in my mind, I shall be glad, for I want to get everything straight from the beginning.

Well, it was in 1826. That seems a long time ago to you, but it is no longer than yesterday to me. I was eighteen years old, and a right smart chunk of a boy for my age. While we were ginning and packing cotton our overseer left us, and my father turned the whole business over to me. Now, you may think that was a small thing, because this railroad business has turned your head, but, as a matter of fact, it was a very big thing. It fell to me to superintend the ginning and the packing of the cotton, and then I was to go to Augusta in charge of two wagons. I never worked harder before nor since. You see we had no packing-screws nor cotton-presses in those days. The

1

planter that was able to afford it had his gin, and the cotton was packed in round bales by a nigger who used something like a crowbar to do the packing. He trampled the lint cotton with his feet, and beat it down with his iron bar until the bagging was full, and then the bale weighed about three hundred pounds. Naturally you laugh at this sort of thing, but it was no laughing matter; it was hard work.

Well, when we got the cotton all prepared, we loaded the wagons and started for Augusta. We hadn't got more than two miles from home, before I found that Crooked-leg Jake, my best driver, was drunk. He was beastly drunk. Where he got his dram, I couldn't tell you to save my life, for it was against the law in those days to sell whiskey to a nigger. But Crooked-leg Jake had it and he was full of it, and he had to be pulled off of the mule and sent to roost on top of the cotton-bags. It was not a very warm roost either, but it was warm enough for a nigger full of whiskey.

This was not a good thing for me at all, but I had to make the best of it. Moreover, I had to do what I had never done before—I had to drive six mules, and there was only one rein to drive them with. This was the fashion, but it was a very difficult matter for a youngster to get the hang of it. You jerk, jerk, jerked, if you wanted the lead mule to turn to the right, and you pull, pull, pulled if you wanted her to go the left. While we were going on in this way, with a stubborn mule at the wheel and a drunken nigger on the wagon, suddenly there came out of the woods a thick-set, dark-featured, black-bearded man with a bag slung scross his shoulder.

"Hello!" says he; "you must be a new hand."

"It would take a very old hand," said I, "to train a team of mules to meet you in the road."

"Now, there you have me," said he; and he laughed as if he were enjoying a very good joke.

"Who hitched up your team?" he asked.

"That drunken nigger," said I.

"To be sure," said he; "I might have known it. The lead-mule is on the off side."

"Why, how do you know that?" I asked.

"My two eyes tell me," he replied; "they are pulling crossways." And with that, without asking anybody's permission, he unhitched the traces, unbuckled the reins and changed the places of the two front mules. It was all done in a jiffy, and in such a light-hearted manner that no protest could be made; and, indeed, no protest was necessary, for the moment the team

2

started I could see that the stranger was right. There was no more jerking and whipping to be done. We went on in this way for a mile or more, when suddenly I thought to ask the stranger, who was trudging along good-humoredly by the side of the wagon, if he would like to ride. He laughed and said he wouldn't mind it if I would let him straddle the saddle-mule; and for my part I had no objections.

So I crawled up on the cotton and lay there with Crooked-leg Jake. I had been there only a short time when the nigger awoke and saw me. He looked scared.

"Who dat drivin' dem mules, Marse Isaiah?" he asked.

"I couldn't tell you even if you were sober," said I. "The lead-mule was hitched on the off-side, and the man that is driving rushed out of the woods, fixed her right, and since then we have been making good time."

"Is he a sho' 'nuff w'ite man, Marse Isaiah?" asked Jake.

"Well, he looks like he is," said I; "but I'm not certain about that."

With that Jake crawled to the front of the wagon, and looked over at the driver. After a while he came crawling back.

"Tell me what you saw," said I.

"Well, sir," said he, "I dunner whe'er dat man's a w'ite man or not, but he's a-settin' sideways on dat saddle-mule, en every time he chirps, dat lead-mule know what he talkin' about. Yasser. She do dat. Did you say he come outen de woods?"

"I don't know where he came from," said I. "He's there, and he's driving the mules."

"Yasser. Dat's so. He's dar sho', kaze I seed 'im wid my own eyes. He look like he made outen flesh en blood, en yit he mought be a ha'nt; dey ain't no tellin'. Dem dar mules is gwine on mos' too slick fer ter suit me."

Well, the upshot of it was that the stranger continued to drive. He made himself useful during the day, and when night came, he made himself musical; for in the pack slung across his back was a fiddle, and in the manipulation of this instrument he showed a power and a mastery which are given to few men to possess. I doubt whether he would have made much of a show on the stage, but I have heard some of your modern players, and none of them could approach him, according to my taste. I'll tell you why. They all seem to play the music for the music itself, but this man played it for the sake of what it reminded him of. I remember that when he took out his fiddle at night, as he invariably did if nobody asked him to, I used to shut my eyes and dream dreams that I have never dreamed since, and see visions that are given

3

to few men to see. If I were younger I could describe it to you, but an old man like me is not apt at such descriptions.

We journeyed on, and, as we journeyed, we were joined by other wagons hauling cotton, until, at last, there was quite a caravan of them—twenty, at least, and possibly more. This made matters very lively, as you may suppose, especially at night, when we went into camp. Then there were scenes such as have never been described in any of the books that profess to tell about life in the South before the war. After the teams had been fed and supper cooked, the niggers would sing, dance and wrestle, and the white men would gather to egg them on, or sit by their fires and tell stories or play cards. Sometimes there would be a fight, and that was exciting; for in those days, the shotgun was mighty handy and the dirk was usually within reach. In fact, there was every amusement that such a crowd of people could manage to squeeze out of such an occasion. In our caravan there were more than a dozen fiddlers, white and black, but not one of them that attracted as much attention as the stranger who drove my team. When he was in the humor he could entrance the whole camp; but it was not often that he would play, and it frequently happened that he and I would go to bed under our wagon while the rest of the teamsters were frolicking. I had discovered that he was a good man to have along. He knew just how to handle the mules, he knew all the roads, he knew just where to camp, and he knew how to keep Crooked-leg Jake sober. One night after we had gone to bed he raised himself on his elbow and said:

"To-morrow night, if I make no mistake, we will camp within a few miles of the Sandhills. There my journey ends, and yet you have never asked me my name."

"Well," said I, "you are a much older man than I am, and I had a notion that if you wanted me to know your name you would tell me. I had no more reason for asking it than you have for hiding it."

He lay over on his back and laughed.

"You'll find out better than that when you are older," he said, and then he continued laughing—though whether it was what I said or his own thoughts that tickled him, I had no means of knowing.

"Well," he went on, after a while, "you are as clever a youngster as ever I met, and I've nothing to hide from you. My name is Willis Featherstone, and I am simply a vagabond, else you would never have seen me trudging along the public road with only a fiddle at my back; but I have a rich daddy hereabouts, and I'm on my way to see how he is getting along. Now," he con-

4

tinued, "I'll give you a riddle. If you can't unriddle it, it will unriddle itself. A father had a son. He sent him to school in Augusta, until he was fifteen. By that time, the father grew to hate the son, and one day, in a fit of anger, sold him to a nigger speculator."

"How could that be?" I asked.

"That is a part of the riddle," said he.

"Are you the son?"

"That is another part of the same riddle."

"Where was the son's mother?" I asked.

"In the riddle—in the riddle," he replied.

I could not unriddle the riddle, but it seemed to hint at some such villainy as I had read about in the books in my father's library. Here was a man who had sold his son; that was enough for me. It gave me matter to dream on, and as I was a pretty heavy feeder in those days, my dreams followed hard on each other. But it isn't worth while to relate them here, for the things that actually happened were infinitely worse than any dream could be.

As Featherstone had foretold, we camped the next night not far from the Sandhills, where the rich people of Augusta went every summer to escape the heat and malaria of the city. We might have gone on and reached Augusta during the night, but both men and mules were tired, and of the entire caravan only one wagon went forward. I shall remember the place as long as I live. In a little hollow, surrounded by live-oaks—we call them water-oaks up here—was a very bold spring, and around and about was plenty of grass for the mules. It was somewhat dry, the time being November, but it made excellent forage. On a little hill beyond the spring was a dwelling-house. I came to have a pretty good view of it afterward, but in the twilight it seemed to be a very substantial building. It was painted white and had green blinds, and it sat in the midst of a beautiful grove of magnolias and cedars. I remember, too,—it is all impressed on my mind so vividly—that the avenue leading to the house was lined on each side with Lombardy poplars, and their spindling trunks stood clearly out against the sky.

While I was helping Featherstone unhitch and unharness the mules, he suddenly remarked:

"That's the place."

"What place?" I asked.

"The place the riddle tells about—where the son was sold by his father."

"Well," said I, by way of saying something, "what can't be cured must be endured."

5

"You are a very clever chap," he said, after a while. "In fact you are the best chap I have seen for many a long day, and I like you. I've watched you like a hawk, and I know you have a mother at home."

"Yes," said I, "and she's the dearest old mother you ever saw. I wish you knew her."

He came up to me, laid his hand on my shoulder, and looked into my face with an air I can never forget.

"That is the trouble," said he; "I don't know her. If I did I would be a better man. I never had much of a mother."

With that he turned away, and soon I heard him singing softly to himself as he mended a piece of the harness. All this time Crooked-leg Jake was cooking our supper beneath the live-oak trees. Other teamsters were doing the same, so that there were two dozen camp-fires burning brightly within an area of not more than a quarter of a mile. The weather was pleasant, too, and the whole scene struck me as particularly lively.

Crooked-leg Jake was always free-handed with his cooking. He went at it with a zest born of his own insatiate appetite, and it was not long before we were through with it; and while the other campers were fuming and stewing over their cooking, Jake was sitting by the fire nodding, and Featherstone was playing his fiddle. He never played it better than he did that night, and he played it a long time, while I sat listening. Meanwhile quite a number of the teamsters gathered around, some reclining in the leaves smoking their pipes, and others standing around in various positions. Suddenly I discovered that Featherstone had a new and an unexpected auditor. Just how I discovered this I do not know; it must have been proned in upon me, as the niggers say. I observed that he gripped the neck of his fiddle a little tighter, and suddenly he swung off from "Money-musk" into one of those queer serenades which you have heard now and again on the plantation. Where the niggers ever picked up such tunes the Lord only knows, but they are heart-breaking ones.

Following the glance of Featherstone's eyes, I looked around, and I saw, standing within the circle of teamsters, a tall mulatto woman. She was a striking figure as she stood there gazing with all her eyes, and listening with all her ears. Her hair was black and straight as that of an Indian, her cheeks were sunken, and there was that in her countenance that gave her a wolfish aspect. As she stood there rubbing her skinny hands together and moistening her thin lips with her tongue, she looked like one distraught. When Featherstone stopped playing, pretending to be tuning his fiddle, the mulatto woman

6

drew a long breath, and made an effort to smile. Her thin lips fell apart and her white teeth gleamed in the firelight like so many fangs. Finally she spoke, and it was an ungracious speech:—

"Ole Giles Featherstone, up yonder—he's my marster—he sont me down here an' tole me to tell you-all dat, bein's he got some vittles lef' over fum dinner, he'll be glad ef some un you would come take supper 'long wid 'im. But, gentermens"—here she lowered her voice, giving it a most tragic tone— "you better not go, kaze he ain't got nothin' up dar dat's fittin' ter eat—some cole scraps an' de frame uv a turkey. He scrimps hisse'f, an' he scrimps me, an' he scrimps eve'ybody on de place, an' he'll scrimp you-all ef you go dar. No, gentermens, ef you des got corn-bread an' bacon you better stay 'way."

Whatever response the teamsters might have made was drowned by Featherstone's fiddle, which plunged suddenly into the wild and plaintive strains of a plantation melody. The mulatto woman stood like one entranced; she caught her breath, drew back a few steps, stretched forth her ebony arms, and cried out:—

"Who de name er God is dat man?"

With that Featherstone stopped his playing, fixed his eyes on the woman, and exclaimed:—

"*Where's Duncan?*"

For a moment the woman stood like one paralyzed. She gasped for breath, her arms jerked convulsively, and there was a twitching of the muscles of her face pitiful to behold; then she rushed forward and fell on her knees at the fiddler's feet, hugging his legs with her arms.

"Honey, who is you?" she cried in a loud voice. "In de name er de Lord, who is you! Does you know me? Say, honey, does you?"

Featherstone looked at the writhing woman serenely.

"Come, now," he said, "I ask you once more, *Where's Duncan?*"

His tone was most peculiar: it was thrilling, indeed, and it had a tremendous effect on the woman. She rose to her feet, flung her bony arms above her head, and ran off into the darkness, screaming:—

"He sold 'im!—he sold Duncan! He sold my onliest boy!"

This she kept on repeating as she ran, and her voice died away like an echo in the direction of the house on the hill. There was not much joking among the teamsters over this episode, and somehow there was very little talk of any kind. None of us accepted the invitation. Featherstone put his fiddle in his bag, and walked off toward the wagons, and it was not long before everybody had turned in for the night.

I suppose I had been asleep an hour when I felt some one shaking me by the shoulder. It was Crooked-leg Jake.

"Marse Isaiah," said he, "dey er cuttin' up a mighty rippit up dar at dat house on de hill. I 'spec' somebody better go up dar."

"What are they doing?" I asked him drowsily.

"Dey er cussin' an' gwine on scan'lous. Dat ar nigger 'oman, she's a-cussin' out de white man, an' de white man, he's a-cussin' back at her."

"Where's Featherstone?" I inquired, still not more than half awake.

"Dat what make me come atter you, suh. Dat white man what bin 'long wid us, he's up dar, an' it look like ter me dat he's a-aggin' de fuss on. Dey gwine ter be trouble up dar, sho ez you er born."

"Bosh!" said I, "the woman's master will call her up, give her a strapping, and that will be the end of it."

"No, suh! no, suh!" exclaimed Jake; "dat ar nigger 'oman done got dat white man hacked. Hit's des like I tell you, mon!"

I drove Jake off to bed, turned over on my pallet, and was about to go to sleep again, when I heard quite a stir in the camp. The mules and horses were snorting and tugging at their halters, the chickens on the hill were cackling, and somewhere near, a flock of geese was screaming. Just then Crooked-leg Jake came and shook me by the shoulder again. I spoke to him somewhat sharply, but he didn't seem to mind it.

"What I tell you, Marse Isaiah?" he cried. "Look up yonder! Ef dat house ain't afire on top, den Jake's a liar!"

I turned on my elbow, and, sure enough, the house on the hill was outlined in flame. The hungry, yellow tongues of fire reached up the corners and ran along the roof, lapping the shingles, here and there, as if blindly searching for food. They found it, too, for by the time I reached the spot, and you may be sure I was not long getting there, the whole roof was in a blaze. I had never seen a house on fire before, and the sight of it made me quake; but in a moment I had forgotten all about the fire, for there, right before my eyes, was a spectacle that will haunt me to my dying day. In the dining-room—I suppose it must have been the dining-room, for there was a sideboard with a row of candles on it—I saw the mulatto woman (the same that had acted so queerly when Featherstone had asked her about Duncan) engaged in an encounter with a gray-haired white man. The candles on the sideboard and the flaring flames without lit up the affair until it looked like some of the spectacles I have since seen in theatres, only it was more terrible.

It was plain that the old man was no match for the woman, but he fought

8

manfully for his life. Whatever noise they made must have been drowned by the crackling and roaring of the flames outside; but they seemed to be making none except a snarling sound when they caught their breath, like two bull-dogs fighting. The woman had a carving-knife in her right hand, and she was endeavoring to push the white man against the wall. He, on his side, was trying to catch and hold the hand in which the woman held the knife, and was also making a frantic effort to keep away from the wall. But the woman had the advantage; she was younger and stronger, and desperate as he was, she was more desperate still.

Of course, it is a very easy matter to ask why some of my companions or myself didn't rush to the rescue. I think such an attempt was made; but the roof of the house was ablaze and crackling from one end to the other, and the heat and smoke were stifling. The smoke and flames, instead of springing upward, ranged downward, so that before anything could be done, the building appeared to be a solid sheet of fire; but through it all could be seen the writhing and wrestling of the nigger woman and the white man. Once, and only once, did I catch the sound of a voice; it was the voice of the nigger woman; she had her carving-knife raised in the air in one hand, and with the other she had the white man by the throat.

"*Where's Duncan?*" she shrieked.

If the man had been disposed to reply, he had no opportunity, for the woman had no sooner asked the question than she plunged the carving-knife into his body, not only once, but twice. It was a sickening sight, indeed, and I closed my eyes to avoid seeing any more of it; but there was no need of that, for the writhing and struggling bodies of the two fell to the floor and so disappeared from sight.

Immediately afterward there was a tremendous crash. The roof had fallen in, and this was followed by an eruption of sparks and smoke and flame, accompanied by a violent roaring noise that sounded like the culmination of a storm. It was so loud that it aroused the pigeons on the place, and a great flock of them began circling around the burning building. Occasionally one more frightened than the rest would dart headlong into the flames, and it was curious to see the way it disappeared. There would be a fizz and a sputter, and the poor bird would be burnt harder than a crackling. I observed this and other commonplace things with unusual interest—an interest sharpened, perhaps, by the fact that there could be no hope for the two human beings on whom the roof had fallen.

Naturally, you will want to ask me a great many questions. I have asked

9

them myself a thousand times, and I've tried to dream the answers to them while I sat dozing here in the sun, but when I dream about the affair at all, the fumes of burning flesh seem to fill my nostrils. Crooked-leg Jake insisted to the day of his death that the man who had driven our team sat in a chair in the corner of the dining-room, while the woman and the man were fighting, and seemed to be enjoying the spectacle. It may be so. At any rate none of us ever saw him again. As for the rest, you know just as much about it as I do.

Blue Dave

THE ATMOSPHERE of mystery that surrounds the Kendrick Place in Putnam County is illusive, of course; but the illusion is perfect. The old house, standing a dozen yards from the roadside, is picturesque with the contrivances of neglect and decay. Through a door hanging loose upon its hinges the passer-by may behold the evidences of loneliness and gloom,—the very embodiment of desolation,—a void, a silence, that is almost portentous. The roof, with its crop of quaint gables, in which proportion has been sacrificed to an effort to attain architectural liveliness, is covered with a greenish-gray moss on the north side, and has long been given over to decay on all sides. The cat-squirrels that occasionally scamper across the crumbling shingles have as much as they can do, with all their nimbleness, to find a secure foothold. The huge wooden columns that support the double veranda display jagged edges at top and bottom, and no longer make even a pretence of hiding their grim hollowness. The well, hospitably placed within arm's reach of the highway, for the benefit of the dead and buried congregation that long ago met and worshipped at Bethesda meetinghouse, is stripped of windlass, chain, and bucket. All the outhouses have disappeared, if they ever had an existence; and nothing remains to tell the story of a flourishing era, save a fig-tree which is graciously green and fruitful in season. This fig-tree has grown to an extraordinary height, and covers a large area with its canopy of limbs and leaves, giving a sort of Oriental flavor to the illusion of mystery and antiquity. It is said of this fig-tree that sermons have been preached and marriages solemnized under its wide-spreading branches; and there is a vague tradition to the effect that a duel was once fought in its shadow by some of the hot-bloods. But no harm will come of respectfully but firmly doubting this tradition; for it is a fact, common to both memory and observation, that duels, even in the old days, when each and every one of us was the pink of chivalry and the soul of honor, were much rarer than the talk of them. Nevertheless, the confession may be made that without such a tradition a fig-tree surrounded by so many evidences of neglect and decay would be a tame affair indeed.

The house, with its double veranda, its tall chimneys, and its curious collection of gables, was built as late as 1836 by young Felix Kendrick, in order, as Grandsir Kendrick declared, to show that "some folks was as good as other folks." Whether Felix succeeded in this or not, it is impossible to gather from either local history or tradition; but there is no doubt that the house attracted attention, for its architectural liveliness has never to this day been duplicated in that region. In those days the Kendrick family was a new one, so to speak, but ambitious. Grandsir Kendrick—a fatal title in itself— was a hatter by trade, who had come to Georgia in search of a precarious livelihood. He obtained permission to build him a little log hut by the side of a running stream; and, for a year or two, people going along the road could hear the snap and twang of his bow-string as he whipped wool or rabbit fur into shape. Some said he was from North Carolina; others said he was from Connecticut; but whether from one State or the other, what should a hatter do away off in the woods in Putnam County? Grandsir Kendrick, who was shrewd, close-fisted, and industrious, did what any sensible man would have done; he became an overseer. In this business, which required no capital, he developed considerable executive ability. The plantations he had charge of paid large profits to their owners, and he found his good management in demand. He commanded a large salary, and saved money. This money he invested in negroes, buying one at a time and hiring them out. He finally came to be the owner of seven or eight stout field hands; whereupon he bought two hundred acres of choice land and set himself up as a patriarch.

Grandsir Kendrick kept to his sober ways, continued his good management, and, in the midst of much shabbiness, continued to put aside money in the shape of negroes. He also reared a son who contrived somehow to have higher notions than his father. These notions of young Felix Kendrick were confirmed and enlarged by his marriage to the daughter of a Methodist circuit-rider. This young lady had been pinched by poverty often enough to know the value of economy, while the position of her father had given her advantages which the most fortunate young ladies of that day might have envied. In short, Mrs. Felix turned out to be a very superior woman in all respects. She was proud as well as pretty, and managed to hold her own with the element which Grandsir Kendrick sometimes dubiously referred to as "the quality." The fact that Mrs. Felix's mother was a Barksdale probably had something to do with her energy and tact; but whatever the cause of her popularity may have been, Grandsir Kendrick was very proud of his son's wife. He had no sympathy with, and no part in, her high notions; but their manifestation afforded him the spectacle of an experience entirely foreign to his own. Here was his son's wife stepping high, and compelling his son to step high. So far as Grandsir Kendrick was concerned, however, it was merely a spectacle. To the day of his death, he never ceased to higgle over a thrip, and it was his constant boast that in his own experience it had always been convenient to give prudence the upper hand of pride.

In 1850 the house was not showing many signs of decay, but young Mrs. Felix had become the Widow Kendrick, her daughter Kitty had grown to be a beautiful young woman, and her son Felix was a lad of remarkable promise. The loss of her husband was a great blow to Mrs. Kendrick. With all her business qualities, her affection for her family and her home was strongly marked, and her husband stood first as the head and centre of each. Felix Kendrick died in the latter part of November, 1849, and his widow made him a grave under the shadow of a tree he had planted when a boy, and in full view of her window. The obsequies were very simple. A prayer was said, and a song was sung; that was all. But it was understood that the funeral sermon would be preached at the house by Mrs. Kendrick's brother, who was on his way home from China, where he had been engaged in converting (to use a neighborhood phrase) the "squinch-eyed heathen."

The weeks went by, and the missionary brother returned; and one Sunday morning in February it was given out at Bethesda that "on the first Sabbath after the second Tuesday in March, the funeral sermon of Brother Felix Kendrick will be preached at the house by Brother Garwood." On the morning of this particular Sunday, which was selected because it did not conflict with the services of the Bethesda congregation, two neighbors met in the forks of the public road that leads to Rockville. Each had come from a different direction. One was riding and one was walking; and both were past the middle time of life.

"Well met, Brother Roach!" exclaimed the man on horseback.

"You've took the words from my mouth, Brother Brannum. I hope you are well. I'm peart myself, but not as peart as I thought I was, bekaze I find that the two or three miles to come is sticking in my craw."

"Ah, when it comes to that, Brother Roach," said the man on horseback, "you and me can be one another's looking-glass. Look on me and you'll see what time has done for you."

"Not so, Brother Brannum! Not so!" exclaimed the other. "There's some furrows on your forrud, and a handful of bird-tracks below your eyes that would ill become me; and I'm plumper in the make-up, you'll allow."

"Yes, yes, Brother Johnny Roach," said Brother Brannum, frowning a little; "but what of that? Death takes no time to feel for wrinkles and furrows, and nuther does plumpness stand in the way. Look at Brother Felix Kendrick,—took off in the very pulse and power of his prime, you may say. Yet, Providence permitting, I am to hark to his funeral today."

"Why, so am I,—so am I," exclaimed Brother Roach. "We seem to agree, Brother Brannum, like the jay-bird and the joree,—one in the tree and t' other on the ground."

Brother Brannum's grim sense of superiority showed itself in his calm smile.

"Yet I'll not deny," continued Brother Roach, flinging his coat, which he had been carrying on his arm, across his shoulder, "that sech discourses go ag'in the grain. It frets me in the mind for to hear what thundering great men folks git to be arter they are dead, though I hope we may both follow suit, Brother Brannum."

"But how, Brother Johnny Roach?"

"Why, by the grace of big discourses, Brother Brannum. There's many a preacher could close down the Bible on his hankcher and make our very misdeeds smell sweet as innocence. It's all in the lift of the eyebrow, and the gesticures of the hand. So old Neighbor Harper says, and he's been a lawyer and a schoolmaster in his day and time."

"Still," said Brother Brannum, as if acknowledging the arguments, "I think Sister Kendrick is jestified in her desires."

"Oh, yes,—oh, yes!" replied Brother Roach, heartily; "none more so. Felix Kendrick's ways is in good shape for some preacher wi' a glib tongue. Felix was a good man; he wanted his just dues, but not if to take them would hurt a man. He was neighborly; who more so? And, sir, when you got to rastlin' wi' trouble, he'd find you and fetch you out. I only hope the Chinee preacher'll be jedgmatical enough for to let us off wi' the simple truth."

"They say," said Brother Brannum, "that he's a man full of grace and fire."

"Well, sir," said Johnny Roach, "if he but makes me disremember that I left the bay mar' at home, I'll thank him kindly."

14

"Mercy, Brother Roach," exclaimed Brother Brannum, taking this as a neighborly hint, "mount up here and rest yourself, whilst I stretch my legs along this level piece of ground."

"I'd thank you kindly, Brother Brannum, if you wouldn't so misjudge me. It's my will to walk; but if I git my limbs sot to the saddle here and now, they'd ache and crack might'ly when next I called upon 'em. I'll take the will for the deed, Brother Brannum."

Thus these neighbors jogged along to Felix Kendrick's funeral. They found a great crowd ahead of them when they got there, though they were not too late for the services; but the house was filled with sympathetic men and women, and those who came late were compelled to find such accommodations as the yard afforded; and these accommodations were excellent in their way, for there was the cool, green grass under the trees, and there were the rustic seats in the shadow of the fig-tree of which mention has been made.

Coming together, Brother Brannum and Brother Roach stayed together; and they soon found themselves comfortably seated under the fig-tree,—a point of view from which they could observe everything that was going on. Brother Brannum, who was a pillar of Bethesda church and extremely officious withal, seemed to regret that he had not arrived soon enough to find a place in the house near the preacher, but Brother Roach appeared to congratulate himself that he had been crowded out of ear-shot.

"We can set here," he declared in great good-humor, "and hear the singing, and then whirl in and preach each man his own sermon. I know better than the furrin preacher what'd be satisfactual to Felix Kendrick. I see George Denham sailing in and out and flying around; and if the pinch comes, as come it must, Brother Brannum, we can up and ast George for to fetch us sech reports as a hongry man can stomach."

Brother Brannum frowned heavily, but made no response. Presently Brother Roach beckoned to the young man whom he had called George Denham. "Howdy, George! How is Kitty Kendrick? Solemn as the season is, George, I lay 't would be wrong for to let Beauty pine."

The young man suppressed a smile, and raised his hands in protest.

"Uncle Johnny! to joke me at such a time! I shall go to-morrow and cut your mill-race, and you will never know who did it."

"Ah, George! if death changes a man no more'n they say it does, little does Felix Kendrick need to be holp by these dismal takings-on. From first to last, he begrudged no man his banter. But here we are and yan's the preacher. The p'int wi' me, George, is, how kin we-all setting on the back seats know when the preacher gits to his 'amen,' onless his expoundance is too loud to be becoming?"

"Come, now, Uncle Johnny," said young Denham, "no winking, and I'll tell you. I was talking to Miss Kitty just now, and all of a sudden she cried out, 'Why, yonder's Uncle Johnny Roach, and he's walking, too. Uncle Johnny must stay to dinner'; and Mrs. Kendrick says, 'Yes, and Brother Brannum, too.' And so there you are."

"Well, sir," exclaimed Brother Roach, "Kitty always had a piece of my heart, and now she has it all."

"A likely young man, that George Denham," said Brother Brannum, as Denham moved towards the house.

"You never spoke a truer word, Brother Brannum," said Brother Roach, enthusiastically. "Look at his limbs, look at his gait, look at his eye. If the world, the flesh, and the devil don't freeze out his intents, you'll hear from that chap. He's a-gitting high up in the law, and where'll you find a better managed plantation than his'n?"

What else Brother Roach said or might have said must be left to conjecture. In the midst of his eulogy on the living, the preacher in the house began his eulogy of the dead. Those who heard what he said were much edified, and those who failed to hear made a decorous pretense of listening intently. In the midst of the sermon Brother Roach felt himself touched on the arm. Looking up, he saw that Brother Brannum was gazing intently at one of the gables on the roof. Following the direction of Brother Brannum's eyes, Brother Roach beheld, with astonishment not unmixed with awe, the head and shoulders of a powerfully built negro. The attitude of the negro was one of attention. He was evidently trying to hear the sermon. His head was bent, and the expression of his face was indicative of great good-humor. His shirt was ragged and dirty, and had fallen completely away from one arm and shoulder, and the billowy muscles glistened in the sun. While Brother Brannum and Brother Roach were gazing at him with some degree of amazement, an acorn dropped upon the roof from one of the tall oaks. Startled by the sudden noise, the negro glanced hurriedly around, and dropped quickly below the line of vision.

"Well, well, well!" exclaimed Brother Roach, after exchanging a look of amazement with Brother Brannum. "Well, well, well! Who'd 'a' thought it. Once 'twas the nigger in the woodpile; now it's the nigger in the steeple, and arter awhile they'll be a-flying in the air,—mark my words. I call that the impidence of the Old Boy. Maybe you don't know that nigger, Brother Brannum?"

"I disremember if I do, Brother Roach."

"Well, sir, when one of 'em passes in front of your Uncle Johnny, you may up and sw'ar his dagarrytype is took. That nigger, roosting up there so slick and cool, is Bledser's Blue Dave. Nuther more, nuther less."

"Bledser's Blue Dave!" exclaimed Brother Brannum in a voice made sepulchral by amazement.

"The identical nigger! I'd know him if I met him arm-in-arm with the King and Queen of France."

"Why, I thought Blue Dave had made his disappearance five year ago," said Brother Brannum.

"Well, sir, my two eyes tells me different. Time and time ag'in I've been told he's a quare creetur. Some say he's strong as a horse and venomous as a snake. Some say he's swifter than the wind and slicker than a red fox. And many's the time by my own h'a'th-stone I've had to pooh-pooh these relations; yet there's no denying that for mighty nigh seven year that nigger's been trolloping round through the woods foot-loose and scotch-free, bidding defiance to the law of the State and Bill Brand's track dogs."

"Well, sir," said Brother Brannum, fetching his hand down on his knee with a thwack, "we ought to alarm the assemblage."

"Jes so," replied Brother Roach, with something like a chuckle; "but you forgit the time and the occasion, Brother Brannum. I'm a worldly man myself, as you may say, but 'twill be long arter I'm more worldlier than what I am before you can ketch me cuttin' sech a scollop as to wind up a funeral sermon wi' a race arter a runaway nigger."

Brother Brannum agreed with this view, but it was with a poor grace. He had a vague remembrance of certain rewards that had from time to time been offered for the capture of Blue Dave, and he was anxious to have a hand in securing at least a part of these. But he refrained from sounding the alarm. With Brother Roach, he remained at the Kendrick Place after the sermon was over, and took dinner. He rode off shortly afterwards, and the next day Bill Brand and his track dogs put in an appearance; but Blue Dave was gone.

It was a common thing to hear of fugitive negroes; but Blue Dave (so called because of the inky blackness of his skin) had a name and a fame that made him the terror of the women and children, both white and black; and

Kitty Kendrick and her mother were not a little disturbed when they learned that he had been in hiding among the gables of their house. The negro's success in eluding pursuit caused the ignorant-minded of both races to attribute to him the possession of some mysterious power. He grew into a legend; he became a part of the folk-lore of the section. According to popular belief, he possessed strange powers and great courage; he became a giant, a spirit of evil. Women frightened their children into silence by calling his name, and many a youngster crept to bed in mortal fear that Blue Dave would come in the night and whisk him away into the depths of the dark woods. Whatever mischief was done was credited to Blue Dave. If a horse was found in the lot spattered with mud, Blue Dave had ridden it; if a cow was crippled, a hog missing, or a smoke-house robbed, Blue Dave was sure to be at the bottom of it all, so far as popular belief was concerned. The negroes had many stories to tell of him. One had seen him standing by a tall poplar-tree. He was about to speak to him when there came a flash of lightning and a crash of thunder, and Blue Dave disappeared, leaving a sulphurous smell behind him. He had been seen by another negro. He was standing in the middle of the Armour's Ferry road. He was armed with a gleaming reap-hook, and accompanied by a big black dog. As soon as the dog saw the new-comer, it bristled up from head to foot, its eyes shone like two coals of fire, and every hair on its back emitted a fiery spark.

Very little was known of the history of Blue Dave. He was brought to the little village of Rockville in chains in a speculator's train,—the train consisting of two Conestoga wagons and thirty or forty forlorn-looking negroes. The speculator explained that he had manacled Blue Dave because he was unmanageable; and he put him on the block to sell him after making it perfectly clear to everybody that whoever bought the negro would get a bad bargain. Nevertheless Blue Dave was a magnificent specimen of manhood, straight as an arrow, as muscular as Hercules, and with a countenance as open and pleasant as one would wish to see. He was bought by General Alfred Bledser, and put on his River Place. He worked well for a few weeks, but got into trouble with the overseer, and finally compromised matters by taking to the woods. He seemed born for this particular business; for the track dogs failed to find him, and all the arts and artifices employed for capturing and reclaiming runaways failed in his case. It was a desperate sort of freedom he enjoyed; but he seemed suited to it, and he made the most of it.

As might be supposed, there was great commotion in the settlement, and particularly at the Kendrick homestead, when it was known that Blue Dave had been hiding among the gables of the Kendrick house. Mrs. Kendrick and her daughter Kitty possessed their full share of what Brother Roach would have called "spunk"; but there is a large and very important corner of the human mind—particularly if it happens to be a feminine mind—which devotes itself to superstition; and these gentle ladies, while they stood in no terror of Blue Dave as a runaway negro simply, were certainly awed by the spectral figure which had grown up out of common report. The house negroes stood in mortal dread of Blue Dave, and their dismay was not without its effect on Mrs. Kendrick and her daughter. Jenny, the house-girl, refused to sleep at the quarters; and when Aunt Tabby, the cook, started for her cabin after dark, she was accompanied by a number of little negroes bearing lightwood torches. All the stories and legends that clustered around Blue Dave's career were brought to the surface again; and, as we have seen, the great majority of them were anything but reassuring.

While the commotion in the settlement and on the Kendrick Place was at its height, an incident occurred that had a tendency to relieve Kitty Kendrick's mind. Shortly after the funeral the spring rains had set in, and for several days great floods came down from the skies. One evening shortly after dark, Kitty Kendrick stepped out upon the veranda, in an aimless sort of way, to look at the clouds. The rain had ceased, but the warm earth was reeking with moisture. The trees and the ground were smoking with fog, and great banks of vapor were whirling across the sky from the southwest. Kitty sighed. After a while George Denham would go rattling by in his buggy from his law office in Rockville to his plantation, and it was too dark to catch a glimpse of him. At any rate, she would do the best she could. She would put the curtains of the sitting-room back, so the light could shine out, and perhaps George would stop to warm his hands and say a word to her mother. Kitty turned to go in when she heard her name called,—

"Miss Kitty!"

"Well, what is it?" Kitty was startled a little in spite of herself.

"Please, ma'am, don't be skeer'd."

"Why should I be frightened? What do you want?"

"Miss Kitty, I des come by fer ter tell you dat Murder Creek done come way out er its banks, en ef Mars. George Denham come by w'en he gwine on home, I wish you please, ma'am, be so good ez ter tell 'im dat dey ain't no fordin' place fer ter be foun' dar dis night."

The voice was that of a negro, and there was something in the tone of it that arrested Kitty Kendrick's attention.

"Who sent you?" she asked.

"Nobody ain't sont me; I des come by myse'f. I laid off fer ter tell Mars. George, but I year talk he mighty headstrong, en I speck he des laugh at me."

"Are you one of our hands?"

"No, 'm; I don't b'long on de Kendrick Place."

"Come out of the shadow there where I can see you."

"I mos' fear'd, Miss Kitty."

"What is your name?"

"Dey calls me Blue Dave, ma'am."

The tone of the voice was something more than humble. There was an appeal in it for mercy. Kitty Kendrick recognized this; but in spite of it she could scarcely resist an impulse to rush into the house, lock the door, and take steps to rouse the whole plantation. By a great effort she did resist it, and the negro went on:

"Please, ma'am, don't be skeer'd er me, Miss Kitty. De Lord years me w'en I say it, dey ain't a ha'r er yo' head dat I'd hurt, dat dey ain't. I ain't bad like dey make out I is, Miss Kitty. Dey tells some mighty big tales, but dey makes um up dey se'f. Manys en manys de time is I seed you w'en you gwine atter sweet-gum en w'en you huntin' flowers, en I allers say ter myse'f, I did, 'Nobody better not pester Miss Kitty w'iles Blue Dave anywhars 'roun'.' Miss Kitty, I 'clar' 'fo' de Lord I ain't no bad nigger," Blue Dave continued in a tone of the most emphatic entreaty. "You des ax yo' little br'er. Little Mars. Felix, he knows I ain't no bad nigger."

"Why don't you go home, instead of hiding out in the woods?" said Kitty, striving to speak in a properly indignant tone.

"Bless yo' soul, Miss Kitty, hit ain't no home fer me," said Blue Dave, sadly. "Hit mought be a home fer some niggers, but hit ain't no home fer me. I year somebody comin'. Good-by, Miss Kitty; don't fergit 'bout Mars. George."

As noiselessly as the wind that faintly stirs the grass, Blue Dave glided away in the darkness, leaving Kitty Kendrick standing upon the veranda half frightened and wholly puzzled. Her little brother Felix came out to see where she had gone. Felix was eight years old, and had views of his own.

"Sister Kit, what are you doing? Watching for Mr. George to go by?"

"Don't speak to me, you naughty boy!" exclaimed Kitty. "You've disgraced us all. You knew Blue Dave was hiding on top of the house all the while. What would be done with us if people found out we had been harboring a runaway negro?" Kitty pretended to be terribly shocked. Felix gave a long whistle, indicative of astonishment.

"You are awful smart," he said. "How did you find that out? Yes, I did know it," he went on desperately, "and I don't care if I did. If you tell anybody, I'll never run up the road to see if Mr. George is coming as long as I live; I won't never do anything for you."

Kitty's inference was based on what Blue Dave had said; but it filled her with dismay to find it true. She caught the child by the shoulder and gave him a little shake.

"Brother Felix, how dare you do such a thing? If mother knew of it, it would break her heart."

"Well, go and tell her and break her heart," said the boy, sullenly. "It wasn't my fault that Blue Dave was up there. I didn't tote him up, I reckon."

"Oh, how could you do such a thing?" reiterated Kitty, putting her handkerchief to her eyes, as if by this means to expiate her brother's folly.

"Well," said the child, still speaking sullenly, "I heard something moving on top of the house one day when I was in the garret, and I kept on hearing it until I opened the window and went out on the roof. Then, when I got out there, I saw a great big nigger man."

"Weren't you frightened?" exclaimed Kitty, catching her breath. "What did you say?"

"I said 'Hello!' and then he jumped like he was shot. I asked him his name, and he said he was named Blue Dave, and he begged me so hard I promised not to tell he was up there. And then, after that, he used to come in the garret and tell me no end of tales, and I've got a trunk full of chestnuts that he brought me. He's the best nigger man I ever saw, less'n it's old Uncle Manuel, and he'll be as good as Uncle Manuel when he gets that old, 'cause Uncle Manuel said so. And I know it ain't my fault; and if you want to tell mother you can come and tell her right now, and then you won't never be my sister any more, never, never!"

"I think you have acted shamefully," said Kitty. "Suppose he had come in the garret, and made his way downstairs, and murdered us all while we were asleep."

"Well," said Felix, "he could have come any time. I wouldn't be afraid to go out in the woods and stay with Blue Dave this very night, and if I had my way he wouldn't be running from old Bill Brand and his dogs. When I get a man I'm going to save up money and buy Blue Dave. I thought at first I wanted a pony, but I wouldn't have a pony now."

While they were talking, Kitty heard the rattle of buggy wheels. The sound came nearer and nearer. Whoever was driving was singing to pass the time away, and the quick ear of Kitty recognized the voice of George Denham. He went dashing by; but he must have seen the girl standing on the veranda, for he cried out, "Good-night, Miss Kitty!" and then caught up the burden of his song again as he went whirling down the road. Kitty wrung her hands. She went in to her mother with tears in her eyes.

"Oh, mother! George has gone by without stopping. What shall we do?"

Mrs. Kendrick was a very practical woman. Knowing nothing of the freshet in Murder Creek, she was amazed as well as amused at Kitty's tragic attitude.

"Well, it's most too soon for George to begin to take his meals here, I reckon," she said dryly. "You'd better make you a cup of ginger-tea and go to bed."

"But, mother, there's a freshet in Murder Creek. Oh, why didn't he stop?"

Mrs. Kendrick was kneeling on the floor cutting out clothes for the plough-hands,—"slaving for her niggers," as she called it. She paused in her work and looked at Kitty, as if to see whether she had heard her aright.

"Well, upon my word!" she exclaimed, after critically surveying her daughter, "I don't see how girls can be so weak-minded. Many a man as good as George Denham has crossed Murder Creek in a freshet. I don't see but what he's big enough and ugly enough to take care of himself."

"Oh," exclaimed Kitty, going from window to window, and vainly endeavoring to peer out into the darkness, "why didn't he stop?"

"Well," said Mrs. Kendrick, resuming the use of her shears, "if you'll try to worry along and stand it this time, I'll send out and have a fence built across the big road, and get the niggers to light a bonfire; and we'll stop him the next time he comes along. I'll have to do my duty by my own children, I reckon. But don't be alarmed," she continued, perceiving that Kitty's distress was genuine. "You may have to fly around here and get George some supper, after all. I've been waiting on niggers all day; and even if I hadn't, I'm too old and fagged out to be rushing in amongst the pots and kettles to please George Denham."

George Denham rattled down the road, singing of "Barbara Allen," but thinking of Kitty Kendrick. Suddenly his horse shied, and then he heard somebody call him.

"Mars. George! Is dat you, Mars. George?"

"Unless you want to make a ghost of me by frightening my horse," exclaimed the young man, checking the animal with some difficulty. "What do you want?"

"Mars. George, is you see Miss Kitty w'en you come by des now?"

"No, I didn't stop. Is anything the matter?"

"No, sir, nothin' in 'tickler ain't de matter, 'ceppin' dat Miss Kitty had sump'n' ter tell you."

"Are you one of the Kendrick negroes?"

"No, sir; I don't b'long dar."

"Who are you?"

"I 'clar' ter goodness, I skeer'd ter tell you, Mars. George; kaze you mought fly up en git mad."

The young man laughed with such genuine heartiness that it did the negro good to hear it.

"Well, I know who you are," he said; "you are Blue Dave, and you've come to tell me that you want me to carry you to jail, where Bill Brand can get his hands on you."

The negro was thunderstruck. " 'Fo' de Lord, Mars. George! how you know who I is?"

"Why, I know by your looks. You've got horns and a club foot. That's the way the Old Boy fixes himself."

"Now, Mars. George," said the negro, in a grieved tone, "ef you could see me good you wouldn't set dar en say I'm a bad-lookin' nigger."

"Are you really Blue Dave?" the young man asked, dropping his bantering tone and speaking seriously.

"Yasser, Mars. George; I'm dat ve'y nigger."

"What do you want with me?"

"I des wanter tell you, Mars. George, dat dey's a freshet come fum 'bove, en Murder Creek is 'way out'n hits banks. You can't cross dar wid no hoss en buggy dis night."

The young man reflected a moment. He was more interested in the attitude of the negro than he was in the extent of the freshet or the danger of an attempt to cross the creek.

"I've a knack of crossing Murder Creek in a freshet," he said. "But why should you want to keep me out of it?"

"Well, sir, fer one thing," said Blue Dave, shifting about on his feet uneasily, "you look so much like my young marster w'at died in Ferginny.

En den dat day w'en de speckerlater put me up on de block, you 'uz settin' dar straddle er yo' pony, en you 'lowed dat he oughter be 'shame er hisse'f fer ter chain me up dat a-way."

"Oh, I remember. I made quite a fool of myself that day."

"Yasser; en den w'en de man say sump'n' sassy back, little ez you wuz, you spurred de pony at 'im en tole 'im you'd slap 'im in de jaw. He 'uz de skeer'dest w'ite man I ever see. I say ter myse'f den dat I hope de day'd come w'en dat little boy'd grow up en buy me; en dat make I say w'at I does. I want you to keep out'n dat creek dis night, en den I want you ter buy me. Please, sir, buy me, Mars. George; I make you de bes' nigger you ever had."

"Why, great Jerusalem! you wouldn't be on my place a week before you'd get your feelings hurt and rush off to the woods, and I'd never see you any more."

"Des try me, Mars. George! des try me. I'll work my arms off ter de elbows, en den I'll work wid de stumps. Des try me, Mars. George!"

"I expect you would be a right good hand if you hadn't been free so long. Go home and let me see how you can work for your master, and then maybe I'll think about buying you."

"Eh-eh, Mars. George! I better go jump in a burnin' bresh-pile. Ain't you gwine ter tu'n back, Mars. George?"

"Not to-night. Go home and behave yourself."

With that George Denham clucked to his restive horse, and went clattering down the road in the direction of Murder Creek, which crossed the highway a mile farther on. Blue Dave stood still a moment, scratching his head and looking after the buggy.

"Is anybody ever see de beat er dat?" he exclaimed. "Ef Mars. George gits in dat creek dey's got ter be a merakel come 'bout ef he gits out." He stood in the road a moment longer, still scratching his head as if puzzled. Then he addressed himself indignantly. "Looky yer, nigger, w'at you stan'in' yer fer? Whar yo' manners, whar yo' perliteness?"

Thus, half-humorously, half-seriously, talking to himself, Blue Dave went trotting along in the direction taken by George Denham. He moved without apparent exertion, but with amazing swiftness. But the young man in the buggy had also moved swiftly; and, go as fast as he might, Blue Dave could not hope to overtake him before he reached the creek.

For George Denham was impatient to get home,—as impatient as his horse, which did not need even the lightest touch of the whip to urge it forward. He paid no attention to the familiar road. He was thinking of pretty

Kitty Kendrick, and of the day, not very far in the future he hoped, when, in going home, he should be driving towards her instead of away from her. He paid no attention to the fact that, as he neared the creek, his horse subsided from a swinging trot to a mincing gait that betrayed indecision; nor did it strike him as anything unusual that the horse should begin to splash water with his feet long before he had reached the banks of the creek; no doubt it was a pool left standing in the road after the heavy rains. But the pool steadily grew deeper; and while George Denham was picturing Kitty Kendrick sitting on one side of his fireplace and his old mother on the other,— his old mother, with her proud face and her stately ways,—his horse stopped and looked around. Young Denham slapped the animal with the reins, without taking note of his surroundings. Thus reassured, the horse went on; but the water grew deeper and deeper, and presently the creature stopped again. This time it smelt of the water and emitted the low, deeply drawn snort by which horses betray their uneasiness; and when George Denham would have urged it forward, it struck the water impatiently with its forefoot. Aroused by this, the young man looked around; but there was nothing to warn him of his danger. The fence that would otherwise have been a landmark, was gone. There was no loud and angry roaring of the floods. Behind him the shifting clouds, the shining stars, and the blue patches of sky mirrored themselves duskily and vaguely in the slow creeping waters; before him the shadows of the trees that clustered somewhere near the banks of the creek were so deep and heavy that they seemed to merge the dark waters of the flood into the gloom of the night. When the horse was quiet, peering ahead, with its sharp little ears pointed forward, there was no sound save the vague sighing of the wind through the tops of the scrub pines and the gentle ripple of the waters.

As George Denham urged his horse forward, confident of his familiarity with the surroundings, Blue Dave ran up on the little ridge to the left through which the road had been cut or worn.

"Mars. George!" he shouted, "don't you see wharbouts you is! Wait, Mars. George! Pull dat hoss up!"

But Blue Dave was too late. As he spoke, the horse and buggy plunged into the flood, and for a moment they were lost to view. Then the struggling animal seemed to strike rising ground; but the buggy was caught in the resistless current, and, with George Denham clinging to it, it dragged the horse down, and the swirling waters seemed to sweep over and beyond them. Blue Dave lost not a moment. Flinging himself into the flood from the

25

vantage ground on which he stood, a few strokes of his sinewy arms carried him to where he saw George Denham disappear. That young man was an expert swimmer; and though the sudden immersion had taken him at a disadvantage, he would have made his way out with little difficulty but for the fact that a heavy piece of driftwood had been hurled against his head. Stunned, but still conscious, he was making an ineffectual attempt to reach the shore when he was caught by Blue Dave and borne safely back to land. The horse, in its struggles, had succeeded in tearing itself loose from the buggy, and they heard it crawl up the bank on the other side and shake itself. Blue Dave carried George Denham out of the water as one would carry a child. When he had set the young man down in a comparatively dry place, he exclaimed with a grin,

"Dar now, Mars. George! w'at I tell you? Little mo'en de tarrypins would 'a' bin a-nibblin' atter you."

George Denham was dazed as well as weak. He put his hand to his head and tried to laugh.

"You were just in time, old fellow," he said.

Then he got on his feet and tried to walk, but he would have sunk down again but for Blue Dave's arm.

"Why, I'm as weak as a stray cat," he exclaimed feebly. "Let me lie down here a moment."

"Dat I won't, Mars. George! dat I won't! I tuck 'n' brung you out, en now I'm a-gwineter take 'n' ca'er you back dar whar Miss Kitty waitin'."

"Well, you'll have to wait until I can walk."

"No, sir; I'll des squat down, en you kin crawl up on my back des like you useter play hoss."

"Why, you can't carry me, old fellow; I'm too heavy for that."

"Shoo! don't you b'leeve de half er dat, Mars. George. I toted bigger turns dan w'at you is long 'fo' I had de strenk w'at I got now. Grab me 'roun' de neck, Mars. George; git up little higher. Now, den, don't you be fear'd er fallin'."

Blue Dave rose from his stooping posture, steadied himself a moment, and then moved on with his living burden. He moved slowly and cautiously at first, but gradually increased his pace to a swinging walk that carried him forward with surprising swiftness.

To George Denham it all seemed like a dream. He suffered no pain, and it was with a sort of queer elation of mind that he felt the huge muscles of the negro swell and subside under him with the regularity of machinery, and

26

knew that every movement carried him toward Kitty Kendrick and—rest. He was strangely tired, but not otherwise uncomfortable. He felt abundantly grateful to this poor runaway negro, and thought that if he could overcome his mother's prejudices (she had a horror of runaway negroes) he would buy Blue Dave and make him comfortable. Thus they swung along until the negro's swift stride brought them to Mrs. Kendrick's gate. There Blue Dave deposited George Denham, and exclaimed with a laugh as he leaned against the fence,

"You'er right smart chunk er meat, Mars. George, ez sho ez de worl'!"

George Denham also leaned against the fence, but he didn't laugh. He was thinking of what seemed to him a very serious matter.

"Mother will be frightened to death when that horse gets home," he said.

"You go in dar en get wom, Mars. George," said Blue Dave. "I'm gwine 'roun' by de High Bridge en tell um whar you is."

"Why, you'll break yourself down," said George Denham.

"Ah, Lord, Mars. George!" said the negro, laughing, "time you bin in de woods long ez I is de four mile 'twix' yer en yo' house'll look mighty short. Go in dar, Mars. George, 'fo' you git col'!"

Shortly after this, George Denham was in bed and fast asleep. He had been met at the door by Kitty Kendrick, in whose tell-tale face the blushes of that heartiest of all welcomes had chased away the pallor of dread and anxiety. Mrs. Kendrick was less sympathetic in word than in deed. She had known George Denham since he was a little boy in short clothes; and while she approved of him, and had a sort of motherly affection for him, she was disposed to be critical, as are most women who have the knack of management.

"And so you've come back dripping, have you? Well, you ain't the first headstrong, high-strung chap that's found out water is wet when the creek blots out the big road, I reckon. I'm no duck myself. When I see water, I'm like the old cat in the corner; I always feel like shaking my foot. Kitty, call Bob and tell him to make a fire in the big room. He's asleep, I reckon, and you'll have to holler. Set a nigger down and he's snoring directly. You look pale," Mrs. Kendrick continued, turning to George. "You must have gone in over your ears. I should think a drenching like that would take all the conceit out of a man."

"Well, it has taken it all out of me, ma'am," said George, laughing. Then the young man told Mrs. Kendrick of his misadventure, and of the part Blue Dave had borne in it.

"He's the nigger that roosted on top of my house," said Mrs. Felix, bustling around and putting a kettle of water on the fire. "Well, it's a round-about way to pay for his lodging, but it's the best he could do, I reckon. Now, don't you worry yourself, George; in ten minutes you'll be snug in bed, and then you'll drink a cup of composition tea, and to-morrow morning you'll have forgotten all about trying to make a spring branch out of Murder Creek."

As the successful mistress of a household, Mrs. Kendrick knew precisely what was necessary to be done. There was no hitch in her system, no delay in her methods, and no disputing her remedies. George Denham was ordered to bed as if he had been a child; and though the "composition" tea was hot in the mouth and bitter to the palate, it was useless to protest against it. As a consequence of all this, the young man was soon in the land of dreams.

When everything was quiet, Kitty prepared a very substantial lunch. Then, calling her little brother Felix, she went across the yard to the quarters, and stopped at Uncle Manuel's cabin. The door was ajar, and Kitty could see the venerable old negro nodding before the flickering embers. She went in and called his name,

"Uncle Manuel!"

"Eh! Who dat?" Then, looking around and perceiving Kitty, the old negro's weather-beaten face shone with a broad smile of surprise and welcome. "Why, honey! Why, little Mistiss! How come dis? You makes de ole nigger feel proud; dat you does. I fear'd ter ax you ter set down, honey, de cheer so rickety."

"Uncle Manuel," said Kitty, "do you know Blue Dave?"

Uncle Manuel was old, and wise, and cunning. He hesitated a moment before replying; and even then his caution would not allow him to commit himself.

"Blue Dave, he's dat ar runaway nigger, ain't he, honey? I done year talk un 'im lots er times."

"Well," said Kitty, placing her basket upon Uncle Manuel's tool-chest, "here is something for Blue Dave to eat. If you don't see him yourself, per-haps you can send it to him by some one."

Uncle Manuel picked up the basket, weighed it in his hand, and then placed it on the chest again. Then he looked curiously at Kitty, and said,

"Honey, how come you gwine do dis? Ain't you year tell hit's ag'in de law fer ter feed a runaway nigger?"

Kitty blushed as she thought of George Denham. "I send Blue Dave the

28

victuals because I choose to, Uncle Manuel," she said. "The law has nothing to do with that little basket."

She started to go, but Uncle Manuel raised both hands heavenwards.

"Wait, little Mistiss," he cried, the tears running down his furrowed face; "des wait, little Mistiss. 'T won't hurt you, honey. De ole nigger wuz des gwine ter git down ter his pra'rs 'fo' you come in. Dey ain't no riper time dan dis."

Uncle Manuel's voice was husky with suppressed emotion. With his hands still stretched toward the skies, and the tears still running down his face, he fell upon his knees and exclaimed,

"Saviour en Marster er de worl'! draw nigh dis night en look down into dis ole nigger's heart; lissen ter de humblest er de humble. Blessed Marster! some run wild en some go stray, some go hether en some go yan'; but all un um mus' go befo' dy mercy-seat in de een'. Some'll fetch big works en some'll fetch great deeds, but po' ole Manuel won't fetch nothin' but one weak, sinful heart. Dear, blessed Marster! look in dat heart en see w'at in dar. De sin dat's dar, Lord, blot it out wid dy wounded han'. Dear Marster, bless my little Mistiss. Her comin's en her gwines is des like one er dy angels er mercy; she scatters bread en meat 'mongs' dem w'at's lonesome in der ways, en dem w'at runs up en down in de middle er big tribalation. Saviour! Marster! look down 'pon my little Mistiss; gedder her 'nead dy hev'mly wings. Ef trouble mus' come, let it come 'pon me. I'm ole, but I'm tough; I'm ole, but I got de strenk. Lord! let de troubles en de trials come 'pon de ole nigger w'at kin stan' um, en save my little Mistiss fum sheddin' one tear. En den, at de las' fetch us all home ter hev'm, whar dey's res' fer de w'ary. Amen."

Never in her life before had Kitty felt so thrilling a sense of nearness to her Creator as when Uncle Manuel was offering up his simple prayer; and she went out of the humble cabin weeping gently.

The four-mile run to the Denham Plantation was fun for Blue Dave. He was wet and cold, and the exercise acted as a lively invigorant. Once, as he sped along, he was challenged by the patrol; but he disappeared like a shadow, and came into the road again a mile away, singing to himself,

> Run, nigger, run! patter-roller ketch you;
> Run, nigger, run! hit's almos' day!

He was well acquainted with the surroundings at the Denham Plantation, having been fed many a time by the well-cared-for negroes; and he had no hesitation in approaching the premises. The clouds had whirled themselves away, and the stars told him it was ten o'clock. There was a light in the sitting-room, and Blue Dave judged it best to go to the back door. He rapped gently, and then a little louder. Ordinarily the door would have been opened by the trim black housemaid; but to-night it was opened by George Denham's mother, a prim old lady of whom everybody stood greatly in awe without precisely knowing why. She looked out, and saw the gigantic negro looming up on the doorsteps.

"Do you bring news of my son?" she asked. The voice was low, but penetrating; and the calm, even tones told the story of a will too strong to tolerate opposition or even contradiction.

Blue Dave hesitated out of sheer embarrassment at finding such cool serenity where he had probably expected to find grief or some such excitement.

"Did you hear me speak?" the prim old lady asked, before the negro had time to gather his wits. "Do you bring me news of my son?"

"Yessum," said Blue Dave, scratching his head; "dat w'at I come fer. Mars. George gwine ter stay at de Kendrick Place ter-night. I speck he in bed by dis time," he added reassuringly.

"His horse has come home without buggy or harness. Is my son hurt? Don't be afraid to tell me the truth. What has happened to him?"

How could the poor negro—how could anybody—know what a whirlwind of yearning affection, dread, and anxiety was raging behind these cool, level tones?

"Mistiss, I tell you de trufe: Mars. George is sorter hurted, but he ain't hurted much. I met 'im in de road, en I tuck 'n' tole 'im dey wuz a freshet in Murder Creek; but he des laugh at me, en he driv' in des like dey wa'n't no water dar; en den w'en he make his disappearance, I tuck 'n' splunge in atter 'im, en none too soon, n'er, kaze he got strucken on de head wid a log, en w'en I fotch 'im out, he 'uz all dazzle up like. Yit he ain't hurted much, Mistiss."

"What is your name?" the prim old lady asked.

"Blue Dave, ma'am."

"The runaway?"

The negro hesitated, looked around, and then hung down his head. He knew the calm, fearless eyes of this gentlewoman were upon him; he felt the influence of her firm tones. She repeated her question:

30

"Are you Blue Dave, the runaway?"

"Yessum."

The answer seemed to satisfy the lady. She turned and called Eliza, the housemaid.

"Eliza, your master's supper is in the dining-room by the fire. Here are the keys. Take it into the kitchen." Then she turned to Blue Dave. "David," she said, "go into the kitchen and eat your supper."

Then Eliza was sent after Ellick, the negro foreman; and Ellick was not long in finding Blue Dave a suit of linsey-woolsey clothes, a little warmer and a little drier than those the runaway was in the habit of wearing. Then the big grays were put to the Denham carriage, shawls and blankets were thrown in, and Blue Dave was called.

"Have you had your supper, David?" said Mrs. Denham, looking grimmer than ever as she stood on her veranda arrayed in bonnet and wraps.

"Thanky, Mistiss! thanky, ma'am. I ain't had no meal's vittles like dat, not sence I lef' Ferginny."

"Can you drive a carriage, David?" the old lady asked.

"Dat I kin, Mistiss."

Whereupon he seized the reins and let down the carriage steps. Mrs. Denham and her maid got in; but when everything was ready, Blue Dave hesitated.

"Mistiss," he said, rather sheepishly, "w'en I come 'long des now, de patter-rollers holler'd atter me."

"No matter, David," the grim old lady replied; "your own master wouldn't order you off of *my* carriage."

"Keep yo' eye on dat off hoss!" exclaimed Ellick, as the carriage moved off.

"Hush, honey," Blue Dave cried, as exultantly as a child; " 'fo' dey gits ter de big gate, I'll know deze yer hosses better dan ef dey wuz my br'er."

After that, nothing more was said. The road had been made firm and smooth by the heavy beating rain, and the carriage swung along easily and rapidly. The negro housemaid fell back against the cushions, and was soon sound asleep; but Mrs. Denham sat bolt-upright. Hers was an uncompromising nature, it had been said, and certainly it seemed so; but as the carriage rolled along, there grew before her mind's eye the vague, dim outlines of a vision,—a vision of a human creature hiding in the dark swamps, fleeing through the deep woods and creeping swiftly through the pine thickets. It was a pathetic figure, this fleeing human creature, whether chased by dogs and men or pursued only by the terrors that hide themselves behind the vast shadows of the night; and the figure grew more pathetic when, as it seemed, it sprang out of the very elements themselves to snatch her son from the floods. The old lady sighed and pressed her thin lips together. She had made up her mind.

Presently the carriage drew up at the Kendrick Place; and in a little while, after effusive greetings all around, Mrs. Denham was sitting at Mrs. Kendrick's hearth listening to the story of her son's rescue. She wanted to go in and see George at once, but Mrs. Kendrick would consent only on condition that he was not to be aroused.

"It is foolish to say it," said the old lady, smiling at Kitty as she came out of the room in which her son was sleeping; "but my son seems to look to-night just as he did when a baby."

Kitty smiled such a responsive smile, and looked so young and beautiful, that the proud old lady stooped and kissed her.

"I think I shall love you, my dear."

"I reckon I'll have to get even with you," said Mrs. Kendrick, who had a knack of hiding her own emotion, "by telling George that I've fallen in love with him."

This gave a light and half-humorous turn to affairs, and in a moment Mrs. Denham was as prim and as uncompromising in appearance as ever.

"Well!" exclaimed Mrs. Kendrick, after she and Kitty had retired for the night, "the day's worth living if only to find out that Rebecca Denham has got a heart in her insides. I believe actually she'd 'a' cried for a little."

"She did cry, mother," said Kitty, solemnly. "There were tears in her eyes when she leaned over me."

"Well, well, well!" said Mrs. Kendrick, "she always put me in mind of a ghost that can't be laid on account of its pride. But we're what the Lord made us, I reckon, and people deceive their looks. My old turkey gobbler is harmless as a hound puppy; but I reckon he'd bust if he didn't up and strut when strangers are in the front porch."

With that Mrs. Kendrick addressed herself to her prayers and to slumber; but Kitty lay awake a long time, thinking and thinking, until finally her thoughts became the substance of youth's sweetest dreams.

But why should the tender dreams of this pure heart be transcribed here? Indeed, why should these vague outlines be spun out to the vanishing point, like the gossamer threads that float and glance and disappear in the September skies? Some of the grandchildren of George Denham and Kitty Kendrick will read these pages, and wonder, romantic youngsters that they are, why all the love passages have been suppressed; other readers, more practical and perhaps severer, will ask themselves what possible interest there can be in the narrative of a simple episode in the life of a humble fugitive. What reply can be made, what explanation can be offered? Fortunately, what remains to be told may mostly be put in the sententious language of Brother Johnny Roach.

One day, shortly after the events which have been described, Brother Brannum rode up to Brother Roach's mill, dismounted, and hitched his horse to the rack.

"You're mighty welcome, Brother Brannum," said Brother Roach from the door, as cheerful under his covering of meal dust as the clown in the pantomime; "you're mighty welcome. I had as lief talk to my hopper as to most folks; but the hopper knows me by heart, and I dassent take too many liberties wi' it. Come in, Brother Brannum; there's no great head of water on, and the gear is running soberly. Sat'days, when all the rocks are moving, my mill is a female woman; the clatter is turrible. I'll not deny it. I hope you're well, Brother Brannum. And Sister Brannum. I'll never forgit the savor of her Sunday dumplings, not if I live a thousand year."

"We're well as common, Brother Roach, well as common. Yit a twitch here and a twinge there tells us we're moving along to'rds eternity. It's age that's a-feeling of us, Brother Roach; and when we're ripe it'll pluck us."

"It's age ruther than the dumplings, that I'll take the stand on," exclaimed Brother Roach. "Yit, when it comes to that, look at Mizzers Denham; that woman kin look age out of countenance any day. Then there's Giner'l Bledser; who more nimble at a muster than the Giner'l? I see 'em both this last gone Sat'day, and though I was in-about up to my eyes in the toll-bin, I relished the seeing and the hearing of 'em. But I reckon you've heard the news, Brother Brannum," said Brother Roach, modestly deprecating his own sources of information.

"Bless you! Not me, Brother Roach," said Brother Brannum; "I've heard no news. Down in my settlement I'm cut off from the world. Let them caper as they may, we're not pestered wi' misinformation."

"No, nor me nuther, Brother Brannum," said Brother Roach, "bekaze it's as much as I can do for to listen at the racket of my mill. Yit there are some sights meal dust won't begin to hide, and some talk the clatter of the hopper won't nigh drown."

"What might they be, Brother Roach?" Brother Brannum brushed the dust off a box with his coat-tails, and sat down.

"Well, sir," said Brother Roach, pushing his hat back, and placing his thumbs behind his suspenders, "last Sat'day gone I was a-hurrying to and fro, when who should pop in at the door but Giner'l Bledser?

" 'Hello, Johnny!' says he, free and familiar.

" 'Howdy, Giner'l,' says I. 'You look holp up, speaking off-hand,' says I.

" 'That I am, Johnny, that I am,' says he; 'I've made a trade that makes me particular proud,' says he.

" 'How's that, Giner'l?' says I.

" 'Why, I've sold Blue Dave,' says he; 'eight years ago, I bought him for five hundred dollars, and now I've sold him to Mizzers Denham for a thousand,' says he. 'I've got the cold cash in my pocket, and now let 'em ketch the nigger,' says he.

" 'Well, Giner'l,' says I, 'it'll be time for to marvel arter you see the outcome bekaze,' says I, 'when there's business in the wind, Mizzers Denham is as long-headed and as cle'r-sighted as a Philadelphia lawyer,' says I.

"And (would you believe it, Brother Brannum?) the outcome happened then and there right before our very face and eyes."

"In what regards, Brother Roach?" said Brother Brannum, rubbing his bony hands together.

"Well, sir, I glanced my eye out of the door, and I see the Denham carriage coming down yan hill. I p'inted it out to the Giner'l, and he ups and says, says he,

" 'Davy, though she may be a-going to town for to sue me for damages, yit, if Mizzers Denham's in that carriage, I'll salute her now,' says he; and then he took his stand in the door, as frisky as a colt and as smiling as a basket of chips. As they come up, I tetch'd the Giner'l on the shoulder.

" 'Giner'l, says I, 'look clost at that nigger on the carriage,—look clost at him,' says I.

" 'Why, what the thunderation!' says he.

" 'To be certain!' says I; 'that's your Blue Dave, and he looks mighty slick,' says I.

"The Giner'l forgot for to say howdy," continued Brother Roach, laughing until he began to wheeze; "but Mizzers Denham, she leant out of the carriage window, and said, says she,

" 'Good-morning, Giner'l, good-morning! David is a most excellent driver,' says she.

34

"The Giner'l managed for to take off his hat, but he was in-about the worst whipped-out white man I ever see. And arter the carriage got out of hearing, sir, he stood in that there door there and cussed plump tell he couldn't cuss. When a man's been to Congress and back, he's liable for to know how to take the name of the Lord in vain. But don't tell me about the wimmen, Brother Brannum. Don't!"

Blue Dave was happy at last. He became a great favorite with everybody. His voice was the loudest at the corn-shucking, his foot was the nimblest at the plantation frolics, his row was the straightest and the cleanest in the cotton-patch, his hand was the firmest on the carriage-seat, his arm was the strongest at the log-rolling. When his old mistress came to die, her wandering mind dwelt upon the negro who had served her so faithfully. She fancied she was making a journey.

"The carriage goes smoothly along here," she said. Then, after a little pause she asked, "Is David driving?" and the weeping negro cried out from a corner of the room,

" 'Tain't po' Dave, Mistiss! De good Lord done tuck holt er de lines."

And so, dreaming as a little child would dream, the old lady slipped from life into the beatitudes, if the smiles of the dead mean anything.

Balaam and His Master

WHAT FANTASTIC TRICKS are played by fate or circumstance! Here is a horrible war that shall redeem a nation, that shall restore civilization, that shall establish Christianity. Here is a university of slavery that shall lead the savage to citizenship. Here is a conflagration that shall rebuild a city. Here is the stroke of a pen that shall change the destinies of many peoples. Here is the bundle of fagots that shall light the fires of liberty. As in great things, so in small. Tragedy drags comedy across the stage, and hard upon the heels of the hero tread the heavy villain and the painted clown.

What a preface to write before the name of Billville!

Years ago, when one of the ex-Virginian pioneers who had settled in Wilkes County, in the State of Georgia, concluded to try his fortune farther west, he found himself, after a tedious journey of a dozen days, in the midst of a little settlement in middle Georgia. His wagons and his negroes were at once surrounded by a crowd of curious but good-humored men and a swarm of tow-headed children.

"What is your name?" he asked one of the group.

"Bill Jones."

"And yours?" turning to another.

"Bill Satterlee."

The group was not a large one, but in addition to Jones and Satterlee, as the newcomer was informed, Bill Ware, Bill Cosby, Bill Pinkerton, Bill Pearson, Bill Johnson, Bill Thurman, Bill Jessup, and Bill Prior were there present, and ready to answer to their names. In short, fate or circumstance had played one of its fantastic pranks in this isolated community, and every male member of the settlement, with the exception of Laban Davis, who was small and puny-looking, bore the name of Bill.

"Well," said the pioneer, who was not without humor, "I'll pitch my tent in Billville. My name is Bill Cozart."

This is how Billville got its name—a name that has clung to it through thick and thin. A justifiable but futile attempt was made during the war to change the name of the town to Panola, but it is still called Billville, much to the disappointment of those citizens who have drawn both pride and prosperity in the lottery of life.

It was a fortunate day for Billville when Mr. William Cozart, almost by accident, planted his family tree in the soil of the settlement. He was a man of affairs, and at once became the leading citizen of the place. His energy and public spirit, which had room for development here, appeared to be contagious. He bought hundreds of acres of land, in the old Virginia fashion, and made for himself a home as comfortable as it was costly. His busy and unselfish life was an example for his neighbors to follow, and when he died the memory of it was a precious heritage to his children.

Meanwhile Billville, stirred into action by his influence, grew into a thrifty village, and then into a flourishing town; but through all the changes the Cozarts remained the leading family, socially, politically, and financially. But one day in the thirties Berrien Cozart was born, and the wind that blew aside the rich lace of his cradle must have been an ill one, for the child grew up to be a thorn in the side of those who loved him best. His one redeeming quality was his extraordinary beauty. This has, no doubt, been exaggerated; but there are still living in Billville many men and women who knew him, and they will tell you to-day that Berrien Cozart was the handsomest man they have ever seen—and some of them have visited every court in Europe. So far as they are concerned, the old saying, "Handsome is that handsome does," has lost its force. They will tell you that Berrien Cozart was the handsomest man in the world and—probably the worst.

He was willful and wrongheaded from the first. He never, even as a child, acknowledged any authority but his own sweet will. He could simulate obedience whenever it suited his purpose, but only one person in the world had any real influence over him—a negro named Balaam. The day Berrien Cozart was born, his proud and happy father called to a likely negro lad who was playing about in the yard—the day was Sunday—and said:

"How old are you?"

"I dunno 'zackly, marster, but ole Aunt Emmeline she know."

"Do you do any work?"

"Yes, suh; I totes water, an' I drives de cows ter de pastur', an' I keeps off de calfs, an' I runs de chickens out'n de gyardin."

The sprightly and intelligent appearance of the lad evidently made a favorable impression on the master, for he beckoned to him and said:

"Come in here; I want to show you something."

The negro dropped his hat on the ground and followed Mr. Cozart, who led the way to the darkened room where Berrien, the baby, was having his first experience with existence. He lay on the nurse's lap, with blinking eyes and red and wrinkled face, trying to find his mouth with his fists. The nurse, black as she was, was officious, and when she saw the negro boy she exclaimed:

"Balaam, w'at you doin' in yere? Take yo'se'f right out! Dis ain't no place fer you."

"Marster says so," said Balaam, sententiously.

"Balaam," said Mr. Cozart, "this baby will be your master. I want you to look after him and take care of him."

"Yes, suh," said Balaam, regarding his new master with both interest and curiosity. "He look like he older dan w'at he is." With that Balaam retreated to the negro quarters, where he had a strange tale to tell the other children about the new white baby.

Berrien grew and thrived, and when he was a year old Balaam took charge of him, and the two soon became devoted to each other. The negro would take the child on his back and carry him from one end of the plantation to the other, and Berrien was never happy unless Balaam was somewhere in sight. Once, when it was found necessary to correct Balaam with a switch for some boyish offense, his young master fell on the floor in a convulsion of rage and grief. This manifestation made such an impression on the family that no further attempt was ever made to punish Balaam; and so the two grew up together—the young master with a temper of extreme violence and an obstinacy that had no bounds, and the negro with an independence and a fearlessness extremely rare among slaves.

It was observed by all, and was a cause of special wonder among the negroes, that, in spite of Berrien Cozart's violent temper, he never turned his hand against Balaam, not even when he was too young to reason about the matter. Sometimes, when he was seen throwing stones in a peculiarly vicious way at a tree, or at the chickens, or at some of the other children, the older negroes would laughingly shake their heads at one another and say that the child was mad with Balaam.

These queer relations between master and slave grew stronger as the two grew older. When Berrien was ten and Balaam twenty they were even more inseparable than they had been when the negro was trudging about the plantation with his young master on his back. At that time Balaam was not allowed to sleep in the big house; but when Berrien was ten he had a room to himself, and the negro slept on a pallet by the side of the bed.

About this time it was thought necessary to get a private tutor for Berrien. He had a great knack for books in a fitful sort of way, but somehow the tutor, who was an estimable young gentleman from Philadelphia, was not very much to Berrien's taste. For a day or two matters went along smoothly enough, but it was not long before Balaam, lying on the floor outside the door, heard a tremendous racket and clatter in the room. Looking in, he saw his young master pelting the tutor with books and using language that was far from polite. Balaam went in, closing the door carefully behind him, and almost immediately the tumult ceased. Then the negro appeared leading his young master by the arm. They went downstairs and out on the lawn. The tutor, perplexed and astonished by the fierce temper of his pupil, saw the two from the window and watched them curiously. Berrien finally stopped and leaned against a tree. The negro, with his hand on the boy's shoulder, was saying something unpleasant, for the tutor observed one or two fierce gestures of protest. But these soon ceased, and presently Berrien walked rapidly back to the house, followed by Balaam. The tutor heard them coming up the stairway; then the door opened, and his pupil entered and apologized for his rudeness.

For some time there was such marked improvement in Berrien's behavior that his tutor often wondered what influence the negro had brought to bear on his young master; but he never found out. In fact, he soon forgot all about the matter, for the improvement was only temporary. The youngster became so disagreeable and so unmanageable that the tutor was glad to give up his position at the end of the year. After that Berrien was sent to the Academy, and there he made considerable progress, for he was spurred on in his studies by the example of the other boys. But he was a wild youth, and there was no mischief, no matter how malicious it might be, in which he was not the leader. As his character unfolded itself the fact became more and more manifest that he had an unsavory career before him. Some of the older heads predicted that he would come to the gallows, and there was certainly some ground for these gloomy suggestions, for never before had the quiet community of Billville given development to such reckless wickedness as that which marked the daily life of Berrien Cozart as he grew older. Sensual, cruel, impetuous, and implacable, he was the wonder of the mild-mannered people of the county, and a terror to the God-fearing. Nevertheless, he was attractive even to those who regarded him as the imp of the Evil One, and many a love-lorn maiden was haunted by his beautiful face in her dreams.

When Berrien was eighteen he was sent to Franklin College at Athens, which was supposed to divide the responsibility of guardianship with a student's parents. The atmosphere the young man found there in those days suited him admirably. He became the leader of the wildest set at that venerable institution, and proceeded to make a name for himself as the promoter and organizer of the most disreputable escapades the college had ever known. He was an aggressor in innumerable broils, he fought a duel in the suburbs of Athens, and he ended his college career by insulting the chancellor in the lecture-room. He was expelled, and the students and the people of Athens breathed freer when it was known that he had gone home never to return.

There was a curious scene with his father when the wayward youth returned to Billville in disgrace. The people of that town had received some inkling of the sort of education the young man was getting at college, though Mr. Cozart was inclined to look somewhat leniently on the pranks of his son, ascribing them to the hot blood of youth. But when Berrien's creditors began to send in their accounts, amounting to several thousands of dollars, he realized for the first time that the hope and pride of his later years had been vain delusions. Upon the heels of the accounts came Berrien himself, handsomer and more attractive than ever. Dissipation was not one of his vices, and he returned with the bloom of youth on his cheek and the glowing fires of health in his sparkling eyes. He told the story of his expulsion with an air as gay as any cavalier ever assumed. The story was told at the table, and there was company present. But this fact was ignored by Berrien's father. His hand shook as he laid down his knife and fork.

"You have damaged my credit," he said to his son across the table; "you have disgraced your mother's name and mine; and now you have the impudence to make a joke of it at my table, sir. Let me not see your face in this house again until you have returned to college and wiped out the blot you have placed on your name."

"As you please, sir," said Berrien. His eyes were still full of laughter, but some of those who were at the table said his nether lip trembled a little. He rose, bowed, and passed out.

Balaam was in his young master's room when the latter went in. He had unpacked the trunk and the valise and was placing the things in a clothes-press, meanwhile talking with himself, as most negroes will when left to themselves. Berrien entered, humming the tune of a college glee.

40

"I 'lowed you was at dinner, Marse Berry," said Balaam.

"I have finished," said young Cozart. "Have you had yours?"

"Lord! no, suh. Hit'll be 'way yander todes night 'fo' I kin git dese clo'es straightened out."

"Well," said the young man, "you go and get your dinner as soon as you can. This valise must be repacked. Before the sun goes down we must be away from here."

"Good Lord, Marse Berry! I ain't said howdy wid none er de folks yit. How come we got ter go right off?"

"You can stay, if you choose," said Berrien. "I reckon you'd be a better negro if you had stayed at home all the time. Right now you ought to be picking your five hundred pounds of cotton every day."

"Now, you know, Marse Berry, dat if you er gwine, I'm gwine too—you know dat p'intedly; but you come in on me so sudden-like dat you sorter git me flustrated."

"Well," said Berrien, seating himself on the side of the bed and running his fingers through his curling hair, "if you go with me this time you will be taking a big jump in the dark. There's no telling where you'll land. Pap has taken the studs, and I have made up my mind to leave here for good and all. You belong to me, but I'll give you your choice; you can go with me, or you can stay. If you go, I'll probably get into a tight place and sell you; if you stay, Pap will make a pet of you for my sake."

Regarding this as a very good offhand joke, the young man laughed so loud that the sound of it penetrated to the dining-room, and, mellow and hearty as it was, it struck strangely on the ears of those still sitting at the table.

"I knowed in reason dat dey was gwine to be a rippit," said Balaam; "kaze you know how you been gwine on up yander, Marse Berry. I tole an' tole you 'bout it, an' I dunno whar in de name er goodness you'd been ef I hadn't been right dar fer ter look atter you."

"Yes," remarked Berrien, sarcastically, "you were just about drunk enough half the time to look after me like a Dutch uncle."

Balaam held his head down and chuckled. "Yes, suh," he said, "I tuck my dram, dey ain't no 'sputin' er dat; yit I never has tuck so much dat I ain't keep my eye on you. But 't ain't do no good: you des went right 'long; an' dar was ole Mistiss, which she done sick in bed, an' Miss Sally Carter, which she's yo' born cousin—dar dey all was a-specktin' you ter head de whole school gang. An' you did head 'em, mon, but not in de books."

"My fair Cousin Sarah!" exclaimed Berrien in a reminiscent way.

"Yes, suh," said Balaam; "an' dey tells me down in de kitchen dat she comin' yere dis ve'y day."

"Then," said the young man, "it is time for me to be going. Get your dinner. If I am to have your company, you must be ready in an hour; if you want to stay, go to the overseer and tell him to put you to work."

Laughing good-naturedly, Balaam slipped out. After a little while Berrien Cozart went down the stairway and into the room of his mother, who was an invalid. He sat at her bedside and talked a few moments. Then he straightened and smoothed her pillows, stroked her gray hair, gazed into her gentle eyes, and kissed her twice. These things the poor lady remembered long afterwards. Straying into the spacious parlor, the young man looked around on the familiar furniture and the walls covered with portraits. Prominent among these was the beautiful face of Sally Carter. The red curtains in the windows, swaying to and fro in the wind, so swiftly changed the light and shadow that the fair face in the heavy gilt frame seemed to be charged with life. The lustrous eyes seemed to dance and the saucy lips to smile. Berrien remembered his fair cousin with pleasure. She had been his playmate when he was younger, and the impression she made on him had been a lasting one. Beautiful as she was, there was no nonsense about her. She was high-spirited and jolly, and the young man smiled as he recalled some of their escapades together. He raised his hand to salute the portrait, and at that moment a peal of merry laughter greeted his ears. Turning, he saw framed in the doorway the rosy original of the portrait. Before he could recover from his astonishment the young lady had seized and kissed him. Then she held him off at arm's length and looked at him.

"Why, how handsome you have grown," she cried. "Just think of it! I expected to meet a regular border ruffian. My dear boy, you have no idea what a tremendous reputation your friends have given you. Ann Burney— you remember that funny little creature, don't you? as fat as a butterball— Ann told me the other day that you were positively the terror of everybody around Athens. And now I find you here kissing your fingers at my portrait on the wall. I declare, it is too romantic for anything! After this I know you will never call me Sarah Jane."

"You have taken me by surprise," said Berrien, as soon as he could get in a word. "I was admiring the skill of the artist. The lace there, falling against the velvet bodice, is neatly done."

42

"Ah, but you are blushing; you are confused!" exclaimed Miss Carter. "You haven't even told me you are glad to see me."

"There is no need to tell you that," said Berrien. "I was just thinking, when you rushed in on me, how good and kind you always were. You are maturer than the portrait there, but you are more beautiful."

Miss Carter bent low with a mock curtsey, but the color in her face was warmer as she exclaimed:

"Oh! how nice you are! The portrait there is only sixteen, and I am twenty-five. Just think of that! And just think of me at that age—what a tomboy I was! But I must run and tell the rest of the folks howdy."

Berrien Cozart walked out on the veranda, and presently he was joined by his father. "My son," said the old gentleman, "you will need money for your traveling expenses. Here is a check on our Augusta factor; you can have it cashed in Madison. I want you to return to college, make all proper apologies, and redeem yourself."

"Thank you, sir," said Berrien, taking the check and stuffing it into his pocket. His father turned to go indoors, hesitated a moment, and looked at Berrien, who was drumming idly on one of the pillars. Then the old gentleman sighed and went in.

Shortly thereafter Berrien Cozart and Balaam were journeying away from Billville in the conveyance that had brought them there.

On the high hill beyond the "town branch" Balaam leaned out of the hack and looked back at Billville. The town appeared insignificant enough; but the setting sun imparted a rosy glow to the roof of the yellow court-house and to the spire of the old church. Observing the purpose of the negro, Mr. Cozart smiled cynically and flipped the hot ashes of his cigar into Balaam's ear.

"As you are telling the town good-by," said the young man, "I'll help you to bow."

"Yasser!" said Balaam, shaking the ashes from his ear; "I was des a-lookin' back at de place. Dat sun shine red, mon, an' de jail look like she de bigges' house dar. She stan' out mo' bigger dan w'at de chu'ch do."

It may be that this statement made no impression on Berrien, but he leaned back in his seat and for miles chewed the end of his cigar in silence.

It is not the purpose of this chronicle to follow him through all his ad-ventures and escapades. As he rode away from Billville on that memorable day he seemed to realize that his career had just begun. It was a career to which he had served a long and faithful apprenticeship, and he pursued it to the end. From Madison he went to Atlanta, where for months he was a familiar, albeit a striking figure. There were few games of chance in which he was not an adept. No conjurer was so adroit with the cards or the dice; he handled these emblems of fate and disaster as an artist handles his tools. And luck chose him as her favorite; he prospered to such a degree that he grew reckless and careless. Whereupon one fine day luck turned her back on him, and he paraded on fine afternoons in front of Lloyd's Hotel a penniless man. He had borrowed and lost until he could borrow no longer.

Balaam, who was familiar with the situation, was not surprised to learn that his master had made up his mind to sell him.

"Well, suh," said Balaam, brushing his master's coat carefully, "you kin sell me, but de man dat buys Balaam will git a mighty bad bargain."

"What do you mean?" exclaimed Berrien.

"You kin sell me, suh, but I ain't gwine stay wid um."

"You can't help yourself," said the master.

"I got legs, Marse Berry. You know dat yo'se'f."

"Your legs will do you no good. You'll be caught if you go back home."

"I ain't gwine dar, suh. I'm gwine wid you. I hear you say yistiddy night p'intedly dat you gwine 'way f'om dis place, an' I'm gwine wid you. I been 'long wid you all de time, an' ole marster done tole me w'en you was baby dat I got ter stay wid you."

Something in this view seemed to strike Mr. Cozart. He walked up and down the floor a few minutes, and then fell to laughing.

"By George, Balaam, you are a trump,—a royal flush in spades. It will be a famous joke."

Thereupon Berrien Cozart arranged his cards, so to speak, for a more hazardous game than any he had ever yet played. He went with Balaam to a trader who was an expert in the slave market, and who knew its ups and downs, its weak points and its strong points. At first Berrien was disposed to put Balaam on the block and have him auctioned off to the highest bidder; but the trader knew the negro, and had already made a study of his strong points. To be perfectly sure, however, he thumped Balaam on the chest, listened to the beating of his heart, and felt of his muscles in quite a professional way.

"I reckon he ain't noways vicious," said the trader, looking at Balaam's smiling face.

"I have never seen him angry or sullen," said Mr. Cozart. Other questions were asked, and finally the trader jotted down this memorandum in his note-book:

"Buck nigger, Balaam; age 32; 6 feet 1 inch; sound as a dollar; see Colonel Strother."

Then the trader made an appointment with Berrien for the next day, and said he thought the negro could be disposed of at private sale. Such was the fact, for when Berrien went back the next day the trader met him with an offer of fifteen hundred dollars in cash for Balaam.

"Make it eighteen," said Mr. Cozart.

"Well, I'll tell you what I'll do," said the trader, closing his eyes and pursing his mouth in a business-like way. "I'll give you sixteen fifty—no more, no less. Come, now, that's fair. Split the difference."

Thereupon Mr. Cozart said it was a bargain, and the trader paid him the money down after the necessary papers were drawn up. Balaam seemed to be perfectly satisfied. All he wanted, he said, was to have a master who would treat him well. He went with Berrien to the hotel to fetch his little belongings, and if the trader had searched him when he returned he would have found strapped around his body a belt containing fifty dollars in specie.

Having thus, in a manner, replenished his empty purse, Mr. Berrien Cozart made haste to change his field of operations. To his competitors in his own special department of industry he let drop the hint that he was going to Columbus, and thence to Mobile and New Orleans, where he would hang on the outskirts of the racing season, picking up such crumbs and contributions as might naturally fall in the way of a professional gentleman who kept his eyes open and his fingers nimble enough to deal himself a winning hand.

As a matter of fact Mr. Cozart went to Nashville, and he had not been gone many days before Balaam disappeared. He had been missing two days before Colonel Strother, his new master, took any decided action, but on the morning of the fourth day the following advertisement appeared among others of a like character in the columns of the Atlanta "Intelligencer":

 $100 reward will be paid for the apprehension of my negro boy *Balaam.* Thirty-odd years old, but appeared younger; tall, pleasant-looking, quick-spoken, and polite. Was formerly the property of the Hon. William Cozart. He is supposed to be making his way to his old home. Was well dressed when last seen. Milledgeville "Recorder" and "Federal Union" please copy.

BOZEMAN STROTHER,
Atlanta, Georgia.

(d. & w. 1 mo.)

This advertisement duly appeared in the Milledgeville papers, which were published not far from Billville, but no response was ever made; the reward was never claimed. Considering the strength and completeness of the patrol system of that day, Balaam's adventure was a risky one; but, fortunately for him, a wiser head than his had planned his flight and instructed him thoroughly in the part he was to play. The shrewdness of Berrien Cozart had provided against all difficulties. Balaam left Atlanta at night, but he did not go as a fugitive. He was armed with a "pass" which formally set forth to all to whom it might concern that the boy David had express permission to join his master in Nashville, and this "pass" bore the signature of Elmore Avery, a gentleman who existed only in the imagination of Mr. Berrien Cozart. Attached thereto, also, was the signature seal of the judge of ordinary. With this little document Balaam would have found no difficulty whatever in traveling. The people he met would have reasoned that the negro whose master trusted him to make so long a journey alone must be an uncommonly faithful one, but Balaam met with an adventure that helped him along much more comfortably than the pass could have helped him. It is best, perhaps, to tell the story in his own language, as he told it long afterwards.

"I won't say I weren't skeered," said Balaam, "kaze I was; yit I weren't skeered 'nough fer ter go slippin' 'longside er de fences an' 'mongst de pine thickets. I des kep' right in de big road. Atter I got out er town a little piece, I tuck off my shoes an' tied de strings tergedder an' slung 'em 'cross my shoulder, on top my satchel, an' den I sorter mended my gait. I struck up a kind er dog-trot, an' by de time day come a many a mile lay 'twix' me an' Atlanta. Little atter sun-up I hear some horses trottin' on de road de way I come, an' bimeby a man driv up in a double buggy. He say, 'Hello, boy! Whar you gwine?' I pulled off my hat, an' say, 'I gwine whar my marster is, suh.' Den de white man 'low, 'W'at he name?' Well, suh, when de man ax me dat, hit come over me like a big streak er de chill an' fever dat I done clean fergit de name what Marse Berry choosen ter be call by. So I des runned my han' und' de lindin' er my hat an' pulled out de pass, an' say, 'Boss, dis piece er paper kin talk lots better dan I kin.'

"De man look at me right hard, an' den he tuck de pass an' read it out loud. Well, suh, w'en he come ter de name I des grabbed holt un it wid my min', an' I ain't never turned it loose tell yit. De man was drivin' long slow, an' I was walkin' by de buggy. He helt de pass in his han's some little time, den he look at me an' scratch his head. Atter a while he 'low: 'You got a mighty

46

long journey befo' you. Kin you drive? Ef you kin, put on yo' shoes an' mount up here an' take dese lines.'

"Well, suh, I wuz sorter glad, an' yit I wuz sorter skittish, but I tol' de white man thankydo, an' le'pt up in dat buggy like I was de gladdes' nigger in de worl'. De man he keep on lookin' at me, an' bimeby he say, 'I tuck a notion when I fust see you dat you was de boy w'at Cozart had in Atlanta.' Mon! you could er knocked me over wid a feather, I was dat weak; but I bu'st out laughin' an' 'low, 'Lord, boss! ef I wa'n't no better lookin' dan dat ar Cozart nigger I'd quit bein' a nigger an' take up wid de monkey tribe.' De man say, 'I had de idee dat de Cozart nigger was a mighty likely boy. What was his name? Balaam?' I was so skeered it fair make me sick at de stomach, yit I talk right out. I 'low, 'Dey call 'im Balaam, an' dey have ter whale 'im.' De man he laugh, 'He got a great big scyar on de side er his neck now whar somebody hit 'im a diff, an' he lay roun' dem hotels an' drink dram all night long.' De man look sideways at my neck. 'Dat nigger got so bad dat his marster had ter sell 'im, an' dey tells me, suh, dat de man w'at buy 'im ain' no mo' dan paid de money fer 'im dan he have ter take 'im down and strop 'im.'

"Well, suh, de man look at me an laugh so funny dat it make my ve'y limbs ache. Yes, suh. My heart hit up 'g'inst my ribs des like a flutter-mill; an' I wuz so skeered it make my tongue run slicker dan sin. He ax me mo' questions dan I could answer now, but I made answer den des like snappin' my fingers. W'at make me de mo' skeered was de way dat ar white man done. He'd look at me an' laugh, an' de plumper I gin 'im de answer de mo' he'd laugh. I say ter myse'f, I did: 'Balaam, you 'r a goner, dat w'at you is. De man know you, an' de fust calaboose he come ter he gwine slap you in dar.' I had a mighty good notion ter jump out er dat buggy an' make a break fer de woods, but stidder dat I sot right whar I wuz, kaze I knowed in reason dat ef de man want me right bad an' I wuz ter break an' run he'd fetch me down wid a pistol.

"Well, suh, dat man joke an' laugh de whole blessed mornin', an' den bimeby we drove in a town not much bigger dan Bivvle" (which was Balaam's pet name for Billville), "an' dar de white man say we'd stop fer dinner. He ain't say de word too soon fer me, mon, kaze I was so hongry an' tired it make my head swim. We driv up ter tavern, we did, an' de folks dar dey holler, 'Howdy, Judge,' an' de white man he holler 'Howdy' back, an' den he tol' me ter take de horses an' buggy down ter de liberty stable an' have 'em fed, an' den come back an' git my dinner. Dat wuz mighty good

47

news; but whilst I wuz eatin' my dinner I hear dat white man laughin', an' it come over me dat he know who I wuz an' dat he wuz gwine ter gi' me up; yit dat ain't hender my appetite, an' I des sot dar an' stuff myse'f tell I des make de yuther niggers open der eyes. An' den, when I git my belly full, I sot in de sun an' went right fast ter sleep. I 'spec' I tuck a right smart nap, kaze when some un hollered at me an' woke me up de sun wuz gwine down de hill right smartly. I jumped up on my feet, I did, an' I say, 'Who dat callin' me?' Somebody 'low, 'Yo' marster want you.' Den I bawl out, 'Is Marse Berry come?' De niggers all laugh, an' one un 'em say, 'Dat nigger man dreamin', mon. He ain't woke good yit.'

"By dat time I done come ter my senses, an' den I ax dem wharbouts marster is. Bimeby, when I done foun' de white man w'at bring me in his buggy, he look at me sorter funny an' say, 'You know whar you lef' my buggy: well, you go down an' raise up de seat an' fetch me de little box you'll fin' in dar. Wrop it up in de buggy rug an' fetch it an' put it on de table dar.' Well, suh, I went an' got dat box, an' time I put my han' on it I knowed des 'zactly w'at wuz on de inside er it. I done seed too many er 'em. It wuz under lock an' key, but I knowed it wuz a farrar box like dem w'at Marse Berry done his gamblin' wid. By de time I got back ter de room in de tavern de white man done had de table kivered wid a piece er cloff w'at he got out'n his satchel. He tuck de box, onlocked it, rattled de chips in his han', an' shuffled de kyards. Den he look at me an' laugh. He was de quarest white man dat ever I laid eyes on.

"Atter while I ax 'im ef I hadn't better be gitten' 'long todes de eend er my journey. He 'low: 'Lord, no! I want you ter set round yere atter supper an' gi' me luck. You ain't losin' no time, kaze I'm a-gwine plumb to Chattanoogy, an' ef you'll be ez spry ez you kin be I'll take you 'long wid me.' De ups an' odds er it was dat I stayed wid de man. De folks named 'im Judge, an' he was a judge, mon. 'Long 'bout nine dat night he come ter his room, whar I was waitin' fer 'im, an' soon atter dat de young gentlemens 'bout town 'gun ter drap in, an' 't wa'n't long 'fo' de game got started. Look like de man ain't wanter play, but de yuthers dey kep' on coaxin', an' presently he fotch out de box an' opened up. Well, sah, I done seed lots er gamblin' fust an' last, but dat white man beat my time. Dey played poker, stidder farrar, an' it look like ter me dat de man done got de kyards trained. He dealt 'em 'boveboard, an' dey des come in his han' 'zackly like he want 'em ter come. Ef he had any tricks like w'at Marse Berry played on folks,

48

dey was too slick fer my eye, yit he des beated dem yuther mens scand'lous. It was des like one er dese yere great big river cats ketchin' minners.

"Atter dey been playin' some little time, de white man what brung me dar 'low: 'Boy, you better go git some sleep. We'll start soon in de mornin'.' But I say, 'No, suh; I'll des set in de cornder here an' nod, an' I'll be close by ef so be you want me.' I sot dar, I did, an' I had a good chance ter sleep, kaze, bless yo' heart! dem mens ain't make much fuss. Dey des grip der kyards an' sorter hol' der bref. Sometimes one un 'em would break out an' cuss a word er two, but inginer'lly dey'd plank up der scads an' lose 'em des like dey wuz usen ter it. De white man w'at dey call Judge he des wiped 'em up, an' at de een' he wuz des ez fresh ez he wuz at de start. It wuz so nigh day when de game broke up dat Marse Judge 'lowed dat it was too late fer supper an' not quite soon 'nough fer breakfas', an' den he say he wuz gwine ter take a walk an' git some a'r.

"Well, suh, it wuz dat away all de time I wuz wid dat white man— laughin' an' jokin' all day, an' gamblin' all night long. How an' when he got sleep I'll never tell you, kaze he wuz wide awake eve'y time I seed 'im. It went on dis away plumb till we got ter de Tennessy River, dar whar Chatty- noogy is. Atter we sorter rested, de white man tuck me 'cross de river, an' we druv on ter whar de stage changes hosses. Dar we stopped, an' whilst I wuz waitin' fer de stage de white man 'low, 'Balaam!' He kotch me so quick, dat I jump des like I'd been shot, an' hollered out, 'Suh!' Den he laugh sorter funny, an' say: 'Don't look skeered, Balaam; I knowed you fum de off-start. You 'r' a mighty good boy, but yo' marster is a borned rascal. I'm gwine send you whar yoo say he is, an' I want you ter tell 'im dis fum me—dat dough he tried ter rob me, yit fer de sake er his Cousin Sally, I he'ped you ter go whar he is.'

"Den de man got in his buggy an' driv back, an' dat de las' time I ever laid eyes on 'im. When de stage come 'long I got up wid de driver, an' 't wa'n't long 'fo' I wuz wid Marse Berry, an' I ain't no sooner seed 'im dan I knowed he was gwine wrong wuss and wuss: not but w'at he was glad kaze I come, but it look like his face done got mo' harder. Well, suh, it was des dat away. I ain't gwine ter tell you all w'at he done an' how he done it, kaze he was my own marster, an' he never hit me a lick amiss, 'ceppin' it was when he was a little boy. I ain't gwine ter tell you whar we went an' how we got dar, kaze dey done been too much talk now. But we drapped down inter Alabam', an' den inter Massasip', an' den inter Arkansaw, an' back ag'in inter Massasip';

49

an' one night whilst we wuz on one er dem big river boats, Marse Berry he got inter a mighty big row. Dey wuz playin' kyards fer de bigges' kind er stakes, an' fust news I know de lie was passed, an' den de whole gang made fer Marse Berry. Dey whipped out der knives an' der pistols, an' it look like it wuz gwine ter be all night wid Marse Berry. Well, suh, I got so skeered dat I picked up a cheer an' smashed de nighest man, and by dat time Marse Berry had shot one; an', suh, we des cleaned 'em out. Den Marse Berry made a dash fer de low'-mos' deck, an' I dashed atter 'im. Den I hear sumpin' go ker-slosh in de water, an' I 'lowed it was Marse Berry, an' in I splunged head-foremos'. An' den—but, Lord, suh, you know de balance des good ez I does, kaze I hear tell dat dey wuz sumpin' n'er 'bout it in de papers."

This was as far as Balaam ever would go with the story of his adventure. He had made a hero of Berrien Cozart from his youth, and he refused to dwell on any episode in the young man's career that, to his mind, was not worthy of a Cozart. When Berrien leaped to the lower deck of the steamboat his foot touched a stick of wood. This he flung into the river, and then hid himself among the cotton bales that were piled on the forward part of the boat. It will never be known whether he threw the piece of wood into the water knowing that Balaam would follow, or whether his sole intention was to elude pursuit. A shot or two was fired, but the bullets fell wide of their mark, and the boat swept on, leaving the negro swimming around, searching for his master.

At the next landing-place Berrien slipped ashore unseen. But fortune no longer favored him; for the next day a gentleman who had been a passenger on the boat recognized him, and an attempt was made to arrest him. He shot the high sheriff of the county through the head, and became a fugitive indeed. He was pursued through Alabama into Georgia, and being finally captured not a mile away from Billville, was thrown into jail in the town where he was born. His arrest, owing to the standing of his family, created a tremendous sensation in the quiet village. Before he was carried to jail he asked that his father be sent for. The messenger tarried some little time, but he returned alone.

"What did my father say?" Berrien asked with some eagerness.

"He said," replied the messenger, "that he didn't want to see you."

"Did he write that message?" the young man inquired.

"Oh, no!" the messenger declared. "He just waved his arm—so—and said he didn't want to see you."

At once the troubled expression on Berrien Cozart's face disappeared. He looked around on the crowd and smiled.

"You see what it is," he said with a light laugh, "to be the pride of a family! Gentlemen, I am ready. Don't let me keep you waiting." And so, followed by half the population of his native village, he was escorted to jail.

This building was a two-story brick structure, as solid as good material and good work could make it, and there was no fear that any prisoner could escape, especially from the dungeon where Berrien's captors insisted on confining him. Nevertheless the jailer was warned to take unusual precautions. This official, however, who occupied with his family the first story of the jail, merely smiled. He had grown old in the business of keeping this jail, and certainly he knew a great deal more about it than those Mississippi officials who were strutting around and putting on such airs.

To his other duties the jailer added those of tyler of the little lodge of freemasons that had its headquarters in a hall on the public square, and it so happened that the lodge was to meet on the very night that Berrien was put into jail. After supper the jailer, as had been his habit for years, smoked his pipe, and then went down to the village and lighted the lamps in the masonic hall. His wife and daughter, full of the subject of Berrien Cozart's imprisonment, went to a neighbor's not far away for the purpose of discussing the matter. As they passed out of the gate they heard the jailer blowing the tin trumpet which was the signal for the masons to assemble.

It was nearly eleven o'clock when the jailer returned, but he found his wife and daughter waiting for him. Both had a troubled air, and they lost no time in declaring that they had heard weeping and sobbing upstairs in the dungeon. The jailer himself was very sympathetic, having known Berrien for many years, and he took another turn at his pipe by way of consolation. Then, as was his custom, he took his lantern and went around the jail on a tour of inspection to see that everything was safe.

He did not go far. First he stumbled over a pile of bricks, and then his shoulder struck a ladder. He uttered a little cry and looked upward, and there, dim as his lantern was, he could see a black and gaping hole in the wall of the dungeon. He ran into the house as fast as his rheumatic legs could carry him and he screamed to his wife and daughter:

"Raise the alarm! Cozart has escaped! We are ruined!"

Then he ran to the dungeon door, flung it open, and then fell back with a cry of terror. What did he see, and what did the others who joined him there see? On the floor lay Berrien Cozart dead, and crouching beside him was Balaam. How the negro had managed to make his way through the masonry of the dungeon without discovery is still one of the mysteries of Billville. But, prompt as he was, he was too late. His master had escaped through a wider door. He had made his way to a higher court. Death, coming to him in that dark dungeon, must have visited him in the similitude of a happy dream, for there under the light of the lanterns he lay smiling sweetly as a little child that nestles on its mother's breast; and on the floor near him, where it had dropped from his nerveless hand, was a golden locket, from which smiled the lovely face of Sally Carter.

Free Joe and the Rest of the World

THE NAME OF Free Joe strikes humorously upon the ear of memory. It is impossible to say why, for he was the humblest, the simplest, and the most serious of all God's living creatures, sadly lacking in all those elements that suggest the humorous. It is certain, moreover, that in 1850 the sober-minded citizens of the little Georgian village of Hillsborough were not inclined to take a humorous view of Free Joe, and neither his name nor his presence provoked a smile. He was a black atom, drifting hither and thither without an owner, blown about by all the winds of circumstance, and given over to shiftlessness.

The problems of one generation are the paradoxes of a succeeding one, particularly if war, or some such incident, intervenes to clarify the atmosphere and strengthen the understanding. Thus, in 1850, Free Joe represented not only a problem of large concern, but, in the watchful eyes of Hillsborough, he was the embodiment of that vague and mysterious danger that seemed to be forever lurking on the outskirts of slavery, ready to sound a shrill and ghostly signal in the impenetrable swamps, and steal forth under the midnight stars to murder, rapine, and pillage,—a danger always threatening, and yet never assuming shape; intangible, and yet real; impossible, and yet not improbable. Across the serene and smiling front of safety, the pale outlines of the awful shadow of insurrection sometimes fell. With this invisible panorama as a background, it was natural that the figure of Free Joe, simple and humble as it was, should assume undue proportions. Go where he would, do what he might, he could not escape the finger of observation and the kindling eye of suspicion. His lightest words were noted, his slightest actions marked.

Under all the circumstances it was natural that his peculiar condition should reflect itself in his habits and manners. The slaves laughed loudly day by day, but Free Joe rarely laughed. The slaves sang at their work and danced at their frolics, but no one ever heard Free Joe sing or saw him dance. There was something painfully plaintive and appealing in his attitude, something touching in his anxiety to please. He was of the friendliest nature, and seemed to be delighted when he could amuse the little children who had made a playground of the public square. At times he would please them by making his little dog Dan perform all sorts of curious tricks, or he would tell them quaint stories of the beasts of the field and birds of the air; and frequently he was coaxed into relating the story of his own freedom. That story was brief, but tragical.

In the year of our Lord 1840, when a negro-speculator of a sportive turn of mind reached the little village of Hillsborough on his way to the Mississippi region, with a caravan of likely negroes of both sexes, he found much to interest him. In that day and at that time there were a number of young men in the village who had not bound themselves over to repentance for the various misdeeds of the flesh. To these young men the negro-speculator (Major Frampton was his name) proceeded to address himself. He was a Virginian, he declared; and, to prove the statement, he referred all the festively inclined young men of Hillsborough to a barrel of peach-brandy in one of his covered wagons. In the minds of these young men there was less doubt in regard to the age and quality of the brandy than there was in regard to the negro-trader's birthplace. Major Frampton might or might not have been born in the Old Dominion,—that was a matter for consideration and inquiry,—but there could be no question as to the mellow pungency of the peach-brandy.

In his own estimation, Major Frampton was one of the most accomplished of men. He had summered at the Virginia Springs; he had been to Philadelphia, to Washington, to Richmond, to Lynchburg, and to Charleston, and had accumulated a great deal of experience which he found useful. Hillsborough was hid in the woods of Middle Georgia, and its general aspect of innocence impressed him. He looked on the young men who had shown their readiness to test his peach-brandy, as overgrown country boys who needed to be introduced to some of the arts and sciences he had at his command. Thereupon the major pitched his tents, figuratively speaking, and became, for the time being, a part and parcel of the innocence that characterized Hillsborough. A wiser man would doubtless have made the same mistake.

The little village possessed advantages that seemed to be providentially

54

arranged to fit the various enterprises that Major Frampton had in view. There was the auction-block in front of the stuccoed court-house, if he desired to dispose of a few of his negroes; there was a quarter-track, laid out to his hand and in excellent order, if he chose to enjoy the pleasures of horse-racing; there were secluded pine thickets within easy reach, if he desired to indulge in the exciting pastime of cock-fighting; and various lonely and unoccupied rooms in the second story of the tavern, if he cared to challenge the chances of dice or cards.

Major Frampton tried them all with varying luck, until he began his famous game of poker with Judge Alfred Wellington, a stately gentleman with a flowing white beard and mild blue eyes that gave him the appearance of a benevolent patriarch. The history of the game in which Major Frampton and Judge Alfred Wellington took part is something more than a tradition in Hillsborough, for there are still living three or four men who sat around the table and watched its progress. It is said that at various stages of the game Major Frampton would destroy the cards with which they were playing, and send for a new pack, but the result was always the same. The mild blue eyes of Judge Wellington, with few exceptions, continued to overlook "hands" that were invincible—a habit they had acquired during a long and arduous course of training from Saratoga to New Orleans. Major Frampton lost his money, his horses, his wagons, and all his negroes but one, his body-servant. When his misfortune had reached this limit, the major adjourned the game. The sun was shining brightly, and all nature was cheerful. It is said that the major also seemed to be cheerful. However this may be, he visited the court-house, and executed the papers that gave his body-servant his freedom. This being done, Major Frampton sauntered into a convenient pine thicket, and blew out his brains.

The negro thus freed came to be known as Free Joe. Compelled, under the law, to choose a guardian, he chose Judge Wellington, chiefly because his wife Lucinda was among the negroes won from Major Frampton. For several years Free Joe had what may be called a jovial time. His wife Lucinda was well provided for, and he found it a comparatively easy matter to provide for himself; so that, taking all the circumstances into consideration, it is not matter for astonishment that he became somewhat shiftless.

When Judge Wellington died, Free Joe's troubles began. The judge's negroes, including Lucinda, went to his half-brother, a man named Calderwood, who was a hard master and a rough customer generally,—a man of many eccentricities of mind and character. His neighbors had a habit of alluding to him as "Old Spite"; and the name seemed to fit him so completely, that he was known far and near as "Spite" Calderwood. He probably enjoyed the distinction the name gave him, at any rate, he never resented it, and it was not often that he missed an opportunity to show that he deserved it. Calderwood's place was two or three miles from the village of Hillsborough, and Free Joe visited his wife twice a week, Wednesday and Saturday nights.

One Sunday he was sitting in front of Lucinda's cabin, when Calderwood happened to pass that way.

"Howdy, marster?" said Free Joe, taking off his hat.

"Who are you?" exclaimed Calderwood abruptly, halting and staring at the negro.

"I'm name' Joe, marster. I'm Lucindy's ole man."

"Who do you belong to?"

"Marse John Evans is my gyardeen, marster."

"Big name—gyardeen. Show your pass."

Free Joe produced that document, and Calderwood read it aloud slowly, as if he found it difficult to get at the meaning:

"*To whom it may concern: This is to certify that the boy Joe Frampton has my permission to visit his wife Lucinda.*"

This was dated at Hillsborough, and signed "*John W. Evans.*"

Calderwood read it twice, and then looked at Free Joe, elevating his eyebrows, and showing his discolored teeth.

"Some mighty big words in that there. Evans own this place, I reckon. When's he comin' down to take hold?"

Free Joe fumbled with his hat. He was badly frightened.

"Lucindy says she speck you wouldn't min' my comin', long ez I behave, marster."

Calderwood tore the pass in pieces and flung it away.

"Don't want no free niggers 'round here," he exclaimed. "There's the big road. It'll carry you to town. Don't let me catch you here no more. Now, mind what I tell you."

Free Joe presented a shabby spectacle as he moved off with his little dog Dan slinking at his heels. It should be said in behalf of Dan, however, that his bristles were up, and that he looked back and growled. It may be that the dog had the advantage of insignificance, but it is difficult to conceive how a dog bold enough to raise his bristles under Calderwood's very eyes could be as insignificant as Free Joe. But both the negro and his little dog seemed to give a new and more dismal aspect to forlornness as they turned into the road and went toward Hillsborough.

After this incident Free Joe appeared to have clearer ideas concerning his peculiar condition. He realized the fact that though he was free he was more helpless than any slave. Having no owner, every man was his master. He knew that he was the object of suspicion, and therefore all his slender resources (ah! how pitifully slender they were!) were devoted to winning, not kindness and appreciation, but toleration; all his efforts were in the direction of mitigating the circumstances that tended to make his condition so much worse than that of the negroes around him,—negroes who had friends because they had masters.

So far as his own race was concerned, Free Joe was an exile. If the slaves secretly envied him his freedom (which is to be doubted, considering his miserable condition), they openly despised him, and lost no opportunity to treat him with contumely. Perhaps this was in some measure the result of the attitude which Free Joe chose to maintain toward them. No doubt his instinct taught him that to hold himself aloof from the slaves would be to invite from the whites the toleration which he coveted, and without which even his miserable condition would be rendered more miserable still.

His greatest trouble was the fact that he was not allowed to visit his wife; but he soon found a way out of this difficulty. After he had been ordered away from the Calderwood place, he was in the habit of wandering as far in that direction as prudence would permit. Near the Calderwood place, but not on Calderwood's land, lived an old man named Micajah Staley and his sister Becky Staley. These people were old and very poor. Old Micajah had a palsied arm and hand; but, in spite of this, he managed to earn a precarious living with his turning-lathe.

When he was a slave Free Joe would have scorned these representatives of a class known as poor white trash, but now he found them sympathetic and helpful in various ways. From the back door of their cabin he could hear the Calderwood negroes singing at night, and he sometimes fancied he could distinguish Lucinda's shrill treble rising above the other voices. A large poplar grew in the woods some distance from the Staley cabin, and at the foot of this tree Free Joe would sit for hours with his face turned toward Calderwood's. His little dog Dan would curl up in the leaves near by, and the two seemed to be as comfortable as possible.

One Saturday afternoon Free Joe, sitting at the foot of this friendly poplar, fell asleep. How long he slept, he could not tell; but when he awoke little

Dan was licking his face, the moon was shining brightly, and Lucinda his wife stood before him laughing. The dog, seeing that Free Joe was asleep, had grown somewhat impatient, and he concluded to make an excursion to the Calderwood place on his own account. Lucinda was inclined to give the incident a twist in the direction of superstition.

"I'uz settin' down front er de fireplace," she said, "cookin' me some meat, w'en all of a sudden I year sumpin at de do'—scratch, scratch. I tuck'n tu'n de meat over, en make out I aint year it. Bimeby it come dar 'gin—scratch, scratch. I up en open de do', I did, en, bless de Lord! dar wuz little Dan, en it look like ter me dat his ribs done grow tergeer. I gin 'im some bread, en den, w'en he start out, I tuck'n foller 'im, kaze, I say ter myse'f, maybe my nigger man mought be some'rs 'roun'. Dat ar little dog got sense, mon."

Free Joe laughed and dropped his hand lightly on Dan's head. For a long time after that he had no difficulty in seeing his wife. He had only to sit by the poplar-tree until little Dan could run and fetch her. But after a while the other negroes discovered that Lucinda was meeting Free Joe in the woods, and information of the fact soon reached Calderwood's ears. Calderwood was what is called a man of action. He said nothing; but one day he put Lucinda in his buggy, and carried her to Macon, sixty miles away. He carried her to Macon, and came back without her; and nobody in or around Hillsborough, or in that section, ever saw her again.

For many a night after that Free Joe sat in the woods and waited. Little Dan would run merrily off and be gone a long time, but he always came back without Lucinda. This happened over and over again. The "willis-whistlers" would call and call, like phantom huntsmen wandering on a far-off shore; the screech-owl would shake and shiver in the depths of the woods; the night-hawks, sweeping by on noiseless wings, would snap their beaks as though they enjoyed the huge joke of which Free Joe and little Dan were the victims; and the whip-poor-wills would cry to each other through the gloom. Each night seemed to be lonelier than the preceding, but Free Joe's patience was proof against loneliness. There came a time, however, when little Dan refused to go after Lucinda. When Free Joe motioned him in the direction of the Calderwood place, he would simply move about uneasily and whine; then he would curl up in the leaves and make himself comfortable.

One night, instead of going to the poplar-tree to wait for Lucinda, Free Joe went to the Staley cabin, and, in order to make his welcome good, as he expressed it, he carried with him an armful of fat-pine splinters. Miss Becky Staley had a great reputation in those parts as a fortune-teller, and the school-girls, as well as older people, often tested her powers in this direction, some in jest and some in earnest. Free Joe placed his humble offering of light-wood in the chimney-corner, and then seated himself on the steps, dropping his hat on the ground outside.

"Miss Becky," he said presently, "whar in de name er gracious you reckon Lucindy is?"

"Well, the Lord he'p the nigger!" exclaimed Miss Becky, in a tone that seemed to reproduce, by some curious agreement of sight with sound, her general aspect of peakedness. "Well, the Lord he'p the nigger! haint you been a-seein' her all this blessed time? She's over at old Spite Calderwood's, if she's anywheres, I reckon."

"No'm, dat I aint, Miss Becky. I aint seen Lucindy in now gwine on mighty nigh a mont'."

"Well, it haint a-gwine to hurt you," said Miss Becky, somewhat sharply. "In my day an' time it wuz allers took to be a bad sign when niggers got to honeyin' 'roun' an' gwine on."

"Yessum," said Free Joe, cheerfully assenting to the proposition—"yessum, dat's so, but me an' my ole 'oman, we 'uz raise tergeer, en dey aint bin many days w'en we 'uz 'way fum one 'n'er like we is now."

"Maybe she's up an' took up wi' some un else," said Micajah Staley from the corner. "You know what the sayin' is, 'New master, new nigger.' "

"Dat's so, dat's de sayin', but tain't wid my ole 'oman like 'tis wid yuther niggers. Me en her wuz des natally raise up tergeer. Dey's lots likelier niggers dan w'at I is," said Free Joe, viewing his shabbiness with a critical eye, "but I knows Lucindy mos' good ez I does little Dan dar—dat I does."

There was no reply to this, and Free Joe continued,

"Miss Becky, I wish you please, ma'am, take en run yo' kyards en see sump'n n'er 'bout Lucindy; kaze ef she sick, I'm gwine dar. Dey ken take en take me up en gimme a stroppin', but I'm gwine dar."

Miss Becky got her cards, but first she picked up a cup, in the bottom of which were some coffee-grounds. These she whirled slowly round and round, ending finally by turning the cup upside down on the hearth and allowing it to remain in that position.

"I'll turn the cup first," said Miss Becky, "and then I'll run the cards and see what they say."

As she shuffled the cards the fire on the hearth burned low, and in its fitful light the gray-haired, thin-featured woman seemed to deserve the weird reputation which rumor and gossip had given her. She shuffled the cards for some moments, gazing intently in the dying fire; then, throwing a piece of pine on the coals, she made three divisions of the pack, disposing them about in her lap. Then she took the first pile, ran the cards slowly through her fingers, and studied them carefully. To the first she added the second pile. The study of these was evidently not satisfactory. She said nothing, but frowned heavily; and the frown deepened as she added the rest of the cards until the entire fifty-two had passed in review before her. Though she frowned, she seemed to be deeply interested. Without changing the relative position of the cards, she ran them all over again. Then she threw a larger piece of pine on the fire, shuffled the cards afresh, divided them into three piles, and subjected them to the same careful and critical examination.

"I can't tell the day when I've seed the cards run this a-way," she said after a while. "What is an' what aint, I'll never tell you; but I know what the cards sez."

"W'at does dey say, Miss Becky?" the negro inquired, in a tone the solemnity of which was heightened by its eagerness.

"They er runnin' quare. These here that I'm a-lookin' at," said Miss Becky, "they stan' for the past. Them there, they er the present; and the t'others, they er the future. Here's a bundle,"—tapping the ace of clubs with her thumb,—"an' here's a journey as plain as the nose on a man's face. Here's Lucinda"—

"Whar she, Miss Becky?"

"Here she is—the queen of spades."

Free Joe grinned. The idea seemed to please him immensely.

"Well, well, well!" he exclaimed. "Ef dat don't beat my time! De queen er spades! W'en Lucindy year dat hit'll tickle 'er, sho'!"

Miss Becky continued to run the cards back and forth through her fingers.

"Here's a bundle an' a journey, and here's Lucinda. An' here's ole Spite Calderwood."

She held the cards toward the negro and touched the king of clubs.

"De Lord he'p my soul!" exclaimed Free Joe with a chuckle. "De faver's dar. Yesser, dat's him! W'at de matter 'long wid all un um, Miss Becky?"

The old woman added the second pile of cards to the first, and then the third, still running them through her fingers slowly and critically. By this time the piece of pine in the fireplace had wrapped itself in a mantle of flame illuminating the cabin and throwing into strange relief the figure of Miss Becky as she sat studying the cards. She frowned ominously at the cards and mumbled a few words to herself. Then she dropped her hands in her lap and gazed once more into the fire. Her shadow danced and capered on the wall and floor behind her, as if, looking over her shoulder into the future, it could behold a rare spectacle. After a while she picked up the cup that had been turned on the hearth. The coffee-grounds, shaken around, presented what seemed to be a most intricate map.

"Here's the journey," said Miss Becky, presently; "here's the big road, here's rivers to cross, here's the bundle to tote." She paused and sighed. "They haint no names writ here, an' what it all means I'll never tell you. Cajy, I wish you'd be so good as to han' me my pipe."

"I haint no hand wi' the kyards," said Cajy, as he handed the pipe, "but I reckon I can patch out your misinformation, Becky, bekaze the other day, whiles I was a-finishin' up Mizzers Perdue's rollin'-pin, I hearn a rattlin' in the road. I looked out, an' Spite Calderwood was a-drivin' by in his buggy an' thar sot Lucinda by him. It'd in-about drapt out er my min'."

Free Joe sat on the door-sill and fumbled at his hat, flinging it from one hand to the other.

"You aint see um gwine back, is you, Mars Cajy?" he asked after a while.

"Ef they went back by this road," said Mr. Staley, with the air of one who is accustomed to weigh well his words, "it must 'a' bin endurin' of the time whiles I was asleep, bekaze I haint bin no furder from my shop than to yon bed."

"Well, sir!" exclaimed Free Joe in an awed tone, which Mr. Staley seemed to regard as a tribute to his extraordinary powers of statement.

"Ef it's my beliefs you want," continued the old man, "I'll pitch 'em at you fair and free. My beliefs is that Spite Calderwood is gone an' took Lucindy outen the county. Bless your heart and soul! when Spite Calderwood meets the Old Boy in the road they'll be a turrible scuffle. You mark what I tell you."

Free Joe, still fumbling with his hat, rose and leaned against the door-facing. He seemed to be embarrassed. Presently he said,

"I speck I better be gittin' 'long. Nex' time I see Lucindy, I'm gwine tell 'er w'at Miss Becky say 'bout de queen er spades—dat I is. Ef dat don't tickle 'er, dey ain't no nigger 'oman never bin tickle'."

He paused a moment, as though waiting for some remark or comment, some confirmation of misfortune, or, at the very least, some endorsement of his suggestion that Lucinda would be greatly pleased to know that she had figured as the queen of spades; but neither Miss Becky nor her brother said any thing.

"One minnit ridin' in the buggy 'longside er Mars Spite, en de nex' highfalutin' 'roun' playin' de queen er spades. Mon, deze yer nigger gals gittin' up in de pictur's; dey sholy is."

With a brief "Good-night, Miss Becky, Mars Cajy," Free Joe went out into the darkness, followed by little Dan. He made his way to the poplar, where Lucinda had been in the habit of meeting him, and sat down. He sat there a long time; he sat there until little Dan, growing restless, trotted off in the direction of the Calderwood place. Dozing against the poplar, in the gray dawn of the morning Free Joe heard Spite Calderwood's fox-hounds in full cry a mile away.

"Shoo!" he exclaimed, scratching his head, and laughing to himself, "dem ar dogs is des a-warmin' dat old fox up."

But it was Dan the hounds were after, and the little dog came back no more. Free Joe waited and waited, until he grew tired of waiting. He went back the next night and waited, and for many nights thereafter. His waiting was in vain, and yet he never regarded it as in vain. Careless and shabby as he was, Free Joe was thoughtful enough to have his theory. He was convinced that little Dan had found Lucinda, and that some night when the moon was shining brightly through the trees, the dog would rouse him from his dreams as he sat sleeping at the foot of the poplar-tree, and he would open his eyes and behold Lucinda standing over him, laughing merrily as of old; and then he thought what fun they would have about the queen of spades.

How many long nights Free Joe waited at the foot of the poplar-tree for Lucinda and little Dan, no one can ever know. He kept no account of them, and they were not recorded by Micajah Staley nor by Miss Becky. The season ran into summer and then into fall. One night he went to the Staley cabin, cut the two old people an armful of wood, and seated himself on the door-steps, where he rested. He was always thankful—and proud, as it seemed—when Miss Becky gave him a cup of coffee, which she was sometimes thoughtful enough to do. He was especially thankful on this particular night.

"You er still layin' off for to strike up wi' Lucindy out thar in the woods, I reckon," said Micajah Staley, smiling grimly. The situation was not without its humorous aspects.

"Oh, dey er comin', Mars Cajy, dey er comin', sho," Free Joe replied. "I boun' you dey'll come; en w'en dey does come, I'll des take en fetch um yer, whar you kin see um wid your own eyes, you en Miss Becky."

"No," said Mr. Staley, with a quick and emphatic gesture of disapproval.

"Don't! don't fetch 'em anywheres. Stay right wi' 'em as long as may be."

Free Joe chuckled, and slipped away into the night, while the two old people sat gazing in the fire. Finally Micajah spoke.

"Look at that nigger; look at 'im. He's pine-blank as happy now as a killdee by a mill-race. You can't 'faze 'em. I'd in-about give up my t'other hand ef I could stan' flat-footed, an' grin at trouble like that there nigger."

"Niggers is niggers," said Miss Becky, smiling grimly, "an' you can't rub it out; yit I lay I've seed a heap of white people lots meaner'n Free Joe. He grins,—an' that's nigger,—but I've ketched his under jaw a-trimblin' when Lucindy's name uz brung up. An' I tell you," she went on, bridling up a little, and speaking with almost fierce emphasis, "the Old Boy's done sharpened his claws for Spite Calderwood. You'll see it."

"Me, Rebecca?" said Mr. Staley, hugging his palsied arm; "me? I hope not."

"Well, you'll know it then," said Miss Becky, laughing heartily at her brother's look of alarm.

The next morning Micajah Staley had occasion to go into the woods after a piece of timber. He saw Free Joe sitting at the foot of the poplar, and the sight vexed him somewhat.

"Git up from there," he cried, "an' go an' arn your livin'. A mighty purty pass it's come to, when great big buck niggers can lie a-snorin' in the woods all day, when t'other folks is got to be up an' a-gwine. Git up from there!"

Receiving no response, Mr. Staley went to Free Joe, and shook him by the shoulder; but the negro made no response. He was dead. His hat was off, his head was bent, and a smile was on his face. It was as if he had bowed and smiled when death stood before him, humble to the last. His clothes were ragged; his hands were rough and callous; his shoes were literally tied together with strings; he was shabby in the extreme. A passer-by, glancing at him, could have no idea that such a humble creature had been summoned as a witness before the Lord God of Hosts.

The Colonel's "Nigger Dog"

ONE MORNING Colonel Rivers of Jasper, standing on his back porch, called to a negro man who was passing through the yard.

"Ben!"

"Yasser!"

"How's everything at the home place?"

"Tollerble, suh,—des tollerble."

"Tell Shade I want to see him this morning."

"Unk Shade done gone, suh. He sho is. He done gone!"

"Gone where?"

"He done tuck ter de woods, suh. Yasser! he done gone!"

A frown clouded the colonel's otherwise pleasant brow.

"What is the matter with the old simpleton?"

"Some kinder gwines on 'twix him an' Marse Preston, suh. I dunno de rights un it. But Unk Shade done gone, suh!"

"When did he go?"

"Yistiddy, suh."

The colonel turned and went into the house, and the negro passed on, shaking his head and talking to himself. The colonel walked up and down the wide hall a little while, and then went into his library and flung himself into an easy-chair. As it happened, the chair sat facing his writing-desk, and over the desk hung a large portrait of his mother. It was what people call "a speaking likeness," and the colonel felt this as he looked at it. The face was full of character. Firmness shone in the eyes and played about the lips. The colonel regarded the portrait with an interest that was almost new. Old Shade in the woods,—old Shade a runaway! What would his mother say if she were alive? The colonel felt, too,—he could not help but feel,—that he was largely responsible for the fact that old Shade was a fugitive.

When Mary Rivers married Jack Preston, the colonel, Mary's father, insisted that the couple should live at the old home place. The desire was natural. Mary was the apple of his eye, and he wanted to see her rule in the home over which his mother had reigned. The colonel himself had been born there, and his mother had lived there for more than forty years. His father had died in 1830, but his mother lived until the day after the fiftieth anniversary of her wedding.

For near a quarter of a century this excellent lady had been the manager of her own estate, and she had succeeded, by dint of hard and pinching economy and untiring energy, in retrieving the fortune which her husband had left in a precarious condition. It was said of the colonel's father, William Rivers, that he was a man perverse in his ways and with a head full of queer notions, and it seems to be certain that he frittered away large opportunities in pursuit of small ones.

When William Rivers died he left his widow as a legacy four small boys—the colonel, the oldest, was in his teens—a past-due mortgage on the plantation, and a whole raft (as you may say) of small debts. She had one consolation that she breathed often to her little boys,—their father had lived temperately and died a Christian. Besides that consolation, she had an abundance of hope and energy. She could have sold a negro or two, but there were only a dozen of them, big and little, and they were all members of one family. The older ones had grown up with their mistress, and the younger ones she had nursed and attended through many an hour's sickness. She would have parted with her right hand sooner than sell one of them. She took her little boys from school—the youngest was ten and the oldest fourteen—and put them to work in the fields with the negroes for one year. At the end of that period she began to see daylight, as it were, and then the boys went back to school, but their vacations for several years afterward were spent behind the plough. She was as uncompromising in her business as in her religion. In one she stickled for the last thrip that was her due; in the other she believed in the final perseverance of the saints.

It is enough to say that she succeeded. She transacted her own business. She did it well at the very beginning, and thereafter with an aptitude that was constantly growing. She paid the estate out of debt, and added to it, and when her oldest son graduated at Princeton, she had the finest and most profitable plantation in Jasper County. All the old people said that if her father, Judge Walthall, could have returned to life, he would have been proud of the success of his daughter, which was in that day and still remains the most remarkable event in the annals of Jasper County.

The main dependence of Mrs. Rivers, even after her boys grew up, was a negro man named Shadrach. He grew old with his mistress and imbibed many of her matter-of-fact ways and methods. At first he was known as Uncle Shed, but the negro pronunciation lengthened this to Shade, and he was known by everybody in the counties round as Uncle Shade.

Uncle Shade knew how important his services were to his mistress and what store she set by his energy and faithfulness, and the knowledge made him more independent in his attitude and temper than the average negro. The truth is, he was not an average negro, and he knew it. He knew it by the fact that the rest of the negroes obeyed his most exacting orders with as much alacrity as they obeyed those of white men, and were quite as anxious to please him. He knew it, too, by the fact that his mistress had selected him in preference to his own father to take charge of the active management of the plantation business.

The selection was certainly a good one. Whatever effect it may have had on Uncle Shade, it was the salvation of the plans of his mistress. The negro seemed to have a keen appreciation of the necessities of the situation. He worked the hands harder than any white man could have worked them, and kept them in a good humor by doing as much as any two of them. The Saturday half-holiday was abolished for a time, and the ploughs and the hoes were kept going just as long as the negroes could see how to run a furrow.

A theory of the neighborhood was that Uncle Shade was afraid of going to the sheriff's block, and if this theory was wrong it was at least plausible. The majority of those who worked under Uncle Shade were his own flesh and blood, but his mistress had made bold to hire four extra negroes in order to carry out the plans she had in view, and these four worked as hard and as cheerfully as any of the rest.

Such was the energy with which Uncle Shade managed the rougher details of the plantation work, that at the end of the first year his mistress saw her way clear to enlarging her plans. She found that within five years she would be able to pay off all the old debts and make large profits to boot. So she sent her boys back to school, bought two of the four hired hands, and hired four more. These new ones, under Uncle Shade's management, worked as willingly as the others. In this way the estate was cleared of debt, and gradually enlarged, and Mrs. Rivers had been able, in the midst of it all, to send her boys to Princeton, where they took high rank in their studies.

The youngest drifted to California in the fifties, and disappeared; the second went into business in Charleston as a cotton factor and commission merchant. The oldest, after taking a law course, settled down at home, practiced law a little and farmed a great deal. He finally fell in love with a school-ma'am from Connecticut. His mother, who had been through the mill, as the saying is, and knew all about the dignity and lack of dignity there is in labor, rather approved the match, although some of the neighbors, whose pretensions were far beyond their possessions, shook their heads and said that the young man might have done better.

Nevertheless, the son did very well indeed. He did a great deal better than some of those who criticised his choice, for he got a wife who knew how to put her shoulder to the wheel when there was any necessity for it, and how to economize when her husband's purse was pinched. The son, having married the woman of his choice, built him a home within a stone's throw of his mother's, and during her life not a day passed but he spent a part of it in her company. He had always been fond of his mother, and as he grew older, his filial devotion was fortified and strengthened by the profound impression which her character made on him. It was a character that had been moulded on heroic lines. As a child, she had imbibed the spirit of the Revolution, and everything she said and did was flavored with the energy and independence that gave our colonial society its special and most beautiful significance,—the significance of candor and simplicity.

Something of his mistress's energy and independence was reflected in the character of Uncle Shade, and the result of it was that he was not very popular with those that did not know him well. The young master came back from college with a highly improved idea of his own importance. His mother, although she was secretly proud of his airs, told him with trenchant bluntness that his vanity stuck out like a pot-leg and must be lopped off. This was bad enough, but when Uncle Shade let it be understood that he wasn't going to run hither and yon at the beck and call of a boy, nothing prevented a collision but the firm will that controlled everything on the plantation. After that, both the young master and the negro were more considerate of each other, but neither forgot the little episode.

When the young man married, he and Uncle Shade saw less of each other, and there was no more friction between them for four or five years. But in 1850 the negro's mistress died, and he and the rest of the negroes, together with the old home place, became the property of the son, who was now a prosperous planter, looked up to by his neighbors, and given the title of colonel by those who knew no other way of showing their respect and esteem. But in her will the colonel's mother made ample provision, as she thought, for the protection of Uncle Shade. He was to retain, under all circumstances, his house on the home place; he was never to be sold, and he was to be treated with the consideration due to a servant who had cheerfully given more than the best part of his life to the service of the family.

The terms of the will were strictly complied with. The colonel had loved his mother tenderly, and he respected her memory. He made it a point to treat Uncle Shade with consideration. He appealed to his judgment whenever opportunity offered, and frequently found it profitable to do so. But the old negro still held himself aloof. Whether from grief at the death of his mistress, or for other reasons, he lost interest in the affairs of the plantation. The other negroes said he was "lonesome," and this description of his condition, vague as it was, was perhaps the best that could be given. Except in the matter of temper, Uncle Shade was not the negro he was before his old mistress died.

This was the state of affairs when the colonel's daughter, Mary, married Jack Preston in 1861. When this event occurred, the colonel insisted that the young couple should take up their abode at the old home place. He had various sentimental reasons for this. For one thing, Mary was very much like her grandmother, in spite of her youth and beauty. Those who had known the old lady remarked the "favor"—as they called it—as soon as they saw the granddaughter. For another, the old home place was close at hand, almost next door, and the house and grounds had been kept in apple-pie order by Uncle Shade. The flower-garden was the finest to be seen in all that region, and the house itself and every room of it was as carefully kept as if the dead mistress had simply gone on a visit and was likely to return at any moment.

Naturally, the young couple found it hard to resist the entreaties of the colonel, particularly as Mary objected very seriously to living in town. So they went to the old home place, and were affably received by Uncle Shade. They found everything arranged to their hands.

Their first meal at the old home place was dinner. The colonel had told Uncle Shade that he would have company at noon, and they found the dinner smoking on the table when they arrived. A young negro man was set to wait on the table. He made some blunder, and instantly a young negro girl came in, smiling, to take his place. Uncle Shade, who was standing in the door of the dining-room, dressed in his Sunday best, took the offender by the arm as he passed out, and in a little while those who were at table heard the swish of a buggy whip as it fell on the negro's shoulders. The unusual noise set the chickens to cackling, the turkeys to gobbling, and the dogs to barking.

"Old man," said Preston, when Uncle Shade had gravely resumed his place near the dining-room door, "take 'em farther away from the house the next time you kill em."

"I'll do so, suh," replied Uncle Shade dryly, and with a little frown.

Matters went along smoothly enough for all concerned, but somehow Preston failed to appreciate the family standing and importance of Uncle Shade. The young man was as genial and as clever as the day is long, but he knew nothing of the sensitiveness of an old family servant. On the other hand, Uncle Shade had a dim idea of Preston's ignorance, and resented it. He regarded the young man as an interloper in the family, and made little effort to conceal his feelings.

One thing led to another until finally there was an explosion. Preston would have taken harsh measures, but Uncle Shade gathered up a bundle of "duds," and took to the woods.

Nominally he was a runaway, but he came and went pretty much as suited his pleasure, always taking care to keep out of the way of Preston.

At last the colonel, who had made the way clear for Uncle Shade to come back and make an apology, grew tired of waiting for that event; the longer he waited, the longer the old negro stayed away.

The colonel made one or two serious efforts to see Uncle Shade, but the old darky, misunderstanding his intentions, made it a point to elude him. Finding his efforts in this direction unavailing, the colonel grew angry. He had something of his mother's disposition—a little of her temper if not much of her energy—and he decided to take a more serious view of Uncle Shade's capers. It was a shame and a disgrace, anyhow, that one of the Rivers negroes should be hiding in the woods without any excuse, and the colonel determined to put an end to it once for all. He would do more—he would teach Uncle Shade once for all that there was a limit to the forbearance with which he had been treated.

Therefore, after trying many times to capture Uncle Shade and always without success, the colonel announced to his wife that he had formed a plan calculated to bring the old negro to terms.

"What is it?" his wife asked.

"Well, I'll tell you," said the colonel, hesitating a little. "I'm going to get me a nigger dog and run old Shade down and catch him, if it takes me a year to do it."

The wife regarded the husband with amazement.

"Why, Mr. Rivers, what are you thinking of?" she exclaimed. "You don't mean to tell me that you are going to put yourself on a level with Bill Favers and go trolloping around the country, hunting negroes with hound-dogs? I never heard you say that any of your family ever stooped to such as that."

"They never did," the colonel rejoined testily. "But they never had such a rantankerous nigger to deal with."

"Just as he is, just so he was made," was Mrs. Rivers's matter-of-fact comment.

"I know that mighty well," said the colonel. "But the time has come when he ought to be taken in hand. I could get Bill Favers's dogs and run him down in an hour, but I'm going to catch my own nigger with my own nigger dog."

"Why, Mr. Rivers, you haven't a dog on the place that will run a pig out of the garden, much less catch a negro. There are ten or fifteen hound-dogs around the yard, and they are actually too no-account to scratch the fleas off."

"Well," replied the colonel, wincing a little, "Matt Kilpatrick has promised to give me one of his beagles, and I'm going to take him and train him to track niggers."

"Another dog on the place!" exclaimed Mrs. Rivers. "Well, you'll have to sell some negroes. We can't afford to feed a lot of no-account negroes and no-account dogs without selling something. You can't even give the dogs away—and I wouldn't let you impose on anybody that way, if you could; so you'll have to sell some of the negroes. They are lazy and no-account enough, goodness knows, but they can manage to walk around and pick up chips and get a thimbleful of milk from twenty cows, and sweep off the porch when there's anybody to keep them awake."

Nevertheless, the colonel got his beagle, and he soon came to take more interest in it than in all his other dogs. He named it Jeff, after Matt Kilpatrick's old beagle, and Jeff turned out to be the cutest little dog ever seen in that section. The colonel trained him assiduously. Twice a day he'd hold Jeff and make one of the little negroes run down by the spring-house and out across the cow-lot. When the little negro was well out of sight the colonel would unleash Jeff and away the miniature hunt would go across the fields, the colonel cheering it on in regulation style.

The colonel's "nigger dog" was eight months old when he was taken in hand, and by the time he was a year old he had developed amazingly. The claim was gravely made that he had a colder nose than Bill Favers's dog Sound, who could follow a scent thirty-six hours old. It is not to be supposed that the training of Jeff went no farther than tracking the little negroes within sight of the house. The time speedily came when he was put on the trails of negroes who had hours the start,—negroes who crept along on fences and waded wide streams in their efforts to baffle the dog.

But Jeff was not easily baffled. He developed such intelligence and such powers of discriminating scent as would have put to shame the lubberly and inefficient dogs known as bloodhounds. Bloodhounds have figured very largely in fiction and in the newspapers as the incarnation of ferocity and intelligence. As a matter of fact, Jeff, the little beagle, could have whipped a shuck-pen full of them without ever showing his teeth, and he could run half a mile while a bloodhound was holding his senseless head in the air to give tongue.

Naturally the colonel was very proud of Jeff. He had the dog always at his heels, whether going to town or about the plantation, and he waited for the opportunity to come when he might run Uncle Shade to his hiding-place in the swamps of Murder Creek and capture him. The opportunity was not long in coming, though it seemed long to the colonel's impatience.

There was this much to be said about Uncle Shade. He had grown somewhat wary, and he had warned all the negroes on both plantations that if they made any reports of his movements, the day of wrath would soon come for them. And they believed him fully, so that, for some months, he might have been whirled away on a cloud or swallowed by the earth for all the colonel could hear or discover.

But one day, while he was dozing in his library, he heard a dialogue between the housemaid and the cook. The housemaid was sweeping in the rear hall, and the cook was fixing things in the dining-room. They judged by the stillness of the house that there was no one to overhear them.

"Mighty quare 'bout Unk Shade," said the house-girl.

"Huh! dat ole nigger-man de devil, mon!" replied the cook, rattling the dishes.

"I boun' ef 'twuz any er we-all gwine on dat away runnin' off an' comin' back when we git good an' ready, an' eatin' right dar in de house in broad daylight, an' marster gwine right by de do'—I boun' you we'd be kotch an' fotch back," remarked the girl, in an injured tone.

"La! I ain't studyin' 'bout ole Shade kingin' it 'roun' here," exclaimed the cook. "He been gwine on dat away so long dat 't ain't nothin' new." Here she paused and laughed heartily.

"What you laughin' at?" inquired the girl, pausing in her work.

"At de way dat ole nigger man been gwine on," responded the cook. "I hear tell dat marster got dat ar little houn'-dog trainin' now fer ter track ole Shade down. Dar de dog an' dar old Shade, but dey ain't been no trackin' done yit. Dat dog bleedzter be no 'count, kaze all he got ter do is to go down dar by the house whar ole Shade live at 'twix' daybreak an' sun-up, an' dar he'll fin' de track er dat ole nigger man hot an' fresh."

"I don't keer ef dey does ketch 'im," said the house-girl, by way of comment. "De wuss frailin' I ever got he gi' me. He skeer'd me den, an' I been skeer'd un 'im fum dat day."

"De white folks kin git 'im any time dey want 'im," said the cook. "But you hear me!—dey don't want 'im."

"Honey, I b'lieve you," exclaimed the girl.

At this juncture the colonel raised his head and uttered an exclamation of anger. Instantly there was the most profound silence in the dining-room and in the hall. The house-girl slipped up the stairway as noiselessly as a ghost, and the cook disappeared as if by magic.

The colonel called both negroes, but they seemed to be out of hearing. Finally the cook answered. Her voice came from the spring lot, and it was the voice of conscious innocence. It had its effect, too, for the colonel's heavy frown cleared away, and he indulged in a hearty laugh. When the cook came up, he told her to have breakfast the next morning by sunrise.

The woman knew what this meant, and she made up her mind accordingly. In spite of the fact that she pretended to despise Uncle Shade, she had a secret respect for his independence of character, and she resolved to repair, as far as she knew how, the damage her unbridled tongue had wrought.

Thus it was that when Uncle Shade made his appearance that night he found the cook nodding by the chimney corner, while his wife was mending some old clothes. A covered skillet sat near the fire, and a little mound of ashes in one corner showed where the ashcake was baking or the sweet potatoes roasting. Uncle Shade said nothing. He came in silently, placed his tin bucket in the hearth, and seated himself on a wooden stool. There was no greeting on the part of his wife. She laid aside her mending, and fixed his supper on a rude table close at hand.

"I speck you mus' be tired," she said when everything was ready—"tired and hongry too."

Uncle Shade made no response. He sat gazing steadily into the pine-knot flame in the fireplace that gave the only light in the room.

"De Lord knows I'd quit hidin' out in de woods ef I wuz you," said his wife. "I wouldn't be gwine 'roun' like some wil' varmint—dat I wouldn't!—I'd let um come git me an' do what dey gwine ter do. Dey can't kill you."

"Dat's so," exclaimed the cook, by way of making herself agreeable.

Uncle Shade raised his eyebrows and looked at the woman until she moved about in her chair uneasily.

"How come you ain't up yonder whar you b'long?" he asked. He was not angry; the tone of his voice was not even unkind; but the cook was so embarrassed that she could hardly find her tongue.

"I'm here kaze marster tol' me ter get brekkus by sun-up, an' I know by de way he done dat he gwine ter come and put dat ar nigger dog on yo' track."

"What good dat gwine ter do?" Uncle Shade asked.

"Now, ez ter dat," replied the cook, "I can't tell you. It may do harm, an' it may not, but what good it gwine ter do, I'm never is ter tell you."

"What de dog gwine ter do?" inquired Uncle Shade.

The cook looked at the other woman and laughed, and then rose from her seat, adjusting her head handkerchief as she did so.

"You mos' too much fer me," she remarked as she went toward the door. "Mos' a long ways too much. Ef you kin git off de groun' an' walk in de elements, de dog ain't gwine do nothin'. Maybe you kin do dat; I dunno. But ef you can't dat ar dog'll track you down sho ez you er settin' dar." Then she went out.

Uncle Shade ate his supper and then sat before the fire smoking his pipe. After a while he got a piece of candle out of an old cigar-box, lit it, and proceeded to ransack a wooden chest which seemed to be filled with all sorts of odds and ends,—gimlets, hinges, horn buttons, tangled twine, quilt pieces, and broken crockery. At the bottom he found what he was looking for,—a letter that had been rolled in cylindrical shape. Around it had been wrapped a long strip of cloth. He unrolled the package, took the letter out and looked at it, rolled it up again, and then placed it carefully in his hat.

"Well, den," said his wife, "what you gwine ter do?"

"I'll tell you," he said. He leaned over and placed one hand on her knee. "Ef he don't ketch me, I ain't comin' back. Ef he ketch me, I'll show 'im dat,"—indicating the letter,—"an' ef dat ain't do no good, I'm gwine ter jump off Injun Bluff in de river."

"Sho nuff?" his wife asked, in a low voice.

"Sho nuff!" he answered, in a voice as low.

The woman sighed as she rose from her chair to clear away the little table. In a little while she began to sing a hymn, and by that time Uncle Shade, lying across the foot of the bed, was fast asleep.

The cook, out of abundant caution, gave her master his breakfast before sunrise. The colonel called Jeff into the dining-room and gave him some substantial scraps of warm victuals—an unheard-of proceeding in that house.

After breakfast the colonel mounted his horse, which was standing saddled at the gate, and rode over to the old home place. He rode straight to Uncle Shade's house, called a negro to hold his horse, and went in, followed by Jeff.

"Where did Shade sleep last night?" he asked of Shade's wife.

"Well, suh, what little sleepin' he done, he done right dar, suh—right dar in de baid, suh."

The colonel pulled off one of the blankets, made Jeff smell of it, and then went out and mounted his horse. Once in the saddle, he spoke an encouraging word to the dog. The task set for Jeff was much more difficult than the colonel thought it was. The dog circled around the house, once, twice, thrice, his nose to the ground. Then he ran back to the door, and tried to unravel the riddle again. He went off a little way, flung back, and entered the house, nosed the bed carefully, and then came out, giving tongue for the first time.

Near by was a low wooden bench. Jeff leaped upon it and gave tongue again. A piece of bacon-rind lay on the bench. The dog nosed around it very carefully. The colonel clenched his teeth together. "If he eats that meat-skin," he thought, "I'll go get my gun and kill him." But Jeff did no such thing. He had solved a problem that had puzzled his intelligent nose, and he sprang away from the bench with a ringing challenge.

Some of the negroes who had been watching the dog looked at each other and shook their heads. As a matter of fact, Uncle Shade had sat on that bench and greased the soles of his shoes with the bacon-rind. He had a theory of his own that the dog would be unable to follow him after his shoes were greased.

It is certain that Jeff had considerable difficulty in getting away from the negro quarters, for Uncle Shade, true to his habits, had gone to several of the cabins and issued his orders, laying off a week's work for the plough-hands, and telling them what to do in the event that rains suspended their operations. Patiently Jeff threaded the maze of the old negro's comings and goings, and at last he found the final clue at the stile that led from the negro quarters into the avenue.

74

The colonel rode around by the big gate, and when he passed through Jeff was going down the big avenue at a pretty lively clip, but he was not running as freely as his custom was. Where a bush or a weed touched the footpath, he would examine it with his nose, but he kept the colonel's horse in a canter. When he left the avenue for the public road he ran in a more assured manner, and the colonel was compelled to force the canter into a gallop.

This was nothing like a fox-hunt, of course. The excitement of companionship and rivalry, and the thrill of the restless and eager-moving pack were lacking, but the enthusiasm of the colonel was mingled with pride as he rode after the dog that was guiding him so swiftly and unerringly. The enthusiasm was as persistent as the pride. But Jeff had no room for such emotions. The path of duty, straight or crooked, lay before him, and he followed it up as nimbly as he could.

The colonel was puzzled by the route they were taking. He had heard a good deal of runaway negroes, and had seen some after they were caught, but he had always imagined that they went into the deep woods or into the dim swamps for shelter and safety. But here was old Shade going poling down the public road where every passer-by could see him. Or was the dog at fault? Was it some visiting negro who had called in to see the negroes at the home place, and had then gone home by the road?

While the colonel was nursing these suspicions, Jeff paused and ran back toward him. At a low place in the fence, the dog hesitated and then flung himself over, striking into a footpath. This began to look like business. The path led to a ravine, and the ravine must naturally lead to a swamp. But the path really led to a spring, and before the colonel could throw a few rails from the fence and remount his horse, Jeff had reached the spring and was clicking up the hill beyond in the path that led back to the road.

It appeared that Uncle Shade had rested at the spring a while, for the dog went forward more rapidly. The spring was six miles from the colonel's house, and he began to have grave doubts as to the sagacity of Jeff. What could have possessed old Shade to run away by this public route? But if the colonel had doubts, Jeff had none. He pressed forward vigorously, splashing through the streams that crossed the road and going as rapidly up hill as he went down.

The colonel's horse was a good one, but the colonel himself was a heavy weight, and the pace began to tell on the animal. Nevertheless, the colonel kept him steadily at his work. Four or five miles farther they went, and then

Jeff, after casting about for a while, struck off through an old sedge field.

Here, at last, there was no room for doubt, for Jeff no longer had to put his nose to the ground. The tall sedge held the scent, and the dog plunged through it almost as rapidly as if he had been chasing a rabbit. The colonel, in his excitement, cheered the dog on lustily, and the chase from that moment went at top speed.

Uncle Shade, moving along on a bluff overlooking Little River, nearly a mile away, heard it and paused to listen. He thought he knew the voices of man and dog, but he was not sure, so he lifted a hand to his ear and frowned as he listened. There could be no doubt about it. He was caught. He looked all around the horizon and up at the glittering sky. There was no way of escape. So he took his bundle from the end of his cane, dropped it at the foot of a huge hickory-tree, and sat down.

Presently Jeff came in sight, running like a quarter-horse. Uncle Shade thought if he could manage to kill the dog, there would still be a chance for him. His master was not in sight, and it would be an easy matter to slip down the bluff and so escape. But, no; the dog was not to be trapped. His training and instinct kept him out of the old negro's reach. Jeff made a wide circle around Uncle Shade and finally stopped and bayed him, standing far out of harm's way.

The old negro took off his hat, folded it once and placed it between his head and the tree as a sort of cushion. And then the colonel came galloping up, his horse in a lather of sweat. He drew rein and confronted Uncle Shade. For a moment he knew not what to say. It seemed as though his anger choked him; and yet it was not so. He was nonplussed. Here before him was the object of his pursuit, the irritating cause of his heated and hurried journey. There was in the spectacle that which drove the anger out of his heart, and the color out of his face. Here he saw the very essence and incarnation of helplessness,—an old man grown gray and well-nigh decrepit in the service of the family, who had witnessed the very beginning and birth, as it were, of the family fortune.

What was to be done with him? Here in the forest that was almost a wilderness, the spirit of justice threatened to step forth from some convenient covert and take possession of the case. But the master had inherited obstinacy, and pride had added to the store. Anger returned to her throne.

"What do you mean by defying me in this way?" the colonel asked hotly. "What do you mean by running away, and hiding in the bushes? Do you suppose I am going to put up with it?"

76

The colonel worked himself up to a terrible pitch, but the old negro looked at his master with a level and disconcerting eye.

"Well, suh," replied Uncle Shade, fumbling with a pebble in his hand, "ef my mistiss wuz 'bove groun' dis day I'd be right whar she wuz at,—right dar doin' my work, des like I usen ter. Dat what I mean, suh."

"Do you mean to tell me, you impudent rascal, that because your mistress is dead you have the privilege of running off and hiding in the woods every time anybody snaps a finger at you? Why, if your mistress was alive to-day she'd have your hide taken off."

"She never is done it yet, suh, an' I been live wid 'er in about fifty year."

"Well, I'm going to do it," cried the colonel excitedly. He rode under a swinging limb and tied his horse. A leather strap fixed to a wooden handle hung from the horn of his saddle. "Take off that coat," he exclaimed curtly.

Uncle Shade rose and began to search in his pockets. "Well, suh," he said, " 'fo' I does dat I got sump'n here I want you to look at."

"I want to see nothing," cried the colonel. "I've put up with your rascality until I'm tired. Off with that coat!"

"But I got a letter fer you, suh, an' dey tol' me to put it in yo' han' de fus time you flew'd up an' got mad wid me."

It is a short jump from the extreme of one emotion to the extreme of another. The simplicity and earnestness of the old negro suddenly appealed to the colonel's sense of the ridiculous, and once more his anger took wings. Uncle Shade searched in his pockets until he suddenly remembered that he had placed it in the lining of his hat. As he drew it forth with a hand that shook a little from excitement, it seemed to be a bundle of rags. "It's his conjure-bag," the colonel said to himself, and at the thought of it he could hardly keep his face straight.

Carefully unrolling the long strip of cloth, which the colonel immediately recognized as part of a dress his mother used to wear, Uncle Shade presently came to a yellow letter. This he handed to the colonel, who examined it curiously. Though the paper was yellow with age and creased, the ink had not faded.

"What is this?" the colonel asked mechanically, although he had no diffi-culty in recognizing the writing as that of his mother,—the stiff, uncom-promising, perpendicular strokes of the pen could not be mistaken. "What is this?" he repeated.

"Letter fer you, suh," said Uncle Shade.

"Where did you get it?" the colonel inquired.

"I tuck it right out'n mistiss' han', suh," Uncle Shade replied.

The colonel put on his spectacles and spread the letter out carefully. This is what he read:

MY DEAR SON: I write this letter to commend the negro Shade to your special care and protection. He will need your protection most when it comes into your hand. I have told him that in the hour when you read these lines he may surely depend on you. He has been a faithful servant to me—and to you. No human being could be more devoted to my interests and yours than he has been. Whatever may have been his duty, he has gone far beyond it. But for him, the estate and even the homestead would have gone to the sheriff's block long ago. The fact that the mortgages have been paid is due to his devotion and his judgment. I am grateful to him, and I want my gratitude to protect him as long as he shall live. I have tried to make this plain in my will, but there may come a time when he will especially need your protection, as he has frequently needed mine. When that time comes I want you to do as I would do. I want you to stand by him as he has stood by us. To this hour he has never failed to do more than his duty where your interests and mine were concerned. It will never be necessary for him to give you this letter while I am alive; it will come to you as a message from the grave. God bless you and keep you is the wish of your

MOTHER.

The colonel's hands trembled a little as he folded the letter, and he cleared his throat in a somewhat boisterous way. Uncle Shade held out his hand for the letter.

"No, no!" the colonel cried. "It is for me. I need it a great deal worse than you do."

Thereupon he put the document in his pocket. Then he walked off a little way and leaned against a tree. A piece of crystal quartz at his feet attracted his attention. A mussel shell was lying near. He stooped and picked them both up and turned them over in his hand.

"What place is this?" he asked.

"Injun Bluff, suh."

"Didn't we come out here fishing once, when I was a little boy?"

"Yasser," replied Uncle Shade, with some animation. "You wa'n't so mighty little, nudder. You wuz a right smart chunk of a chap, suh. We tuck 'n' come'd out here, an' fished, an' I got you a hankcher full er deze here quare rocks, an' you played like dey wuz diamon's, an' you up'd an' said that you liked me better'n you liked anybody 'ceppin' yo' own blood kin. But times done change, suh. I'm de same nigger, but yuther folks ain't de same."

The colonel cleared his throat again and pulled off his spectacles, on which a mist had gathered.

"Whose land is this?" he asked presently.

"Stith Ingram's, suh."

"How far is his house?"

"Des cross dat fiel', suh."

"Well, take my hankcher and get me some more of the rocks. We'll take 'em home."

Uncle Shade gathered the specimens of quartz with alacrity. Then the two, Uncle Shade leading the horse, went across the field to Stith Ingram's, and, as they went, Jeff, the colonel's "nigger dog," fawned first on one and then on the other with the utmost impartiality, although he was too weary to cut up many capers.

Mr. Ingram himself, fat and saucy, was sitting on his piazza when the small procession came in sight. He stared at it until he saw who composed it, and then he began to laugh.

"Well, I declare!" he exclaimed. "Well, the great Tecumseh! Why, colonel! Why, what in the world! I'm powerful glad to see you! Is that you, Shade? Well, take your master's horse right round to the lot and brush him up a little. Colonel, come in! It's been a mighty long time since you've darkened this door. Where've you been?"

"I've just been out training my nigger dog," the colonel replied. "Old Shade started out before day, and just kept moving. He was in one of his tantrums, I reckon. But I'm glad of it. It gives me a chance to take dinner with you."

"Glad!" exclaimed Mr. Ingram. "Well, you ain't half as glad as I am. That old Shade's a caution. Maybe he was trying to get away, sure enough."

"Oh, no," replied the colonel. "Shade knows well enough he couldn't get away from Jeff."

That afternoon, Mr. Ingram carried the colonel and Jeff home in his buggy, and Uncle Shade rode the colonel's horse.

Daddy Jake, the Runaway

ONE FINE DAY in September, in the year 1863, there was quite an uproar on the Gaston plantation, in Putnam County, in the State of Georgia. Uncle Jake, the carriage-driver, was missing. He was more than fifty years old, and it was the first time he had been missing since his mistress had been big enough to call him. But he was missing now. Here was his mistress waiting to order the carriage; here was his master fretting and fuming; and here were the two little children, Lucien and Lillian, crying because they didn't know where Uncle Jake was—"Daddy Jake," who had heretofore seemed always to be within sound of their voices, ready and anxious to amuse them in any and every way.

Then came the news that Daddy Jake had actually run away. This was, indeed, astounding news, and although it was brought by the son of the overseer, none of the Gastons would believe it, least of all Lucien and Lillian. The son of the overseer also brought the further information that Daddy Jake, who had never had an angry word for anybody, had struck the overseer across the head with a hoe-handle, and had then taken to the woods. Dr. Gaston was very angry, indeed, and he told the overseer's son that if anybody was to blame it was his father. Mrs. Gaston, with her eyes full of tears, agreed with her husband, and Lucien and Lillian, when they found that Daddy Jake was really gone, refused to be comforted. Everybody seemed to be dazed. As it was Saturday, and Saturday was a holiday, the negroes stood around their quarters in little groups discussing the wonderful event. Some of them went so far as to say that if Daddy Jake had taken to the woods it was time for the rest of them to follow suit; but this proposition was hooted down by the more sensible among them.

Nevertheless, the excitement on the Gaston plantation ran very high when it was discovered that a negro so trusted and so trustworthy as Daddy

Jake had actually run away; and it was not until all the facts were known that the other negroes became reconciled to Daddy Jake's absence. What were the facts? They were very simple, indeed; and yet, many lads and lasses who read this may fail to fully comprehend them.

In the first place, the year in which Daddy Jake became a fugitive was the year 1863, and there was a great deal of doubt and confusion in the South at that time. The Conscription Act and the Impressment Law were in force. Under the one, nearly all the able-bodied men and boys were drafted into the army; and under the other, all the corn and hay and horses that the Confederacy needed were pressed into service. This state of things came near causing a revolt in some of the States, especially in Georgia, where the laws seemed to bear most heavily. Something of this is to be found in the history of that period, but nothing approaching the real facts has ever been published. After the Conscription Act was passed the planters were compelled to accept the services of such overseers as they could get, and the one whom Dr. Gaston had employed lacked both experience and discretion. He had never been trained to the business. He was the son of a shoemaker, and he became an overseer merely to keep out of the army. A majority of those who made overseeing their business had gone to the war either as volunteers or substitutes, and very few men capable of taking charge of a large plantation were left behind.

At the same time overseers were a necessity on some of the plantations. Many of the planters were either lawyers or doctors, and these, if they had any practice at all, were compelled to leave their farming interests to the care of agents; there were other planters who had been reared in the belief that an overseer was necessary on a large plantation; so that, for one cause and another, the overseer class was a pretty large one. It was a very respectable class, too; for, under ordinary circumstances, no person who was not known to be trustworthy would be permitted to take charge of the interests of a plantation, for these were as varied and as important as those of any other business.

But in 1863 it was a very hard matter to get a trustworthy overseer; and Dr. Gaston, having a large practice as a physician, had hired the first person who applied for the place, without waiting to make any inquiries about either his knowledge or his character; and it turned out that his overseer was not only utterly incompetent, but that he was something of a rowdy besides. An experienced overseer would have known that he was employed, not to exercise control over the house-servants, but to look after the farm-hands;

but the new man began business by ordering Daddy Jake to do various things that were not in the line of his duty. Naturally, the old man, who was something of a boss himself, resented this sort of interference. A great many persons were of the opinion that he had been spoiled by kind treatment; but this is doubtful. He had been raised with the white people from a little child, and he was as proud in his way as he was faithful in all ways. Under the circumstances, Daddy Jake did what other confidential servants would have done; he ignored the commands of the new overseer, and went about his business as usual. This led to a quarrel—the overseer doing most of the quarreling. Daddy Jake was on his dignity, and the overseer was angry. Finally, in his fury, he struck the old negro with a strap which he was carrying across his shoulders. The blow was a stinging one, and it was delivered full in Daddy Jake's face. For a moment the old negro was astonished. Then he became furious. Seizing an ax-handle that happened to be close to his hand, he brought it down upon the head of the overseer with full force. There was a tremendous crash as the blow fell, and the overseer went down as if he had been struck by a pile-driver. He gave an awful groan, and trembled a little in his limbs, and then lay perfectly still. Daddy Jake was both dazed and frightened. He would have gone to his master, but he remembered what he had heard about the law. In those days a negro who struck a white man was tried for his life, and if his guilt could be proven, he was either branded with a hot iron and sold to a speculator, or he was hanged.

The certainty of these punishments had no doubt been exaggerated by rumor, but even the rumor was enough to frighten the negroes. Daddy Jake looked at the overseer a moment, and then stopped and felt of him. He was motionless and, apparently, he had ceased to breathe. Then the old negro went to his cabin, gathered up his blanket and clothes, put some provisions in a little bag, and went off into the woods. He seemed to be in no hurry. He walked with his head bent, as if in deep thought. He appeared to understand and appreciate the situation. A short time ago he was the happy and trusted servant of a master and mistress who had rarely given him an unkind word; now he was a fugitive—a runaway. As he passed along by the garden palings he heard two little children playing and prattling on the other side. They were talking about him. He paused and listened.

"Daddy Jake likes me the best," Lucien was saying, "because he tells me stories."

"No," said Lillian, "he likes me the best, 'cause he tells me all the stories and gives me some gingercake, too."

The old negro paused and looked through the fence at the little children, and then he went on his way. But the youngsters saw Daddy Jake, and went running after him.

"Let me go, Daddy Jake!" cried Lucien. "Le' me go, too!" cried Lillian. But Daddy Jake broke into a run and left the children standing in the garden, crying.

It was not very long after this before the whole population knew that Daddy Jake had knocked the overseer down and had taken to the woods. In fact, it was only a few minutes, for some of the other negroes had seen him strike the overseer and had seen the overseer fall, and they lost no time in raising the alarm. Fortunately the overseer was not seriously hurt. He had received a blow severe enough to render him unconscious for a few minutes, —but this was all; and he was soon able to describe the fracas to Dr. Gaston, which he did with considerable animation.

"And who told you to order Jake around?" the doctor asked.

"Well, sir, I just thought I had charge of the whole crowd."

"You were very much mistaken, then," said Doctor Gaston, sharply; "and if I had seen you strike Jake with your strap, I should have been tempted to take my buggy-whip and give you a dose of your own medicine."

As a matter of fact, Doctor Gaston was very angry, and he lost no time in giving the new overseer what the negroes called his "walking-papers." He paid him up and discharged him on the spot, and it was not many days before everybody on the Gaston plantation knew that the man had fallen into the hands of the Conscription officers of the Confederacy, and that he had been sent on to the front.

At the same time, as Mrs. Gaston herself remarked, this fact, however gratifying it might be, did not bring Daddy Jake back. He was gone, and his absence caused a great deal of trouble on the plantation. It was found that half-a-dozen negroes had to be detailed to do the work which he had voluntarily taken upon himself—one to attend to the carriage-horses, another to look after the cows, another to feed the hogs and sheep, and still others to look after the thousand and one little things to be done about the "big house." But not one of them, nor all of them, filled Daddy Jake's place.

Many and many a time Doctor Gaston walked up and down the veranda wondering where the old negro was, and Mrs. Gaston, sitting in her rocking-chair, looked down the avenue day after day, half expecting to see Daddy Jake make his appearance, hat in hand and with a broad grin on his face. Some of the neighbors, hearing that Daddy Jake had become a fugitive, wanted to get Bill Locke's "track-dogs" and run him down, but Doctor Gaston and his wife would not hear to this. They said that the old negro wasn't used to staying in the woods, and that it wouldn't be long before he would come back home.

Doctor Gaston, although he was much troubled, looked at the matter from a man's point of view. Here was Daddy Jake's home; if he chose to come back, well and good; if he didn't, why, it couldn't be helped, and that was an end of the matter. But Mrs. Gaston took a different view. Daddy Jake had been raised with her father; he was an old family servant; he had known and loved her mother, who was dead; he had nursed Mrs. Gaston herself when she was a baby; in short, he was a fixture in the lady's experience, and his absence worried her not a little. She could not bear to think that the old negro was out in the woods without food and without shelter. If there was a thunderstorm at night, as there sometimes is in the South during September, she could hardly sleep for thinking about the old negro.

Thinking about him led Mrs. Gaston to talk about him very often, especially to Lucien and Lillian, who had been in the habit of running out to the kitchen while Daddy Jake was eating his supper and begging him to tell a story. So far as they were concerned, his absence was a personal loss. While Daddy Jake was away they were not only deprived of a most agreeable companion, but they could give no excuse for not going to bed. They had no one to amuse them after supper, and, as a consequence, their evenings were very dull. The youngsters submitted to this for several days, expecting that Daddy Jake would return, but in this they were disappointed. They waited and waited for more than a week, and then they began to show their impatience.

"I used to be afraid of runaways," said Lillian one day, "but I'm not afraid now, 'cause Daddy Jake is a runaway." Lillian was only six years old, but she had her own way of looking at things.

"Pshaw!" exclaimed Lucien, who was nine, and very robust for his age; "I never was afraid of runaways. I know mighty well they wouldn't hurt me. There was old Uncle Fed; he was a runaway when Papa bought him. Would he hurt anybody?"

"But there might be some bad ones," said Lillian, "and you know Lucinda says Uncle Fed is a real, sure-enough witch."

"Lucinda!" exclaimed Lucien, scornfully. "What does Lucinda know about witches? If one was to be seen she wouldn't stick her head out of the door to see it. She'd be scared to death."

"Yes, and so would anybody," said Lillian, with an air of conviction. "I know I would."

"Well, of course,—a little girl," explained Lucien. "Any little girl would be afraid of a witch, but a great big double-fisted woman like Lucinda ought to be ashamed of herself to be afraid of witches, and that, too, when everybody knows there aren't any witches at all, except in the stories."

"Well, I heard Daddy Jake telling about a witch that turned herself into a black cat, and then into a big black wolf," said Lillian.

"Oh, that was in old times," said Lucien, "when the animals used to talk and go on like people. But you never heard Daddy Jake say he saw a witch,—now, did you?"

"No," said Lillian, somewhat doubtfully; "but I heard him talking about them. I hope no witch will catch Daddy Jake."

"Pshaw!" exclaimed Lucien. "Daddy Jake carried his rabbit-foot with him, and you know no witch can bother him as long as he has his rabbit-foot."

"Well," said Lillian, solemnly, "if he's got his rabbit-foot and can keep off the witches all night, he won't come back any more."

"But he *must* come," said Lucien. "I'm going after him. I'm going down to the landing to-morrow, and I'll take the boat and go down the river and bring him back."

"Oh, may I go, too?" asked Lillian.

"Yes," said Lucien, loftily, "if you'll help me get some things out of the house and not say anything about what we are going to do."

Lillian was only too glad to pledge herself to secrecy, and the next day found the two children busily preparing for their journey in search of Daddy Jake.

The Gaston plantation lay along the Oconee River in Putnam County, not far from Roach's Ferry. In fact, it lay on both sides of the river, and, as the only method of communication was by means of a bateau, nearly everybody on the plantation knew how to manage the boat. There was not an hour during the day that the bateau was not in use. Lucien and Lillian had been carried across hundreds of times, and they were as much at home in the boat as they were in a buggy. Lucien was too young to row, but he knew how to guide the bateau with a paddle while others used the oars.

This fact gave him confidence, and the result was that the two children quietly made their arrangements to go in search of Daddy Jake. Lucien was the "provider," as he said, and Lillian helped him to carry the things to the boat. They got some meal-sacks, two old quilts, and a good supply of biscuits and meat. Nobody meddled with them, for nobody knew what their plans were, but some of the negroes remarked that they were not only unusually quiet, but very busy—a state of things that is looked upon by those who are acquainted with the ways of children as a very bad sign, indeed.

The two youngsters worked pretty much all day, and they worked hard; so that when night came they were both tired and sleepy. They were tired and sleepy, but they managed to cover their supplies with the meal-sacks, and the next morning they were up bright and early. They were up so early, indeed, that they thought it was a very long time until breakfast was ready; and, at last, when the bell rang, they hurried to the table and ate ravenously, as became two travelers about to set out on a voyage of adventure.

It was all they could do to keep their scheme from their mother. Once Lillian was on the point of asking her something about it, but Lucien shook his head, and it was not long before the two youngsters embarked on their journey. After seating Lillian in the bateau, Lucien unfastened the chain from the stake, threw it into the boat, and jumped in himself. Then, as the clumsy affair drifted slowly with the current, he seized one of the paddles, placed the blade against the bank, and pushed the bateau out into the middle of the stream.

It was the beginning of a voyage of adventure, the end of which could not be foretold; but the sun was shining brightly, the mocking-birds were singing in the water-oaks, the blackbirds were whistling blithely in the reeds, and the children were light-hearted and happy. They were going to find Daddy Jake and fetch him back home, and not for a moment did it occur to them that the old negro might have gone in a different direction. It seemed somehow to those on the Gaston plantation that whatever was good, or great, or wonderful had its origin "down the river." Rumor said that the biggest crops were grown in that direction, and that there the negroes were happiest.

The river, indeed, seemed to flow to some far-off country where everything was finer and more flourishing. This was the idea of the negroes themselves, and it was natural that Lucien and Lillian should be impressed with the same belief. So they drifted down the river, confident that they would find Daddy Jake. They had no other motive—no other thought. They took no account of the hardships of a voyage such as they had embarked on.

Lazily, almost reluctantly as it seemed, the boat floated down the stream.

86

At first, Lucien was inclined to use the broad oar, but it appeared that when he paddled on one side the clumsy boat tried to turn its head up stream on the other side, and so, after a while, he dropped the oar in the bottom of the boat.

The September sun was sultry that morning, but, obeying some impulse of the current, the boat drifted down the river in the shade of the water-oaks and willows that lined the eastern bank. On the western bank the Gaston plantation lay, and as the boat floated lazily along the little voyagers could hear the field-hands singing as they picked the opening cotton. The song was strangely melodious, though the words were ridiculous.

> My dog's a 'possum dog,
> *Here, Rattler! here!*
> He cross de creek upon a log,
> *Here, Rattler! here!*
>
> He run de 'possum up a tree,
> *Here, Rattler! here!*
> He good enough fer you an' me,
> *Here, Rattler! here!*
>
> Kaze when it come his fat'nin' time,
> *Here, Rattler! here!*
> De 'possum eat de muscadine,
> *Here, Rattler! here!*
>
> He eat till he kin skacely stan',
> *Here, Rattler! here!*
> An' den we bake him in de pan,
> *Here, Rattler! here!*

It was to the quaint melody of this song that the boat rocked and drifted along. One of the negroes saw the children and thought he knew them, and he called to them, but received no reply; and this fact was so puzzling that he went back and told the other negroes that there was some mistake about the children. "Ef dey'd' a' bin our chillun," he said, "dey'd' a' hollered back at me, sho'." Whereupon the field-hands resumed their work and their song, and the boat, gliding southward on the gently undulating current, was soon lost to view.

To the children it seemed to be a very pleasant journey. They had no thought of danger. The river was their familiar friend. They had crossed and recrossed it hundreds of times. They were as contented in the bateau as they would have been in their mother's room. The weather was warm, but on the river and in the shade of the overhanging trees the air was cool and refreshing. And after a while the current grew swifter, and the children, dipping their hands in the water, laughed aloud.

Once, indeed, the bateau, in running over a long stretch of shoals, was caught against a rock. An ordinary boat would have foundered, but this boat, clumsy and deep-set, merely obeyed the current. It struck the rock, recoiled, touched it again, and then slowly turned around and pursued its course down the stream. The shoals were noisy but harmless. The water foamed and roared over the rocks, but the current was deep enough to carry the bateau safely down. It was not often that a boat took that course, but Lucien and Lillian had no sense of fear. The roaring and foaming of the water pleased them, and the rushing and whirling of the boat, as it went dashing down the rapids, appeared to be only part of a holiday frolic. After they had passed the shoals, the current became swifter, and the old bateau was swept along at a rapid rate. The trees on the river bank seemed to be running back toward home, and the shadows on the water ran with them.

Sometimes the boat swept through long stretches of meadow and marsh lands, and then the children were delighted to see the sandpipers and killdees running along the margin of the water. The swallows, not yet flown southward, skimmed along the river with quivering wing, and the kingfishers displayed their shining plumage in the sun. Once a moccasin, fat and rusty, frightened by the unexpected appearance of the young voyagers, dropped into the boat; but, before Lucien could strike him with the unwieldy oar, he tumbled overboard and disappeared. Then the youngsters ate their dinner. It was a very dry dinner; but they ate it with a relish. The crows, flying lazily over, regarded them curiously.

"I reckon they want some," said Lucien.

"Well, they can't get mine," said Lillian, " 'cause I *jest* about got enough for myself."

They passed a white man who was sitting on the river bank, with his coat off, fishing.

"Where under the sun did you chaps come from?" he cried.

"Up the river," replied Lucien.

"Where in the nation are you going?"

"Down the river."

"Maybe he knows where Daddy Jake is," said Lillian. "Ask him."

"Why, he wouldn't know Daddy Jake from a side of sole leather," exclaimed Lucien.

By this time the boat had drifted around a bend in the river. The man on the bank took off his hat with his thumb and forefinger, rubbed his head with the other fingers, drove away a swarm of mosquitoes, and muttered, "Well, I'll be switched!" Then he went on with his fishing.

Meanwhile the boat drifted steadily with the current. Sometimes it seemed to the children that the boat stood still, while the banks, the trees, and the fields moved by them like a double panorama. Queer-looking little birds peeped at them from the bushes; fox-squirrels chattered at them from the trees; green frogs greeted them by plunging into the water with a squeak; turtles slid noiselessly off the banks at their approach; a red fox that had come to the river to drink disappeared like a shadow before the sun; and once a great white crane rose in the air, flapping his wings heavily.

Altogether it was a very jolly journey, but after a while Lillian began to get restless.

"Do you reckon Daddy Jake will be in the river when we find him?" she asked.

Lucien himself was becoming somewhat tired, but he was resolved to go right on. Indeed, he could not do otherwise.

"Why, who ever heard of such a thing?" he exclaimed. "What would Daddy Jake be doing in the water?"

"Well, how are we's to find him?"

"Oh, we'll find him."

"But I want to find him right now," said Lillian, "and I want to see Mamma, and Papa, and my dollies."

"Well," said Lucien with unconscious humor, "if you don't want to go, you can get out and walk back home." At this Lillian began to cry.

"Well," said Lucien, "if Daddy Jake was over there in the bushes and was to see you crying because you didn't want to go and find him, he'd run off into the woods and nobody would see him any more."

Lillian stopped crying at once, and, as the afternoon wore on, both children grew more cheerful; and even when twilight came, and after it the darkness, they were not very much afraid. The loneliness—the sighing of the wind through the trees, the rippling of the water against the sides of the boat, the hooting of the big swamp-owl, the cry of the whippoorwill, and the answer of its cousin, the chuck-will's-widow—all these things would have awed and frightened the children. But, shining steadily in the evening sky, they saw the star they always watched at home. It seemed to be brighter than ever, this familiar star, and they hailed it as a friend and fellow-traveler.

89

They felt that home couldn't be so far away, for the star shone in its accustomed place, and this was a great comfort.

After a while the night grew chilly, and then Lucien and Lillian wrapped their quilts about them and cuddled down in the bottom of the boat. Thousands of stars shone overhead, and it seemed to the children that the old bateau, growing tired of its journey, had stopped to rest; but it continued to drift down the river.

You may be sure there was trouble on the Gaston place when night came and the children did not return. They were missed at dinner-time; but it frequently happened that they went off with some of the plantation wagons, or with some of the field-hands, and so nothing was thought of their absence at noon; but when night fell and all the negroes had returned from their work, and there was still no sign of the children, there was consternation in the big house and trouble all over the plantation. The field-hands, returned from their work, discussed the matter at the doors of their cabins and manifested considerable anxiety.

At first the house-servants were sent scurrying about the place hunting for the truants. Then other negroes were pressed into service, until, finally, every negro on the place was engaged in the search, and torches could be seen bobbing up and down in all parts of the plantation. The negroes called and called, filling the air with their musical halloos, but there was no reply save from the startled birds, or from the dogs, who seemed to take it for granted that everybody was engaged in a grand 'possum hunt, and added the strength of their own voices to the general clamor.

While all this was going on, Mrs. Gaston was pacing up and down the long veranda wringing her hands in an agony of grief. There was but one thought in her mind—the *river*, the RIVER! Her husband in the midst of his own grief tried to console her, but he could not. He had almost as much as he could do to control himself, and there was in his own mind—the RIVER!

The search on the plantation and in its vicinity went on until nearly nine o'clock. About that time Big Sam, one of the plough-hands, who was also a famous fisherman, came running to the house with a frightened face.

"Marster," he exclaimed, "de boat gone—she done gone!"

"Oh, I knew it!" exclaimed Mrs. Gaston—"the river, the river!"

"Well!" said Doctor Gaston, "the boat must be found. Blow the horn!"

Big Sam seized the dinner-horn and blew a blast that startled the echoes for miles around. The negroes understood this to be a signal to return, and most of them thought that the children had been found, so they came back laughing and singing, and went to the big house to see the children.

"Wh'abouts you fine um, marster?" asked the foreman.

"They haven't been found, Jim," said Dr. Gaston. "Big Sam says that the boat is gone from the landing, and that boat must be found to-night."

"Marster," said a negro, coming forward out of the group, "I seed a boat gwine down stream dis mornin'. I wuz way up on de hill—"

"And you didn't come and tell me?" asked Dr. Gaston in a severe tone.

"Well, suh, I hollered at um, an' dey ain't make no answer, an' den it look like ter me 't wuz dem two Ransome boys. Hit mos' drap out'n my min'. An' den you know, suh, our chillun ain't never had no doin's like dat—gittin' in de boat by dey own-alone se'f an' sailin' off dat a-way."

"Well," said Dr. Gaston, "the boat must be found. The children are in it. Where can we get another boat?"

"I got one, suh," said Big Sam.

"Me, too, marster," said another negro.

"Then get them both, and be quick about it!"

"Ah-yi, suh," was the response, and in a moment the group was scattered, and Big Sam could be heard giving orders in a loud and an energetic tone of voice. For once he was in his element. He could be foreman on the Oconee if he couldn't in the cotton-patch. He knew every nook and cranny of the river for miles up and down; he had his fish-baskets sunk in many places, and the overhanging limbs of many a tree bore the marks of the lines of his set-hooks. So for once he appointed himself foreman, and took charge of affairs. He and Sandy Bill (so-called owing to the peculiar color of his hair) soon had their boats at the landing. The other negroes were assembled there, and the most of them had torches.

"Marster," said Big Sam, "you git in my boat, an' let little Willyum come fer ter hol' de torch. Jesse, you git in dar wid Sandy Bill. Fling a armful er light'ood in bofe boats, boys, kaze we got ter have a light, and dey ain't no tellin' how fur we gwine."

The fat pine was thrown in, everything made ready, and then the boats started. With one sweep of his broad paddle, Big Sam sent his boat into the middle of the stream, and, managed by his strong and willing arms, the clumsy old bateau became a thing of life. Sandy Bill was not far behind him.

The negroes used only one paddle in rowing, and each sat in the stern of his boat, using the rough but effective oar first on one side and then the other.

From a window, Mrs. Gaston watched the boats as they went speeding down the river. By her side was Charity, the cook.

"Isn't it terrible!" she exclaimed, as the boats passed out of sight. "Oh, what shall I do?"

" 'T would be mighty bad, Mist'iss, *ef* dem chillun wuz los'; but dey ain't no mo' los' dan I is, an' I'm a-standin' right yer in de cornder by dish yer cheer."

"Not lost! Why, of course they are lost. Oh, my darling little children!"

"No 'm, dey ain't no mo' los' dan you is. Dey tuck dat boat dis mornin', an' dey went atter ole man Jake—dat's whar dey er gone. Dey ain't gone nowhar else. Dey er in dat boat right now; dey may be asleep, but dey er in dar. Ain't I year um talkin' yistiddy wid my own years? Ain't I year dat ar Marse Lucien boy 'low ter he sister dat he gwine go fetch ole man Jake back? Ain't I miss a whole can full er biscuits? Ain't I miss two er dem pies w'at I lef' out dar in de kitchen? Ain't I miss a great big hunk er light-bread? An' who gwine dast ter take um less'n it's dem ar chillun? Dey don't fool me, mon. I'm one er de oldest rats in de barn—I is dat!"

Charity's tone was emphatic and energetic. She was so confident that her theory was the right one that she succeeded in quieting her mistress some-what.

"An' mo' 'n dat," she went on, seeing the effect of her remarks, "dem chillun'll come home yer all safe an' soun'. Ef Marster an' dem niggers don't fetch um back, dey'll come deyse'f; an' old man Jake'll come wid um. You min' w'at I tell you. You go an' go ter bed, honey, an' don't pester yo'se'f 'bout dem chillun. I'll set up yer in the cornder an' nod, an' keep my eyes on w'at 's gwine on outside."

But Mrs. Gaston refused to go to bed. She went to the window, and away down the river she could see the red light of the torches projected against the fog. It seemed as if it were standing still, and the mother's heart sank within her at the thought. Perhaps they had found the boat—empty! This and a thousand other cruel suggestions racked her brain.

But the boats were not standing still; they were moving down the river as rapidly as four of the stoutest arms to be found in the county could drive them. The pine torches lit up both banks perfectly. The negroes rowed in silence a mile or more, when Big Sam said:

"Marster, kin we sing some?"

"Does it seem to be much of a singing matter, Sam?" Dr. Gaston asked, grimly.

92

"No, suh, it don't; but singin' he'ps 'long might'ly w'en you workin', mo'
speshually ef you er doin' de kind er work whar you kin sorter hit a lick wid
the chune—kinder keepin' time, like."

Dr. Gaston said nothing, and Big Sam went on:

" 'Sides dat, Marster, we-all useter sing ter dem chillun, an' dey knows our
holler so well dat I boun' you ef dey wuz ter year us singin' an' gwine on,
dey'd holler back."

"Well," said Dr. Gaston, struck by the suggestion, "sing."

"Bill," said Big Sam to the negro in the other boat, "watch out for me;
I'm gwine away."

"You'll year fum me w'en you git whar you gwine," Sandy Bill replied.

With that Big Sam struck up a song. His voice was clear and strong, and
he sang with a will.

> Oh, Miss Malindy, you er lots too sweet for me;
>   I cannot come to see you
> Ontil my time is free—
>   Oh, den I'll come ter see you,
> An' take you on my knee.
>
> Oh, Miss Malindy, now don't you go away;
>   I cannot come to see you
> Ontil some yuther day—
>   Oh, den I'll come ter see you—
> Oh, den I'll come ter stay.
>
> Oh, Miss Malindy, you is my only one;
>   I cannot come ter see you
> Ontil de day is done—
>   Oh, den I'll come ter see you,
> And we'll have a little fun.
>
> Oh, Miss Malindy, my heart belongs ter you;
>   I cannot come ter see you
> Ontil my work is thoo'.
>   Oh, den I'll come ter see you,
> I'll come in my canoe.

The words of the song, foolish and trivial as they are, do not give the
faintest idea of the melody to which it was sung. The other negroes joined in,
and the tremulous tenor of little Willyum was especially effective. The deep
dark woods on either side seemed to catch up and echo back the plaintive
strain. To a spectator on the bank, the scene must have been an uncanny one

—the song with its heart-breaking melody, the glistening arms and faces of the two gigantic blacks, the flaring torches, flinging their reflections on the swirling waters, the great gulfs of darkness beyond—all these must have been very impressive. But these things did not occur to those in the boats, least of all to Dr. Gaston. In the minds of all there was but one thought—the children.

The negroes rowed on, keeping time to their songs. Their arms appeared to be as tireless as machinery that has the impulse of steam. Finally Big Sam's boat grounded.

"Hol' on dar, Bill!" he shouted. "Watch out!" He took the torch from the little negro and held it over his head, and then behind him, peering into the darkness beyond. Then he laughed.

"De Lord he'p my soul!" he exclaimed; "I done clean fergit 'bout Moccasin Shoals! Back yo' boat, Bill." Suiting the action to the word, he backed his own, and they were soon away from the shoals.

"Now, den," he said to Bill, "git yo' boat in line wid mine, an' hol' yo' paddle in yo' lap." Then the boats, caught by the current, moved toward the shoals, and one after the other touched a rock, turned completely around, and went safely down the rapids, just as the children's boat had done in the forenoon. Once over the shoals, Big Sam and Sandy Bill resumed their oars and their songs, and sent the boats along at a rapid rate.

A man, sitting on the river bank, heard them coming, and put out his torch by covering it with sand. He crouched behind the bushes and watched them go by. After they had passed he straightened himself, and remarked:

"Well, I'll be switched!" Then he relighted his torch, and went on with his fishing. It was the same man that Lucien and Lillian had seen.

The boats went on and on. With brief intervals the negroes rowed all night long, but Dr. Gaston found no trace of his children. In sheer desperation, however, he kept on. The sun rose, and the negroes were still rowing. At nine o'clock in the morning the boats entered Ross's mill-pond. This Dr. Gaston knew was the end of his journey. If the boat had drifted into this pond, and been carried over the dam, the children were either drowned or crushed on the rocks below. If their boat had not entered the pond, then they had been rescued the day before by some one living near the river.

It was with a heavy heart that Dr. Gaston landed. And yet there were no signs of a tragedy anywhere near. John Cosby, the miller, fat and hearty, stood in the door of the mill, his arms akimbo, and watched the boats curiously. His children were playing near. A file of geese was marching down to the water, and a flock of pigeons was sailing overhead, taking their

94

morning exercise. Everything seemed to be peaceful and serene. As he passed the dam on his way to the mill, Dr. Gaston saw that there was a heavy head of water, but possibly not enough to carry a large bateau over; still—the children were gone!

The puzzled look on the miller's face disappeared as Dr. Gaston approached.

"Well, the gracious goodness!" he exclaimed. "Why, howdy, Doc.—howdy! Why, I'm right down glad to see you. Whichever an' whichaway did you come?"

"My little children are lost," said Dr. Gaston, shaking the miller's hand. The jolly smile on John Cosby's face disappeared as suddenly as if it had been wiped out with a sponge.

"Well, now, that's too bad—too bad," he exclaimed, looking at his own rosy-cheeked little ones standing near.

"They were in a bateau," said Dr. Gaston, "and I thought maybe they might have drifted down here and over the mill-dam."

The miller's jolly smile appeared again. "Oh, no, Doc.—no, no! Whichever an' whichaway they went, they never went over that dam. In time of a freshet, the thing might be did; but not now. Oh, no! Ef it lies betwixt goin' over that dam an' bein' safe, them babies is jest as safe an' soun' as mine is."

"I think," said Dr. Gaston, "that they started out to hunt Jake, my carriage-driver who has run away."

"Jake run away!" exclaimed Mr. Cosby, growing very red in the face. "Why, the impident scoundull! Hit ain't been three days sence the ole rascal wuz here. He come an' 'lowed that some of your wagons was a-campin' out about two mile from here, an' he got a bushel of meal, an' said that if you didn't pay me the money down I could take it out in physic. The impident ole scoundull! An' he was jest as 'umble-come-tumble as you please—a-bowin', an' a-scrapin', an' a-howdy-do-in'."

But the old miller's indignation cooled somewhat when Dr. Gaston briefly told him of the incident which caused the old negro to run away.

"Hit sorter sticks in my gizzard," he remarked, "when I hear tell of a nigger hittin' a white man; but I don't blame Jake much."

"And now," said Dr. Gaston, "I want to ask your advice. You are a level-headed man, and I want to know what you think. The children got in the boat, and came down the river. There is no doubt in my mind that they started on a wild-goose chase after Jake; but they are not on the river now, nor is the boat on the river. How do you account for that?"

"Well, Doc., if you want my naked beliefs about it, I'll give 'em to you, fa'r an' squar'. It's my beliefs that them youngsters have run up agin old Jake somewhar up the river, an' that they are jest as safe an' soun' as you is. Them's my beliefs."

"But what has become of the boat?"

"Well, I'll tell you. Old Jake is jest as cunning as any other nigger. He took an' took the youngsters out, an' arterwards he drawed the boat out on dry land. He rightly thought there would be pursuit, an' he didn't mean to be ketched."

"Then what would you advise me to do?" asked Dr. Gaston.

The old man scratched his head.

"Well, Doc., I'm a-talkin' in the dark, but it's my beliefs them youngsters 'll be at home before you can get there to save your life. Jake may not be there, but if he's found the boy an' gal, he'll carry 'em safe home. Now you mind what I tell you."

Dr. Gaston's anxiety was too great to permit him to put much confidence in the old miller's prediction. What he said seemed reasonable enough, but a thousand terrible doubts had possession of the father's mind. He hardly dared go home without the children. He paced up and down before the mill, a most miserable man. He knew not where to go or what to do.

Mr. Cosby, the miller, watched him awhile, and shook his head. "If Doc. don't find them youngsters," he said to himself, "he'll go plum deestracted." But he said aloud:

"Well, Doc, you an' the niggers must have a breathing-spell. We'll go up to the house an' see ef we can't find somethin' to eat in the cubberd, an' arterwards, in the time you are restin', we'll talk about findin' the youngsters. If there's any needcessity, I'll go with you. My son John can run the mill e'en about as good as I can. We'll go up yan to 'Squire Ross's an' git a horse or two, an' we'll scour the country on both sides of the river. But you've got to have a snack of somethin' to eat, an' you've got to take a rest. Human natur' can't stand the strain."

Torn as he was by grief and anxiety, Dr. Gaston knew this was good advice. He gratefully accepted John Cosby's invitation to breakfast, as well as his offer to aid in the search for the lost children. After Doctor Gaston had eaten, he sat on the miller's porch and tried to collect his thoughts so as to be able to form some plan of search. While the two men were talking, they heard Big Sam burst out laughing. He laughed so loud and heartily that Mr. Cosby grew angry, and went into the back yard to see what the fun was

96

about. In his heart the miller thought the negroes were laughing at the food his wife had set before them, and he was properly indignant.

"Well, well," said he, "what's this I hear? Two high-fed niggers a-laughin' beca'se their master's little ones are lost and gone! And has it come to this? A purty pass, a mighty purty pass!" Both the negroes grew very serious at this.

"Mars' John, we-all was des projickin' wid one an'er. You know how niggers is w'en dey git nuff ter eat. Dey feel so good dey 'bleege ter holler."

Mr. Cosby sighed, and turned away. "Well," said he, "I hope niggers 's got souls, but I know right p'int-blank that they ain't got no hearts."

Now, what was Big Sam laughing at?

He was laughing because he had found out where Lucien and Lillian were. How did he find out? In the simplest manner imaginable. Sandy Bill and Big Sam were sitting in Mr. Cosby's back yard eating their breakfast, while little Willyum was eating his in the kitchen. It was the first time the two older negroes had had an opportunity of talking together since they started from home the day before.

"Sam," said Sandy Bill, "did you see whar de chillun landed w'en we come 'long des a'ter sunup dis mornin'?"

"Dat I didn't," said Sam, wiping his mouth with the back of his hand— "dat I didn't, an' ef I had I'd a hollered out ter Marster."

"Dat w'at I wuz feared un," said Sandy Bill.

"Feared er what?" asked Big Sam.

"Feared you'd holler at Marster ef you seed whar dey landed. Dat how come I ter run foul er yo' boat."

"Look yer, nigger man, you ain't done gone 'stracted, is you?"

"Shoo, chile! don't talk ter me 'bout gwine 'stracted. I got ez much sense ez Ole Zip Coon."

"Den whyn't you tell Marster? Ain't you done see how he troubled in he min'?"

"I done see dat, en it makes me feel bad; but t'er folks got trouble, too, lots wuss'n Marster."

"Is dey los' der chillun?"

"Yes—Lord! dey done los' eve'body. But Marster ain't los' no chillun yit."

"Den wat we doin' way down yer?" asked Big Sam in an angry tone.

"Le' me tell you," said Sandy Bill, laying his hand on Big Sam's shoulder; "le' me tell you. Right cross dar fum whar I run foul er yo' boat is de biggest cane-brake in all creation."

"I know 'im," said Big Sam. "Dey calls 'im Hudson's cane-brake."

"Now you talkin'," said Sandy Bill. "Well, ef you go dar you'll fin' right in the middle er dat cane-brake a heap er niggers dat you got 'quaintance wid—Randall Spivey, an' Crazy Sue, an' Cupid Mitchell, an' Isaiah Little—dey er all dar; an' ole man Jake, he dar too."

"Look yer, nigger," Sam exclaimed, "how you know?"

"I sent 'im dar. He come by me in de fiel' an' tole me he done kilt de overseer, an' I up an' tell 'im, I did, 'Make fer Hudson's cane-brake,' an' dar's right whar he went."

It was at this point that Big Sam's hearty laughter attracted the attention of Dr. Gaston and Mr. Cosby.

"Now, den," said Sandy Bill, after the miller had rebuked them and returned to the other side of the house, "now, den, ef I'd 'a' showed Marster whar dem chillun landed, en tole 'im whar dey wuz, he'd 'a' gone 'cross dar, en seed dem niggers, an' by dis time nex' week ole Bill Locke's nigger-dogs would 'a' done run um all in jail. You know how Marster is. He think kaze he treat his niggers right dat eve'ybody else treat der'n des dat a-way. But don't you worry 'bout dem chillun."

Was it possible for Sandy Bill to be mistaken?

Lucien and Lillian, cuddled together in the bottom of their boat, were soon fast asleep. In dreams of home their loneliness and their troubles were all forgotten. Sometimes in the starlight, sometimes in the dark shadows of the over-hanging trees, the boat drifted on. At last, toward morning, it was caught in an eddy and carried nearer the bank, where the current was almost imperceptible. Here the clumsy old bateau rocked and swung, sometimes going lazily forward, and then as lazily floating back again.

As the night faded away into the dim gray of morning, the bushes above the boat were thrust softly aside and a black face looked down upon the children. Then the black face disappeared as suddenly as it came. After awhile it appeared again. It was not an attractive face. In the dim light it seemed to look down on the sleeping children with a leer that was almost hideous. It was the face of a woman. Around her head was a faded red handkerchief, tied in a fantastic fashion, and as much of her dress as could be seen was ragged, dirty, and greasy. She was not pleasant to look upon, but the children slept on unconscious of her presence.

Presently the woman came nearer. On the lower bank a freshet had deposited a great heap of sand, which was now dry and soft. The woman sat down on this, hugging her knees with her arms, and gazed at the sleeping children long and earnestly. Then she looked up and down the river, but nothing was to be seen for the fog that lay on the water. She shook her head and muttered:

"Hit's p'izen down yer for dem babies. Yit how I gwine git um out er dar?"

She caught hold of the boat, turned it around, and, by means of the chain, drew it partially on the sand-bank. Then she lifted Lillian from the boat, wrapping the quilt closer about the child, carried her up the bank, and laid her beneath the trees where no dew had fallen. Returning, she lifted Lucien and placed him beside his sister. But the change aroused him. He raised himself on his elbow and rubbed his eyes. The negro woman, apparently by force of habit, slipped behind a tree.

"Where am I?" Lucien exclaimed, looking around in something of a fright. He caught sight of the frazzled skirt of the woman's dress. "Who is there behind that tree?" he cried.

"Nobody but me, honey—nobody ner nothin' but po' ole Crazy Sue. Don't be skeerd er me. I ain't nigh ez bad ez I looks ter be."

It was now broad daylight, and Lucien could see that the hideous ugliness of the woman was caused by a burn on the side of her face and neck.

"Wasn't I in a boat?"

"Yes, honey; I brung you up yer fer ter keep de fog fum pizenin' you."

"I dreamed the Bad Man had me," said Lucien, shivering at the bare recollection.

"No, honey; 't want nobody ner nothin' but po' ole Crazy Sue. De boat down dar on de sand-bank, an' yo' little sissy layin' dar soun' asleep. Whar in de name er goodness wuz you-all gwine, honey?" asked Crazy Sue, coming nearer.

"We were going down the river hunting for Daddy Jake. He's a runaway now. I reckon we'll find him after a while."

"Is you-all Marse Doc. Gaston' chillun?" asked Crazy Sue, with some show of eagerness.

"Why, of course we are," said Lucien.

Crazy Sue's eyes fairly danced with joy. She clasped her hands together and exclaimed:

"Lord, honey, I could shout,—I could des holler and shout; but I ain't gwine do it. You stay right dar by yo' little sissy till I come back; I want ter run an' make somebody feel good. Now, don't you move, honey. Stay right dar."

With that Crazy Sue disappeared in the bushes. Lucien kept very still. In the first place, he was more than half frightened by the strangeness of his surroundings, and, in the second place, he was afraid his little sister would wake and begin to cry. He felt like crying a little himself, for he knew he was many miles from home, and he felt very cold and uncomfortable. Indeed, he felt very lonely and miserable; but just when he was about to cry and call Daddy Jake, he heard voices near him. Crazy Sue came toward him in a half-trot, and behind her—close behind her—was Daddy Jake, his face wreathed in smiles and his eyes swimming in tears. Lucien saw him and rushed toward him, and the old man stooped and hugged the boy to his black bosom.

"Why, honey," he exclaimed, "whar de name er goodness you come f'um! Bless you! ef my eyes wuz sore de sight un you would make um well. How you know whar yo' Daddy Jake is?"

"Me and sister started out to hunt you," said Lucien, whimpering a little, now that he had nothing to whimper for, "and I think you are mighty mean to run off and leave us all at home."

"Now you talkin', honey," said Daddy Jake, laughing in his old fashion. "I boun' I'm de meanes' ole nigger in de Nunited State. Yit, ef I'd 'a' know'd you wuz gwine ter foller me up so close, I'd 'a' fotch you wid me, dat I would! An' dar 's little Missy," he exclaimed, leaning over the little girl, "an' she's a-sleepin' des ez natchul ez ef she wuz in her bed at home. What I tell you-all?" he went on, turning to a group of negroes that had followed him,—Randall, Cupid, Isaiah, and others,—"What I tell you-all? Ain't I done bin' an' gone an' tole you dat deze chillun wuz de out-doin'est chillun on de top-side er de roun' worl'?"

The negroes—runaways all—laughed and looked pleased, and Crazy Sue fairly danced. They made so much fuss that they woke Lillian, and when she saw Daddy Jake she gave one little cry and leaped in his arms. This made Crazy Sue dance again, and she would have kept it up for a long time, but Randall suggested to Daddy Jake that the boat ought to be hauled ashore and hidden in the bushes. Crazy Sue stayed with the children while the negro men went after the boat. They hauled it up the bank by the chain, and then they lifted and carried it several hundred yards away from the river, and hid it in the thick bushes and grass.

"Now," said Daddy Jake, when they had returned to where they left the children, "we got ter git away f'um yer. Dey ain't no tellin' w'at gwine ter

100

happen. Ef deze yer chillun kin slip up on us dis away w'at kin a grown man do?"

The old man intended this as a joke, but the others took him at his word, and were moving off. "Wait!" he exclaimed. "De chillun bleeze ter go whar I go. Sue, you pick up little Missy dar, an' I'll play hoss fer dish yer chap."

Crazy Sue lifted Lillian in her arms, Daddy Jake stooped so that Lucien could climb up on his back, and then all took up their march for the middle of Hudson's cane-brake. Randall brought up the rear in order, as he said, to "stop up de holes."

It was a narrow, slippery, and winding path in which the negroes trod—a path that a white man would have found difficult to follow. It seemed to lead in all directions; but, finally, it stopped on a knoll high and dry above the surrounding swamp. A fire was burning brightly, and the smell of frying meat was in the air. On this knoll the runaway negroes had made their camp, and for safety they could not have selected a better place.

It was not long before Crazy Sue had warmed some breakfast for the children. The negroes had brought the food they found in the boat, and Crazy Sue put some of the biscuits in a tin bucket, hung the bucket on a stick, and held it over the fire. Then she gave them some bacon that had been broiled on a stone, and altogether they made a hearty breakfast.

During the morning most of the negro men stayed in the cane-brake, some nodding and some patching their clothes, which were already full of patches. But after dinner, a feast of broiled fish, roasted sweet potatoes, and ash-cake, they all went away, leaving Crazy Sue to take care of the children. After the men had all gone, the woman sat with her head covered with her arms. She sat thus for a long time. After a while Lucien went to her and put his hand on her shoulder.

"What's the matter?" he asked.

"Nothin', honey; I wuz des a-settin' yer a-studyin' an' a-studyin'. Lots er times I gits took dat a-way."

"What are you studying about?" said Lucien.

" 'Bout folks. I wuz des a-studyin' 'bout folks, an' 'bout how come I whar I is, w'en I oughter be somers else. W'en I set down dis a-way, I gits dat turrified in de min' dat I can't stay on de groun' sca'cely. Look like I want ter rise up in de elements an' fly."

"What made you run away?" Lucien asked with some curiosity.

"Well, you know, honey," said Crazy Sue, after a pause, "my marster ain't nigh ez good ter his niggers ez yo' pa is ter his'n. 'T ain't dat my marster is any mo' strick, but look like hit fret 'im ef he see one er his niggers settin' down anywheres. Well, one time, long time ago, I had two babies, an' dey wuz twins, an' dey wuz des 'bout ez likely little niggers ez you ever did see. De w'ite folks had me at de house doin' de washin' so I could be where I kin nurse de babies. One time I wuz settin' in my house nursin' un um, an' while I settin' dar I went fast ter sleep. How long I sot dar 'sleep, de Lord only knows, but w'en I woked up, Marster wuz stan'in in de do', watchin' me. He ain't say nothin, yit I knowed dat man wuz mad. He des turn on his heel an' walk away. I let you know I put dem babies down an' hustled out er dat house mighty quick.

"Well, sir, dat night de foreman come 'roun' an' tole me dat I mus' go ter de fiel' de nex' mornin'. Soon ez he say dat, I up an' went ter de big house an' ax Marster w'at I gwine do wid de babies ef I went ter de fiel'. He stood an' look at me, he did, an' den he writ a note out er his pocket-book, an' tol' me ter han' it ter de overseer. Dat w'at I done dat ve'y night, an' de overseer, he took an' read de note, an' den he up an' say dat I mus' go wid de hoe-han's, way over ter de two-mile place.

"I went, kaze I bleeze ter go; yit all day long, whiles I wuz hoein' I kin year dem babies cryin'. Look like sometimes dey wuz right at me, an' den ag'in look like dey wuz way off yander. I kep' on a-goin' an' I kep' on a-hoein', an' de babies kep' on a-famishin'. Dey des fade away, an' bimeby dey died, bofe un um on the same day. On dat day I had a fit an' fell in de fier, an' dat how come I burnt up so.

"Look like," said the woman, marking on the ground with her bony forefinger—"look like I kin year dem babies cryin' yit, an' dat de reason folks call me Crazy Sue, kaze I kin year um cryin' an' yuther folks can't. I'm mighty glad dey can't, kaze it 'ud break der heart."

"Why didn't you come and tell Papa about it?" said Lucien, indignantly.

"Ah, Lord, honey!" exclaimed Crazy Sue, "yo' pa is a mighty good man, an' a mighty good doctor, but he ain't got no medicine wa't could 'a' kyored me an' my marster."

In a little while Daddy Jake put in an appearance, and the children soon forgot Crazy Sue's troubles, and began to think about going home.

"Daddy Jake," said Lucien, "when are you going to take us back home?"

"I want to go right now," said Lillian.

Daddy Jake scratched his head and thought the matter over.

"Dey ain't no use talkin'," said he, "I got ter carry you back an' set you down in sight er de house, but how I gwine do it an' not git kotched? Dat w'at troublin' me."

"Why, Papa ain't mad," said Lucien. "I heard him tell that mean old overseer he had a great mind to take his buggy whip to him for hitting you."

"Ain't dat man dead?" exclaimed Daddy Jake in amazement.

"No, he ain't," said Lucien. "Papa drove him off the place."

"Well, I be blest!" said the old man with a chuckle. "W'at kinder head you reckon dat w'ite man got?—Honey," he went on, growing serious again, "is you *sholy sho* dat man ain't dead?"

"Didn't I see him after you went away? Didn't I hear Papa tell him to go away? Didn't I hear Papa tell Mamma he wished you had broken his neck? Didn't I hear Papa tell Mamma that you were a fool for running away?" Lucien flung these questions at Daddy Jake with an emphasis that left nothing to be desired.

"Well," said Daddy Jake, "dat mus' be so, an' dat bein' de case, we'll des start in de mornin' an' git home ter supper. We'll go over yander ter Marse Meredy Ingram's an' borry his carriage an' go home in style. I boun' you, dey'll all be glad to see us."

Daddy Jake was happy once more. A great burden had been taken from his mind. The other negroes when they came in toward night seemed to be happy, too, because the old man could go back home; and there was not one but would have swapped places with him. Randall was the last to come, and he brought a big, fat chicken.

"I wuz comin' 'long cross de woods des now," he said, winking his eye and shaking his head at Daddy Jake, "an', bless gracious, dis chicken flew'd right in my han'. I say ter myse'f, I did, 'Ole lady, you mus' know we got comp'ny at our house,' an' den I clamped down on 'er, an' yer she is. Now, 'bout dark, I'll take 'er up yander an' make Marse Ingram's cook fry 'er brown fer deze chillun, an' I'll make 'er gimme some milk."

Crazy Sue took the chicken, which had already been killed, wet its feathers thoroughly, rolled it around in the hot embers, and then proceeded to pick and clean it.

Randall's programme was carried out to the letter. Mr. Meredith Ingram's cook fried the chicken for him, and put in some hot biscuit for good measure, and the milker gave him some fresh milk, which she said would not be missed.

The children had a good supper, and they would have gone to sleep directly afterward, but the thought of going home with Daddy Jake kept them awake. Randall managed to tell Daddy Jake, out of hearing of the children, that Dr. Gaston and some of his negroes had been seen at Ross's mill that morning.

"Well," said Daddy Jake, "I bleeze ter beat Marster home. Ef he go back dar widout de chillun, my mistiss 'll drap right dead on de flo'." This was his only comment.

Around the fire the negroes laughed and joked, and told their adventures. Lillian felt comfortable and happy, and as for Lucien, he himself felt a hero. He had found Daddy Jake, and now he was going to carry him back home.

Once, when there was a lull in the talk, Lillian asked why the frogs made so much fuss.

"I speck it's kaze dey er mad wid Mr. Rabbit," said Crazy Sue. "Dey er tryin' der best ter drive 'im outen de swamp."

"What are they mad with the Rabbit for?" asked Lucien, thinking there might be a story in the explanation.

"Hit's one er dem ole-time fusses," said Crazy Sue. "Hit's most too ole ter talk about."

"Don't you know what the fuss was about?" asked Lucien.

"Well," said Crazy Sue, "one time Mr. Rabbit an' Mr. Coon live close ter one anudder in de same neighborhoods. How dey does now, I ain't a-tellin' you; but in dem times dey wa'n't no hard feelin's 'twix' um. Dey des went 'long like two ole cronies. Mr. Rabbit, he wuz a fisherman, and Mr. Coon, he wuz a fisherman—"

"And put 'em in pens," said Lillian, remembering an old rhyme she had heard.

"No, honey, dey ain't no William-Come-Trimbletoe in dis. Mr. Rabbit an' Mr. Coon wuz bofe fishermans, but Mr. Rabbit, he kotch fish, an' Mr. Coon, he fished fer frogs. Mr. Rabbit, he had mighty good luck, an' Mr. Coon, he had mighty bad luck. Mr. Rabbit, he got fat an' slick, an' Mr. Coon, he got po' an' sick.

"Hit went on dis a-way tell one day Mr. Coon meet Mr. Rabbit in de big road. Dey shook han's, dey did, an' den Mr. Coon, he 'low:

" 'Brer Rabbit, whar you git sech a fine chance er fish?'

"Mr. Rabbit laugh an' say: 'I kotch um outen de river, Brer Coon. All I got ter do is ter bait my hook,' sezee.

"Den Mr. Coon shake his head an' 'low: 'Den how come I ain't kin ketch no frogs?'

"Mr. Rabbit sat down in de road an' scratched fer fleas, an' den he 'low: 'Hit's kaze you done make um all mad, Brer Coon. One time in de dark er de moon, you slipped down ter de branch an' kotch de ole King Frog; an' ever sence dat time, w'enever you er passin' by, you kin year um sing out, fus' one an' den anudder—*Yer he come! Dar he goes! Hit 'im in de eye; hit 'im in de eye! Mash 'im an' smash 'im; mash 'im an' smash 'im!* Yasser, dat w'at dey say. I year um constant, Brer Coon, an 'dat des w'at day say.'

"Den Mr. Coon up an' say: 'Ef dat de way dey gwine on, how de name er goodness kin I ketch um, Brer Rabbit? I bleeze ter have sump'n ter eat fer me an' my fambly connection.'

"Mr. Rabbit sorter grin in de cornder er his mouf, an' den he say: 'Well, Brer Coon, bein' ez you bin so sociable 'long wid me, an' ain't never showed yo' toofies w'en I pull yo' tail, I'll des whirl in an' he'p you out.'

"Mr. Coon, he say: 'Thanky, thanky-do, Brer Rabbit.'

"Mr. Rabbit hung his fish on a tree lim', an' say: 'Now, Brer Coon, you bleeze ter do des like I tell you.'

"Mr. Coon 'lowed dat he would ef de Lord spared 'im.

"Den Mr. Rabbit say: 'Now, Brer Coon, you des rack down yander, an' git on de big san'-bar 'twix' de river an' de branch. W'en you git dar you mus' stagger like you sick, and den you mus' whirl roun' an' roun' an' drap down like you dead. After you drap down, you must sorter jerk yo' legs once er twice, an' den you mus' lay right still. Ef fly light on yo' nose, let 'im stay dar. Don't move; don't wink yo' eye; don't switch yo' tail. Des lay right dar, an' 't won't be long 'fo' you year f'um me. Yit don't you move till I give de word.'

"Mr. Coon, he paced off, he did, an' done des like Mr. Rabbit tol' 'im. He staggered roun' on de san'-bank, an' den he drapped down dead. Atter so long a time, Mr. Rabbit come lopin' 'long, an' soon's he git dar, he squall out, 'Coon dead!' Dis rousted de frogs, an' dey stuck dey heads up fer ter see w'at all de rippit wuz 'bout. One great big green un up an' holler, *W'at de matter? W'at de matter?* He talk like he got a bad col'.

"Mr. Rabbit 'low: 'Coon dead!'

"Frog say: *Don't believe it! Don't believe it!*

"N'er frog say: *Yes, he is! Yes, he is!* Little bit er one say: *No, he ain't! No, he ain't!*

"Dey kep' on 'sputin' an' 'sputin', tell bimeby hit look like all de frogs in de neighborhoods wuz dar. Mr. Rabbit look like he ain't a-yearin' ner a-keerin' wa't dey do er say. He sot dar in de san' like he gwine in mournin' fer Mr. Coon. De Frogs kep' gittin' closer an' closer. Mr. Coon, he ain't move. W'en a fly 'd git on 'im Mr. Rabbit he'd bresh 'im off.

"Bimeby he 'low: 'Ef you want ter git 'im outen de way, now's yo' time, Cousin Frogs. Des whirl in an' bury him deep in de san'.'

"Big ole Frog say: *How we gwine ter do it? How we gwine ter do it?*

"Mr. Rabbit 'low: 'Dig de san' out fum under 'im an' let 'im down in de hole.'

"Den de Frogs dey went ter work sho nuff. Dey mus' 'a' bin a hunderd un um, an' dey make dat san' fly, mon. Mr. Coon, he ain't move. De Frogs, dey dig an' scratch in de san' tell atter while dey had a right smart hole, an' Mr. Coon wuz down in dar.

"Bimeby big Frog holler: *Dis deep nuff? Dis deep nuff?*

"Mr. Rabbit 'low: 'Kin you jump out?'

"Big Frog say: *Yes, I kin! Yes, I kin!*

"Mr. Rabbit say: 'Den 't ain't deep nuff.'

"Den de Frogs dey dig an' dey dig, tell, bimeby, Big Frog say: *Dis deep nuff? Dis deep nuff?*

Mr. Rabbit 'low: 'Kin you jump out?'

"Big Frog say: *I dess kin! I dess kin!*

"Mr. Rabbit say: 'Dig it deeper.'

"De Frogs keep on diggin' tell bimeby, big Frog holler out: *Dis deep nuff? Dis deep nuff?*

"Mr. Rabbit 'low: 'Kin you jump out?'

"Big Frog say: *No, I can't! No, I can't! Come he'p me! Come he'p me!*

"Mr. Rabbit bust out laughin', and holler out:

"'RISE UP, SANDY, AN' GIT YO' MEAT!' an' Mr. Coon riz."

Lucien and Lillian laughed heartily at this queer story, especially the curious imitation of frogs both big and little that Crazy Sue gave. Lucien wanted her to tell more stories, but Daddy Jake said it was bedtime; and the children were soon sound asleep.

The next morning Daddy Jake had them up betimes. Crazy Sue took Lillian in her arms, and Daddy Jake took Lucien on his back. As they had gone into the cane-brake, so they came out. Randall and some of the other negroes wanted to carry Lillian, but Crazy Sue wouldn't listen to them. She had brought the little girl in, she said, and she was going to carry her out. Daddy Jake, followed by Crazy Sue, went in the direction of Mr. Meredith Ingram's house. It was on a hill, more than a mile from the river, and was in a grove of oak-trees. As they were making their way through a plum orchard, not far from the house, Crazy Sue stopped.

"Brer Jake," she said, "dis is all de fur I'm gwine. I'm 'mos' too close ter dat house now. You take dis baby an' let dat little man walk. 'T ain't many steps ter whar you gwine." Crazy Sue wrung Daddy Jake's hand, stooped and kissed the children, and with a "God bless you all!" disappeared in the bushes, and none of the three ever saw her again.

Mr. Meredith Ingram was standing out in his front yard, enjoying a pipe before breakfast. He was talking to himself and laughing when Daddy Jake and the children approached.

"Howdy, Mars' Meredy," said the old negro, taking off his hat and bowing as politely as he could with the child in his arms. Mr. Ingram looked at him through his spectacles and over them.

"Ain't that Gaston's Jake?" he asked, after he had examined the group.

"Yasser," said Daddy Jake, "an' deze is my marster's little chillun."

Mr. Ingram took his pipe out of his mouth.

"Why, what in the world!—Why, what under the sun!—Well, if this doesn't beat—why, what in the nation!"—Mr. Ingram failed to find words to express his surprise.

Daddy Jake, however, made haste to tell Mr. Ingram that the little ones had drifted down the river in a boat, that he had found them, and wished to get them home just as quickly as he could.

"My marster bin huntin' fer um, suh," said the old negro, "and I want ter beat him home, kaze ef he go dar widout deze chillun, my mistiss 'll be a dead 'oman—she cert'n'y will, suh."

"Well, well, well!" exclaimed Mr. Ingram. "If this don't beat—why, of course, I'll send them home. I'll go with 'em myself. Of course I will. Well, if this doesn't—George! hitch up the carriage. Fetch out Ben Bolt and Rob Roy, and go and get your breakfast. Jake, you go and help him, and I'll take these chaps in the house and warm 'em up. Come on, little ones. We'll have something to eat and then we'll go right home to Pappy and Mammy." They went in, Mr. Ingram muttering to himself, "Well, if this doesn't beat—"

After breakfast Mr. Ingram, the children, Daddy Jake, and George, the driver, were up and away, as the fox-hunters say. Daddy Jake sat on the driver's seat with George, and urged on the horses. They traveled rapidly, and it is well they did, for when they came in sight of the Gaston place, Daddy Jake saw his master entering the avenue that led to the house. The old negro put his hands to his mouth and called so loudly that the horses jumped. Doctor Gaston heard him and stopped, and in a minute more had his children in his arms, and that night there was a happy family in the Gaston house. But nobody was any happier than Daddy Jake.

A Story of the War

WHEN Miss Theodosia Huntingdon, of Burlington, Vermont, concluded to come South in 1870, she was moved by three considerations. In the first place, her brother, John Huntingdon, had become a citizen of Georgia—having astonished his acquaintances by marrying a young lady, the male members of whose family had achieved considerable distinction in the Confederate army; in the second place, she was anxious to explore a region which she almost unconsciously pictured to herself as remote and semi-barbarous; and, in the third place, her friends had persuaded her that to some extent she was an invalid. It was in vain that she argued with herself as to the propriety of undertaking the journey alone and unprotected, and she finally put an end to inward and outward doubts by informing herself and her friends, including John Huntingdon, her brother, who was practicing law in Atlanta, that she had decided to visit the South.

When, therefore, on the 12th of October, 1870—the date is duly recorded in one of Miss Theodosia's letters—she alighted from the cars in Atlanta, in the midst of a great crowd, she fully expected to find her brother waiting to receive her. The bells of several locomotives were ringing, a number of trains were moving in and out, and the porters and baggage-men were screaming and bawling to such an extent that for several moments Miss Huntingdon was considerably confused; so much so that she paused in the hope that her brother would suddenly appear and rescue her from the smoke, and dust, and din. At that moment some one touched her on the arm, and she heard a strong, half-confident, half-apologetic voice exclaim:

"Ain't dish yer Miss Doshy?"

Turning, Miss Theodosia saw at her side a tall, gray-haired negro. Elaborating the incident afterward to her friends, she was pleased to say that the appearance of the old man was somewhat picturesque. He stood towering above her, his hat in one hand, a carriage-whip in the other, and an expectant smile lighting up his rugged face. She remembered a name her brother had often used in his letters, and, with a woman's tact, she held out her hand, and said:

"Is this Uncle Remus?"

"Law, Miss Doshy! how you know de old nigger? I know'd you by de faver; but how you know me?" And then, without waiting for a reply: "Miss Sally, she sick in bed, en Mars John, he bleedzd ter go in de country, en dey tuck'n sont me. I know'd you de minnit I laid eyes on you. Time I seed you, I say ter myse'f, 'I lay dar's Miss Doshy,' en, sho nuff, dar you wuz. You ain't gun up yo' cheeks, is you? Kaze I'll git de trunk sont up by de 'spress waggin."

The next moment Uncle Remus was elbowing his way unceremoniously through the crowd, and in a very short time, seated in the carriage driven by the old man, Miss Huntingdon was whirling through the streets of Atlanta in the direction of her brother's home. She took advantage of the opportunity to study the old negro's face closely, her natural curiosity considerably sharpened by a knowledge of the fact that Uncle Remus had played an important part in her brother's history. The result of her observation must have been satisfactory, for presently she laughed, and said:

"Uncle Remus, you haven't told me how you knew me in that great crowd."

The old man chuckled, and gave the horses a gentle rap with the whip.

"Who? Me! I know'd you by de faver. Dat boy er Mars John's is de ve'y spit en immij un you. I'd a know'd you in New 'Leens, let 'lone down dar in de kyar-shed."

This was Miss Theodosia's introduction to Uncle Remus. One Sunday afternoon, a few weeks after her arrival, the family were assembled in the piazza enjoying the mild weather. Mr. Huntingdon was reading a newspaper; his wife was crooning softly as she rocked the baby to sleep; and the little boy was endeavoring to show his Aunt Dosia the outlines of Kennesaw Mountain through the purple haze that hung like a wonderfully fashioned curtain in the sky and almost obliterated the horizon. While they were thus engaged, Uncle Remus came around the corner of the house, talking to himself.

"Dey er too lazy ter wuk," he was saying, "en dey specks hones' fokes fer ter stan' up en s'port um. I'm gwine down ter Putmon County whar Mars Jeems is—dat's w'at I'm agwine ter do."

"What's the matter now, Uncle Remus?" inquired Mr. Huntingdon, folding up his newspaper.

"Nuthin' 'tall, Mars John, 'ceppin deze yer sunshine niggers. Dey begs my terbacker, en borrys my tools, en steals my vittles, en hit's done come ter dat pass dat I gotter pack up en go. I'm agwine down ter Putmon, dat's w'at."

Uncle Remus was accustomed to make this threat several times a day, but upon this occasion it seemed to remind Mr. Huntingdon of something.

"Very well," he said, "I'll come around and help you pack up, but before you go I want you to tell Sister here how you went to war and fought for the Union.—Remus was a famous warrior," he continued, turning to Miss Theodosia; "he volunteered for one day, and commanded an army of one. You know the story, but you have never heard Remus's version."

Uncle Remus shuffled around in an awkward, embarrassed way, scratched his head, and looked uncomfortable.

"Miss Doshy ain't got no time fer ter set dar an year de ole nigger run on."

"Oh, yes, I have, Uncle Remus!" exclaimed the young lady; "plenty of time."

The upshot of it was that, after many ridiculous protests, Uncle Remus sat down on the steps, and proceeded to tell his story of the war. Miss Theodosia listened with great interest, but throughout it all she observed—and she was painfully conscious of the fact, as she afterward admitted—that Uncle Remus spoke from the standpoint of a Southerner, and with the air of one who expected his hearers to thoroughly sympathize with him.

"Co'se," said Uncle Remus, addressing himself to Miss Theodosia, "you ain't bin to Putmon, en you dunner whar de Brad Slaughter place en Harmony Grove is, but Mars John en Miss Sally, dey bin dar a time er two, en dey knows how de lan' lays. Well, den, it 'uz right 'long in dere whar Mars Jeems lived, en whar he live now. When de war come 'long he wuz livin' dere longer Old Miss en Miss Sally. Ole Miss 'uz his ma, en Miss Sally dar 'uz his sister. De war come des like I tell you, en marters sorter rock along same like dey allers did. Hit didn't strike me dat dey wuz enny war gwine on, en ef I hadn't sorter miss de nabers, en seed fokes gwine outer de way fer ter ax de news, I'd a 'lowed ter myse'f dat de war wuz 'way off 'mong some yuther country. But all dis time de fuss wuz gwine on, en Mars Jeems, he wuz des eatchin' fer ter put in. Ole Miss en Miss Sally, dey tuck on so he didn't git off de fus' year, but bimeby news come down dat times wuz gittin putty hot, en Mars Jeems he got up, he did, en say he gotter go, en go he did. He got a overseer fer ter look atter de place, en he went en jined de army. En he 'uz a fighter, too, mon, Mars Jeems wuz. Many's en many's de time," continued the old man, reflectively, "dat I hatter take'n bresh dat boy on accounter his 'buzin' en beatin' dem yuther boys. He went off dar fer ter fight, en he fit. Ole Miss useter call me up Sunday en read w'at de papers say 'bout Mars Jeems, en it hope 'er up might'ly. I kin see 'er des like it 'uz yistiddy.

" 'Remus,' sez she, 'dish yer's w'at de papers say 'bout my baby,' en den she'd read out twel she couldn't read fer cryin'. Hit went on dis way year in en year out, en dem wuz lonesome times, sho's you bawn, Miss Doshy— lonesome times, sho. Hit got hotter en hotter in de war, en lonesomer en mo' lonesomer at home, en bimeby 'long come de conscrip' man, en he des ever-las'nly scoop up Mars Jeems's overseer. W'en dis come 'bout, old Miss, she sont atter me en say, sez she:

" 'Remus, I ain't got nobody fer ter look arter de place but you,' sez she, en den I up'n say, sez I:

" 'Mistiss, you kin des 'pen' on de ole nigger.'

"I wuz ole den, Miss Doshy—let 'lone w'at I is now; en you better b'leeve I bossed dem han's. I had dem niggers up en in de fiel' long 'fo 'day, en de way dey did wuk wuz a caution. Ef dey didn't earnt der vittles dat season den I ain't name Remus. But dey wuz tuk keer un. Dey had plenty er cloze en plenty er grub, en dey wuz de fattes' niggers in de settlement.

"Bimeby one day, Ole Miss, she call me up en say de Yankees done gone en tuck Atlanty—dish yer ve'y town; den present'y I hear dey wuz a march-in' on down todes Putmon, en, lo en beholes! one day, de fus news I know'd, Mars Jeems he rid up wid a whole gang er men. He des stop long nuff fer ter change hosses en snatch a mouffle er sump'n' ter eat, but 'fo' he rid off, he call me up en say, sez he:

" 'Daddy'—all Ole Miss's chilluns call me daddy—'Daddy,' he say, "pears like dere's gwineter be mighty rough times 'roun' yer. De Yankees, dey er done got ter Madison en Mounticellar, en 'twon't be many days 'fo' dey er down yer. 'Tain't likely dey'll pester mother ner sister; but, daddy, ef de wus come ter de wus, I speck you ter take keer un um,' sezee.

"Den I say, sez I: 'How long you bin knowin' me, Mars Jeems?' sez I.

" 'Sence I wuz a baby,' sezee.

" 'Well, den, Mars Jeems,' sez I, 'you know'd t'wa'nt no use fer ter ax me ter take keer Ole Miss en Miss Sally.'

"Den he tuck'n squoze my han' en jump on de filly I bin savin' fer 'im, en rid off. One time he tu'n 'roun' en look like he wanter say sump'n', but he des waf' his han'—so—en gallop on. I know'd den dat trouble wuz brewin'.

112

Nigger dat knows he's gwineter git thumped kin sorter fix hisse'f, en I tuck'n fix up like de war wuz gwineter come right in at de front gate. I tuck'n got all de cattle en hosses tergedder en driv' um to de fo'-mile place, en I tuck all de corn en fodder en w'eat, en put um in a crib out dar in de woods; en I bilt me a pen in de swamp, en dar I put de hogs. Den, w'en I fix all dis, I put on my Sunday cloze en groun' my axe. Two whole days I groun' dat axe. De grinestone wuz in sight er de gate en close ter de big 'ouse, en dar I tuck my stan'.

"Bimeby one day, yer come de Yankees. Two un um come fus, en den de whole face er de yeath swawm'd wid um. De fus glimpse I kotch un um, I tuck my axe en march inter Ole Miss settin'-room. She done had de sidebode move in dar, en I wish I may drap ef twuzn't fa'rly blazin' wid silver—silver cups en silver sassers, silver plates en silver dishes, silver mugs en silver pitchers. Look like ter me dey wuz fixin' fer a weddin'. Dar sot Ole Miss des ez prim en ez proud ez ef she own de whole county. Dis kinder hope me up, kaze I done seed Ole Miss look dat away once befo' w'en de overseer struck me in de face wid a w'ip. I sot down by de fier wid my axe 'tween my knees. Dar we sot w'iles de Yankees ransack de place. Miss Sally, dar, she got sorter restless, but Ole Miss didn't skasely bat 'er eyes. Bimeby, we hear steps on de peazzer, en yer come a couple er young fellers wid strops on der shoulders, en der sodes a draggin' on de flo', en der spurrers a rattlin'. I won't say I wuz skeer'd," said Uncle Remus, as though endeavoring to recall something he failed to remember, "I wont say I wuz skeer'd, kaze I wuzent; but I wuz took'n wid a mighty funny feelin' in de naberhood er de gizzard. Dey wuz mighty perlite, dem young chaps wuz; but Ole Miss, she never tu'n 'er head, en Miss Sally, she look straight at de fier. Bimeby one un um see me, en he say, sezee:

" 'Hello, ole man, w'at you doin' in yer?' sezee.

" 'Well, boss,' sez I, 'I bin cuttin' some wood fer Ole Miss, en I des stop fer ter wom my han's a little,' sez I.

" 'Hit is cole, dat's a fack,' sezee.

"Wid dat I got up en tuck my stan' behime Ole Miss en Miss Sally, en de man w'at speak, he went up en wom his han's. Fus thing you know, he raise up sudden, en say, sezee:

" 'W'at dat on yo' axe?'

" 'Dat's de fier shinin' on it,' sez I.

" 'Hit look like blood,' sezee, en den he laft.

"But, bless yo' soul, dat man wouldn't never laft dat day ef he'd know'd de wukkins er Remus's mine. But dey didn't bodder nobody ner tech nuthin', en bimeby dey put out. Well, de Yankees, dey kep' passin' all de mawnin' en it look like ter me dey wuz a string un um ten mile long. Den dey commence gittin' thinner en thinner, en den atter w'ile we hear skummishin' in de naberhood er Armer's fe'y, en Ole Miss 'low how dat wuz Wheeler's men makin' persoot. Mars Jeems wuz wid dem Wheeler fellers, en I know'd ef dey wuz dat close I wa'n't doin' no good settin' 'round' de house toas'n my shins at de fier, so I des tuck Mars Jeems's rifle fum behime de do' en put out ter look atter my stock.

"Seem like I ain't never see no raw day like dat, needer befo' ner sence. Dey wa'n't no rain, but de wet des sifted down; mighty raw day. De leaves on de groun' 'uz so wet dey don't make no fuss, en I got in de woods, en w'enever I year de Yankees gwine by, I des stop in my tracks en let um pass. I wuz stan'in' dat away in de aidge er de woods lookin' out 'cross a clearin', w'en—*piff!*—out come a little bunch er blue smoke fum de top er wunner dem big lonesome-lookin' pines, en den—*pow!*

"Sez I ter myse'f, sez I: 'Honey, youer right on my route, en I'll des see w'at kinder bird you got roostin' in you,' en w'iles I wuz a lookin' out bus' de smoke—*piff!* en den—*bang!* Wid dat I des drapt back inter de woods, en sorter skeerted 'roun' so's ter git de tree 'twix' me en de road. I slid up putty close, en wadder you speck I see? Des ez sho's youer settin' dar lissenin' dey wuz a live Yankee up dar in dat tree, en he wuz a loadin' en a shootin' at de boys des ez cool es a cowcumber in de jew, en he had his hoss hitch out in de bushes, kaze I year de creetur tromplin' 'roun'. He had a spy-glass up dar, en w'iles I wuz a watchin' un 'im, he raise 'er up en look thoo 'er, en den he lay 'er down en fix his gun fer ter shoot. I had good eyes in dem days, ef I ain't got um now, en 'way up de big road I see Mars Jeems a comin'. Hit wuz too fur fer ter see his face, but I know'd 'im by de filly w'at I raise fer 'im, en she wuz a prancin' like a school-gal. I know'd dat man wuz gwineter shoot Mars Jeems ef he could, en dat wuz mo'n I could stan'. Manys en manys de time dat I nuss dat boy, en hilt 'im in dese arms, en toted 'im on dis back, en w'en I see day Yankee lay dat gun 'cross a lim' en take aim at Mars Jeems I up wid my ole rifle, en shet my eyes en let de man have all she had."

"Do you mean to say," exclaimed Miss Theodosia, indignantly, "that you shot the Union soldier, when you knew he was fighting for your freedom?"

"Co'se, I know all about dat," responded Uncle Remus, "en it sorter made cole chills run up my back; but w'en I see dat man take aim, en Mars Jeems gwine home ter Ole Miss en Miss Sally, I des disremembered all 'bout freedom en lammed aloose. En den atter dat, me en Miss Sally tuck en nuss de man right straight along. He los' one arm in dat tree bizness, but me en Miss Sally we nuss 'im en we nuss 'im twel he done got well. Des 'bout dat time I quit nuss'n 'im, but Miss Sally she kep' on. She kep' on," continued Uncle Remus, pointing to Mr. Huntingdon, "en now dar he is."

"But you cost him an arm," exclaimed Miss Theodosia.

"I gin 'im dem," said Uncle Remus, pointing to Mrs. Huntingdon, "en I gin 'im deze"—holding up his own brawny arms. "En ef dem ain't nuff fer enny man den I done los' de way."

Ananias

MIDDLE GEORGIA, after Sherman passed through on his famous march to the sea, was full of the direst confusion and despair, and there were many sad sights to be seen. A wide strip of country with desolate plantations, and here and there a lonely chimney standing sentinel over a pile of blackened and smouldering ruins, bore melancholy testimony to the fact that war is a very serious matter. All this is changed now, of course. The section through which the grim commander pushed his way to the sea smiles under the application of new and fresher energies. We have discovered that war, horrible as it is, sometimes drags at its bloody tumbril wheel certain fructifying and fertilizing forces. If this were not so, the contest in which the South suffered the humiliation of defeat, and more, would have been a very desperate affair indeed. The troubles of that unhappy time—its doubts, its difficulties, and its swift calamities—will never be known to posterity, for they have never been adequately described.

It was during this awful period—that is to say, in January, 1866—that Lawyer Terrell, of Macon, made the acquaintance of his friend Ananias. In the midst of the desolation to be seen on every hand, this negro was the forlornest spectacle of all. Lawyer Terrell overtook him on the public highway between Macon and Rockville. The negro wore a ragged blue army overcoat, a pair of patched and muddy blue breeches, and had on the remnants of what was once a military cap. He was leading a lame and broken-down horse through the mud, and was making his way toward Rockville, at what appeared to be a slow and painful gait. Curiosity impelled Lawyer Terrell to draw rein as he came up with the negro.

"Howdy, boss?" said the negro, taking off his tattered cap. Responding to his salutation, the lawyer inquired his name. "I'm name' Ananias, suh," he replied.

The name seemed to fit him exactly. A meaner-looking negro Lawyer Terrell had never seen. There was not the shadow of a smile on his face, and seriousness ill became him. He had what is called a hang-dog look. A professional overseer in the old days would have regarded him as a negro to be watched, and a speculator would have put him in chains the moment he bought him. With a good deal of experience with negroes, Lawyer Terrell had never seen one whose countenance and manner were more repulsive.

"Well," said the lawyer, still keeping along with him in the muddy road, "Ananias is a good name."

"Yasser," he replied; "dat w'at mammy say. Mammy done dead now, but she say dat dey wuz two Ananiases. Dey wuz ole Ananias en young Ananias. One un um wuz de Liar, en de udder wuz de Poffit. Dat w'at mammy say. I'm name' atter de Poffit."

Lawyer Terrell laughed, and continued his cross-examination.

"Where are you going?"

"Who? Me? I'm gwine back ter Marster, suh."

"What is your master's name?"

"Cunnel Benjamime Flewellen, suh."

"Colonel Benjamin Flewellen; yes; I know the colonel well. What are you going back there for?"

"Who? Me? Dat my home, suh. I bin brung up right dar, suh—right 'longside er Marster en my young mistiss, suh."

"Miss Ellen Flewellen," said Lawyer Terrell, reflectively. At this remark the negro showed a slight interest in the conversation; but his interest did not improve his appearance.

"Yasser, dat her name, sho; but we-all call her Miss Nelly."

"A very pretty name, Ananias," remarked Lawyer Terrell.

"Lord! yasser."

The negro looked up at this, but Lawyer Terrell had his eyes fixed on the muddy road ahead of him. The lawyer was somewhat youngish himself, but his face had a hard, firm expression common to those who are in the habit of having their own way in the court-house and elsewhere.

"Where have you been, Ananias?" said the lawyer presently.

"Who? Me? I bin 'long wid Sherman army, suh."

"Then you are quite a soldier by this time."

"Lord! yasser! I bin wid um fum de time dey come in dese parts plum tell dey got ter Sander'ville. You ain't never is bin ter Sander'ville, is you, boss?"

"Not to say right in the town, Ananias, but I've been by there a great many times." Lawyer Terrell humored the conversation, as was his habit.

"Well, suh," said Ananias, "don't you never go dar; special don't you go dar wid no army, kase hit's de longes' en de nasties' road fum dar ter yer w'en you er comin' back, dat I ever is lay my two eyes on."

"Why did you come back, Ananias?"

"Who? Me? Well, suh, w'en de army come 'long by home dar, look like eve'ybody got der eye sot on me. Go whar I would, look alike all de folks wuz a-watchin' me. 'Bout time de army wuz a-pilin' in on us, Marse Wash Jones, w'ich I never is done 'im no harm dat I knows un, he went ter Marster, he did, en he 'low dat ef dey don't keep mighty close watch on Ananias dey'd all be massycreed in deir beds. I know Marse Wash tol' Marster dat, kaze Ma'y Ann, w'ich she wait on de table, she come right outer de house en tol' me so. Right den, suh, I 'gun ter feel sorter skittish. Marster had done got me ter hide all de stock out in de swamp, en I 'low ter myse'f, I did, dat I'd des go over dar en stay wid um. I ain't bin dar so mighty long, suh, w'en yer come de Yankees, en wid um wuz George, de carriage driver, de nigger w'at Marster think mo' uv dan he do all de balance er his niggers. En now, den, dar wuz George a-fetchin' de Yankees right whar he know de stock wuz hid at."

"George was a very handy negro to have around," said Lawyer Terrell.

"Yasser. Marster thunk de worl' en all er dat nigger, en dar he wuz showin' de Yankees whar de mules en hosses wuz hid at. Well, suh, soon ez he see me, George he put out, en I staid dar wid de hosses. I try ter git dem folks not ter kyar um off, I beg um en I plead wid um, but dey des laugh at me, suh. I follered 'long atter um', en dey driv dem hosses en mules right by de house. Marster wuz standin' out in de front porch, en w'en he see de Yankees got de stock, en me 'long wid um, suh, he des raise up his han's—so —en drap um down by his side, en den he tuck 'n tu'n roun' en go in de house. I run ter de do', I did, but Marster done fasten it, en den I run roun' de back way, but de back do' wuz done fassen too. I know'd dey didn't like me," Ananias went on, picking his way carefully through the mud, "en I wuz mos' out'n my head, kaze I ain't know w'at ter do. 'Tain't wid niggers like it is wid white folks, suh. White folks know w'at ter do, kaze dey in de habits er doin' like dey wanter, but niggers, suh—niggers, dey er diffunt. Dey dunner w'at ter do."

"Well, what did you do?" asked Lawyer Terrell.

"Who? Me? Well, suh, I des crope off ter my cabin, en I draw'd up a cheer front er de fier, en stirred up de embers, en sot dar. I ain' sot dar long 'fo'

Marster come ter de do'. He open it, he did, en he come in. He 'low, 'You in dar, Ananias?' I say, 'Yasser.' Den he come in. He stood dar, he did, en look at me. I ain't raise my eyes, suh; I des look in de embers. Bimeby he say, 'Ain't I allers treat you well, Ananias?' I 'low, 'Yasser.' Den he say, 'Ain't I raise you up fum a little baby, w'en you got no daddy?' I 'low, 'Yasser.' He say, 'How come you treat me dis a-way, Ananias? W'at make you show dem Yankees whar my hosses en mules is?' "

Ananias paused as he picked his way through the mud, leading his broken-down horse.

"What did you tell him?" said Lawyer Terrell, somewhat curtly.

"Well, suh, I dunner w'at de name er God come 'cross me. I wuz dat full up dat I can't talk. I tried ter tell Marster des 'zactly how it wuz, but look like I wuz all choke up. White folks kin talk right straight 'long, but niggers is diffunt. Marster stood dar, he did, en look at me right hard, en I know by de way he look dat his feelin's wuz hurted, en dis make me wuss. Eve'y time I try ter talk, suh, sumpin' ne'r kotch me in de neck, en 'fo' I kin come ter myse'f, suh, Marster wuz done gone. I got up en tried ter holler at 'im, but dat ketch wuz dar in my neck, suh, en mo' special wuz it dar, suh, w'en I see dat he wuz gwine 'long wid his head down; en dey mighty few folks, suh, dat ever is see my marster dat a-way. He kyar his head high, suh, ef I do say it myse'f."

"Why didn't you follow after him and tell him about it?" inquired Lawyer Terrell, drawing his lap-robe closer about his knee.

"Dat des zactly w'at I oughter done, suh; but right den en dar I ain't know w'at ter do. I know'd dat nigger like me ain't got no business foolin' 'roun' much, en dat wuz all I did know. I sot down, I did, en I make up my min' dat ef Marster got de idee dat I had his stock run'd off, I better git out fum dar; en den I went ter work, suh, en I pack up w'at little duds I got, en I put out wid de army. I march wid um, suh, plum tell dey got ter Sander'ville, en dar I ax um w'at dey gwine pay me fer gwine wid um. Well, suh, you mayn't b'lieve me, but dem w'ite mens dey des laugh at me. All dis time I bin runnin' over in my min' 'bout Marster en Miss Nelly, en w'en I fin' out dat dey wa'n't no pay fer niggers gwine wid de army I des up en say ter myse'f dat dat kind er business ain't gwine do fer me."

"If they had paid you anything," said Lawyer Terrell, "I suppose you would have gone on with the army?"

"Who? Me? Dat I wouldn't," replied Ananias, emphatically—"dat I wouldn't. I'd 'a got my money, en I'd 'a come back home, kaze I boun' you

I wa'n't a-gwine ter let Marster drap off and die widout knowin' who run'd dem stock off. No, suh. I wuz des 'bleege ter come back."

"Ananias," said Lawyer Terrell, "you are a good man."

"Thanky, suh!—thanky, marster!" exclaimed Ananias, taking off his weather-beaten cap. "You er de fus w'ite man dat ever tol' me dat sence I bin born'd inter de worl'. Thanky, suh!"

"Good-by," said Lawyer Terrell, touching his horse lightly with the whip.

"Good-by, marster!" said Ananias, with unction. "Good-by, marster! en thanky!"

Lawyer Terrell passed out of sight in the direction of Rockville. Ananias went in the same direction, but he made his way over the road with a lighter heart.

It is to be presumed that Ananias's explanation was satisfactory to Colonel Benjamin Flewellen, for he settled down on his former master's place, and proceeded to make his presence felt on the farm as it never had been felt before. Himself and his army-worn horse were decided accessions, for the horse turned out to be an excellent animal. Ananias made no contract with his former master, and asked for no wages. He simply took possession of his old quarters, and began anew the life he had led in slavery times—with this difference: in the old days he had been compelled to work, but now he was working of his own free-will and to please himself. The result was that he worked much harder.

It may be said that though Colonel Benjamin Flewellen was a noted planter, he was not much of a farmer. Before and during the war he had intrusted his plantation and his planting in the care of an overseer. For three hundred dollars a year—which was not much of a sum in slavery times—he could be relieved of all the cares and anxieties incident to the management of a large plantation. His father before him had conducted the plantation by proxy, and Colonel Flewellen was not slow to avail himself of a long-established custom that had been justified by experience. Moreover, Colonel Flewellen had a taste for literature. His father had gathered together a large collection of books, and Colonel Flewellen had added to this until he was owner of one of the largest private libraries in a State where large private libraries were by no means rare. He wrote verse on occasion, and essays in defense of slavery. There are yet living men who believed that his "Reply" to Charles Sumner's attack on the South was so crushing in its argument and its invective—particularly its invective—that it would go far toward putting an end to the abolition movement. Colonel Flewellen's "Reply" filled a page of the New York "Day-Book," and there is no doubt that he made the most of the limited space placed at his disposal.

With his taste and training it is not surprising that Colonel Benjamin Flewellen should leave his plantation interests to the care of Mr. Washington Jones, his overseer, and devote himself to the liberal arts. He not only wrote and published the deservedly famous "Reply" to Charles Sumner, which was afterward reprinted in pamphlet form for the benefit of his friends and admirers, but he collected his fugitive verses in a volume, which was published by an enterprising New York firm "for the author"; and in addition to this he became the proprietor and editor of the Rockville "Vade-Mecum," a weekly paper devoted to "literature, science, politics, and the news."

When, therefore, the collapse came, the colonel found himself practically stranded. He was not only land-poor, but he had no experience in the management of his plantation. Ananias, when he returned from his jaunt with the army, was of some help, but not much. He knew how the plantation ought to be managed, but he stood in awe of the colonel, and he was somewhat backward in giving advice. In fact, he had nothing to say unless his opinion was asked, and this was not often, for Colonel Flewellen had come to entertain the general opinion about Ananias, which was, in effect, that he was a sneaking, hypocritical rascal who was not to be depended on; a good-enough worker, to be sure, but not a negro in whom one could repose confidence.

The truth is, Ananias's appearance was against him. He was ugly and mean-looking, and he had a habit of slipping around and keeping out of the way of white people—a habit which, in that day and time, gave everybody reason enough to distrust him. As a result of this, Ananias got the credit of every mean act that could not be traced to any responsible source. If a smoke-house was broken open in the night, Ananias was the thief. The finger of suspicion was pointed at him on every possible occasion. He was thought to be the head and front of the Union League, a political organization set in motion by the shifty carpet-baggers for the purpose of consolidating the negro vote against the whites. In this way prejudice deepened against him all the while, until he finally became something of an Ishmaelite, holding no intercourse with any white people but Colonel Flewellen and Miss Nelly.

Meanwhile, as may be supposed, Colonel Flewellen was not making much of a success in managing his plantation. Beginning without money, he had as much as he could do to make "buckle and tongue meet," as the phrase goes.

In fact he did not make them meet. He farmed on the old lavish plan. He borrowed money, and he bought provisions, mules, and fertilizers on credit, paying as much as two hundred per cent interest on his debts.

Strange to say, his chief creditor was Mr. Washington Jones, his former overseer. Somehow or other Mr. Jones had thrived. He had saved money as an overseer, being a man of simple tastes and habits, and when the crash came he was comparatively a rich man. When affairs settled down somewhat, Mr. Jones blossomed out as a commission merchant, and he soon established a large and profitable business. He sold provisions and commercial fertilizers, he bought cotton, and he was not above any transaction, however small, that promised to bring him a dime where he had invested a thrip. He was a very thrifty man indeed. In addition to his other business he shaved notes and bought mortgages, and in this way the fact came to be recognized, as early as 1868, that he was what is known as "a leading citizen." He did not hesitate to grind a man when he had him in his clutches, and on this account he made enemies; but as his worldly possessions grew and assumed tangible proportions, it is not to be denied that he had more friends than enemies.

For a while Mr. Washington Jones's most prominent patron was Colonel Benjamin Flewellen. The colonel, it should be said, was not only a patron of Jones, but he patronized him. He made his purchases, chiefly on credit, in a lordly, superior way, as became a gentleman whose hireling Jones had been. When the colonel had money he was glad to pay cash for his supplies, but it happened somehow that he rarely had money. Jones, it must be confessed, was very accommodating. He was anxious to sell to the colonel on the easiest terms, so far as payment was concerned, and he often, in a sly way, flattered the colonel into making larger bills than he otherwise would have made.

There could be but one result, and though that result was inevitable, everybody about Rockville seemed to be surprised. The colonel had disposed of his newspaper long before, and one day there appeared, in the columns which he had once edited with such care, a legal notice to the effect that he had applied to the ordinary of the county, in proper form, to set aside a homestead and personalty. This meant that the colonel, with his old-fashioned ways and methods, had succumbed to the inevitable. He had a house and lot in town, and this was set apart as his homestead by the judge of ordinary. Mr. Washington Jones, you may be sure, lost no time in foreclosing his mortgages, and the fact soon came to be known that he was now the proprietor of the Flewellen place.

Just at this point the colonel first began to face the real problems of life, and he found them to be very knotty ones. He must live—but how? He knew no law, and was acquainted with no business. He was a gentleman and a scholar; but these accomplishments would not serve him; indeed, they stood in his way. He had been brought up to no business, and it was a little late in life— the colonel was fifty or more—to begin to learn. He might have entered upon a political career, and this would have been greatly to his taste, but all the local offices were filled by competent men, and just at that time a Southerner to the manner born had little chance to gain admission to Congress. The Republican "reconstructionists," headed by Thaddeus Stevens, barred the way. The outlook was gloomy indeed.

Nelly Flewellen, who had grown to be a beautiful woman, and who was as accomplished as she was beautiful, gave music lessons; but in Rockville at that time there was not much to be made by teaching music. It is due to the colonel to say that he was bitterly opposed to this project, and he was glad when his daughter gave it up in despair. Then she took in sewing surreptitiously, and did other things that a girl of tact and common sense would be likely to do when put to the test.

The colonel and his daughter managed to get along somehow, but it was a miserable existence compared to their former estate of luxury. Just how they managed, only one person in the wide world knew, and that person was Ananias. Everybody around Rockville said it was very queer how the colonel, with no money and little credit, could afford to keep a servant, and a man-servant at that. But there was nothing queer about it. Ananias received no wages of any sort; he asked for none; he expected none. A child of misfortune himself, he was glad to share the misfortunes of his former master. He washed, he ironed, he cooked, he milked, and he did more. He found time to do little odd jobs around town, and with the money thus earned he was able to supply things that would otherwise have been missing from Colonel Flewellen's table. He was as ugly and as mean-looking as ever, and as unpopular. Even the colonel distrusted him, but he managed to tolerate him. The daughter often had words of praise for the shabby and forlorn-looking negro, and these, if anything, served to lighten his tasks.

But in spite of everything that his daughter or Ananias could do, the colonel continued to grow poorer. To all appearances—and he managed to keep up appearances to the last—he was richer than many of his neighbors, for he had a comfortable house, and he still had credit in the town. Among the shopkeepers there were few that did not respect and admire the colonel for what he had been. But the colonel, since his experience with Mr. Washington Jones, looked with suspicion on the credit business. The result was that he and his daughter and Ananias lived in the midst of the ghastliest poverty.

As for Ananias, he could stand it well enough; so, perhaps, could the colonel, he being a man, and a pretty stout one; but how about the young lady? This was the question that Ananias was continually asking himself, and circumstances finally drove him to answering it in his own way. There was this much to be said about Ananias; when he made up his mind, nothing could turn him, humble as he was; and then came a period in the career of the family to which he had attached himself when he was compelled to make up his mind or see them starve.

At this late day there is no particular reason for concealing the facts. Ananias took the responsibility on his shoulders, and thereafter the colonel's larder was always comparatively full. At night Ananias would sit and nod before a fire in the kitchen, and after everybody else had gone to bed he would sneak out into the darkness, and be gone for many hours; but whether the hours of his absence were many or few, he never returned empty-handed. Sometimes he would bring a "turn" of wood, sometimes a bag of meal or potatoes, sometimes a side of meat or a ham, and sometimes he would be compelled to stop, while yet some distance from the house, to choke a chicken that betrayed a tendency to squall in the small still hours between midnight and morning. The colonel and his daughter never knew whence their supplies came. They only knew that Ananias suddenly developed into a wonderfully good cook, for it is a very good cook indeed that can go on month after month providing excellent meals without calling for new supplies.

But Ananias had always been peculiar, and if he grew a trifle more uncommunicative than usual, neither the colonel nor the colonel's daughter was expected to take notice of the fact. Ananias was a sullen negro at best, but his sullenness was not at all important, and nobody cared whether his demeanor was grave or gay, lively or severe. Indeed, except that he was an object of distrust and suspicion, nobody cared anything at all about Ananias. For his part, Ananias seemed to care nothing for people's opinions, good, bad, or indifferent. If the citizens of Rockville thought ill of him, that was their affair altogether. Ananias went sneaking around, attending to what he conceived to be his own business, and there is no doubt that, in some way, he managed to keep Colonel Flewellen's larder well supplied with provisions.

About this time Mr. Washington Jones, who had hired a clerk for his store, and who was mainly devoting his time to managing, as proprietor, the Flewellen place, which he had formerly managed as overseer, began to discover that he was the victim of a series of mysterious robberies and burglaries. Nobody suffered but Mr. Jones, and everybody said that it was not only very unjust, but very provoking also, that this enterprising citizen should be systematically robbed, while all his neighbors should escape. These mysterious robberies soon became the talk of the whole county. Some people sympathized with Jones, while others laughed at him. Certainly the mystery was a very funny mystery, for when Jones watched his potato hill, his smoke-house was sure to be entered. If he watched his smoke-house, his potato hill would suffer. If he divided his time watching both of these, his store-house would be robbed. There was no regularity about this; but it was generally conceded that the more Jones watched, the more he was robbed, and it finally came to be believed in the county that Jones, to express it in the vernacular, "hollered too loud to be hurt much."

At last one day it was announced that Jones had discovered the thief who had been robbing him. He had not caught him, but he had seen him plainly enough to identify him. The next thing that Rockville knew, a warrant had been issued for Ananias, and he was arrested. He had no commitment trial. He was lodged in the jail to await trial in the Superior Court. Colonel Flewellen was sorry for the negro, as well he might be, but he was afraid to go on his bond. Faithful as Ananias had been, he was a negro, after all, the colonel argued, and if he was released on bond he would not hesitate to run away, if such an idea should occur to him.

Fortunately for Ananias, he was not permitted to languish in jail. The Superior Court met the week after he was arrested, and his case was among the first called. It seemed to be a case, indeed, that needed very little trying. But a very curious incident happened in the court-room.

Among the lawyers present was Mr. Terrell, of Macon. Mr. Terrell was by all odds the greatest lawyer practising in that circuit. He was so great, indeed, that he was not called "major," or "colonel," or "judge." He ranked with Stephens and Hill, and like these distinguished men his title was plain "Mr." Mr. Terrell practised in all the judicial circuits of the State, and had important cases in all of them. He was in Rockville for the purpose of arguing a case to be tried at term, and which he knew would be carried to the Supreme Court of the State, no matter what the verdict of the lower court might be. He was arranging and verifying his authorities anew, and he was very busy when the sheriff came into the court-house bringing Ananias. The judge on the bench thought he had never seen a more rascally-looking prisoner; but even rascally-looking prisoners have their rights, and so, when Ananias's case was called, the judge asked him in a friendly way if he had counsel—if he had engaged a lawyer to defend him.

Ananias did not understand at first, but when the matter was made plain to him he said he could get a lawyer. Whereupon he walked over to where Mr. Terrell sat immersed in his big books, and touched him on the shoulder. The lawyer looked up.

"I'm name' Ananias, suh," said the negro.

"I remember you," said Mr. Terrell. "What are you doing here?"

"Dey got me up fer my trial, suh, en I 'ain't got nobody fer ter speak de word fer me, suh, en I 'low'd maybe—"

Ananias paused. He knew not what else to say. He had no sort of claim on this man. He saw everybody around him laughing. The great lawyer himself smiled as he twirled his eye-glasses on his fingers. Ananias was embarrassed.

"You want me to speak the word?" said Mr. Terrell.

"Yes, suh, if you please, suh."

"You need not trouble yourself, Mr. Terrell," said the judge, affably. "I was about to appoint counsel."

"May it please your honor," said Mr. Terrell, rising. "I will defend this boy. I know nothing whatever of the case, but I happen to know something of the negro."

There was quite a little stir in the courtroom at this announcement. The loafers outside the railings of the bar, who had seen Ananias every day for a good many years, leaned forward to take another look at him. The lawyers inside the bar also seemed to be interested in the matter. Some thought that the great lawyer had taken the negro's case by way of a joke, and they promised themselves a good deal of enjoyment, for it is not every day that a prominent man is seen at play. Others knew not what to think; so that between those who regarded it as a practical joke and those who thought that Mr. Terrell might be in a serious mood, the affair caused quite a sensation.

"May it please the court," said Mr. Terrell, his firm voice penetrating to every part of the large room, "I know nothing of this case; therefore I will ask half an hour's delay to look over the papers and to consult with my client."

126

"Certainly," said the judge, pleasantly. "Mr. Sheriff, take the prisoner to the Grand Jury room, so that he may consult with his counsel."

The sheriff locked the prisoner and the lawyer in the Grand Jury room, and left his deputy there to open the door when Mr. Terrell announced that the conference was over. In the mean time the court proceeded with other business. Cases were settled, dismissed, or postponed. A couple of young lawyers fell into a tumultuous wrangle over an immaterial point, which the judge disposed of with a wave of his hand.

In the Grand Jury room Ananias was telling his volunteer counsel a strange tale.

"And do you mean to tell me that you really stole these things from Jones?" said Mr. Terrell, after he had talked a little with his client.

"Well, suh," replied Ananias, unabashed, "I didn't zackly steal um, suh, but I tuck um; I des tuck um, suh."

"What call had you to steal from Jones? Weren't you working for Colonel Flewellen? Didn't he feed you?" inquired the lawyer. Ananias shifted about from one foot to the other, and whipped his legs with his shabby hat, which he held in his hand. Lawyer Terrell, seated in a comfortable chair, and thoroughly at his ease, regarded the negro curiously. There appeared to be a pathetic element even in Ananias's manner.

"Well, suh," he said, after a while, seeing that he could not escape from the confession, "ef I hadn't a-tuck dem things fum Marse Wash Jones, my Marster en my young mistiss would 'a sot dar en bodaciously starve deyse'f ter deff. I done seed dat, suh. Dey wuz too proud ter tell folks dey wuz dat bad off, suh, en dey'd 'a sot dar, en des bodaciously starve deyse'f ter deff, suh. All dey lifetime, suh, dey bin use ter havin' deir vittles put right on de table whar dey kin git it, en w'en de farmin' days done gone, suh, dey wa'n't nobody but Ananias fer put de vittles dar; en I des hatter scuffle 'roun' en git it de bes' way I kin. I 'spec', suh," Ananias went on, his countenance brightening up a little, "dat ef de wuss had a-come ter de wuss, I'd 'a' stole de vittles; but I 'ain't had ter steal it, suh; I des went en tuck it fum Marse Wash Jones, kaze it come off'n Marster's lan', suh."

"Why, the land belongs to Jones," said Lawyer Terrell.

"Dat w'at dey say, suh; but eve'y foot er dat lan' b'longded ter de Flewellen fambly long 'fo' Marse Wash Jones' daddy sot up a hat-shop in de neighborhoods. I dunner how Marse Wash git dat lan', suh; I know it

127

b'longded in de Flewellen fambly sence 'way back, en dey got deir graveyard dar yit."

Lawyer Terrell's unusually stern face softened a little. He saw that Ananias was in earnest, and his sympathies were aroused. He had some further conversation with the negro, questioning him in regard to a great many things that assumed importance in the trial.

When Lawyer Terrell and his client returned to the court-room they found it filled with spectators. Somehow, it became generally known that the great advocate was to defend Ananias, and a large crowd of people had assembled to watch developments. In some way the progress of Ananias and the deputy-sheriff through the crowd that filled all the aisles and doorways had been delayed; but when the negro, forlorn and wretched-looking, made his appearance in the bar for the purpose of taking a seat by his counsel, there was a general laugh. Instantly Lawyer Terrell was upon his feet.

"May it please your honor, what *is* the duty of the sheriff of this county, if it is not to keep order in this court-room?"

The ponderous staff of the sheriff came down on the floor with a thump; but it was unnecessary. Silence had fallen on the spectators with the first words of the lawyer. The crowd knew that he was a game man, and they admired him for it. His whole attitude, as he gazed at the people around him, showed that he was full of fight. His heavy blond hair, swept back from his high forehead, looked like the mane of a lion, and his steel-gray eyes glittered under his shaggy and frowning brows.

The case of the State *versus* Ananias Flewellen, *alias* Ananias Harper—a name he had taken since freedom—was called in due form. It was observed that Lawyer Terrell was very particular to strike certain names from the jury list, but this gave no cue to the line of his defense. The first witness was Mr. Washington Jones, who detailed, as well as he knew how, the circumstances of the various robberies of which he had been the victim. He had suspected Ananias, but had not made his suspicions known until he was sure, —until he had caught him stealing sweet-potatoes.

The cross-examination of the witness by Ananias's counsel was severe. The fact was gradually developed that Mr. Jones caught the negro stealing potatoes at night; that the night was dark and cloudy; that he did not actually catch the negro, but saw him; that he did not really see the negro clearly, but knew "in reason" that it must be Ananias.

The fact was also developed that Mr. Jones was not alone when he saw Ananias, but was accompanied by Mr. Miles Cottingham, a small farmer in the neighborhood, who was well known all over the county as a man of undoubted veracity and of the strictest integrity.

At this point Lawyer Terrell, who had been facing Mr. Jones with severity painted on his countenance, seemed suddenly to recover his temper. He turned to the listening crowd, and said, in his blandest tones, "Is Mr. Miles Cottingham in the room?"

There was a pause, and then a small boy perched in one of the windows, through which the sun was streaming, cried out, "He's a-standin' out yander by the horse-rack."

Whereupon a subpoena was promptly made out by the clerk of the court, and the deputy sheriff, putting his head out of a window, cried:

"Miles G. Cottingham! Miles G. Cottingham! Miles G. Cottingham! Come into court."

Mr. Cottingham was fat, rosy, and cheerful. He came into court with such a dubious smile on his face that his friends in the room were disposed to laugh, but they remembered that Lawyer Terrell was somewhat intolerant of these manifestations of good-humor. As for Mr. Cottingham himself, he was greatly puzzled. When the voice of the court crier reached his ears he was in the act of taking a dram, and, as he said afterward, he "come mighty nigh drappin' the tumbeler." But he was not subjected to any such mortification. He tossed off his dram in fine style, and went to the court-house, where, as soon as he had pushed his way to the front, he was met by Lawyer Terrell, who shook him heartily by the hand, and told him his testimony was needed in order that justice might be done.

Then Mr. Cottingham was put on the stand as a witness for the defense.

"How old are you, Mr. Cottingham?" said Lawyer Terrell.

'Ef I make no mistakes, I'm a-gwine on sixty-nine," replied the witness.

"Are your eyes good?"

"Well, sir, they er about ez good ez the common run; not so good ez they mought be, en yit good enough fer me."

"Did you ever see that negro before?" The lawyer pointed to Ananias.

"Which nigger? That un over there? Why, that's thish yer God-forsakin' Ananias. Ef it had a-bin any yuther nigger but Ananias I wouldn't 'a' bin so certain and shore; bekaze sence the war they er all so mighty nigh alike I can't tell one from t'other sca'cely. All eckceppin' of Ananias; I'd know Ananias ef I met 'im in kingdom come wi' his hair all swinjed off."

The jury betrayed symptoms of enjoying this testimony; seeing which, the State's attorney rose to his feet to protest.

"May it please the court"—

"One moment, your honor!" exclaimed Lawyer Terrell. Then, turning to the witness: "Mr. Cottingham, were you with Mr. Jones when he was watching to catch a thief who had been stealing from him?"

"Well, sir," replied Mr. Cottingham, "I sot up wi' him one night, but I disremember in pertickler what night it wuz."

"Did you see the thief?"

"Well, sir," said Mr. Cottingham, in his deliberate way, looking around over the court-room with a more judicial air than the judge on the bench, "ef you push me close I'll tell you. Ther wuz a consid'able flutterment in the neighborhoods er whar we sot, an' me an' Wash done some mighty sly slippin' up en surrounderin'; but ez ter seein' anybody, we didn't see 'im. We heerd 'm a-scufflin' an' a-runnin', but we didn't ketch a glimpse un 'im, nuther har ner hide."

"Did Mr. Jones see him?"

"No more'n I did. I wuz right at Wash's elbow. We heerd the villyun a-runnin', but we never seed 'im. Atterwards, when we got back ter the house, Wash he 'lowed it must 'a bin that nigger Ananias thar, an' I 'lowed it jess mought ez well be Ananias ez any yuther nigger, bekaze you know yourself—"

"That will do, Mr. Cottingham," said Mr. Lawyer Terrell, blandly. The State's attorney undertook to cross-examine Mr. Cottingham; but he was a blundering man, and the result of his cross-examination was simply a stronger and more impressive repetition of Mr. Cottingham's testimony.

After this, the solicitor was willing to submit the case to the jury without argument, but Mr. Terrell said that if it pleased the court he had a few words to say to the jury in behalf of his client. The speech made by the State's attorney was flat and stale, for he was not interested in the case; but Lawyer Terrell's appeal to the jury is still remembered in Rockville. It was not only powerful, but inimitable; it was humorous, pathetic, and eloquent. When he concluded, the jury, which was composed mostly of middle-aged men, was in tears. The feelings of the spectators were also wrought up to a very high pitch, and when the jury found a verdict of "not guilty," without retiring, the people in the court-room made the old house ring again with applause.

And then something else occurred. Pressing forward through the crowd came Colonel Benjamin Flewellen. His clothes were a trifle shabby, but he had the air of a prince of the blood. His long white hair fell on his shoulders, and his movements were as precise as those of a grenadier. The spectators made way for him. Those nearest noticed that his eyes were moist, and that his nether lip was a-tremble, but no one made any remark. Colonel Flewellen pressed forward until he reached Ananias, who, scarcely comprehending the situation, was sitting with his hands folded and his head bent down. The colonel placed his hand on the negro's shoulder.

"Come, boy," he said, "let's go home."

"Me, Marster?" said the negro, looking up with a dazed expression. It was the tone, and not the words, that Ananias heard.

"Yes, old fellow, your Miss Nelly will be waiting for us."

"Name er God!" exclaimed Ananias, and then he arose and followed his old master out of the court-room. Those who watched him as he went saw that the tears were streaming down his face, but there was no rude laughter when he made a futile attempt to wipe them off with his coattail. This display of feeling on the part of the negro was somewhat surprising to those who witnessed it, but nobody was surprised when Ananias appeared on the streets a few days after with head erect and happiness in his face.

Aunt Fountain's Prisoner

IT IS CURIOUS how the smallest incident, the most unimportant circumstance, will recall old friends and old associations. An old gentleman, who is noted far and near for his prodigious memory of dates and events, once told me that his memory, so astonishing to his friends and acquaintances, consisted not so much in remembering names and dates and facts, as in associating each of these with some special group of facts and events; so that he always had at command a series of associations to which he could refer instantly and confidently. This is an explanation of the system of employing facts, but not of the method by which they are accumulated and stored away.

I was reminded of this some years ago by a paragraph in one of the county newspapers that sometimes come under my observation. It was a very commonplace paragraph; indeed, it was in the nature of an advertisement,—an announcement of the fact that orders for "gilt-edged butter" from the Jersey farm on the Tomlinson Place should be left at the drug-store in Rockville, where the first that came would be the first served. This business-like notice was signed by Ferris Trunion. The name was not only peculiar, but new to me; but this was of no importance at all. The fact that struck me was the bald and bold announcement that the Tomlinson Place was the site and centre of trading and other commercial transactions in butter. I can only imagine what effect this announcement would have had on my grandmother, who died years ago, and on some other old people I used to know. Certainly they would have been horrified; and no wonder, for when they were in their prime the Tomlinson Place was the seat of all that was high, and mighty, and grand, in the social world in the neighborhood of Rockville. I remember that everybody stood in awe of the Tomlinsons. Just why this was so, I never could make out. They were very rich; the Place embraced several thousand acres; but if the impressions made on me when a child are worth any thing, they were extremely simple in their ways. Though, no doubt, they could be formal and conventional enough when occasion required.

I have no distinct recollection of Judge Addison Tomlinson, except that he was a very tall old gentleman, much older than his wife, who went about the streets of Rockville carrying a tremendous gold-headed cane carved in a curious manner. In those days I knew more of Mrs. Tomlinson than I did of the judge, mainly because I heard a great deal more about her. Some of the women called her Mrs. Judge Tomlinson; but my grandmother never called her any thing else but Harriet Bledsoe, which was her maiden name. It was a name, too, that seemed to suit her, so that when you once heard her called Harriet Bledsoe, you never forgot it afterward. I do not know now, any more than I did when a child, why this particular name should fit her so exactly; but, as I have often been told, a lack of knowledge does not alter facts.

I think my grandmother used to go to church to see what kind of clothes Harriet Bledsoe wore; for I have often heard her say, after the sermon was over, that Harriet's bonnet, or Harriet's dress, was perfectly charming. Certainly Mrs. Tomlinson was always dressed in the height of fashion, though it was a very simple fashion when compared with the flounces and furbelows of her neighbors. I remember this distinctly, that she seemed to be perfectly cool the hottest Sunday in summer, and comfortably warm the coldest Sunday in winter; and I am convinced that this impression, made on the mind of a child, must bear some definite relation to Mrs. Tomlinson's good taste.

Certainly my grandmother was never tired of telling me that Harriet Bledsoe was blessed with exceptionally good taste and fine manners; and I remember that she told me often how she wished I was a girl, so that I might one day be in a position to take advantage of the opportunities I had had of profiting by Harriet Bledsoe's example. I think there was some sort of attachment between my grandmother and Mrs. Tomlinson, formed when they were at school together, though my grandmother was much the older of the two. But there was no intimacy. The gulf that money sometimes makes between those who have it and those who lack it lay between them. Though I think my grandmother was more sensitive about crossing this gulf than Mrs. Tomlinson.

I was never in the Tomlinson house but once when a child. Whether it was because it was two or three miles away from Rockville, or whether it was because I stood in awe of my grandmother's Harriet Bledsoe, I do not know. But I have a very vivid recollection of the only time I went there as a boy.

One of my playmates, a rough-and-tumble little fellow, was sent by his mother, a poor sick woman, to ask Mrs. Tomlinson for some preserves. I think this woman and her little boy were in some way related to the Tomlinsons. The richest and most powerful people, I have heard it said, are not so rich and powerful but they are pestered by poor kin, and the Tomlinsons were no exception to the rule.

I went with this little boy I spoke of, and I was afraid afterward that I was in some way responsible for his boldness. He walked right into the presence of Mrs. Tomlinson, and, without waiting to return the lady's salutation, he said in a loud voice,—

"Aunt Harriet, ma says send her some of your nicest preserves."

"*Aunt Harriet*, indeed!" she exclaimed, and then she gave him a look that was cold enough to freeze him, and hard enough to send him through the floor.

I think she relented a little, for she went to one of the windows, bigger than any door you see nowadays, and looked out over the blooming orchard; and then after a while she came back to us, and was very gracious. She patted me on the head; and I must have shrunk from her touch, for she laughed and said she never bit nice little boys. Then she asked me my name; and when I told her, she said my grandmother was the dearest woman in the world. Moreover, she told my companion that it would spoil preserves to carry them about in a tin bucket; and then she fetched a big basket, and had it filled with preserves, and jelly, and cake. There were some ginger-preserves among the rest, and I remember that I appreciated them very highly; the more so, since my companion had a theory of his own that ginger-preserves and fruit-cake were not good for sick people.

I remember, too, that Mrs. Tomlinson had a little daughter about my own age. She had long yellow hair and very black eyes. She rode around in the Tomlinson carriage a great deal, and everybody said she was remarkably pretty, with a style and a spirit all her own. The negroes used to say that she was as affectionate as she was wilful, which was saying a good deal. It was characteristic of Harriet Bledsoe, my grandmother said, that her little girl should be named Lady.

I heard a great many of the facts I have stated from old Aunt Fountain, one of the Tomlinson negroes, who, for some reason or other, was permitted to sell ginger-cakes and persimmon-beer under the wide-spreading China-trees in Rockville on public days and during court-week. There was a theory among certain envious people in Rockville,—there are envious people everywhere,—that the Tomlinsons, notwithstanding the extent of their landed estate and the number of their negroes, were sometimes short of ready cash; and it was hinted that they pocketed the proceeds of Aunt Fountain's persimmon-beer and ginger-cakes. Undoubtedly such stories as these were the outcome of pure envy. When my grandmother heard such gossip as this, she sighed, and said that people who would talk about Harriet Bledsoe in that way would talk about anybody under the sun. My own opinion is, that Aunt Fountain got the money and kept it; otherwise she would not have been so fond of her master and mistress, nor so proud of the family and its position. I spent many an hour near Aunt Fountain's cake and beer stand, for I liked to hear her talk. Besides, she had a very funny name, and I thought there was always a probability that she would explain how she got it. But she never did.

I had forgotten all about the Tomlinsons until the advertisement I have mentioned was accidentally brought to my notice, whereupon memory suddenly became wonderfully active. I am keenly alive to the happier results of the war, and I hope I appreciate at their full value the emancipation of both whites and blacks from the deadly effects of negro slavery, and the wonderful development of our material resources that the war has rendered possible; but I must confess it was with a feeling of regret that I learned that the Tomlinson Place had been turned into a dairy-farm. Moreover, the name of Ferris Trunion had a foreign and an unfamiliar sound. His bluntly worded advertisement appeared to come from the mind of a man who would not hesitate to sweep away both romance and tradition if they happened to stand in the way of a profitable bargain.

I was therefore much gratified, some time after reading Trunion's advertisement, to receive a note from a friend who deals in real estate, telling me that some land near the Tomlinson Place had been placed in his hands for sale, and asking me to go to Rockville to see if the land and the situation were all they were described to be. I lost no time in undertaking this part of the business, for I was anxious to see how the old place looked in the hands of strangers, and unsympathetic strangers at that.

It is not far from Atlanta to Rockville,—a day and a night,—and the journey is not fatiguing; so that a few hours after receiving my friend's request I was sitting in the veranda of the Rockville Hotel, observing, with some degree of wonder, the vast changes that had taken place—the most of them for the better. There were new faces and new enterprises all around me, and there was a bustle about the town that must have caused queer sensations in the minds of the few old citizens who still gathered at the post-office for the purpose of carrying on ancient political controversies with each other.

Among the few familiar figures that attracted my attention was that of Aunt Fountain. The old China-tree in the shade of which she used to sit had been blasted by lightning or fire; but she still had her stand there, and she was keeping the flies and dust away with the same old turkey-tail fan. I could see no change. If her hair was grayer, it was covered and concealed from view by the snow-white handkerchief tied around her head. From my place I could hear her humming a tune,—the tune I had heard her sing in precisely the same way years ago. I heard her scolding a little boy. The gesture, the voice, the words, were the same she had employed in trying to convince me that my room was much better than my company, especially in the neighborhood of her cake-stand. To see and hear her thus gave me a peculiar feeling of homesickness. I approached and saluted her. She bowed with old-fashioned politeness, but without looking up.

"De biggest uns, dee er ten cent," she said, pointing to her cakes; "en de littlest, dee er fi' cent. I make um all myse'f, suh. En de beer in dat jug—dat beer got body, suh."

"I have eaten many a one of your cakes, Aunt Fountain," said I, "and drank many a glass of your beer; but you have forgotten me."

"My eye weak, suh, but dee ain' weak nuff fer dat." She shaded her eyes with her fan, and looked at me. Then she rose briskly from her chair. "De Lord he'p my soul!" she exclaimed enthusiastically. "W'y, I know you w'en you little boy. W'at make I ain' know you w'en you big man? My eye weak, suh, but dee ain' weak nuff fer dat. Well, suh, you mus' eat some my ginger-cake. De Lord know you has make way wid um w'en you wuz little boy."

The invitation was accepted, but somehow the ginger-cakes had lost their old-time relish; in me the taste and spirit of youth were lacking.

We talked of old times and old friends, and I told Aunt Fountain that I had come to Rockville for the purpose of visiting in the neighborhood of the Tomlinson Place.

"Den I gwine wid you, suh," she cried, shaking her head vigorously. "I gwine wid you." And go she did.

"I been layin' off ter go see my young mistiss dis long time," said Aunt Fountain, the next day, after we had started. "I glad I gwine deer in style. De niggers won' know me skacely, ridin' in de buggy dis away."

"Your young mistress?" I inquired.

"Yes, suh. You know Miss Lady w'en she little gal. She grown woman now."

136

"Well, who is this Trunion I have heard of?"

"He monst'ous nice w'ite man, suh. He married my young mistiss. He monst'ous nice w'ite man."

"But who is he? Where did he come from?"

Aunt Fountain chuckled convulsively as I asked these questions.

"We-all des pick 'im up, suh. Yes, suh; we-all des pick 'im up. Ain' you year talk 'bout dat, suh? I dunner whar you bin at ef you ain' never is year talk 'bout dat. He de fus' w'ite man w'at I ever pick up, suh. Yes, suh; de ve'y fus' one."

"I don't understand you," said I; "tell me about it."

At this Aunt Fountain laughed long and loudly. She evidently enjoyed my ignorance keenly.

"De Lord know I oughtn' be laughin' like dis. I ain' laugh so hearty sence I wuz little gal mos', en dat wuz de time w'en Marse Rowan Tomlinson come 'long en ax me my name. I tell 'im, I did, 'I'm name Flew Ellen, suh.' Marse Rowan he deaf ez any dead hoss. He 'low, 'Hey?' I say, 'I'm name Flew Ellen, suh.' Marse Rowan say, 'Fountain! Huh! he quare name.' I holler en laugh, en w'en de folks ax me w'at I hollerin' 'bout, I tell um dat Marse Rowan say I'm name Fountain. Well, suh, fum dat day down ter dis, stedder Flew Ellen, I'm bin name Fountain. I laugh hearty den en my name got change, en I feared ef I laugh now de hoss'll run away en turn de buggy upperside down right spang on top er me."

"But about this Mr. Trunion?" said I.

"Name er de Lord!" exclaimed Aunt Fountain, "ain' you never is bin year 'bout dat? You bin mighty fur ways, suh, kaze we all bin knowin' 'bout it fum de jump."

"No doubt. Now tell me about it."

Aunt Fountain shook her head, and her face assumed a serious expression.

"I dunno 'bout dat, suh. I year tell dat niggers ain' got no business fer go talkin' 'bout fambly doin's. Yit dar wuz yo' gran'mammy. My mistiss sot lots by her, en you been bornded right yer 'long wid um. I don't speck it'll be gwine so mighty fur out'n de fambly ef I tell you 'bout it."

I made no attempt to coax Aunt Fountain to tell me about Trunion, for I knew it would be difficult to bribe her not to talk about him. She waited a while, evidently to tease my curiosity; but as I betrayed none, and even made an effort to talk about something else, she began:

"Well, suh, you ax me 'bout Marse Fess Trunion. I know you bleeze ter like dat man. He ain' b'long ter we-all folks, no furder dan he my young mistiss ole man, but dee ain' no finer w'ite man dan him. No, suh; dee ain'. I tell you dat p'intedly. De niggers, dee say he mighty close en pinchin', but deze is mighty pinchin' times—you know dat yo'se'f, suh. Ef a man don' fa'rly fling 'way he money, dem Tomlinson niggers, dee'll say he mighty pinchin'. I hatter be pinchin' myse'f, suh, kaze I know time I sell my ginger-cakes dat ef I don't grip onter de money, dee won' be none lef' fer buy flour en 'lasses fer make mo'. It de Lord's trufe, suh, kaze I done had trouble dat way many's de time. I say dis 'bout Marse Fess Trunion, ef he ain' got de blood, he got de breedin'. Ef he ain' good ez de Tomlinsons, he lots better dan some folks w'at I know."

I gathered from all this that Trunion was a foreigner of some kind, but I found out my mistake later.

"I pick dat man up myse'f, en I knows 'im 'most good ez ef he wuz one er we-all."

"What do you mean when you say 'you picked him up'?" I asked, unable to restrain my impatience.

"Well, suh, de fus' time I see Marse Fess Trunion wuz terreckerly atter de Sherman army come 'long. Dem wuz hot times, suh, col' ez de wedder wuz. Dee wuz in-about er million un um look like ter me, en dee des ravage de face er de yeth. Dee tuck all de hosses, en all de cows, en all de chickens. Yes, suh; dee cert'n'y did. Man come 'long, en 'low, 'Aunty, you free now,' en den he tuck all my ginger-cakes w'at I bin bakin' 'g'inst Chris'mus; en den I say, 'Ef I wuz free ez you is, suh, I'd fling you down en take dem ginger-cakes 'way fum you.' Yes, suh. I tole 'im dat. It make me mad fer see de way dat man walk off wid my ginger-cakes.

"I got so mad, suh, dat I foller 'long atter him little ways; but dat ain' do no good, kaze he come ter whar dee wuz some yuther men, en dee 'vide up dem cakes till dee want no cake lef'. Den I struck 'cross de plan'ation, en walked 'bout in de drizzlin' rain tell I cool off my madness, suh, kaze de flour dat went in dem cakes cos' me mos' a hunderd dollars in good Confederick money. Yes, suh; it did dat. En I work for dat money mighty hard.

"Well, suh, I ain' walk fur 'fo' it seem like I year some un talkin'. I stop, I did, en lissen, en still I year um. I ain' see nobody, suh, but still I year um. I walk fus' dis away en den dat away, en den I walk 'roun' en 'roun', en den it pop in my min' 'bout de big gully. It ain' dar now, suh, but in dem days we call it de big gully, kaze it wuz wide en deep. Well, suh,' fo' I git dar I see hoss-tracks, en dee led right up ter de brink. I look in, I did, en down dar dee wuz a man en a hoss. Yes, suh; dee wuz bofe down dar. De man wuz layin' out flat on he back, en de hoss he wuz layin' sorter up en down de gully en right on top er one er de man legs, en eve'y time de hoss'd scramble en try fer git up de man 'ud talk at 'im. I know dat hoss mus' des nata'lly a groun' dat man legs in de yeth, suh. Yes, suh. It make my flesh crawl w'en I look at um. Yit de man ain' talk like he mad. No, suh, he ain'; en it make me feel like somebody done gone en hit me on de funny-bone w'en I year 'im talkin' dat away. Eve'y time de hoss scuffle, de man he 'low, 'Hol' up, ole fel, you er mashin' all de shape out'n me.' Dat w'at he say, suh. En den he 'low, 'Ef you know how you hurtin', ole fel, I des know you'd be still.' Yes, suh. Dem he ve'y words.

"All dis time de rain wuz a-siftin' down. It fall mighty saft, but 'twuz monst'ous wet, suh. Bimeby I crope up nigher de aidge, en w'en de man see me he holler out, 'Hol' on, aunty; don't you fall down yer!'

"I ax 'im, I say, 'Marster, is you hurted much?' Kaze time I look at 'im I know he ain' de villyun w'at make off wid my ginger-cakes. Den he 'low, 'I speck I hurt purty bad, aunty, en de wuss un it is dat my hoss keep hurtin' me mo'.'

"Den nex' time de hoss move it errortate me so, suh, dat I holler at 'im loud ez I ken, 'Wo dar, you scan'lous villyun! Wo!' Well, suh, I speck dat hoss mus a-bin use'n ter niggers, kaze time I holler at 'im he lay right still, suh. I slid down dat bank, en I kotch holter dat bridle—I don't look like I'm mighty strong, does I, suh?" said Aunt Fountain, pausing suddenly in her narrative to ask the question.

"Well, no," said I, humoring her as much as possible. "You don't seem to be as strong as some people I've seen."

"Dat's it, suh!" she exclaimed. "Dat w'at worry me. I slid down dat bank, en I kotch dat hoss by de bridle. De man say, 'Watch out dar, aunty! don't let he foot hit you. Dee one cripple too much now.' I ain' pay no 'tention, suh. I des grab de bridle, en I slew dat hoss head roun', en I fa'rly lif' 'im on he foots. Yes, suh, I des lif' 'im on he foots. Den I led 'im down de gully en turnt 'im a-loose, en you ain' never see no hoss supjued like dat hoss wuz, suh. Den I went back whar de man layin', en ax 'im ef he feel better, en he' low dat he feel like he got a big load lif' offen he min', en den, mos' time he say dat, suh, he faint dead away. Yes, suh. He des faint dead away. I ain' never is see no man like dat, w'at kin be jokin' one minnit en den de nex' be dead, ez you may say. But dat's Marse Fess Trunion, suh. Dat's him up en down.

"Well, suh, I stan' dar, I did, en I ain' know w'at in de name er de Lord I gwine do. I wuz des ez wringin' wet ez if I'd a-bin baptize in de water; en de man he wuz mo' wetter dan w'at I wuz, en goodness knows how long he bin layin' dar. I run back ter de big-'ouse, suh, mighty nigh a mile, en I done my level bes' fer fin' some er de niggers en git um fer go wid me back dar en git de man. But I ain' fin' none un um, suh. Dem w'at ain' gone wid de Sherman army, dee done hide out. Den I went in de big-'ouse, suh, en tell Mistiss 'bout de man down dar in de gully, en how he done hurted so bad he ain' kin walk. Den Mistiss—I speck you done fergit Mistiss, suh—Mistiss, she draw herse'f up en ax w'at business dat man er any yuther man got on her plan'ation. I say, 'Yassum, dat so; but he done dar, en ef he stay dar he gwine die dar.' Yes, suh; dat w'at I say. I des put it at Mistiss right pine-blank.

"Den my young mistiss—dat's Miss Lady, suh—she say dat dough she spize um all dez bad az she kin, dat man mus' be brung away from dar. Kaze, she say, she don't keer how yuther folks go on, de Tomlinsons is bleeze to do like Christun people. Yes, suh; she say dem ve'y words. Den Mistiss, she 'low dat de man kin be brung up, en put in de corn-crib, but Miss Lady she say no, he mus' be brung en put right dar in de big 'ouse in one er de up-sta'rs rooms, kaze maybe some er dem State er Georgy boys mought be hurted up dar in de Norf, en want some place fer stay at. Yes, suh; dat des de way she talk. Den Mistiss, she ain' say nothin', yit she hol' her head mighty high.

"Well, suh, I went back out in de yard, en den I went 'cross ter de nigger-quarter, en I ain' gone fur tell I year my ole man prayin' in dar some'r's. I know 'im by he v'ice, suh, en he wuz prayin' des like it wuz camp-meetin' time. I hunt 'roun' fer 'im, suh, en bimeby I fin' 'im squattin' down behime de do'. I grab 'im, I did, en I shuck 'im, en I 'low, 'Git up fum yer, you nasty, stinkin' ole villyun, you!' Yes, suh; I wuz mad. I say, 'Wat you doin' squattin' down on de flo'? Git up fum dar en come go 'long wid me!' I hatter laugh, suh, kaze w'en I shuck my ole man by de shoulder, en holler at 'im, he put up he two han', suh, en squall out, 'Oh, pray marster! don't kill me dis time, en I ain' never gwine do it no mo'!'

"Atter he 'come pacify, suh, den I tell him 'bout de man down dar in de gully, en yit we ain' know w'at ter do. My ole man done hide out some er de mules en hosses down in de swamp, en he feard ter go atter um, suh, kaze he skeerd de Sherman army would come marchin' back en fine um, en he 'low dat he mos' know dee er comin' back atter dat man down dar. Yes, suh; he de skeerdest nigger w'at I ever see, if I do say it myse'f. Yit, bimeby he put out atter one er de hosses, en he brung 'im back; en we hitch 'im up in de spring-waggin, en atter dat man we went. Yes, suh; we did dat. En w'en we git dar, dat ar man wuz plum ravin' deestracted. He wuz laughin' en talkin' wid hese'f, en gwine on, tell it make yo' blood run col' fer lissen at 'im. Yes, suh.

"Me en my ole man, we pick 'im up des like he wuz baby. I come mighty nigh droppin' 'im, suh, kaze one time, wiles we kyarn 'im up de bank, I year de bones in he leg rasp up 'g'inst one er n'er. Yes, suh. It make me blin' sick, suh. We kyard 'im home en put 'im up st'ars, en dar he stayed fer many's de long day."

"Where was Judge Tomlinson?" I asked. At this Aunt Fountain grew more serious than ever,—a seriousness that was expressed by an increased particularity and emphasis in both speech and manner.

"You axin' 'bout Marster? Well, suh, he wuz dar. He wuz cert'n'y dar wid Mistiss en Miss Lady, suh, but look like he ain' take no intruss in w'at gwine on. *Some* folks 'low, suh, dat he ain' right in he head, but dee ain' know 'im—dee ain' know 'im, suh, like we-all. Endurin' er de war, suh, he wuz strucken wid de polzy, en den w'en he git well, he ain' take no intruss in w'at gwine on. Dey'd be long days, suh, w'en he ain' take no notice er no-body ner nuttin' but Miss Lady. He des had dem spells; en den, ag'in, he'd set out on de peazzer en sing by hese'f, en it make me feel so lonesome dat I bleeze ter cry. Yes, suh; it's de Lord's trufe.

"Well, suh, dat man w'at I fin' out dar in de gully wuz Marse Fess Trunion. Yes, suh, de ve'y same man. Dee ain' no tellin' w'at dat po' creetur gone thoo wid. He had fever, he had pneumony, en he had dat broke leg. En all 'long wid dat dee want skacely no time w'en he want laughin' en jokin'. Our w'ite folks, dee des spized 'im kase he bin wid Sherman army. Dee say he wuz Yankee; but I tell um, suh, dat ef Yankee look dat away dee wuz cert'n'y mighty like we-all. Mistiss, she ain' never go 'bout 'im wiles he sick; en Miss Lady, she keep mighty shy, en she tu'n up her nose eve'y time she year 'im laugh. Oh, yes, suh; dee cert'n'y spize de Yankees endurin' er dem times. Dee hated um rank, suh. I tell um, I say, 'You-all des wait. Dee ain' no nicer man dan w'at he is, en you-all des wait tell you know 'im.' *Shoo!* I des might ez well talk ter de win', suh,—dee hate de Yankees dat rank.

"By de time dat man git so he kin creep 'bout on crutches, he look mos' good ez he do now. He wuz dat full er life, suh, dat he bleeze ter go down-sta'rs, en down he went. Well, suh, he wuz mighty lucky dat day. Kase ef he'd a run up wid Mistiss en Miss Lady by hese'f, dee'd er done sumpn' ner fer ter make 'im feel bad. Dee cert'n'y would, suh. But dee wuz walkin' 'roun' in de yard, en he come out on de peazzer whar Marster wuz sunnin' hese'f and singin'. I wouldn' b'lieve it, suh, ef I ain' see it wid my two eyes; but Marster got up out'n he cheer, en straighten hese'f, en shuck han's wid Mars Fess, en look like he know all 'bout it. Dee sot dar, suh, en talk en laugh, en laugh en talk, tell bimeby I 'gun ter git skeerd on de accounts er bofe un um. Dee talk 'bout de war, en dee talk 'bout de Yankees, en dee talk politics right straight 'long des like Marster done 'fo' he bin strucken wid de polzy. En he talk sense, suh. He cert'n'y did. Bimeby Mistiss en Miss Lady come back fum dee walk, en dee look like dee gwine drap w'en dee see w'at gwine on. Dem two mens wuz so busy talkin', suh, dat dee ain' see de wimmen folks, en dee des keep right on wid dee argafyin'. Mistiss en Miss Lady, dee ain' know w'at ter make er all dis, en dee stan' dar lookin' fus' at Marster en den at one er n'er. Bimeby dee went up de steps en start to go by, but Marster he riz up en stop um. Yes, suh. He riz right up en stop um, en right den en dar, suh, he make um interjuced ter one an'er. He stan' up, en he say, 'Mr. Trunion, dis my wife; Mr. Trunion, dis my daughter.'

"Well, suh, I wuz stannin' back in de big hall, en we'n I see Marster gwine on dat away my knees come mighty nigh failin' me, suh. Dis de fus' time w'at he reckermember anybody name, en de fus' time he do like he useter, sence he bin sick wid de polzy. Mistiss en Miss Lady, dee come 'long in atter w'ile, en dee look like dee skeerd. Well, suh, I des far'ly preach at um. Yes, suh; I did dat. I say, 'You see dat? You see how Marster doin'? Ef de han' er de Lord ain' in dat, den he han' ain' bin in nuttin' on de top side er dis yeth.' I say, 'You see how you bin cuttin' up 'roun' dat sick w'ite man wid yo' biggity capers, en yit de Lord retch down en make Marster soun' en well time de yuther w'ite man tetch 'im.' Well, suh, dey wuz dat worked up dat dey sot down en cried. Yes, suh; dey did dat. Dey cried. En I ain' tellin' you no lie, suh, I stood dar en cried wid um. Let 'lone dat, I des far'ly boohooed. Yes, suh; dat's me. W'en I git ter cryin' sho' nuff, I bleeze ter boohoo.

"Fum dat on, Marster do like hese'f, en talk like hese'f. It look like he bin sleep long time, suh, en de sleep done 'im good. All he sense come back; en you know, suh, de Tomlinsons, w'en dey at deese'f, got much sense ez dee want en some fer give way. Mistiss and Miss Lady, dee wuz mighty proud 'bout Marster, suh, but dee ain' fergit dat de yuther man wuz Yankee, en dee hol' deese'f monst'ous stiff. He notice dat hese'f, en he want ter go 'way, but Marster, he 'fuse ter lissen at 'im right pine-plank, suh. He say de dead Tomlinsons would in-about turn over in dee graves ef dee know he sont a cripple man 'way from he 'ouse. Den he want ter pay he board, but Marster ain' lissen ter dat, en needer is Mistiss; en dis mighty funny, too, kaze right dat minnit dee want a half er dollar er good money in de whole fambly, ceppin' some silver w'at I work fer, en w'at I hide in er chink er my chimbly. No, suh. Dee want er half er dollar in de whole fambly, suh. En yit dee won't take de greenbacks w'at dat man offer um.

"By dat time, suh, de war wuz done done, en dee wuz tough times. Dee cert'n'y wuz, suh. De railroads wuz all broke up, en eve'y thing look like it gwine helter-skelter right straight ter de Ole Boy. Dey want no law, suh, en dey want no nuttin'; en ef it hadn't er bin fer me en my ole man, I speck de Tomlinsons, proud ez dee wuz, would er bin mightily pincht fer fin' bread en meat. But dee ain' never want fer it yit, suh, kaze w'en me en my ole man git whar we can't move no furder, Marse Fess Trunion, he tuck holt er de place en he fetcht it right side up terreckerly. He say ter me dat he gwine pay he board dat away, suh, but he ain' say it whar de Tomlinsons kin year 'im, kaze den dee'd a-bin a fuss, suh. But he kotch holt, en me, en him, en my ole man, we des he't eve'y thing hot. Mo' speshually Marse Fess Trunion, suh. You ain' know 'im, suh, but dat ar w'ite man, he got mo' ways ter work, en mo' short cuts ter de ways, suh, dan any w'ite man w'at I ever see, en I done see lots un um. It got so, suh, dat me en my ole man ain' have ter draw no mo' rashuns fum de F'eedman Bureau; but dee wuz one spell, suh, w'en wuss rashuns dan dem wuz on de Tomlinson table.

"Well, suh, dat w'ite man, he work en he scuffle; he hire niggers, and he turn um off; he plan, en he projick; en 'tain' so mighty long, suh, 'fo' he got eve'y thing gwine straight. How he done it, I'll never tell you, suh; but do it he did. He put he own money in dar, suh, kaze dee wuz two times dat I knows un w'en he git money out'n de pos'-office, en I see 'im pay it out ter de niggers, suh. En all dat time he look like he de happies' w'ite man on top er de groun', suh. Yes, suh. En w'en he at de 'ouse Marster stuck right by 'im, en ef he bin he own son he couldn't pay him mo' 'tention. Dee wuz times, suh, w'en it seem like ter me dat Marse Fess Trunion wuz a-cuttin' he eye at Miss Lady, en den I 'low ter myse'f, 'Shoo, man! you mighty nice en all dat, but you Yankee, en you nee'nter be a-drappin' yo' wing 'roun' Miss Lady, kaze she too high-strung fer dat.'

"It look like he see it de same way I do, suh, kaze atter he git eve'y thing straight he say he gwine home. Marster look like he feel mighty bad, but Mistiss en Miss Lady, dee ain' say nuttin' 'tall. Den, atter w'ile, suh, Marse Fess Trunion fix up, en off he put. Yes, suh. He went off whar he come fum, en I speck he folks wuz mighty glad ter see 'im atter so long, kaze ef dee ever wuz a plum nice man it wuz dat man. He want no great big man, suh, en he ain' make much fuss, yit he lef' a mighty big hole at de Tomlinson Place w'en he pulled out fum dar. Yes, suh; he did dat. It look like it lonesome all over de plan'ation. Marster, he' gun ter git droopy, but eve'y time de dinner bell ring he go ter de foot er de sta'rs en call out, 'Come on, Trunion!' Yes, suh. He holler dat out eve'y day, en den, wiles he be talkin', he'd stop en look roun' en say, 'Whar Trunion?' It ain' make no diffunce who he talkin' wid, suh, he'd des stop right still en ax, 'Whar Trunion?' Den de niggers, dee got slack, en eve'y thing 'gun ter go een'-ways. One day I run up on Miss Lady settin' down cryin', en I ax her w'at de name er goodness de matter, en she say nuff de matter. Den I say she better go ask her pappy whar Trunion, en den she git red in de face, en 'low I better go 'ten' ter my business; en den I tell her dat ef somebody ain' tell us whar Trunion is, en dat mighty quick, dee won't be no business on dat place fer 'ten' ter. Yes, suh. I tol' her dat right p'intedly, suh.

"Well, suh, one day Marse Fess Trunion come a-drivin' up in a shiny double buggy, en he look like he des step right out'n a ban'-box; en ef ever I wuz glad ter see anybody, I wuz glad ter see dat man. Marster wuz glad; en dis time, suh, Miss Lady wuz glad, en she show it right plain; but Mistiss, she still sniff de a'r en hol' her head high. T'want long, suh, 'fo' we all knowd dat Marse Fess wuz gwine marry Miss Lady. I ain' know how dee fix it, kaze Mistiss never is come right out en say she 'greeable 'bout it, but Miss Lady wuz a Bledsoe too, en a Tomlinson ter boot, en I ain' never see nobody w'at impatient nuff fer ter stan' out 'g'inst dat gal. It ain' all happen, suh, quick ez I tell it, but it happen; en but fer dat, I dunno w'at in de name er goodness would er 'come er dis place."

A few hours later, as I sat with Trunion on the veranda of his house, he verified Aunt Fountain's story, but not until after he was convinced that I was familiar with the history of the family. There was much in that history he could afford to be proud of, modern though he was. A man who believes in the results of blood in cattle is not likely to ignore the possibility of similar results in human beings; and I think he regarded the matter in some such practical light. He was a man, it seemed, who was disposed to look lightly on trouble, once it was over with; and I found he was not so much impressed with his struggle against the positive scorn and contempt of Mrs. Tomlinson,—a struggle that was infinitely more important and protracted than Aunt Fountain had described it to be,—as he was with his conflict with Bermuda grass. He told me laughingly of some of his troubles with his hot-headed neighbors in the early days after the war, but nothing of this sort seemed to be as important as his difficulties with Bermuda grass. Here the practical and progressive man showed himself; for I have a very vivid recollection of the desperate attempts of the farmers of that region to uproot and destroy this particular variety.

As for Trunion, he conquered it by cultivating it for the benefit of himself and his neighbors; and I suspect that this is the way he conquered his other opponents. It was a great victory over the grass, at any rate. I walked with him over the place, and the picture of it all is still framed in my mind,—the wonderful hedges of Cherokee roses, and the fragrant and fertile stretches of green Bermuda through which beautiful fawn-colored cattle were leisurely making their way. He had a theory that this was the only grass in the world fit for the dainty Jersey cow to eat.

There were comforts and conveniences on the Tomlinson Place not dreamed of in the old days, and I think there was substantial happiness there too. Trunion himself was a wholesome man, a man full of honest affection, hearty laughter, and hard work,—a breezy, companionable, energetic man. There was something boyish, unaffected, and winsome in his manners; and I can easily understand why Judge Addison Tomlinson, in his old age, insisted on astonishing his family and his guests by exclaiming, "Where's Trunion?" Certainly he was a man to think about and inquire after.

I have rarely seen a lovelier woman than his wife, and I think her happiness helped to make her so. She had inherited a certain degree of cold stateliness from her ancestors; but her experience after the war, and Trunion's unaffected ways, had acted as powerful correctives, and there was nothing in the shape of indifference or haughtiness to mar her singular beauty.

As for Mrs. Tomlinson,—the habit is still strong in me to call her Harriet Bledsoe,—I think that in her secret soul she had an ineradicable contempt for Trunion's extraordinary business energy. I think his "push and vim," as the phrase goes, shocked her sense of propriety to a far greater extent than she would have been willing to admit. But she had little time to think of these matters; for she had taken possession of her grandson, Master Addison Tomlinson Trunion, and was absorbed in his wild and boisterous ways, as grandmothers will be. This boy, a brave and manly little fellow, had Trunion's temper, but he had inherited the Tomlinson air. It became him well, too, and I think Trunion was proud of it.

"I am glad," said I, in parting, "that I have seen Aunt Fountain's Prisoner."

"Ah!" said he, looking at his wife, who smiled and blushed, "that was during the war. Since then I have been a Prisoner of Peace."

I do not know what industrial theories Trunion has impressed on his neighborhood by this time; but he gave me a practical illustration of the fact that one may be a Yankee and a Southerner too, simply by being a large-hearted, whole-souled American.

Mom Bi

THE LITTLE TOWN of Fairleigh, in South Carolina, was a noted place before the war, whatever it may be now. It had its atmosphere, as Judge Waynecroft used to say, and that atmosphere was one of distinction. It was a very quiet town, but there was something aristocratic, something exclusive, even in its repose. It was a rough wind that could disturb the stateliness of the live oaks with which the streets were lined, and it was indeed an inhospitable winter that could suppress the tendency of the roses to bloom.

Fairleigh made no public boast that it was not a commercial town, but there can be no doubt that it prided itself on the fact. Even the piney-woods crackers found a slow market there for the little "truck" they had to sell, for it was the custom of the people to get their supplies of all kinds from "the city." It was to "the city," indeed, that Fairleigh owed its prominence, and its inhabitants were duly mindful of that fact.

As late as 1854 there was no more insignificant village in South Carolina than Fairleigh; but in the summer of that year the fever plague flapped its yellow wings above Charleston, and the wealthier families sought safety in flight. Some went North and some went West; some went one way and some another; but the choice few, following the example of Judge Waynecroft, went no further than Fairleigh, which was far enough in the interior to be out of reach of the contagion.

They found the situation of the little village so convenient, and its climate so perfect, that they proceeded—still following the example of Judge Waynecroft—to build summer homes there; and in time Fairleigh became noted as a resort for the wealthiest and most refined people of Charleston.

Of this movement, as has been intimated, Judge Waynecroft was the pioneer; and for this and other reasons he was highly esteemed by the natives of Fairleigh. To their minds the Judge was an able and a public-spirited citizen, whom it was their pleasure to admire. In addition to this, he had a most charming household, in which simplicity lent grace to dignity.

There was one feature of Judge Waynecroft's household, however, which the natives of Fairleigh did not admire, and that was "Mom Bi." Perhaps they were justified in this. Mom Bi was a negro woman, who appeared to be somewhat past middle age, just how far past no one could guess. She was tall and gaunt, and her skin was black as jet. She walked rapidly, but with a sidewise motion, as if she had been overtaken with rheumatism or partial paralysis. Her left arm was bent and withered, and she carried it in front of her and across her body, as one would hold an infant. Her head-handkerchief was queerly tied. The folds of it stood straight up in the air, giving her the appearance of a black Amazon. This impression was heightened by the peculiar brightness of her eyes. They were not large eyes, but they shone like those of a wild animal that is not afraid of the hunter. Her nose was not flat, nor were her lips thick like those of the typical negro. Her whole appearance was aggressive. Moreover, her manner was abrupt, and her tongue sharp, especially when it was leveled at any of the natives of Fairleigh.

To do Mom Bi justice, her manner was abrupt and her tongue sharp even in her master's family, but there these matters were understood. Practically, she ruled the household, and though she quarreled from morning till night, and sometimes far into the night, everything she said was taken in a Pickwickian sense. She was an old family servant who not only had large privileges, but was defiantly anxious to take advantage of all of them.

Whatever effect slavery may have had on other negroes, or on negroes in general, it is certain that Mom Bi's spirit remained unbroken. Whoever crossed her in the least, white or black, old or young, got "a piece of her mind," and it was usually a very large piece. Naturally enough, under the circumstances, Mom Bi soon became as well known in Fairleigh and in all the region round about as any of the "quality people." To some, her characteristics were intensely irritating; while to others they were simply amusing; but to all she was a unique figure, superior in her methods and ideas to the common run of negroes.

Once, after having a quarrel with her mistress—a quarrel which was a one-sided affair, however—Mom Bi heard one of the house girls making an effort to follow her example. The girl was making some impertinent remarks to her mistress, when Mom Bi seized a dog-whip that was hanging in the hall, and used it with such effect that the pert young wench remembered it for many a long day.

148

This was Mom Bi's way. She was ready enough to quarrel with each and every member of her master's family, but she was ready to defend the entire household against any and all comers. Altogether she was a queer combination of tyrant and servant, of virago and "mammy." Yet her master and mistress appreciated and respected her, and the children loved her. Her strong individuality was not misunderstood by those who knew her best.

No one knew just how old she was, and no one knew her real name. Probably no one cared: but there was a tradition in the Waynecroft family that her name was Viola, and that it had been corrupted by the children into Bi—Mom Bi. As to her age, it is sufficient to say that she was the self-constituted repository of the oral history of three generations of the family. She was a young woman when her master's grandfather died in 1799. Good, bad or indifferent, Mom Bi knew all about the family; and there were passages in the careers of some of its members that she was fond of retailing to her master and mistress, especially when in a bad humor.

Insignificant as she was, Mom Bi made her influence felt in Fairleigh. She was respected in her master's family for her honesty and faithfulness, but outsiders shrank from her frank and fearless criticism. The "sandhillers"—the tackies—that marketed their poor little crops in and around the village, were the special objects of her aversion, and she lost no opportunity of harassing them. Whether these queer people regarded Mom Bi as a humorist of the grimmer sort, or whether they were indifferent to her opinions, it would be difficult to say, but it is certain that her remarks, no matter how personal or bitter, made little impression on them. The men would rub their thin beards, nudge each other and laugh silently, while the women would push their sunbonnets back and stare at her as if she were some rare curiosity on exhibition. At such times Mom Bi would laugh loudly and maliciously, and cry out in a shrill and an irritating tone:

"De Lord know, I glad I nigger. Ef I ain't bin born black, dee ain't no tellin, what I mought bin born. I mought bin born lak some deze white folks what eat dirt un set in de chimerly-corner tell dee look lak dee bin smoke-dried. De Lord know what make Jesse Waynecroft fetch he famerly 'mongst folk lak deze."

This was mildness itself compared with some of Mom Bi's harangues later on, when the "sandhillers," urged by some of the energetic citizens of the village, were forming a military company to be offered to the Governor of Virginia for the defense of that State. This was in the summer of 1861. There was a great stir in the South. The martial spirit of the people had been aroused by the fiery eloquence of the political leaders, and the volunteers were mustering in every town and village. The "sandhillers" were not particularly enthusiastic—they had but vague ideas of the issues at stake—but the military business was something new to them, and therefore alluring. They volunteered readily if not cheerfully, and it was not long before there was a company of them mustering under the name of the Rifle Rangers—an attractive title to the ear if not to the understanding.

Mom Bi was very much interested in the maneuvers of the Rifle Rangers. She watched them with a scornful and a critical eye. Even in their uniforms, which were of the holiday pattern, their appearance was the reverse of soldierly. They were hollow-chested and round-shouldered, and exceedingly awkward in all their movements. Their maneuvers on the outskirts of the village, accompanied by the music of fife and drum, always drew a crowd of idlers, and among these interested spectators Mom Bi was usually to be found.

"Dee gwine fight," she would say to the Waynecroft children, in her loud and rasping voice. "Dee gwine kill folks right un left. Look at um! I done git skeer'd myse'f, dee look so 'vigrous. Ki! dee gwine eat dem Yankee up fer true. I sorry fer dem Yankee, un I skeer'd fer myse'f! When dee smell dem vittle what dem Yankee got, 't is good-by, Yankee! Look at um, honey! dee gwine fight fer rich folks' nigger."

The drilling and mustering went on, however, and Mom Bi was permitted to say what she pleased. Some laughed at her, others regarded her with something like superstitious awe, while a great many thought she was merely a harmless simpleton. Above all, she was Judge Waynecroft's family servant, and this fact was an ample apology in Fairleigh and its environs for anything that she might say.

The mustering of the "sandhillers" irritated Mom Bi; but when the family returned to Charleston in the winter, the preparations for war that she saw going on made a definite and profound impression on her. At night she would go into her mistress's room, sit on the hearth in a corner of the fireplace, and watch the fire in the grate. Nursing her withered arm, she would sit silent for an hour at a time, and when she did speak it seemed as if her tongue had lost something of its characteristic asperity.

"I think," said Mrs. Waynecroft, on one occasion, "that Mom Bi is getting religion."

"Well, she'll never get it any younger," the Judge replied.

Mom Bi, sitting in her corner, pretended not to hear, but after a while she said: "Ef de Lord call me in de chu'ch, I gwine; ef he no call I no gwine—enty? I no yerry him call dis long time."

"Well," remarked the Judge, "something has cooled you off and toned you down, and I was in hopes you were in the mourners' seat."

"Huh!" exclaimed Mom Bi. "How come I gwine go in mourner seat? What I gwine do in dey?" Then pointing to a portrait of Gabriel Waynecroft hanging over the mantel, she cried out: "Wey he bin gone at?"

Gabriel was the eldest son, the hope and pride of the family. The Judge and his wife looked at each other.

"I think you know where he has gone," said Mrs. Waynecroft, gently. "He has gone to fight for his country."

"Huh!" the old woman grunted. Then after a pause, "Wey dem san'hillers bin gone at? Wey de country what dee fight fer?"

"Why, what are you talking about?" said Judge Waynecroft, who had been listening behind his newspaper. "This is their country too, and they have gone to fight for it."

" 'Longside dat boy?" Mom Bi asked. Her voice rose as she pointed at Gabriel's picture.

"Why, certainly," said the Judge.

"*Pishou!*" exclaimed Mom Bi, with a hiss that was the very essence of scorn, contempt and unbelief. "Oona nee'n' tell me dat ting. I nuttin' but nigger fer true, but I know better dun dat. I bin nuss dat boy, un I know um troo un troo. Dat boy, 'e cut 'e t'roat fus' fo' 'e fight 'longside dem trash. When 'e be en tell-a you 'e gwine fight 'longside dem whut de Lord done fersooken dis long time?"

The Judge smiled, but Mrs. Waynecroft looked serious; Mom Bi rocked backward and forward, as if nursing her withered arm.

"Whut dem po' white trash gwine fight fer? Nuttin' 't all ain't bin tell me dat. Dee ain't bin had no nigger; dee ain't bin had no money; dee ain't bin had no lan'; dee ain't bin had nuttin' 't all. Un den 'pun top er dat, yer come folks fer tell me dat dat boy gwine fight 'longside dem creeturs."

Mom Bi laughed loudly, and shook her long finger at the portrait of young Gabriel Waynecroft. As a work of art the portrait was a failure, having been painted by an ambitious amateur; but, crude as it was, it showed a face of wonderful refinement. The features were as delicate as those of a woman, with the exception of the chin, which was full and firm. The eyes, large and lustrous, gazed from the canvas with a suggestion of both tenderness and fearlessness.

During the long and dreary days that followed—days of waiting, days of suffering and of sorrow—there were many changes in the Waynecroft household, but Mom Bi held her place. She remained as virile and as active as ever. If any change was noticeable it was that her temper was more uncertain and her voice shriller. All her talk was about the war; and as the contest wore on, with no perceptible advantage to the Confederates, she assumed the character and functions of a prophetess. Among the negroes, especially those who had never come in familiar contact with the whites, she was looked upon as a person to be feared and respected. Naturally, they argued that any black who talked to the white people as Mom Bi did must possess at least sufficient occult power to escape punishment.

Sometimes, in the pleasant weather, while walking with her mistress and the children on the battery at Charleston she would reach forth her hand and exclaim:

"Oona see dem wharfs? Dee gwine be fill wid Yankee ships! Dee gwine sail right stret up, un nuttin' 't all gwine stop um."

Then, turning to the town, she would say:

"Oona see dem street? Dee gwine fair swarm wid Yankee! Dee gwine march troo 'um, un nuttin' 't all gwine stop um. Oona see dem gang er nigger down dey? Dee gwine be free, un nuttin' 't all gwine stop um. Dee'l be free, un ole Bi gwine be free. Ah, Lord! when de drum start fer beat, un de trumpet start fer blow, de white folks gwine los de nigger. Ki! I mos' yeddy dem now."

This was repeated, not once, but hundreds of times—in the house and on the streets, wherever Mom Bi went. At the market, while the venders were weighing out supplies for the Waynecroft household, Mom Bi would take advantage of the occasion to preach a sermon about the war and to utter prophecies about the freedom of the negroes. Her fearlessness was her best protection. Those who heard her had no doubt that she was a lunatic, and so she was allowed to come and go in peace, at a time when the great mass of the negroes were under the strictest surveillance. It made no difference to Mom Bi, however, whether one or a thousand eyes were watching her, or whether the whole world thought she was crazy. She was in earnest, and thus presented a spectacle that is rarer than a great many people are willing to admit.

The old woman went her way, affording amusement to some and to others food for thought; and the rest of the world went its way, especially that part of it that was watching events from rifle-pits and trenches. To those at home the years seemed to drag, though they went fast enough, no doubt, for those at the front. They went fast enough to mark some marvelous changes and developments. Hundreds of thousands of times, it happened that a gun fired in Virginia sorely wounded the hearts of a household far away.

On the Shenandoah, one night, a sharpshooter in blue heard the clatter of a horse's hoofs on the turnpike, and the jangling of sword, spurs and bit. As the horseman came into view in the moonlight, the sharpshooter leveled his rifle. There was a flash, a puff of smoke, and a report that broke into a hundred crackling echoes on the still night air. The horse that had been held so well in hand galloped wildly away with an empty saddle. The comrades of the cavalryman, who had been following him at a little distance, rushed forward at the report of the gun, and found their handsome young officer lying in the road, dead. They scoured the country for some distance around, but they saw nothing and heard nothing, and finally they lifted the dead soldier to a horse, and carried him back to their camp.

The sharpshooter had aimed only at the dashing young cavalryman, but his shot struck a father and a mother in Charleston, and an old negro woman who was supposed to be crazy; and the wounds that it made were grievous. The cavalryman was young Gabriel Waynecroft, and with the ending of his life the hope and expectations of the family seemed to be blotted out. He had been the darling of the household, the pride of his father, the joy of his mother, and the idol of Mom Bi. When the news of his death came, the grief of the household took the shape of consternation. It was terrible to behold. The mother was prostrated and the father crushed. Their sorrow was voiceless. Mom Bi went about wringing her hands and moaning and talking to herself day after day.

Once, Judge Waynecroft, passing through the hall in slippered feet, thought he heard voices in the sitting-room. In an aimless way, he glanced in the room, and the sight made him pause. Mom Bi was sitting in the middle of the room in a low chair, gazing at the portrait of Gabriel Waynecroft, and talking to it. She spoke in a soft and tender tone, in strange contrast to the usual rasping and irritating quality of her voice.

"Look at me, honey," she was saying; "look at you' ole nigger mammy! Whut make dee lef' you fer go way down, dey wey one folks kill turrer folks? Tell de ole nigger mammy dat, honey. Whaffer dee no lef' dem no 'count san'hillers fer do all de fightin'? Who gwine fer cry wun dee git kilt? Fightin' fer nigger! Whaffer you' daddy no sen' he niggers fer fight? De

153

Lord know dee plenty un um. Nummine, honey! 'Tain't gwine fer be long, 'fo' dee'll all know whut de Lord know, un whut ole Bi know. Gi' um time, honey! des gi' um time!"

Judge Waynecroft turned away with a groan. To behold the bewildered grief of this old negro woman was to add a new pang to his own sorrow. Mom Bi paused, but did not turn her head. She heard her master pass down the hall with uncertain step, and then she heard the library door shut.

" 'Tis de gospel troot 'e bin yeddy me preachin'," she exclaimed. Then she turned again to the portrait and gazed at it steadily and in silence for a long while, rocking herself and nursing her withered arm.

When the body of Gabriel Waynecroft was brought home, Mom Bi kneeled on the floor at the foot of the coffin and stayed there, giving utterance to the wildest lamentations. Some friend or acquaintance of the family made an attempt to remove her.

"This will never do," he said kindly, but firmly. "You must get up and go away. The noise you are making distresses and disturbs the family."

Trembling with mingled grief and rage, Mom Bi turned upon the officious person.

"I ain't, I ain't, I ain't!" she almost shrieked. "I gwine fer stay right wey I is. Take you' han' fum off me, man! I bin cry on count dat chile mos' 'fo' he own mammy is. I bin nuss um, I bin worry wid um, I bin stay 'wake wid um wun ev'body wuz sleep, un I bin hol' um in my lap day un night, wun 'e sick un wun 'e well. I ain't gwine out! I ain't! I ain't!"

In fine, Mom Bi, made a terrible scene and the officious person who wanted to drive her out was glad to get out himself, which he was compelled to do in order to escape the clamor that he had unwittingly raised.

The death and burial of Gabriel Waynecroft was a gloomy episode in Mom Bi's experience, and it left its marks upon her. She lost none of her old-time vigor, but her temper became almost unbearable. She was surly, irritable and sometimes violent, especially toward the negroes on the place, who regarded her with a superstitious fear that would be difficult to explain or describe. Left to herself she did well enough. She loved to sit in the sun and talk to herself. The other negroes had a theory that she saw spirits and conversed with them; but they were welcome to their theories, so far as Mom Bi was concerned, provided they didn't pester her.

Meanwhile, Sherman's army was marching through Georgia to Savannah, and in Virginia Grant was arranging the plans of his last campaign. Savannah fell, and then came the information that Sherman's army was moving on

Charleston. The city could be defended in only one direction: all its bristles pointed seaward; and the Confederate troops prepared to evacuate. All these movements were well known to the negroes, especially to Mom Bi, and she made use of her information to renew her prophecies. She stood in the porch of her master's house and watched the Confederates file by, greeting them occasionally with irritating comment.

"Hi! Wey you gwine? Whaffer you no stop fer tell folks good-by? Nummine! Dem Yankee buckra, dee gwine shaky you by de han'. Dee mek you hot fer true. Wey you no stop fer see de nigger come free?"

Most of Mom Bi's prophecies came true. Sherman marched northward, and then came Appomattox. One day, shortly after the surrender, Mom Bi appeared before Judge Waynecroft and his wife rigged out in her best clothes. She was rather more subdued than usual. She entered the room, and then stood still, looking first at one and then at the other.

"Well, Bi," said the Judge, kindly, "what can we do for you?"

"Nuttin' 't all. I gwine down dey at Sawanny, wey my daughter is bin live."

"Do you mean Maria?"

"My daughter 'Ria, w'at you bin sell to John Waynecroft. I gwine down dey wey she live at."

"Why, you are too old to be gadding about," said the Judge. "Why not stay here where you have a comfortable home?"

"I think you are very foolish to even dream of such a thing, Mom Bi. Maria is not able to take care of you."

"I gwine down dey wey my daughter bin live at," persisted Mom Bi. Then she looked at the portrait of Gabriel Waynecroft. The beautiful boyish face seemed to arouse her. Turning suddenly, she exclaimed:

"De Lord know I done bin fergive you-all fer sellin' 'Ria 'way fum me. De Lord know I is! Wun I bin see you set down un let dat chile go off fer git kill' "—Mom Bi pointed her long and quivering finger at Gabriel's portrait —"wun I see dis, I say 'hush up, nigger! don't bodder 'bout 'Ria.' De Lord know I done bin fergive you!"

With this Mom Bi turned to the door and passed out.

"Won't you tell us good-by?" the Judge asked.

"I done bin fergive you," said Mom Bi.

"I think you might tell us good-by," said Mrs. Waynecroft, with tears in her eyes and voice.

"I done bin fergive you," was the answer.

This was in June. One morning months afterward Judge Waynecroft was informed by a policeman that a crazy old negro woman had been arrested in the cemetery.

"She is continually talking about Gabriel Waynecroft," said the officer, "and the Captain thought you might know something about her. She's got the temper of Old Harry," he continued, "and old and crippled as she is, she's as strong as a bull yearling."

It was Mom Bi, and she was carried to her old master's home. Little by little she told the story of her visit to Savannah. She found her daughter and her family in a most deplorable condition. The children had the small-pox, and finally Maria was seized with the disease. For lack of food and proper attention they all died, and Mom Bi found herself alone and friendless in a strange city. How she managed to make her way back home it is impossible to say, but she returned.

The Mom Bi who returned, however, was not the same Mom Bi that went away. Old age had overtaken her in Savannah. Her eyes were hollow, her face was pinched and shrunken, the flesh on her bones had shriveled, and her limbs shook as with the palsy. When she was helped into the house that had so long been her home she looked around at the furniture and the walls. Finally her eyes rested on the portrait of Gabriel Waynecroft. She smiled a little and then said feebly:

"I done bin come back. I bin come back fer stay; but I free, dough!"

In a little while she was freer still. She had passed beyond the reach of mortal care or pain; and, as in the old days, she went without bidding her friends good-by.

An Evening with the Ku-Klux

THE HAPPIEST, the most vivid, and certainly the most critical period of a man's life is combined in the years that stretch between sixteen and twenty-two. His responsibilities do not sit heavily on him, he has hardly begun to realize them, and yet he has begun to see and feel, to observe and absorb; he is for once and for the last time an interested, and yet an irresponsible, spectator of the passing show.

This period I had passed very pleasantly, if not profitably, at Halcyondale in Middle Georgia, directly after the great war, and the town and the people there had a place apart, in my mind. When, therefore, some ten years after leaving there, I received a cordial invitation to attend the county fair, which had been organized by some of the enterprising spirits of the town and county, among whom were Paul Conant and his father-in-law, Major Tumlin Perdue, it was natural that the fact should revive old memories.

The most persistent of these memories were those which clustered around Major Perdue, his daughter Vallie, and his brother-in-law, Colonel Bolivar Blasengame, and Aunt Minervy Ann Perdue. Curiously enough, my recollection of this negro woman was the most persistent of all. Her individuality seemed to stand out more vitally than the rest. She was what is called "a character," and something more besides. The truth is, I should have missed a good deal if I had never known Aunt Minervy Ann Perdue, who, as she described herself, was "Affikin fum 'way back yander 'fo' de flood, an' fum de word go"—a fact which seriously interferes with the somewhat complacent theory that Ham, son of Noah, was the original negro.

It is a fact that Aunt Minervy Ann's great-grandmother, who lived to be a hundred and twenty years old, had an eagle tattooed on her breast, the mark of royalty. The brother of this princess, Qua, who died in Augusta at the age of one hundred years, had two eagles tattooed on his breast. This, taken in connection with his name, which means The Eagle, shows that he was either the ruler of his tribe or the heir apparent. The prince and princess were very small, compared with the average African, but the records kept by a member of the Clopton family show that during the Revolution Qua performed some wonderful feats, and went through some strange adventures in behalf of liberty. He was in his element when war was at its hottest—and it has never been hotter in any age or time, or in any part of the world, savage or civilized, than it was then in the section of Georgia now comprised in the counties of Burke, Columbia, Richmond, and Elbert.

However, that has nothing to do with Aunt Minervy Ann Perdue; but her relationship to Qua and to the royal family of his tribe, remote though it was, accounted for the most prominent traits of her character, and many contradictory elements of her strong and sharply defined individuality. She had a bad temper, and was both fierce and fearless when it was aroused; but it was accompanied by a heart as tender and a devotion as unselfish as any mortal ever possessed or displayed. Her temper was more widely advertised than her tenderness, and her independence more clearly in evidence than her unselfish devotion, except to those who knew her well or intimately.

And so it happened that Aunt Minervy Ann, after freedom gave her the privilege of showing her extraordinary qualities of self-sacrifice, walked about in the midst of the suspicion and distrust of her own race, and was followed by the misapprehensions and misconceptions of many of the whites. She knew the situation and laughed at it, and if she wasn't proud of it her attitude belied her.

It was at the moment of transition from the old conditions to the new that I had known Aunt Minervy Ann and the persons in whom she was so profoundly interested, and she and they, as I have said, had a place apart in my memory and experience. I also remembered Hamp, Aunt Minervy Ann's husband, and the queer contrast between the two. It was mainly on account of Hamp, perhaps, that Aunt Minervy Ann was led to take such a friendly interest in the somewhat lonely youth who was editor, compositor, and pressman of Halcyondale's ambitious weekly newspaper in the days following the collapse of the confederacy.

When a slave, Hamp had belonged to an estate which was in the hands of the Court of Ordinary (or, as it was then called, the Inferior Court), to be administered in the interest of minor heirs. This was not a fortunate thing for the negroes, of which there were above one hundred and fifty. Men, women, and children were hired out, some far and some near. They came back home

158

at Christmastime, enjoyed a week's frolic, and were then hired out again, perhaps to new employers. But whether to new or old, it is certain that hired hands in those days did not receive the consideration that men gave to their own negroes.

This experience told heavily on Hamp's mind. It made him reserved, suspicious, and antagonistic. He had few pleasant memories to fall back on, and these were the days of his early youth, when he used to trot around holding to his old master's coattails—the kind old master who had finally been sent to the insane asylum. Hamp never got over the idea (he had heard some of the older negroes talking about it) that his old master had been judged to be crazy simply because he was unusually kind to his negroes, especially the little ones. Hamp's after-experience seemed to prove this, for he received small share of kindness, as well as scrimped rations, from the majority of those who hired him.

It was a very good thing for Hamp that he married Aunt Minervy Ann, otherwise he would have become a wanderer and a vagabond when freedom came. It was a fate he didn't miss a hair's breadth; he "broke loose," as he described it, and went off, but finally came back and tried in vain to persuade Aunt Minervy Ann to leave Major Perdue. He finally settled down, but acquired no very friendly feelings toward the white race.

He joined the secret political societies, strangely called "Union Leagues," and aided in disseminating the belief that the whites were only awaiting a favorable opportunity to re-enslave his race. He was only repeating what the carpet-baggers had told him. Perhaps he believed the statement, perhaps not. At any rate, he repeated it fervently and frequently, and soon came to be the recognized leader of the negroes in the county of which Halcyondale was the capital. That is to say, the leader of all except one. At church one Sunday night some of the brethren congratulated Aunt Minervy Ann on the fact that Hamp was now the leader of the colored people in that region.

"What colored people?" snapped Aunt Minervy Ann.

"We-all," responded a deacon, emphatically.

"Well, he can't lead *me*, I'll tell you dat right now!" exclaimed Aunt Minervy Ann.

Anyhow, when the time came to elect members of the Legislature (the constitutional convention had already been held), Hamp was chosen to be the candidate of the negro Republicans. A white man wanted to run, but the negroes said they preferred their own color, and they had their way. They had their way at the polls, too, for, as nearly all the whites who would have voted had served in the Confederate army, they were at that time disfranchised.

So Hamp was elected overwhelmingly, "worl' widout een'," as he put it, and the effect it had on him was a perfect illustration of one aspect of human nature. Before and during the election (which lasted three days) Hamp had been going around puffed up with importance. He wore a blue army overcoat and a stove-pipe hat, and went about smoking a big cigar. When the election was over, and he was declared the choice of the county, he collapsed. His dignity all disappeared. His air of self-importance and confidence deserted him. His responsibilities seemed to weigh him down.

He had once "rolled" in the little printing-office where the machinery consisted of a No. 2 Washington hand-press, a wooden imposing-stone, three stands for the cases, a rickety table for "wetting down" the paper, and a tub in which to wash the forms. This office chanced to be my headquarters, and the day after the election I was somewhat surprised to see Hamp saunter in. So was Major Tumlin Perdue, who was reading the exchanges.

"He's come to demand a retraction," remarked the Major, "and you'll have to set him right. He's no longer plain Hamp; he's the Hon. Hamp—what's your other name?" turning to the negro.

"Hamp Tumlin my fergiven name, suh. I thought 'Nervy Ann tol' you dat."

"Why, who named you after me?" inquired the Major, somewhat angrily.

"Me an' 'Nervy Ann fix it up, suh. She say it's about de purtiest name in town."

The Major melted a little, but his bristles rose again, as it were.

"Look here, Hamp!" he exclaimed in a tone that nobody ever forgot or misinterpreted; "don't you go and stick Perdue onto it. I won't stand that!"

"No, suh!" responded Hamp. "I started ter do it, but 'Nervy Ann say she ain't gwine ter have de Perdue name bandied about up dar whar de Legislatur's at."

Again the Major thawed, and though he looked long at Hamp it was with friendly eyes. He seemed to be studying the negro—"sizing him up," as the saying is. For a newly elected member of the Legislature, Hamp seemed to take a great deal of interest in the old duties he once performed about the office. He went first to the box in which the "roller" was kept, and felt of its surface carefully.

"You'll hatter have a bran' new roller 'fo' de mont's out," he said, "an' I won't be here to he'p you make it."

160

Then he went to the roller-frame, turned the handle, and looked at the wooden cylinders. "Dey don't look atter it like I use ter, suh; an' dish yer frame monst'us shackly."

From there he passed to the forms where the advertisements remained standing. He passed his thumb over the type and looked at it critically. "Dey er mighty skeer'd dey'll git all de ink off," was his comment. Do what he would Hamp couldn't hide his embarrassment.

Meanwhile, Major Perdue scratched off a few lines in pencil. "I wish you'd get this in Tuesday's paper," he said. Then he read: "The Hon. Hampton Tumlin, recently elected a member of the Legislature, paid us a pop-call last Saturday. We are always pleased to meet our distinguished fellow-townsman and representative. We trust Hon. Hampton Tumlin will call again when the Ku-Klux are in."

"Why, certainly," said I, humoring the joke.

"Sholy you-all ain't gwine put dat in de paper, is you?" inquired Hamp, in amazement.

"Of course," replied the Major; "why not?"

"Kaze, ef you does, I'm a ruint nigger. Ef 'Nervy Ann hear talk 'bout my name an' entitlements bein' in de paper, she'll quit me sho. Uh-uh! I'm gwine 'way fum here!" With that Hamp bowed and disappeared. The Major chuckled over his little joke, but soon returned to his newspaper. For a quarter of an hour there was absolute quiet in the room, and, as it seemed, in the entire building, which was a brick structure of two stories, the stairway, being in the centre. The hallway was, perhaps, seventy-five feet long, and on each side, at regular intervals, there were four rooms, making eight in all, and, with one exception, variously occupied as lawyers' offices or sleeping apartments, the exception being the printing-office in which Major Perdue and I were sitting. This was at the extreme rear of the hallway.

I had frequently been struck by the acoustic properties of this hallway. A conversation carried on in ordinary tones in the printing-office could hardly be heard in the adjoining room. Transferred to the front rooms, however, or even to the sidewalk facing the entrance to the stairway, the lightest tone was magnified in volume. A German professor of music, who for a time occupied the apartment opposite the printing-office, was so harassed by the thunderous sounds of laughter and conversation rolling back upon him that he tried to remedy the matter by nailing two thicknesses of bagging along the floor from the stairway to the rear window. This was, indeed, something of a help, but when the German left, being of an economical turn of mind, he took his bagging away with him, and once more the hallway was torn and rent, as you may say, with the lightest whisper.

Thus it happened that, while the Major and I were sitting enjoying an extraordinary season of calm, suddenly there came a thundering sound from the stairway. A troop of horse could hardly have made a greater uproar, and yet I knew that fewer than half a dozen people were ascending the steps. Some one stumbled and caught himself, and the multiplied and magnified reverberations were as loud as if the roof had caved in, carrying the better part of the structure with it. Some one laughed at the misstep, and the sound came to our ears with the deafening effect of an explosion. The party filed with a dull roar into one of the front rooms, the office of a harum-scarum young lawyer who had more empty bottles behind his door than he had ever had briefs on his desk.

"Well, the great Gemini!" exclaimed Major Perdue, "how do you manage to stand that sort of thing?"

I shrugged my shoulders and laughed, and was about to begin anew a very old tirade against caves and halls of thunder, when the Major raised a warning hand. Some one was saying—

"He hangs out right on ol' Major Perdue's lot. He's got a wife there."

"By jing!" exclaimed another voice; "is that so? Well, I don't wanter git mixed up wi' the Major. He may be wobbly on his legs, but I don't wanter be the one to run up ag'in 'im."

The Major pursed up his lips and looked at the ceiling, his attitude being one of rapt attention.

"Shucks!" cried another; "by the time the ol' cock gits his bellyful of dram, thunder wouldn't roust 'im."

A shrewd, foxy, almost sinister expression came over the Major's rosy face as he glanced at me. His left hand went to his goatee, an invariable signal of deep feeling, such as anger, grief, or serious trouble. Another voice broke in here, a voice that we both knew to be that of Larry Pulliam, a big Kentuckian who had refugeed to Halcyondale during the war.

"Blast it all!" exclaimed Larry Pulliam, "I hope the Major will come out. Me an' him hain't never butted heads yit, an' it's gittin' high time. Ef he comes out, you fellers jest go ahead with your rat-killin'. I'll 'ten' to him."

"Why, you'd make two of him, Pulliam," said the young lawyer.

"Oh, I'll not hurt 'im; that is, not *much*—jest enough to let 'im know I'm

162

livin' in the same village," replied Mr. Pulliam. The voice of the town bull could not have had a more terrifying sound.

Glancing at the Major, I saw that he had entirely recovered his equanimity. More than that, a smile of sweet satisfaction and contentment settled on his rosy face, and stayed there.

"I wouldn't take a hundred dollars for that last remark," whispered the Major. "That chap's been a-raisin' his hackle at me ever since he's been here, and every time I try to get him to make a flutter he's off and gone. Of course it wouldn't do for me to push a row on him just dry so. But now—" The Major laughed softly, rubbed his hands together, and seemed to be as happy as a child with a new toy.

"My son," said he after awhile, "ain't there some way of finding out who the other fellows are? Ain't you got some word you want Seab Griffin"— this was the young lawyer—"to spell for you?"

Spelling was the Major's weakness. He was a well-educated man, and could write vigorous English, but only a few days before he had asked me how many *f*'s there are in *graphic*.

"Let's see," he went on, rubbing the top of his head. "Do you spell *Byzantium* with two *y*'s, or with two *i*'s, or with one *y* and one *i*? It'll make Seab feel right good to be asked that before company, and he certainly needs to feel good if he's going with that crowd."

So, with a manuscript copy in my hand, I went hurriedly down the hall and put the important question. Mr. Griffin was all politeness, but not quite sure of the facts in the case. But he searched in his books of reference, including the Geographical Gazette, until finally he was able to give me the information I was supposed to stand in need of.

While he was searching, Mr. Pulliam turned to me and inquired what day the paper came out. When told that the date was Tuesday, he smiled and nodded his head mysteriously.

"That's good," he declared; "you'll be in time to ketch the news."

"What news?" I inquired.

"Well, ef you don't hear about it before to-morrer night, jest inquire of Major Perdue. He'll tell you all about it."

Mr. Pulliam's tone was so supercilious that I was afraid the Major would lose his temper and come raging down the hallway. But he did nothing of the kind. When I returned he was fairly beaming, and seemed to be perfectly happy. The Major took down the names in his note-book—I have forgotten

163

all except those of Buck Sanford and Larry Pulliam; they were all from the country except Larry Pulliam and the young lawyer.

After my visit to the room, the men spoke in lower tones, but every word came back to us as distinctly as before.

"The feed of the horses won't cost us a cent," remarked young Sanford. "Tom Gresham said he'd 'ten' to that. They're in the stable right now. And we're to have supper in Tom's back room, have a little game of ante, and along about twelve or one we'll sa'nter down and yank that darned nigger from betwixt his blankets, ef he's got any, and leave him to cool off at the cross-roads. Won't you go 'long, Seab, and see it well done?"

"I'll go and see if the supper's well done, and I'll take a shy at your ante," replied Mr. Griffin. "But when it comes to the balance of the programme—well, I'm a lawyer, you know, and you couldn't expect me to witness the affair. I might have to take your cases and prove an alibi, you know, and I couldn't conscientiously do that if I was on hand at the time."

"The Ku-Klux don't have to have alibis," suggested Larry Pulliam.

"Perhaps not, still—" Apparently Mr. Griffin disposed of the matter with a gesture.

When all the details of their plan had been carefully arranged, the amateur Ku-Klux went filing out, the noise they made dying away like the echoes of a storm.

Major Perdue leaned his head against the back of his chair, closed his eyes, and sat there so quietly that I thought he was asleep. But this was a mistake. Suddenly he began to laugh, and he laughed until the tears ran down his face. It was laughter that was contagious, and presently I found myself joining in without knowing why. This started the Major afresh, and we both laughed until exhaustion came to our aid.

"Oh Lord!" cried the Major, panting, "I haven't had as much fun since the war, and a long time before. That blamed Pulliam is going to walk into a trap of his own setting. Now you jest watch how he goes out ag'in."

"But I'll not be there," I suggested.

"Oh, yes!" exclaimed the Major, "you can't afford to miss it. It'll be the finest piece of news your paper ever had. You'll go to supper with me—" He paused. "No, I'll go home, send Valentine to her Aunt Emmy's, get Blasengame to come around, and we'll have supper about nine. That'll fix it. Some of them chaps might have an eye on my house, and I don't want 'em to see anybody but me go in there. Now, if you don't come at nine, I'll send Blasengame after you."

"I shall be glad to come, Major. I was simply fishing for an invitation."

"*That* fish is always on your hook, and you know it," the Major insisted.

As it was arranged, so it fell out. At nine, I lifted and dropped the knocker on the Major's front door. It opened so promptly that I was somewhat taken by surprise, but in a moment the hand of my host was on my arm, and he pulled me inside unceremoniously.

"I was on the lookout," the Major explained. "Minervy Ann has fixed to have waffles, and she's crazy about havin' 'em just right. If she waits too long to make 'em, the batter'll spoil; and if she puts 'em on before everybody's ready, they won't be good. That's what she says. Here he is, you old Hessian!" the Major cried, as Minervy Ann peeped in from the dining-room. "Now slap that supper together and let's get at it."

"I'm mighty glad you come, suh," said Aunt Minervy Ann, with a curtsey and a smile, and then she disappeared. In an incredibly short time supper was announced, and though Aunt Minervy has since informed me confidentially that the Perdues were having a hard time of it at that period, I'll do her the justice to say that the supper she furnished forth was as good as any to be had in that town—waffles, beat biscuit, fried chicken, buttermilk, and coffee that could not be surpassed.

"How about the biscuit, Minervy Ann?" inquired Colonel Blasengame, who was the Major's brother-in-law, and therefore one of the family.

"I turned de dough on de block twelve times, an' hit it a hundred an forty-sev'm licks," replied Aunt Minervy Ann.

"I'm afeared you hit it one lick too many," said Colonel Blasengame, winking at me.

"Well, suh, I been hittin' dat away a mighty long time," Aunt Minervy Ann explained, "and I ain't never hear no complaints."

"Oh, I'm not complainin', Minervy Ann." Colonel Blasengame waved his hand. "I'm mighty glad you did hit the dough a lick too many. If you hadn't, the biscuit would 'a' melted in my mouth, and I believe I'd rather chew on 'em to get the taste."

"He des runnin' on, suh," said Aunt Minervy Ann to me. "Marse Bolivar know mighty well dat he got ter go 'way fum de Nunited State fer ter git any better biscuits dan what I kin bake."

Then there was a long pause, which was broken by an attempt on the part of Major Perdue to give Aunt Minervy Ann an inkling of the events likely to happen during the night. She seemed to be both hard of hearing and dull of understanding when the subject was broached; or she may have suspected the Major was joking or trying to "run a rig" on her. Her questions and comments, however, were very characteristic.

"I dunner what dey want wid Hamp," she said. "Ef dey know'd how no-count he is, dey'd let 'im 'lone. What dey want wid 'im?"

"Well, two or three of the country boys and maybe some of the town chaps are going to call on him between midnight and day. They want to take him out to the cross-roads. Hadn't you better fix 'em up a little snack? Hamp won't want anything, but the boys will feel a little hungry after the job is over."

"Nobody ain't never tell me dat de Legislatur' wuz like de Free Masons, whar dey have ter ride a billy goat an' go down in a dry well wid de chains a-clankin'. I done tol' Hamp dat he better not fool wid white folks' doin's."

"Only the colored members have to be initiated," explained the Major, solemnly.

"What does dey do wid um?" inquired Aunt Minervy Ann.

"Well," replied the Major, "they take 'em out to the nearest cross-roads, put ropes around their necks, run the ropes over limbs, and pull away as if they were drawing water from a well."

"What dey do dat fer?" asked Aunt Minervy Ann, apparently still oblivious to the meaning of it all.

"They want to see which'll break first, the ropes or the necks," the Major explained.

"Ef dey takes Hamp out," remarked Aunt Minervy Ann, tentatively—feeling her way, as it were—"what time will he come back?"

"You've heard about the Resurrection Morn, haven't you, Minervy Ann?" There was a pious twang in the Major's voice as he pronounced the words.

"I hear de preacher say sump'n 'bout it," replied Aunt Minervy Ann.

"Well," said the Major," along about that time Hamp will return. I hope his record is good enough to give him wings."

"Shuh! Marse Tumlin! you-all des fool'in me. I don't keer—Hamp ain't gwine wid um. I tell you dat right now."

"Oh, he may not want to go," persisted the Major, "but he'll go all the same if they get their hands on him."

"My life er me!" exclaimed Aunt Minervy Ann, bristling up, "does you-all 'speck I'm gwine ter let um take Hamp out dat away? De fus' man come ter my door, less'n it's one er you-all, I'm gwine ter fling a pan er hot embers in his face ef de Lord'll gi' me de strenk. An' ef dat don't do no good, I'll scald um wid b'ilin' water. You hear dat, don't you?"

"Minervy Ann," said the Major, sweetly, "have you ever heard of the Ku-Klux?"

"Yasser, I is!" she exclaimed with startling emphasis. She stopped still and gazed hard at the Major. In response, he merely shrugged his shoulders and raised his right hand with a swift gesture that told the whole story.

"Name er God! Marse Tumlin, is you an' Marse Bolivar and dish yer young genterman gwine ter set down here flat-footed and let dem Ku-kluckers scarify Hamp?"

"Why should *we* do anything? You've got everything arranged. You're going to singe 'em with hot embers, and you're going to take their hides off with scalding water. What more do you want?" The Major spoke with an air of benign resignation.

Aunt Minervy Ann shook her head vigorously. "Ef dey er de Kukluckers, fire won't do um no harm. Dey totes der haids in der han's."

"Their heads in their hands?" cried Colonel Blasengame, excitedly.

"Dat what dey say, suh," replied Aunt Minervy Ann.

Colonel Blasengame looked at his watch. "Tumlin, I'll have to ask you to excuse me to-night," he said. "I—well, the fact is, I have a mighty important engagement up town. I'm obliged to fill it." He turned to Aunt Minervy Ann: "Did I understand you to say the Ku-Klux carry their heads in their hands?"

"Dat what folks tell me. I hear my own color sesso," replied Aunt Minervy Ann.

"I'd be glad to stay with you, Tumlin," the Colonel declared; "but—well, under the circumstances, I think I'd better fill that engagement. Justice to my family demands it."

"Well," responded Major Perdue, "if you are going, I reckon we'd just as well go, too."

"Huh!" exclaimed Aunt Minervy Ann, "ef gwine's de word, dey can't nobody beat me gittin' way fum here. Dey may beat me comin' back, I ain't 'sputin' dat; but dey can't beat me gwine 'way. I'm ol', but I got mighty nigh ez much go in me ez a quarter-hoss."

Colonel Blasengame leaned back in his chair and studied the ceiling. "It seems to me, Tumlin, we might compromise on this. Suppose we get Hamp to come in here. Minervy Ann can stay out there in the kitchen and throw a rock against the back door when the Ku-Klux come."

Aunt Minervy Ann fairly gasped. "*Who? Me?* I'll die fust. I'll t'ar dat do' down; I'll holler twel ev'ybody in de neighborhood come a-runnin'. Ef you don't b'lieve me, you des try me. I'll paw up dat back-yard."

Major Perdue went to the back door and called Hamp, but there was no answer. He called him a second time, with the same result.

"Well," said the Major, "they've stolen a march on us. They've come and carried him off while we were talking."

"No, suh, dey ain't, needer. I know right whar he is, an' I'm gwine atter 'im. He's right 'cross de street dar, colloguin' wid dat ol' Ceely Ensign. Dat's right whar he is."

"Old! Why, Celia is young," remarked the Major. "They say she's the best cook in town."

Aunt Minervy Ann whipped out of the room and was gone some little time. When she returned, she had Hamp with her, and I noticed that both were laboring under excitement which they strove in vain to suppress.

"Here I is, suh," said Hamp. " 'Nervy Ann say you call me."

"How is Celia to-night?" Colonel Blasengame inquired, suavely.

This inquiry, so suddenly and unexpectedly put, seemed to disconcert Hamp. He shuffled his feet and put his hand to his face. I noticed a blue welt over his eye, which was not there when he visited me in the afternoon.

"Well, suh, I 'speck she's tolerbul."

"*Is she? Is she? Ah-h-h!*" cried Aunt Minervy Ann.

"She must be pretty well," said the Major. "I see she's hit you a clip over the left eye."

"Dat's some er 'Nervy Ann's doin's, suh," replied Hamp, somewhat disconsolately.

"Den what you git in de way fer?" snapped Aunt Minervy Ann.

"Marse Tumlin, dat ar 'oman ain't done nothin' in de roun' worl'. She say she want me to buy some hime books fer de church when I went to Atlanty, an' I went over dar atter de money."

"*I himed 'er an' I churched 'er!*" exclaimed Aunt Minervy Ann.

"Here de money right here," said Hamp, pulling a small roll of shin-plasters out of his pocket; "an' whiles we settin' dar countin' de money, 'Nervy Ann come in dar an' frail dat 'oman out."

"Ain't you hear dat nigger holler, Marse Tumlin?" inquired Minervy Ann. She was in high good-humor now. "Look like ter me dey could a-heerd 'er blate in de nex' county ef dey'd been a-lis'nin'. 'Twuz same ez a picnic, suh, an' I'm gwine 'cross dar 'fo' long an' pay my party call."

Then she began to laugh, and pretty soon went through the whole episode for our edification, dwelling with unction on that part where the unfortunate victim of her jealousy had called her "Miss 'Nervy." The more she laughed the more serious Hamp became.

At the proper time he was told of the visitation that was to be made by the Ku-Klux, and this information seemed to perplex and worry him no little. But his face lit up with genuine thankfulness when the programme for the occasion was announced to him. He and Minervy Ann were to remain in the house and not show their heads until the Major or the Colonel or their guest came to the back door and drummed on it lightly with the fingers.

Then the arms—three shot-guns—were brought out, and I noticed with some degree of surprise, that as the Major and the Colonel began to handle these, their spirits rose perceptibly. The Major hummed a tune and the Colonel whistled softly as they oiled the locks and tried the triggers. The Major, in coming home, had purchased four pounds of mustard-seed shot, and with this he proceeded to load two of the guns. In the third he placed only powder. This harmless weapon was intended for me, while the others were to be handled by Major Perdue and Colonel Blasengame. I learned afterward that the arrangement was made solely for my benefit. The Major and the Colonel were afraid that a young hand might become excited and fire too high at close range, in which event mustard-seed shot would be as dangerous as the larger variety.

At twelve o'clock I noticed that both Hamp and Aunt Minervy were growing restless.

"You hear dat clock, don't you, Marse Tumlin?" said Minervy as the chimes died away. "Ef you don't min', de Kukluckers'll be a-stickin' der haids in de back do'."

But the Major and the Colonel were playing a rubber of seven-up (or high-low-Jack) and paid no attention. It was a quarter after twelve when the game was concluded and the players pushed their chairs back from the table.

"Ef you don't fin' um in de yard waitin' fer you, I'll be fooled might'ly," remarked Aunt Minervy Ann.

"Go and see if they're out there," said the Major.

"*Me*, Marse Tumlin? *Me?* I wouldn't go out dat do' not for ham."

The Major took out his watch. "They'll eat and drink until twelve or a little after, and then they'll get ready to start. Then they'll have another drink all 'round, and finally they'll take another. It'll be a quarter to one or after when they get in the grove in the far end of the lot. But we'll go out

169

now and see how the land lays. By the time they get here, our eyes will be used to the darkness."

The light was carried to a front room, and we groped our way out at the back door the best we could. The night was dark, but the stars were shining. I noticed that the belt and sword of Orion had drifted above the tree-tops in the east, following the Pleiades. In a little while the darkness seemed to grow less dense, and I could make out the outlines of trees twenty feet away.

Behind one of these trees, near the outhouse in which Hamp and Aunt Minervy lived, I was to take my stand, while the Major and the Colonel were to go farther into the wood-lot so as to greet the would-be Ku-Klux as they made their retreat, of which Major Perdue had not the slightest doubt.

"You stand here," said the Major in a whisper. "We'll go to the far-end of the lot where they're likely to come in. They'll pass us all right enough, but as soon as you see one of 'em, up with the gun an' lam aloose, an' before they can get away give 'em the other barrel. Then you'll hear from us."

Major Perdue and Colonel Blasengame disappeared in the darkness, leaving me, as it were, on the inner picket line. I found the situation somewhat ticklish, as the saying is. There was not the slightest danger, and I knew it, but if you ever have occasion to stand out in the dark, waiting for something to happen, you'll find there's a certain degree of suspense attached to it. And the loneliness and silence of the night will take a shape almost tangible. The stirring of the half-dead leaves, the chirping of a belated cricket, simply emphasized the loneliness and made the silence more profound. At intervals, all nature seemed to heave a deep sigh, and address itself to slumber again.

In the house I heard the muffled sound of the clock chime one, but whether it was striking the half-hour or the hour I could not tell. Then I heard the stealthy tread of feet. Someone stumbled over a stick of timber, and the noise was followed by a smothered exclamation and a confused murmur of voices. As the story-writers say, I knew that the hour had come. I could hear whisperings, and then I saw a tall shadow steal from behind Aunt Minervy's house, and heard it rap gently on the door. I raised the gun, pulled the hammer back, and let drive. A stream of fire shot from the gun, accompanied by a report that tore the silence to atoms. I heard a sharp exclamation of surprise, then the noise of running feet, and off went the other barrel. In a moment the Major and the Colonel opened on the fugitives. I heard a loud cry of pain from one, and, in the midst of it all, the mustard-seed shot rattled on the plank fence like hominy-snow on a tin roof.

The next instant I heard someone running back in my direction, as if for dear life. He knew the place apparently, for he tried to go through the orchard, but just before he reached the orchard fence, he uttered a half-strangled cry of terror, and then I heard him fall as heavily as if he had dropped from the top of the house.

It was impossible to imagine what had happened, and it was not until we had investigated the matter that the cause of the trouble was discovered. A wire clothes-line, stretched across the yard, had caught the would-be Ku-Klux under the chin, his legs flew from under him, and he had a fall, from the effects of which he was long in recovering. He was a young man about town, very well connected, who had gone into the affair in a spirit of mischief. We carried him into the house, and administered to his hurts the best we could; Aunt Minervy Ann, be it said to her credit, being more active in this direction than any of us.

On the Tuesday following, the county paper contained the news in a form that remains to this day unique. It is hardly necessary to say that it was from the pen of Major Tumlin Perdue.

"Last Saturday afternoon our local editor was informed by a prominent citizen that if he would apply to Major Perdue he would be put in possession of a very interesting piece of news. Acting upon this hint, ye local yesterday went to Major Perdue, who, being in high good-humor, wrote out the following with his own hand:

" 'Late Saturday night, while engaged with a party of friends in searching for a stray dog on my premises, I was surprised to see four or five men climb over my back fence and proceed toward my residence. As my most intimate friends do not visit me by climbing over my back fence, I immediately deployed my party in such a manner as to make the best of a threatening situation. The skirmish opened at my kitchen-door, with two rounds from a howitzer. This demoralized the enemy, who promptly retreated the way they came. One of them, the leader of the attacking party, carried away with him two loads of mustard-seed shot, delivered in the general neighborhood and region of the coattails, which, being on a level with the horizon, afforded as fair a target as could be had in the dark. I understand on good authority that Mr. Larry Pulliam, one of our leading and deservedly popular citizens, has had as much as a quart of mustard-seed shot picked from his carcass. Though hit in a vulnerable spot, the wound is not mortal.—T. PERDUE.' "

I did my best to have Mr. Pulliam's name suppressed, but the Major would not have it so.

"No, sir," he insisted; "the man has insulted me behind my back, and he's got to cut wood or put down the axe."

Naturally this free and easy card created quite a sensation in Halcyondale and the country round about. People knew what it would mean if Major Perdue's name had been used in such an off-hand manner by Mr. Pulliam, and they naturally supposed that a fracas would be the outcome. Public expectation was on tiptoe, and yet the whole town seemed to take the Major's card humorously. Some of the older citizens laughed until they could hardly sit up, and even Mr. Pulliam's friends caught the infection. Indeed, it is said that Mr. Pulliam, himself, after the first shock of surprise was over, paid the Major's audacious humor the tribute of a hearty laugh. When Mr. Pulliam appeared in public, among the first men he saw was Major Perdue. This was natural, for the Major made it a point to be on hand. He was not a ruffler, but he thought it was his duty to give Mr. Pulliam a fair opportunity to wreak vengeance on him. If the boys about town imagined that a row was to be the result of this first meeting, they were mistaken. Mr. Pulliam looked at the Major and then began to laugh.

"Major Perdue," he said, "I'd a heap rather you'd pull your shot-gun on me than your pen."

And that ended the matter.

How Aunt Minervy Ann Ran Away
and Ran Back Again

In the matter of attending the fair at Halcyondale, Aunt Minervy Ann's hospitable wishes jumped with my own desires, and it was not difficult to give her a hard and fast promise in the matter; nor did it take the edge off my desires to entertain a suspicion, verified long afterward, that Aunt Minervy Ann's anxiety was based on a hope, expressed by Major Perdue, that the fair would be properly handled in the Atlanta papers.

The directors of the fair were represented at the little railway station, at Halcyondale, by a committee, and into the hands of this committee fell every man, woman, and child that stepped from the passing trains. It mattered little what the business of these incoming travellers was; whether they came to visit the fair or to attend to their own private affairs. They were seized, bag and baggage, by the committee and borne triumphantly to the hotel, or to a boarding-place, or to some private house. The members of the committee had a duty to perform, and they performed it with an energy and a thoroughness that was amazing if not altogether satisfactory. As I remember, this vigorous body was called the Committee on Public Comfort, and most heroically did it live up to its name and its duties.

These things I learned by observation and not by experience, for before the train on which I was a passenger had cleared the suburbs of Atlanta, I caught a glimpse of Major Tumlin Perdue, who had long been a prominent citizen of Halcyondale. He had changed but little during the ten years. His hair was whiter, and he was a trifle thinner, but his complexion was still rosy and his manners as buoyant as ever. I doubted whether he would know me again, though he had been very friendly with me in the old days, seeming to know by instinct just when and how to drop a word of encouragement and appreciation, and so I forebore to renew the acquaintance. The Major could be boisterous enough in those times when in the humor, but when at his best he had more ways like those of a woman (and a noble and tender-hearted woman at that) than any man I had ever known. He had a woman's tact, intuition, and sympathy; and these qualities were so exquisitely developed in him that they lifted him high in the estimation of a young man who was living away from his mother, and who was somewhat lonely on that account.

Presently, the Major came along the aisle for a drink of water. As he was in the act of drinking, his eyes met mine, and he recognized me instantly. He swallowed the water with a gulp.

"Why, bless my soul!" he exclaimed, greeting me with the simple cordiality that springs from an affectionate nature. "Why, I wouldn't take ten dollars for this! I was thinking about you this very day. Don't you remember the night we went out to ku-klux the Ku-Klux, and the chap that mighty nigh broke his neck running into a wire clothes-line? I saw him to-day. He would hardly speak to me," the Major went on, laughing heartily. "He's never got over that night's business. I thought about you, and I started to hunt you up; but you know how it is in Atlanta. Folks ain't got time to eat, much less to tell you where anybody lives. A man that's too busy is bound to worry, and worry will kill him every bit and grain as quick as John Barley-corn. Business is bound to be the ruin of this country, and if you don't live to see it, your children will."

Thus the Major talked, blending wisdom with impracticable ideas in the most delightful way. He seemed to be highly pleased when he found that I was to spend a week at Halcyondale, attending the fair and renewing old friendships.

"Then you belong to me!" he exclaimed. "It's no use," he went on, shaking his head when I would have protested against imposing on his good-nature; "you needn't say a word. The tavern is stuffed full of people, and even if it wasn't, you'd go to my house. If you ain't been ruined by living in Atlanta, it'll seem like home to you. Dang it all! I'll *make* it seem like home to you anyhow."

Now, the affectation of hospitality is one of the commonest hypocrisies in life, and, to a thoughtful man, one of the most sinister; but the Major's hospitality was genuine. It was brought over from the times before the war, and had stood the test of age and long usage, and, most trying of all, the test of poverty. "If you were welcome when I was well off, how much more welcome you'll be now that I am poor!" This was not said by the Major, but by one of his contemporaries. The phrase fitted a whole generation of noble

174

men and women, and I thank Heaven that it was true at one time even if it is not true now.

When the train, with much clinking and clanking and hissing, came to a standstill at Halcyondale, the Major hustled me off on the side opposite the station, and so I escaped the ordeal of resisting the efforts of the Committee on Public Comfort to convey me to a lodging not of my own selection. The Major's buggy was in waiting, with a negro driver, who got out to make room for me. He bowed very politely, calling me by name.

"You remember Hamp, I reckon," said the Major. "He was a member of the Legislature when you lived here."

Certainly I remembered Hamp, who was Aunt Minervy Ann's husband. I inquired about her, and Hamp, who had swung up to the trunk-rack as the buggy moved off, replied that she was at home and as well as she could be.

"Yes," said the Major, "she's at my house. You may *see* somebody else besides Minervy Ann, but you won't *hear* anybody else. She owns the whole place and the people on it. I had a Boston man to dinner some time ago, one of Conant's friends—you remember Paul Conant, don't you?—and I stirred Minervy Ann up just to see what the man would say. We had a terrible quarrel, and the man never did know it was all in fun. He said they never would have such a lack of discipline among the servants in Boston. I told him I would give him any reasonable amount if he would go out and discipline Minervy Ann, just to show me how it was done. It would have been better than a circus. You heard her, didn't you, Hamp?"

Hamp chuckled good-naturedly. "Yasser, I did, an' it make col' chills run over me ter hear how Minervy Ann went on. She cert'n'y did try herse'f dat day."

The Major smiled a little proudly as I thought, slapped the horse—a bob-tailed black—with the left rein, and we went skimming along the level, sandy street at a three-minute gait. In a short while we were at the Major's house, where I received a warm welcome from his daughter, whom I had known when she was a school-girl. She was now Mrs. Paul Conant, and even more beautiful as a matron than she had been as a girl. I had also known her husband, who had begun his business career in the town a year or two before I left, and even at that time he was one of the most prominent and promising young business men in the town.

He had served in the army the last year of the war, and the service did him a world of good, physically and mentally. His faculties were broadened and enlarged. Contact with all sorts and conditions of men gave him ample knowledge of his kind, and yet he kept in touch with the finer issues of life. He was ripened and not hardened.

The surrender had no such crushing effects on him as it had on older men. It left him youth, and where youth is there must be hope and energy. He returned home, remained a few weeks, sold a couple of horses he had picked up in the track of Sherman's army, and then went into the office of a cotton factor in Savannah, giving his services for the knowledge and experience he desired to gain. In a very short time he learned all the secrets of sampling and grading the great staple. He might have remained in the office at a salary, for his aptness had made him useful, but he preferred to return to Halcyondale, where he engaged in buying cotton on his own account. There was just enough risk in this to stimulate his energies, and not enough to lead to serious speculation.

To this business he added others as his capital grew, and he was soon the most prosperous man in the town. He had formed the stock company under whose auspices the county fair was held, and was president of the board of directors.

Aunt Minervy Ann was very much in evidence, for she acted as cook, nurse, and house-girl. The first glimpse I had of her, she had a bucket of water in her right hand and Conant's baby—a bouncing boy—on her left arm. Just then Major Perdue hustled me off to my room, thus postponing, as I thought, the greeting I had for Aunt Minervy Ann. But presently I heard her coming upstairs talking to herself.

"Ef dey gwine ter have folks puttin' up wid um, dey better tell me in de due time, so I can fix up fer um. Dey ain't been no fresh water in deze rooms sence dat baby wuz born'd."

She went on to the end of the hall and looked in each of the rooms. Then, with an exclamation I failed to catch, she knocked at my door, which was promptly opened. As she saw me a broad smile flashed over her good-natured face.

"I 'low'd 'twuz you," she said, "an' I'm mighty glad you come." She started to pour the water from can to pitcher, when suddenly she stayed her hand. With the exclamation, "Well, ef dis don't bang my time!" she went to the head of the stairs and cried out: "Miss Vallie! Miss Vallie! you don't want no town folks stuck in dish yer back room, does you?"

"Why, certainly not!" cried the lady. "What could father have been thinking of?"

"Shoo! he like all de men folks," responded Aunt Minervy Ann.

176

With that she seized my valise with one hand, and, carrying the can of water in the other, escorted me to one of the front rooms. It was an improvement on the back room only because it had more windows to admit the air and light. I put in a word for the Major, which I hoped would be carried to the ears of the daughter.

"The Major gave me that room because he wanted to treat me as if I were one of the home folks. Now you've brought me here, and I'll feel as uncomfortable as if I were company, sure enough."

"Dey's sump'n in dat, I 'speck," replied Aunt Minervy Ann, laughing; "but, lawsy, massy! you done been in dis house too much ter talk dat-a-way. When kin folks come home, we allus gin um de bes' dey is fer de fus' week er so. Atter dat dey kin rustle 'roun' fer deyse'f."

It is hardly necessary to say that Aunt Minervy Ann took very good care that I should want for none of those little attentions that sharpen the appreciation of a guest; and, in her case, obtrusiveness was not a fault, for her intentions shone clearly and unmistakably through it all.

Major Perdue had the art of entertainment at his fingers' ends, which, though it is very simple, not one man in a hundred learns. It is the knack of leaving the guest to his own devices without seeming to do so. Most fortunate in his gifts is the host who knows how to temper his attentions!

In his efforts to get the fair under way, Paul Conant found it impossible to come to dinner, but sent his apologies.

"You'll think it is a mighty small concern when you see it," said the Major, "but it takes all that Paul can do to keep it from getting into a tangle. He has to be here, there, and everywhere, and there hasn't been a minute for a week or more but what forty people were hollering at him at once, and forty more pulling and hauling him about. If he wasn't a steam-engine, he couldn't hold out half an hour."

"Well, he'll soon straighten matters out," said I, "and then they'll stay so."

"That's so," remarked the Major; "but when that's done, he'll have to rush around from post to pillar to keep 'em straight."

"Did he seem to be greatly worried?" Valentine asked.

"No-o-o-o," replied the Major, slowly and hesitatingly, "but I'm afear'd his shoulder has begun to trouble him again." He leaned back in his chair and looked at the ceiling, apparently lost in thought.

"Why should you think that, father?"

"Once or twice, whilst he was rustling about I saw him fling his hand to his shoulder and hold it there, and I'm mightily afear'd it's hurting him."

The Major drew a deep sigh as he spoke, and silence fell on all. It was brief, but it was long enough for one to know that an unpleasant subject had been touched on—that there was something more behind it all than a pain in Conant's shoulder. Aunt Minervy Ann, who was equal to every emergency, created a diversion with the baby, and the Major soon pulled himself together.

Paul Conant came home to supper, and in the sitting-room, before the meal was announced, I observed that the Major was as solicitous about him as a mother is of her baby. His eyes were constantly on his son-in-law, and if the latter showed any sign of worry, or frowned as if in pain, a shadow would pass over the Major's genial face.

This intense solicitude was something out of the usual order, and I wondered what was behind it. But the next day it was forgotten, nor was it remembered until Aunt Minervy Ann reminded me of it. I had been faithful in my attendance on the fair, had listened patiently to the speeches, and had then tried to refresh my benumbed faculties with such fare as could be found on the grounds—barbecue, pickles, and ginger-cakes. But the occasion had been too much for me, and so, about two o'clock in the afternoon, I decided to return to my quarters at Major Perdue's home and rest my weary limbs. The very thought of the quiet and cool house was refreshing, and so, without waiting for a conveyance, I set out on foot, going through the woods in preference to the public highway, thereby cutting the distance short by nearly a mile.

A great many others had taken advantage of the short-cut through the woods, so that I had no lack of company. Among them I noticed Aunt Minervy and her husband, Hamp, the latter carrying the Conant baby, which, having had enough of the pomps and vanities of this life for the time being, was now fast asleep. I soon came up with the trio, and we went along home together.

"You toughed it out mighty well, suh," remarked Aunt Minervy Ann, after some talk about the various attractions of the fair. "Up dar in Atlanty deze kinder doin's would be laughed at, I 'speck, but hit's de bes' we-all kin do. Me an' Miss Vallie had some truck dar, speshually dat ar grape jelly on de right han' side. Ef dat jelly don't git de blue ribbon er sump'n better, hit'll be bakaze dem ar jedgment men ain't got no sense—I don't keer who dey is. Ain't you see dat ar quilt hangin' up dar wid a pattern in it like a well-whorl, only de middle er de whorl was shape like de mornin' star? Dat ar quilt is older dan what you is, suh—lots older. Me an' Mistiss made dat quilt long 'fo' Miss Vallie wuz born, an' dish yer baby'll tell you she ain't no chicken. Ef dey's any purtier quilt on dat hill dey had it hid ter-day; dey ain't brung it out whar folks kin look at it. I dunno much, but I knows dat much."

We reached the house after awhile, and I lost no time in stretching myself out on a lounge that sat invitingly in the hall behind the stairway. It was not the coolest place in the world; but, really, when one is fagged out, it is unnecessary to try to find all the comforts of life in one spot. Sleep fell on me unawares, and when I awoke, Aunt Minervy Ann was sitting near the head of the lounge fanning me. Such courtesy was surprising, as well as pleasing, but I chid her for taking so much trouble, for I had slept nearly two hours. But she made light of it, saying she had nothing else to do, the baby being in his cradle and sleeping like a log.

Then, to enjoy a smoke, I drew a rocking-chair into the back porch, and proceeded to fill my pipe with what I regarded as a very good brand of tobacco, offering some to Aunt Minervy Ann. She soon found her pipe—clay bowl and reed stem—cleaned it out carefully and filled it from my pouch.

"It look mighty pale, suh," she remarked. "I 'speck dey steam it 'fo' dey mash it up." She seated herself on the top step, lit her pipe, took a few whiffs, and then shook her head. " 'Tain't nigh rank 'nuff for me, suh. Hit tas'e like you er dreamin' 'bout smokin' an' know all de time 'tain't nothin' but a dream." She knocked the tobacco out, and then refilled the pipe with the crumbs and cutting from the end of a plug. This she smoked with an air of supreme satisfaction.

"I 'speck you got de idee dat I better be seein' 'bout supper, stidder settin' up here lookin' biggity. But 'tain't no use, suh. Marse Tumlin and Miss Vallie never is ter come home dis day less'n dey bring Marse Paul wid um. I done hear um sesso. An' I know mighty well, deyer gwine ter come back late, bekaze Paul Conant's one er dem kinder folks what go twel dey can't go, an' when dey git down dey make motions like dey gwine. Dey puts me in mind uv a lizard's tail, suh. Knock it off, an' it'll hop 'bout an' work an' wiggle plum twel de sun go down."

I suggested that the illustration was somewhat inapt (though not in those words), for the reason that Paul Conant's energy was not expended blindly. But I found that Aunt Minervy knew what she was saying.

"I ain't talkin' 'bout his own business, suh, bekaze dey ain't nobody beat 'im at dat. No, suh; I'm talkin' 'bout dem ar doin's out dat at de fair groun's. He's a-workin' at dat lots harder dan he has ter work fer hisse'f. Maybe you tuck notice uv de way dem yuther folks done out dar, suh. Dey stood 'round wid dey mouf open, an' de ribbon pinned on der coats, an' when sump'n had ter be done, dey'd call out fer Conant. It 'uz 'Conant!' here an' 'Conant!' dar, an' ef Conant wuz out er hearin' de whole shebang had ter stop right still an' wait twel Conant kin be dragged up. I watched um p'intedly, suh, an' it's des like I tell you."

Aunt Minervy Ann's characterization of the directors was so acute and so unexpected that I laughed—not at what she said, but at the vivid picture of a lot of helpless men standing about, full of dignity, and yet waiting for young Conant to tell them what to do.

"You may laugh, suh," Aunt Minervy Ann went on with a little frown, "but I'm tellin' you de Lord's trufe. I kep' my eyes on um, an' 'twuz dat-a-way fum soon dis mornin' 'twel I got mad an' come home. You kin ax Hamp, suh, an' he'll tell you de same. I reckon you heer'd Marse Tumlin las' night at de table ax Marse Paul ef his shoulder hurted 'im. I know you did, suh, bekaze I tuck notice how you looked, an' I tried ter shake de baby up so he'd cry, but dat wuz one er de times, suh, when he wouldn't be shuck up. Any udder time dat chil' would er laid back an' blated twel you'd hafter put yo' fingers in yo' years. I wuz mad wid 'im, suh, but I wuz bleedz ter laugh. Chillun mighty funny. When you don't want um ter cry, dey'll holler der heads off, an' when you want um ter cry, dey'll laugh in yo' face. I bet you dey's a blue place on dat baby's arm whar I pinched 'im, but he didn't no mo' min' it dan nothin'."

"Well," said I, "there was something peculiar in the way all of you looked and acted when the Major asked about Mr. Conant's shoulder. It was a very simple question."

"Ah, Lord!" exclaimed Aunt Minervy Ann, raising her right hand on high, "dey better ax 'bout dat shoulder. Yesser! ev'y day an' ev'y night, an' in betwixt times."

"Is Mr. Conant troubled with rheumatism?" I inquired.

"Rheumatiz! bless yo' soul, honey! Ef 'twuz rheumatiz dey wouldn't be no Paul Conant 'round dis house, ner no Conant baby."

Here is something decidedly interesting, I thought, but held my peace, knowing that whatever it was would be more quickly disclosed if there were any disclosure to make.

"Ain't you never hear 'bout it, suh? Well dat bangs me! An' you right up dar in Atlanty, too! No, suh; you must er been in Savanny, bekaze 'twuz de town talk in Atlanty. Anyhow, wharsomever you wuz er might er been,

180

dey ain't no rheumatiz de matter wid Marse Paul Conant's shoulder-blade. I know dat much, an' I know it mighty well, bekaze I wuz right here in dis house, an' nowhars else 'cep'n 'roun' de lot an' up town an' back.

"Well, den, suh, ef you ain't never hear 'bout dat, I mos know you ain't never hear tell er how I run'd off, and how I run'd back, bekaze nobody ain't never talk 'bout dat—leas'ways, not as I knows un."

I declared to Aunt Minervy Ann that I never heard a whisper of it. She leaned back against the railing of the steps and drew a long whiff from her pipe.

" 'Tain't no use ter tell you, suh, how times wuz right atter de war. You wuz right in um, an' ef you don't know, it's bekaze you didn't look 'roun' an' see um. I hear um say, suh, dat niggers wuz po' when dey come free. Dey wuz, suh; dey wuz rank pizen po'; but dey never wuz in dis worl' a nigger ez po' ez some er our white folks wuz. You may shake yo' haid, suh, but I'm givin' you de straight gov'nment trufe. Niggers is use ter bein' po', an' dey never wuz dat po' dat dey can't scuffle 'roun' an' make out somehow. Dey er been po' so long dey er usen ter it. But white folks what been rich! I hope de Lord'll call me home 'fo' I see again what I done saw in dem days. I know in reason, suh, dat I seed mo' er de trouble dan what you did, kaze you couldn't go in at de back gates like me; an' what trouble folks does have dey allers keep it somers betwix' de bedroom an' de back gate.

"De Perdues wa'n't no wuss off dan nobody else. Marse Tumlin had dish yer house an' lot, an' de plantation, an' some lan' way off yander. But all de hosses an' mules an' cattle been tuck off, an' de niggers all gone. Ef he'd er stayed on de plantation, de niggers would 'a' been dar yit, but stay he wouldn't, an' stay he didn't, an' so dar he wuz.

"Do sump'n? What he gwine do? Fo' de big turmoil he done some lawin' an' a heap er farmin'. Leas'ways my ol' Mistiss done de farmin', an' Marse Tumlin, he done de lawin'. He had 'im a office here in town, an' on set days he'd come in an' look arter de cases what he had. But how anybody gwine ter do any lawin' dat-a-way? Marse Tumlin ain't keerin' whedder he git one case er none. He ain't bleedze ter do no lawin'. An' den 'pon top er dat he went off whar dey battlin', an' dar he stayed, an' when he come back, look like de kinder lawin' what he use ter do done gone outer fashion. Ef he hadn't er been holp out, suh, I dunner what'd 'a' come un 'im. An' 'twa'n't only Marse Tumlin. Dey wuz a whole passel un um, too young ter die an' too ol' ter win money in dem kinder times. Ef you ain't ol' 'nuff ter 'member dem times, suh, you kin thank de Lord, kaze dey sho did look like tetotal ruination.

"Now, you know yo'se'f, suh, dat you can't eat a house an' lot an' live dar too; an' you can't eat lan' des dry so less'n you got a mighty appetite fer dirt. Whyn't he sell de lan'? You oughter be de las' one ter ax me dat, suh. Who gwine buy it? Dem what ain't got lan' ain't had no money, an' dem what had money sholy lived a mighty long ways fum here. Day in an' day out, suh, I wuz de wuss pester'd nigger you ever laid eyes on. I ain't know what ter do.

"An' den 'pon top er dat, dar wuz Hamp, my ol' man. When freedom come out, he tuck de notion dat we better go off some'rs an' change de name what we got so dey can't put us back in slave'y. Night an' day it fair rankle in his min', an' he kep' groanin' an' growlin' 'bout it twel I got stirred up. I oughtn't ter tell it, suh, but hit's de Lord's trufe. I got mad, I did, an' I tol' Hamp I'd go. An' den I wa'n't doin' no good stayin' here. 'Twuz des one mo' mouf ter feed, an' mo' dan one, countin' Hamp. So, bimeby, one day, when I wuz sorter fretted, I tol' Hamp ter go on out dar in de country, whar his daddy live at, an' I'd meet 'im dar 'fo' night.

"When de time come, I went in de house an' hunt fer Miss Vallie. She 'uz settin' in de parlor by de winder, but behime de curtain like, so nobody can't see 'er. She 'uz settin' dar wid 'er han's crossed on 'er lap, an' she look so little, an' pale, an' weak, dat I come mighty nigh gwine right back in de kitchen. But she seed me too quick. Den I up'n tell 'er dat I'm gwine out in de country, ter whar Hamp daddy live at. She look at me right hard an' say, 'When you comin' back, Aunt Minervy Ann?' I 'low, 'I'm comin' back des ez soon ez I kin make my 'rangements, honey.' She say, 'Well, I hope you'll have a good time while you er gone.' I 'low, 'Thanky, ma'm.' Wid dat I went an' got my bundle an' put opt fum dar—an' I ain't look back nudder, bekaze I had a mighty weakness in de knees, an' a mighty risin' in my th'oat.

"I went on down de road, an' ef anybody had so much ez said *boo* ter me, I'd 'a' turned right 'roun' an' gone back home. I went on, I did, twel I come ter de mile branch. I see somebody crossin' on de log, an' when I come up wid um, who should it 'a' been but Marse Tumlin. An' he had *one chicken!* He had been out ter de plantation—sev'm mile ef its fifty yards—an' here he wuz comin' back wid one chicken—an' him a walkin', him dat use ter ride 'roun' in his carriage! Walkin' an' totin' one little chicken! Man, suh! I don't never want ter feel again like I felt den. Whedder 'twuz de chicken, er what, I never did see Marse Tumlin Perdue look ez ol' an' ez weasly ez he did den. He look at me an' sorter laugh like I done cotch 'im doin' sump'n he ain't got no business ter do. But dey wa'n't no laugh in me; no, suh, not by a jugful.

"He say, 'Hello, Minervy Ann! whar *you* gwine?' I 'low, I did, 'I'm des gwine out yander whar Hamp kinnery live at.'

"He sorter pull his goatee, an' look down at de dus' on his shoes—an' dey wuz fair kiver'd wid it—an' den he say, 'Well, Minervy Ann, I wish you mighty well. You sho is done a mighty good part by me an' mine. Ef yo' Miss Mary wuz 'live she'd know what ter say—I don't, 'cep' dis'—he straighten up an' stretch out his han'—' 'cep' dis: whenever you want ter come back home, you'll fin' de do' open. Ef you come at night, des knock. We'll know yo' knock.'

"You ain't never seed no fool nigger 'oman cut up, is you? Well, ef you does see one, suh, I hope ter goodness 'twon't be me! Marse Tumlin ain't no mo'n got de words out'n his mouf, suh, 'fo' I tuck de bundle what I had in my han', an' flung it fur ez I could send it.

"Marse Tumlin look at me hard, an' den he say 'Dam ef I don't b'lieve youer crazy!' Time he say it, I 'low, '*I don't keer er dam ef I is!*'

"Yasser! I say it sho, an' den I drapt down on de groun' dar an' holler an' cry like somebody wuz beatin' de life out'n me. Marse Tumlin stood dar pullin at his goatee all dat time, an' bimeby I got up. I wa'n't feelin' much better, but I done had my cry an' dat's sump'n. I got up, I did, an' start back de way I come.

"Marse Tumlin say, 'Whar you gwine, Minervy Ann?' I 'low, 'I'm gwine back home—dat's whar I'm gwine!' He say, 'Pick up yo' bundle.' Wid dat I turn 'roun' on him an' 'low, 'I ain't gwine ter do it! Ef it hadn't er been fer dat ar muslin dress in dar, what Miss Vallie make over an' gi' me, I'd been at home right dis minute.'

"He 'low, 'What dat got ter do wid it, Minervy Ann?' I make answer, 'Bekaze ol' Satan make me want ter put it on an' sho' off 'fo' dem country niggers out dar whar Hamp's folks live at.' Wid dat I start back home, but Marse Tumlin holler at me—'Minervy Ann, take dis chicken.' I tuck it, I did, an' made off up de road. Bimeby I sorter flung my eye 'roun', an', bless gracious! dar wuz Marse Tumlin comin' 'long totin' my bundle. Well, suh, it flewed all over me like fier. I got so mad wid myse'f dat I could 'a' bit a piece out'n my own flesh.

"I waited in de road twel he come up, an' den I snatched de bundle out er his han'. I 'low, 'I ain't gwine ter have you totin' none er my bundles in de public road—no, ner no chickens, needer.' He say, 'Well, don't fling it 'way,

Minervy Ann. De time may come when yo' Miss Vallie'll need dat ar muslin dress.'

"When we got back home I went in de kitchen, an' fix ter clean an' kill de chicken. I 'speck Marse Tumlin must 'a' tol' Miss Vallie 'bout it, bekaze 'twan't long 'fo' I hear her runnin' 'long de plank walk ter de kitchen. She whipt in de do' she did, an' grab me an' cry like I done riz fum de dead. Well, suh, niggers ain't got no sense, you kin take um de world over. No sooner is Miss Vallie start ter cry dan I chuned up, an' dar we had it.

" 'Bout dat time, Marse Tumlin, he come out—men folks is allers gwine some'rs dey got no business. He 'low, '**What** you all blubberin' 'bout?' I make answer, 'We er cryin' over dese two chickens.' He ax, 'What two chickens?' I 'low, 'I'm cryin' over dis un, kaze it's so little, an' Miss Vallie cryin' over de one what you ain't brung. He say 'Well, I be dang!' an' wid dat he went back in de house.

"An' den, atter supper, such ez 'twuz, here come Hamp, an' he say he come ter lay de law down. I 'speck I like my ol' man 'bout ez good ez any udder 'oman what's lawfully married, but ef I didn't put a flea in Hamp year dat night you may shoot me dead. Ef he'd 'a' waited a day er two, hit might er been diffunt; but, manlike, he had ter come at de wrong time, an' he ain't open his mouf 'fo' I wuz fightin' mad. Ol' Miss allers use ter tell me I wuz a bad nigger when I got my dander up, but I never did look at myse'f dat-a-way twel dat night.

"Well, Hamp he come an' stood in de do', but I ain't say nothin'. Den he come in de kitchen, an' stan' 'roun', but still I ain't say nothin'. Den he sot down next de chimbley, but all dat time I ain't say nothin'. He look right pitiful, suh, an' ef I hadn't been mad, I'd 'a' been sorry fer 'im. But I ain't say nothin'.

"Bimeby, he 'low, ' 'Nervy'—he allers call me 'Nervy—' 'Nervy, whyn't you go whar you say you gwine?' I flung myse'f 'roun' at 'im an' say, 'Bekaze I ain't choosen ter go—dar you got it!' He 'low, 'Well, you start ter go, kaze I seed you!' I say, 'Yes, an' I start ter come back, an' you'd 'a' seed dat ef you'd 'a' looked right close.' He 'low, ' 'Nervy, don't you know dem folks in yander'll think you b'long to um?' I say, 'I does. Ain't I free? Can't I b'long to um ef I wanter? I'd like ter see de one ter hender me. What dey done ter you? An' what's I done ter you dat you want ter drag me 'way fum my white folks? You go drag you'se'f—you can't drag *me*.' He 'low, 'Dey done begin ter call you a white-folks nigger, an' dey say you gwine back on yo' own color.' "

Aunt Minervy Ann paused here to laugh. "Mad ez I wuz, suh, de minnit Hamp said dat I know'd I had ter change my chune. I 'low, 'I know right pine-blank who tol' you dat. 'Twan't nobody in de roun' worl' but ol' Cely Ensign, an' she ain't tell you dat in comp'ny, needer. She tol' you whar nobody can't hear 'er but you. Don't you fret! des ez soon ez I git thoo wid supper, I'm gwine 'roun' dar an' drag 'er out an' gi' 'er de wuss frailin' any nigger ever got sence de overseers quit bizness. I ain't fergot dat ar' possum you toted off ter her house.'

"Well, suh, I had 'im! He caved in. He 'low, ' 'Twan't no 'possum; 'twan't nothin' in de roun' worl' but a late watermillion.' I holler, '*Ah-yi! watermillion!* Well, den, ef you want ter drag anybody off fum der white folks, go an' drag ol' Cely Ensign—bekaze you can't drag me.'

"We jowered right smart, but I had Hamp in a cornder. He went off an' stayed maybe a mont', an' den he come back, an' atter 'while he got 'lected ter de legislature. He done mighty well, suh. He got nine dollars a day, an' ev'y Sat'dy night he'd fetch de bigges' part uv it home. 'Twuz mighty handy, too, suh, kaze ef hadn't been fer dat legislatur' money I dunner what me and Miss Vallie an' Marse Tumlin would 'a' done.

"Dat wuz 'bout de time, suh, dat de town boys wanter ku-kluck Hamp, an' you an' Marse Tumlin went out an' ku-klucked dem. Hamp ain't never forgot it, suh. He'd walk fum here to Atlanty fer you ef 'twould do you any good. He don't say much, but I know how he feel. I hear 'im calling me now, suh."

"You haven't told me about Paul Conant," I suggested.

"I'll tell you, suh, 'fo' you go."

In half a minute I heard Aunt Minervy Ann quarrelling and laughing at Hamp in the same breath.

How Aunt Minervy Ann Joined
the Georgia Legislature

Tʜᴇ sᴇᴄᴏɴᴅ ᴅᴀʏ of the fair, I saw more of Paul Conant. He insisted on taking charge of me, and, in his buggy, we visited every part of the fairgrounds, which had been laid out on a most liberal scale. When dinner-time came I was glad enough to excuse myself and hurry back to the refreshing shade of Major Perdue's veranda. There I found Aunt Minervy Ann swinging the baby in a hammock.

"I 'lowed maybe you'd git tired an' come back, suh; an' so I des let dinner sorter simmer whiles I got dish yer baby ter sleep. I dunner how you all does in Atlanty, but down here we has soon dinner. Dem what wanter kin have two meals a day, but dem what does sho 'nuff work better eat three. Me! I want three, whedder I works er not."

The baby stirred, and Aunt Minervy paused. At that moment a group of men, wearing badges, passed by, evidently officials of the fair going to dinner. They were evidently engaged in a very earnest discussion.

"I'm for Conant," said one, with considerable emphasis.

"Oh, so am I," assented another. "When Jim told me this morning that he was a candidate for the Legislature, I told him flat and plain that I was for Paul Conant."

"That's right," remarked a third. "We want a man there with some business sense, and Conant's the man."

Aunt Minervy Ann laughed. "Ef de Legislatur' up dar in Atlanty is like it wuz when I b'long'd ter it, dey can't drag Marse Paul in dar; no, suh! dey can't drag him in dar."

Amazement must have shown in my face, for Aunt Minervy Ann immediately became solemn. "Ain't you never hear tell 'bout my j'inin' de Legislatur'? You may look an' you may laugh, but dat don't wipe out de trufe. Dey wuz a time when I jined de Legislatur' an' when I b'long'd ter de gang same ez Hamp did. You don't 'spute but what Hamp b'long'd ter de Legislatur', suh?" asked Aunt Minervy Ann, anxious to make out the title of her own membership. No, I didn't dispute Hamp's credentials. He had been elected and he had served.

"I know'd you couldn't 'spute dat, suh," Aunt Minervy Ann went on, " 'kaze you wuz down dar when dey choosen'd 'im, an' you wuz dar when dem ar white folks come mighty nigh ku-kluckin' 'im; you wuz right dar wid Marse Tumlin an' Marse Bolivar. I never is ter fergit dat, suh, ner Hamp nudder; an' ef you don't b'lieve it, you des sen' us word you want us. Ef we git de word at midnight we'll git up, an' ef de railroad track is tore up we'll git a waggin, an' ef we can't git a waggin, we'll walk, but what we'll come."

"Well," said I, "tell us about your joining the Legislature."

"I may be long in tellin' it, suh, but 'tain't no long tale," replied Aunt Minervy Ann. "Atter Hamp come up here an' tuck his seat—dat what dey call it den, ef dey don't call it dat now—well, atter come up an' been here some little time, I tuck notice dat he 'gun ter hol' his head mighty high; a little too high fer ter suit me. He want me ter go up dar wid 'im an' stay dar, 'kaze he sorter skittish 'bout comin' home when dem country boys mought be hangin' 'roun' de depot. But I up an' tol' 'im flat an' plain dat I wa'n't gwine ter leave Miss Vallie an' let er' git usen ter strange niggers. I tol' 'im he mought go an' stay ef he want ter, but de fus' week he miss comin' home, I wuz gwine atter 'im, an' ef I fotch 'im home he won't go back in a hurry; I tol' 'im dat, flat an' plain.

"Well, suh, he done mighty well; I'll say dat fer 'im. He want too many clean shirts an' collars fer ter suit me, but he say he bleeze ter have um dar whar he at, an' I ain't make no complaint 'bout dat; but I took notice dat he wuz sorter offish wid Marse Tumlin. Mo' dan dat, I tuck notice dat needer Marse Tumlin ner Marse Bolivar so much ez look at 'im when dey pass 'im by. I know'd by dat dat sump'n wuz up.

"Now, Hamp ain't had no reg'lar time fer comin' home. Sometimes he'd come We'n'sday, an' den ag'in he'd come Friday. I ax 'im why he ain't stay de week out an' 'ten' ter his work like he oughter. He say he gettin' des much pay when he at home loafin' 'roun' ez he do when he up yer. Well, suh, dat 'stonish me. You know yo'se'f, suh, dat when folks is gittin' pay fer dat what dey ain't doin', dey's boun' ter be swindlin' gwine on some'rs, ef not wuss, an' dat what I tol' 'im. He laugh an' say dat's on account er politics an' de erpublican party, an' I make answer dat ef dat de case, dey er bofe rank an' rotten; desso.

"We went on fum one thing ter an'er, twel bimeby I ax 'im what dey is 'twixt 'im an' Marse Tumlin an' Marse Bolivar. Hamp say dey ain't nothin' 'ceppin' dat dey done ax 'im fer ter do sump'n dat ain't in 'cordance wid erpublican pencerpuls, an' he bleeze ter effuse um. Well, suh, dis kinder riled me. I know'd right pine-blank dat Hamp ain't know no mo' 'bout erpublican pencerpuls dan I is, an' I wouldn't a-know'd um ef I'd a met um in de road wid der name painted on um; so I ax 'im what erpublican pencerpuls hender'd 'im fum doin' what Marse Tumlin ax 'im ter do. He sot dar an' hummed an' haw'd, an' squirm'd in his cheer, an' chaw'd on de een' er his segyar. I wait long 'nuff, an' den I ax 'im ag'in. Well, suh, dat's been twenty years ago, an' he ain't never tol' me yit what dem erpublican pencerpuls wuz. I ain't flingin' off on um, suh. I 'speck dey wuz a bairlful er dem erpublican pencerpuls, an' maybe all good uns, but I know'd mighty well dat dey ain't hender dat nigger man fum doin' what Marse Tumlin ax 'im ter do.

"So de nex' chance I git, I up'n ax Marse Tumlin what de matter wuz 'twix' him an' Hamp. He say 'twa'n't nothin' much, 'cep' dat Hamp had done come up here in Atlanta an' sol' hisse'f out to a passel er kyarpit-baggers what ain't no intruss down here but ter git han's on all de money in sight. I say, 'He may 'a' gi' hisse'f 'way, Marse Tumlin, but he sho' ain't sell hisse'f, 'kaze I ain't seen one er de money.' Marse Tumlin 'low, 'Well, any-how, it don't make much diffunce, Minervy Ann. Dem kyarpit-baggers up dar, dey pat 'im on de back an' tell 'im he des ez good ez what dey is. I had de idee, Minervy Ann,' he say, 'dat Hamp wuz lots better dan what dey is, but he ain't; he des 'bout good ez dey is.'

"Marse Tumlin do like he don't wanter talk 'bout it, but dat ain't nigh satchify me. I say, 'Marse Tumlin, what did you want Hamp ter do?' He drum on de arm er de cheer wid his fingers, an' sorter study. Den he say, 'Bein' it's all done an' over wid, I don't min' tellin' you all about it. Does you know who's a-runnin' dis county now?' I had a kinder idee, but I say, 'Who, Marse Tumlin?' He 'low, 'Mahlon Botts an' his br'er Mose; dey er runnin' de county, an' dey er ruinin' it'.

"Den he ax me ef I know de Bottses. Know um! I'd been a-knowin' um sence de year one, an' dey wuz de ve'y drugs an' offscourin's er creation. I ax Marse Tumlin how come dey ter have holt er de county, an' he say dey make out dey wuz good erpublicans, des ter make de niggers vote um in office—so dey kin make money an' plunder de county. Den I ax 'im what he want Hamp ter do. He say all he want Hamp ter do wuz ter he'p 'im git er

188

whatyoumaycallum—yasser, dat's it, a bill; dat's de ve'y word he say—he want Hamp ter he'p 'im git a bill th'oo de Legislatur'; an' den he went on an' tell me a long rigamarolious 'bout what 'twuz, but I'll never tell you in de roun' worl'."

[The proceedings of the Georgia Legislature reported in the Atlanta *New Era*, of November 10, 1869, show that the measure in question was a local bill to revive the polling-places in the militia districts of the county represented by the Hon. Hampton Tumlin, and to regulate elections so that there could be no repeating. This verification of Aunt Minervy Ann's statement was made long ago after she told the story, and purely out of curiosity. The discussions shed an illuminating light over her narrative, but it is impossible to reproduce them here, even in brief.]

"He tol' me dat, suh, an' den he le'nt back in de cheer, an' kinder hummed a chune. An' me—I stood up dar by de fireplace an' studied. Right den an' dar I made up my min' ter one thing, an' I ain't never change it, needer; I made up my min' dat ef we wuz all gwine ter be free an' live in de same neighborhoods—dat ef we wuz gwine ter do dat, whatsomever wuz good fer de white folks bleeze ter be good fer de niggers, an' whatsomever wuz good fer Marse Tumlin an' Miss Vallie wuz des ez good fer me an' Hamp.

"I 'low, 'Marse Tumlin, when you gwine up dar whar Hamp at?' He say, 'Oh, I dunno; I'm tired er de infernal place,' desso. Den he look at me right hard. 'What make you ax?' sez he. I 'low, ' 'Kaze ef youer gwine right soon, I'm gwine wid you.' He laugh an' say, 'What de dickunce you gwine up dar fer?' I 'low, 'I gwine up dar fer ter jine de Legislatur'. I ain't hear tell dat dem what jines hatter be baptize in runnin' water, an' ef dey ain't, den I'll jine long wid Hamp.' Marse Tumlin say, 'You reckin Hamp would be glad fer to see you, Minervy Ann?' I 'low, 'He better had be, ef he know what good fer 'im.' Marse Tumlin say, 'Ef I wuz you, Minervy Ann, I wouldn't go up dar spyin' atter Hamp. He'll like you none de better fer it. De las' time I wuz up dar, Hamp wuz havin' a mighty good time. Ef you know what's good fer you, Minervy Ann, you won't go up dar a-doggin' atter Hamp.'

"Well, suh, right at dat time I had de idee dat Marse Tumlin wuz prankin' an' projeckin'; you know how he runs on; but he wa'n't no mo' prankin' dan what I am right now. (Nummine! I'll git back ter Hamp terreckly.) I laugh an' say, 'I ain't gwine ter dog atter Hamp, Marse Tumlin; I des wanter go up dar an' see how he gittin' on, an' fin' out how folks does when dey sets up dar in de Legislatur'. An' ef you'll put dat ar whatshisname—bill; dat's right, suh; bill wuz de word—ef you'll put dat ar bill in yo' pocket, I'll see what Hamp kin do wid it.' Marse Tumlin 'low, ' 'Tain't no use fer ter see Hamp, Minervy Ann. He done tol' me he can't do nothin'. I lef' de bill wid 'im.'

"I say, 'Marse Tumlin, you dunner nothin' 'tall 'bout Hamp. He must er change mighty sence dey 'fo' yistidy if he erfuse ter do what I tell 'im ter do. Ef dat de case, I'll go up dar an' frail 'im out an' come on back home an' ten' ter my work.'

"Marse Tumlin look at me wid his eyes half shot an' kinder laugh way down in his stomach. He 'low, 'Minervy Ann, I been livin' a long time, an' I been knowin' a heap er folks, but you er de bangin'est nigger I ever is see. Free ez you is, I wouldn't take two thousan' dollars fer you, cash money. I'll git Bolivar, an' we'll go up dar on de mornin' train. Vallie kin stay wid er aunt. 'Tain't gwine ter hurt you ter go; I want you ter see some things fer yo'se'f.'

"Well, suh, sho' 'nuff, de nex' mornin' me an' Marse Tumlin an' Marse Bolivar, we got on de train, an' put out, an' 'twa'n't long 'fo' we wuz pullin' in under de kyar-shed. Dat 'uz de fus' time I ever is been ter dis town, an' de racket an' de turmoil kinder tarrify me, but when I see 't'er folks gwine 'long 'tendin' ter der bizness, 'twa'n't no time 'fo' I tuck heart, 'kaze dar wuz Marse Tumlin an' Marse Bolivar right at me, an' dey wuz bowin' an' shakin' han's wid mos' eve'ybody dat come 'long. Dey wuz two mighty pop'lous white men, suh; you know dat yo'se'f.

"I 'speck de train must 'a' got in 'fo' de Legislatur' sot down, 'kaze when we went th'oo a narrer street an' turn inter de one what dey call Decatur, whar dey carry on all de devilment, I hear Marse Tumlin say dat we wuz 'bout a hour too soon. Right atter dat Marse Bolivar say, 'Tumlin, dat ar nigger man 'cross dar wid de gals is got a mighty familious look ter me; I done been seed 'im somewhar, sho'.' Marse Tumlin say, 'Dat's a fac'; I used ter know dat man some'rs.' Well, suh, I lookt de way dey wuz a-lookin', an' dar wuz Hamp! Yassar! Hamp! Hamp an' two mulatter gals. An' I wish you could 'a' seed um; I des wish you could! Dar wuz Hamp all diked out in his Sunday cloze which I tol' 'im p'intedly not ter w'ar while he workin' in de Legislatur'. He had a segyar in his mouf mos' ez big an' ez long ez a waggin-spoke, an' dar he wuz a-bowin' an' scrapin', an' scrapin' an' gigglin', an' de mulatter gals wuz gigglin' an' snickerin' an' squealin'—I *declaire*, Mr. Tumlin! you oughter be *'shame* er yo'se'f; oh, youer too *b-a-a-a-d!*' "

With powers of mimicry unequalled, Aunt Minervy Ann illustrated the bowing and scraping of Hamp, and reproduced the shrill but not unmusical voices of the mulatto girls.

190

"I tell you de trufe, suh, whiles you could count ten you might 'a' pusht me over wid a straw, an' den, suh, my dander 'gun ter rise. I must 'a' show'd it in my looks, 'kaze Marse Tumlin laid his han' on my shoulder an' say, 'Don't kick up no racket, Minervy Ann; you got Hamp right whar you want 'im. You know what we come fer.' Well, suh, I hatter stan' dar an' swaller right hard a time er two, 'kaze I ain't got no use fer mulatters; to make um, you got ter spile good white blood an' good nigger blood, an' when dey er made dey got in um all dat's mean an' low down on bofe sides, an' ef dey yever is ter be saved, dey'll all hatter be baptize twice han' runnin'—once fer de white dat's in um, and once fer de black. De Bible mayn't sesso, but common-sense'll tell you dat much.

"Well, suh, I stood dar some little time watchin' Hamp's motions, an' he wuz makin' sech a big fool er hisse'f dat I des come mighty nigh laughin' out loud, but all dat time Marse Tumlin had de idee dat I wuz mad, an' when I start to'rds Hamp, wid my pairsol grabbed in de middle, he 'low, 'Min' yo' eye, Minervy Ann.' I walk up, I did, an' punch Hamp in de back wid de pairsol. Ef I'd 'a' hit 'im on de head wid a pile-driver, he couldn't 'a' been mo' dum'founder'd. He look like he wuz gwine th'oo de sidewalk. I say, 'When you git time, I'd like ter have a little chat wid you.' He 'low, 'Why, why'—an' wid dat he stuck de lit een' er his segyar in his mouf. Well, suh, you may b'lieve you done seed splutterin' an' splatterin', but you ain't never seed none like dat. He made a motion, Hamp did, like he wanter make me 'quainted wid de mulatter gals, but I say, 'When you git time fum yo' Legislatur', I got a sesso fer you ter hear.'

"Wid dat, suh, I turn 'roun' an' cross de street an' foller on atter Marse Tumlin an' Marse Bolivar. I ain't mo'n git 'cross, 'fo' here come Hamp. He 'low, 'Why, honey, whyn't you tell me you wuz comin'? When'd you come?' I say, 'Oh, I'm *honey*, is I? Well, maybe you'll fin' a bee in de comb.' He 'low, 'Whyn't you tell me you wuz comin' so I kin meet you at de train?' I say, 'I wanter see what kinder fambly you got in dis town. An' I seed it! I seed it!'

"Well, suh, I 'speck I'd 'a' got mad ag'in, but 'bout dat time we cotch up wid Marse Tumlin an' Marse Bolivar. Marse Tumlin turn 'roun', he did, an' holler out, 'Well, ef here ain't Minervy Ann! What you doin' up here, an' how did you lef' yo' Miss Vallie?' He shuck han's des like he ain't see me befo' in a mont', an' Marse Bolivar done de same. I humor'd um, suh, but I ain't know what dey wuz up ter fer long atterwards. Dey don't want Hamp ter know dat I come 'long wid um. Den dey went on, an' me an' Hamp went ter whar he stay at.

"When I got 'im off by hisse'f, suh, he sot in ter tellin' me how come 'im ter be wid dem ar gals, an' he want me ter know um, an' he know mighty well I'd like um—you know how men–folks does, suh. But dey wa'n't na'er minit in no day dat yever broke when Hamp kin fool me, an' he know'd it. But I let 'im run on. Bimeby, when he get tired er splanifyin', I 'low, 'What dat paper what Marse Tumlin ax you ter put in de Legislatur'?' He say, 'How you know 'bout dat?' I 'low, 'I hear Marse Tumlin tellin' Miss Vallie 'bout it, an' I hear Miss Vallie wonder an' wonder what de matter wid you.'

"I fotch Miss Vallie in, suh, bekaze Hamp think dey ain't nobody in de worl' like Miss Vallie. One time, des 'fo' de big turmoil, when Marse Tumlin hire Hamp fum de Myrick 'state, he fell sick, an' Miss Vallie (she wa'n't nothin' but a school-gal den) she got sorry fer 'im 'kaze he wuz a hired nigger, an' she'd fill a basket wid things fum de white folks' table an' tote um to 'im. Mo' dan dat, she'd set dar whiles he's eatin' an' ax 'bout his folks. Atter dat, suh, de groun' whar Miss Vallie walk wuz better'n any yuther groun' ter Hamp. So when I call her name up, Hamp ain't say nothin' fer long time.

"Den he shuck his head an' say dey ain't no use talkin', he des can't put dat ar paper in de Legislatur'. He say ef he wuz ter, 'twon't do no good, 'kaze all de erpublicans would jump on it, an' den dey'd jump on him ter boot. I 'low, 'Whar you reckon I'll be whiles all dat jumpin' gwine on?' He say, 'You'll be on de outside, an' ef you wuz on de inside, dey'd hike you out.' 'An' who'd do de hikin'?' sez I. 'De surgeon er de armies,' sez he. 'White er black?' sez I. 'Yaller,' sez Hamp. I 'low, 'Good 'nuff; we'll see which un'll be hiked.' An' I told Hamp right den an' dar, dat ef he erfuse ter put dat paper in, I'll do it myse'f.

"Well, suh, whiles we settin' dar talkin', dey come a-rappin' at de do' an' in walk a big bushy-head mulatter, an' I ain't tellin' you no lie, he de mos' venomous-lookin' creetur you ever laid yo' eyes on. His ha'r wuz all spread out like a scourin' mop, an' he had a grin on 'im ez big ez dat gate dar. Hamp call 'im Arion Alperiar Ridley."

At this point I was compelled to come to the rescue of Aunt Minervy Ann's memory. The statesman's real name was Aaron Alpeora Bradley, and he was one of the most corrupt creatures of that corrupt era. He had a superficial education that only added to the density of his ignorance, but it gave him considerable influence with the negro members of the Legislature. Aunt Minervy Ann accepted the correction with alacrity.

"I fergot his name, suh, but I ain't never fergit him. He so mean-lookin' he make de col' chills run over me. He wuz a low-country mulatter, an' you know how dey talk. Eve'y time he look at me, he'd bow, an' de mo' he bowed de mo' I 'spized 'im. He call Hamp 'Mistooah Tummalin,' an' eve'y time he say sump'n' he'd gi' one er dem venomous grins. I declar' ter gracious, suh, I oughtn't ter talk 'bout dat man dis way, but de way he look wuz scan'lous. I done fergive 'im for dat long time 'go on 'count er what he done; but when I hear white folks 'busin' 'im in dat day an' time I know'd dey had mighty good groun', bekaze dey ain't no human kin look like dat man an' not be mean at bottom.

"Well, suh, Hamp, he up'n tol' dis yer Alpory er Alpiry (whatsomever his name mought be) what I come ter town fer, an' Alpory, he say, 'Mistooah Tummalin, you kyarn't do it. Hit would-er ruin you in de-er party, suh—er ruin you.' I kinder fired up at dat. I 'low, 'How come he can't do it? Ain't he free?' Ol' Alpory, he grin an' he talk, he talk an' he grin, but he ain't budge me. At de offstart I say ef Hamp don't put dat paper in de Legislatur', I'll put it in myse'f, an' at de windin' up I still say dat ef he don't put Marse Tumlin's paper in de Legislatur', den I'll be de one ter do it. Ol' Alpory say, 'You-er is got no marster, ma'am.' Den I snapt 'im up an' cut 'im off short; I say, 'I got one ef I want one. Ain't I free?' Den he went on wid a whole passel er stuff dat I can't make head er tail un, ner him needer, fer dat metter, twel bimeby I say, 'Oh, hush up an' go on whar you gwine.'

"Hamp look so broke up at dis dat I wuz kinder sorry I say it, but dat's de only way ter deal wid dem kind er folks, suh. Ol' Alpory wuz des famishin', suh, fer some un ter b'lieve he's a big Ike; dat 'uz all de matter wid 'im an' I know'd it. So he quit his jawin' when I snapped 'im up, an' he sot dar some time lookin' like a cow does when her cud don't rise. Bimeby he ax Hamp fer ter let 'im see de paper what I want 'im ter put in de Legislatur'. He tuck it, he did, an' look at it sideways an' upside down, an' eve'ywhichaway. Ez ef dat wa'n't 'nuff, he took off his goggles an' wiped um an' put um on ag'in, an' read de paper all over ag'in, noddin' his head an' movin' his mouf, an' grinnin'.

"Atter he got th'oo, he fol' de paper up an' han' it back ter Hamp. He say he can't see no harm in it ter save his life, an' he 'low dat ef Hamp'll put it in at one een' er de Legislatur', he'll put in it at de 't'er een'. Dey call one part a house, but nobody ain't never tell me why dey call a wranglin' gang er men a house. Dey des might ez well call um a hoss an' buggy; eve'y bit an' grain. Well, suh, de house wuz de part what Hamp b'longs ter, an' de 't'er part wuz whar ol' Alpory b'long'd at, an' by de time dey wuz ready fer set in dar dey had e'en 'bout 'greed fer put de paper in at bofe een's.

193

"I went 'long wid Hamp, suh, an' he show'd me de way ter de gall'ry, an' I sot up dar an' look down on um, an' wonder why all un um, white an' black, wa'n't at home yearnin' der livin' 'stidder bein' in dat place a-wranglin' an' callin' names, an' howlin' an' wavin' der arms an' han's. Dey wuz a big fat white man settin' up in de pulpit, an' he kep' on a-maulin' it wid a mallet. I dunner what his name wuz, but I hear one big buck nigger call 'im Mr. Cheer. Marse Tumlin tol' me atterwards dat de man wuz de speaker, but all de res' done lots mo' speakin' dan what he did; all un um 'cep' Hamp.

"Yasser; all un um 'cep' Hamp, an' he sot dar so still dat 'twa'n't long 'fo' I 'gun ter git shame un him. He sot dar an' fumble wid some papers, an' helt his head down, an' look like he skeer'd. I watch 'im, suh, twel I got so res'less in de min' I can't set still. Bimeby I got up an' went down ter de front do'; I wuz gwine ter make my way in dar whar Hamp wuz at, an' kinder fetch 'im out'n his dreams, ef so be he wuz dreamin'. An' I'd a gone in, but a nigger man at de do' barred de way. He say, 'Who you want ter see?' I 'low, 'I wanter see Hamp Tumlin, dat's who.' He say, 'Does you mean de Honnerbul Hampton Tumlin?' I 'low, 'Yes, I does ef you wanter put it dat away. *Go in dar an' tell 'im dat de Honnerbul Minervy Ann Perdue is out here waitin' fer 'im, an' he better come quick ef he know what good fer 'im.'*

"Wid dat, suh, I hear somebody laugh, an' look up an' dar wuz Marse Tumlin standin' not fur fum de do' talkin' wid an'er white man. He 'low, 'Scott, dis is Minervy Ann. She got mo' sense an' grit dan half de white folks you meet.' Well, suh, de man come up, he did, an' shuck han's an' say he mighty glad ter see me. I never is ter fergit his name on 'count er what happen atterwards. 'Bout dat time Hamp come out an' Marse Tumlin an' de 't'er man draw'd off up de hall.

"I say, 'Hamp, why in de name er goodness ain't you 'ten' ter yo' bizness? What you waitin' fer? Is you skeer'd?' He vow an' declair' dat he des waitin' a chance fer ter put de paper in. I tol' 'im dat de way ter git a chance wuz ter make one, an' wid dat he went on in, an' I went back in de gall'ry. Well, suh, 'twa'n't long 'fo' Hamp put in de paper. A man at de foot er de pulpit read it off, an' den a white man settin' not fur fum Hamp jump up an' say he want sump'n done wid it, I dunner what. Hamp say sump'n back at 'im, an' den de white man say he sorry fer ter see de honnerbul gemman gwine back on de erpublican party. Den Mose Bently—I know'd Mose mighty well—he riz an' say ef de erpublican party is got ter be led 'roun' by men like de one what des tuck his seat, it's high time fer honest folks ter turn der backs on it.

"Well, suh, when Mose say dat, I clap my han's, I did, an' holla 'Good!

194

good! now you got it!' I couldn't he'p it fer ter save my life. De man in de pulpit maul de planks wid de mallet like he tryin' ter split um, an' he 'low dat ef folks in de gall'ry don't keep still, he'll have um cle'r'd out. I holla back at 'im, 'You better some er dat gang down dar cle'r'd out!' Quick ez a flash, suh, dat ar Mr. Scott what been talkin' wid Marse Tumlin jump up an' 'low, 'I secon's de motion!' De man in de pulpit say, 'What motion does de gemman fum Floyd secon'?' Den Mr. Scott fling his head back an' 'low, 'De Honnerbul Minervy Ann Perdue done move dat de flo' be cle'r'd 'stidder de gall'ry. I secon's de motion.'

"Den fum dat he went on an' 'buze de erpublican party, speshually dat ar man what had de 'spute wid Hamp. Mr. Scott say dey got so little sense dat dey go ag'in a paper put in by one er der own party. He say he ain't keer nothin' 'tall 'bout de paper hisse'f, but he des wanter show um up fer what dey wuz.

"He totch'd um, suh, ez you may say, on de raw, an' when he git th'oo he say, 'Now, I hope de cheer will deal wid de motion of de Honnerbul Minervy Ann Perdue.' Mr. Scott say, 'She settin' up dar in de gall'ry an' she got des ez much right ter set on dis flo' ez nineteen out er twenty er dem settin' here.' De man in de pulpit look at me right hard, an' den he 'gun ter laugh. I say, 'You nee'n ter worry yo'se'f 'bout me. You better 'ten' ter dem ar half-drunk niggers an' po' white trash down dar. I wouldn't set wid 'em ef I never did fin' a place fer ter set at.'

"Wid dat, suh, I pickt up my pairsol an' make my way out, but ez I went I hear um whoopin' an' hollerin'."

"Well, they didn't pass the bill, did they?" I asked.

"What? dat paper er Marse Tumlin's? Bless yo' soul, suh, dey run'd over one an'er tryin' ter pass it. Mr. Scott fit it like he fightin' fire, an' make out he wuz terribly ag'in it, but dat des make um wuss. Hamp say dat inginer'lly dem ar laws has ter wait an' hang fire; but dey tuck up dat un, an' shove it th'oo. Dey tuck mo' time in de 't'er een' er de Legislatur', whar ol' Alpory wuz at, but it went th'oo when it start. I hope dey don't have no sech gwines-on now, suh. Ef dey does de whole county can't drag Paul Conant in dar. I'll jine um myse'f, 'fo' I'll let 'im git in dat kind er crowd."

How Aunt Minervy Ann Frailed
the Gossett Boys

DURING THE PROGRESS of the fair, there was some discussion of financial matters in Major Perdue's family. As I remember, someone had given Paul Conant a check which was thrown out by the Atlanta bank on which it was drawn. The sum was not a considerable one, but it was sufficiently large to attract Aunt Minervy Ann's attention.

"I 'speck dey got mo' banks in Atlanty dan what we-all got down here," she remarked, the next time I had an opportunity to talk with her. She laughed so heartily as she made the remark that I regarded her with some astonishment. "You may look, suh, but I ain't crazy. When I hear anybody say 'bank' it allers puts me in min' er de time when me an' Marse Tumlin frailed out de Gossett boys."

"Frailed out the Gossett boys?" I exclaimed.

"Yasser, frailed is de word."

"But what has that to do with a bank?" I inquired.

"Hit got all ter do wid it, suh," she replied. We were in the sitting-room, and Aunt Minervy Ann sank down on a footstool and rested one arm on the lounge. "Right atter freedom dey wa'n't nothin' like no bank down whar we live at; you know dat yo'se'f, suh. Folks say dat banks kin run widout money, but 'fo' you start um, dey got ter have money, er sump'n dat look like money. An' atter freedom dey wa'n't no money 'roun' here 'cep' dat kin' what nobody ain't hankerin' atter.

"But bimeby it 'gun ter dribble in fum some'rs; fus' dem ar little shin-plasters, an' den de bigger money come 'long. It kep' on dribblin' in an' dribblin' in twel atter while you could git a dollar here an' dar by workin' yo' han's off, er sprainin' yo' gizzard to git it. Bimeby de news got norated 'roun' dat ol' Joshaway Gossett gwine ter start a bank. Yasser! ol' Joshaway

196

Gossett. Dat make folks open der eyes an 'shake der head. I 'member de time, suh, when ol' Joshaway wuz runnin' a blacksmith shop out in de country. Den he sot in ter make waggins. Atter dat, he come ter be overseer fer Marse Bolivar Blasengame, but all de time he wuz overseein' he wuz runnin' de blacksmith shop an' de waggin fact'ry.

"When de war come on, suh, dey say dat ol' Joshaway tuck all de money what he been savin' an' change it inter gol'; de natchul stuff. An' he had a pile un it. He kep' dat up all endurin' er de turmoil, and by de time freedom come out he had mo' er de natchul stuff dan what Cyarter had oats. Dat what folks say, suh, an' when eve'ybody talk one way you may know dey ain't fur fum de trufe. Anyhow, de word went 'roun' dat ol' Joshaway gwine ter start a bank. Folks wa'n't 'stonished 'kaze he had money, but bekaze he gwine ter start a bank, an' he not much mo' dan knowin' B fum bullfoot. Some snicker, some laugh, an' some make fun er ol' Joshaway, but Marse Tumlin say dat ef he know how ter shave a note, he bleeze ter know how ter run a bank. I ain't never see nobody shave a note, suh, but dat 'zackly what Marse Tumlin say.

"But ol' Joshaway, he ain't a-keerin' what folks say. He start de bank, an' he kep' it up twel de time I'm gwine tell you 'bout. He bought 'im a big strong safe, an' he had it walled up in de back er de bank, an' dar 'twuz. Don't make no diffunce what folks say 'bout ol' Joshaway, dey can't say he ain't honest. He gwine ter have what's his'n, an' he want yuther folks fer ter have what's der'n. When dat de case, 'tain't no trouble ter git folks ter trus' you. Dey put der money in ol' Joshaway's bank, whar he kin take keer un it, bekaze dey know'd he wa'n't gwine ter run off wid it.

"Well, suh, de bank wuz runnin' 'long des like 'twuz on skids, an' de skids greased. Ol' Joshaway ain't move ter town, but he hired 'im a clerk, an' de clerk stayed in de bank night an' day, an' I hear folks say de town wuz better'n bigger on 'count er ol' Joshaway's bank. I dunner how dey make dat out, 'kaze de bank wa'n't much bigger dan de kitchen back dar. Anyhow, dar she wuz, and dar she stayed fer a time an' a time.

"But one day Marse Tumlin Perdue tuck de notion dat he got ter borry some money. He seed yuther folks gwine in dar an' borryin' fum ol' Joshaway, an' he know he got des much bizness fer ter borry ez what dey is. Mo' dan dat, when he had plenty er money an' niggers, he done ol' Joshaway many a good turn. I know'd dat myse'f, suh, an' 'tain't no hearsay; I done seed it wid my own eyes. On de day I'm talkin' 'bout, Miss Vallie sont me up town fer ter ax Marse Tumlin kin he spar' two dollars—dat wuz befo' Miss

Vallie wuz married; 'bout a mont' befo', an' she wuz makin' up her weddin' fixin's.

" 'Twa'n't no trouble ter fin' Marse Tumlin. He wuz settin' in de shade wid a passel er men. He seed me, he did, an' he come ter meet me. When I tell 'im what Miss Vallie want, he kinder scratch his head an' look sollum. He studied a minit, an' den he tell me ter come go 'long wid 'im. He cut 'cross de squar' an' went right ter ol' Joshaway's bank, me a-follerin' right at his heels. He went in, he did, an' 'low, 'Hello, Joshaway!' Ol' Joshaway, he say, 'Howdy, Maje?' He wuz settin' in dar behime a counter what had wire palin's on top un it, an' he look fer all de worl' like some ongodly creetur what dey put in a cage for ter keep 'im fum doin' devilment.

"Marse Tumlin 'low, 'Joshaway, I want ter borry a hundred dollars for a mont' er so.' Ol' Joshaway kinder change his cud er terbacker fum one side ter de yuther, an' cle'r up his th'oat. He say, 'Maje, right dis minit, I ain't got fifty dollars in de bank.' Nigger ez I is, I know'd dat wuz a lie, an' I couldn't help fum gruntin' ef I wuz gwine to be kilt fer it. At dat ol' Joshaway look up. Marse Tumlin stood dar drummin' on de counter. Bimeby ol' Joshaway say, 'Spoze'n I had it, Maje, who you gwine git fer yo skyority?' des so. Marse Tumlin 'low, 'Fer my what?' 'Fer yo' skyority,' sez ol' Joshaway. I up an' say, 'Des lissen at dat!' Marse Tumlin 'low, 'Who went yo' skyority when I use ter loan you money?' 'Times is done change, Maje,' sez ol' Joshaway. Marse Tumlin flirted de little gate open, an' went 'roun' in dar so quick it made my head swim. He say, '*I* ain't change!' an' wid dat, he took ol' Joshaway by de coat-collar an' cuff'd 'im 'roun' considerbul. He ain't hurt ol' Joshaway much, but he call 'im some names dat white folks don't fling at one an'er widout dey's gwine ter be blood-lettin' in de neighbor-hoods.

"Den Marse Tumlin come out fum behime de counter, an' stood in de do' an' look up town. By dat time I wuz done out on de sidewalk, 'kaze I don't want no pistol-hole in my hide. When it come ter fa'r fis' an' skull, er a knock-down an' drag-out scuffle, I'm wid you; I'm right dar; but deze yer guns an' pistols what flash an' bang an' put out yo' lights—an' maybe yo' liver—when it come ter dem, I lots druther be on t'er side de fence. Well, suh, I fully 'spected ol' Joshaway to walk out atter Marse Tumlin wid de double-bairl gun what I seed behime de counter; an' Marse Tumlin 'spected it, too, 'kaze he walk up an' down befo' de bank, an' eve'y once in a while he'd jerk his wescut down in front like he tryin' ter t'ar de bindin' off. Bimeby I see Marse Bolivar Blasengame git up fum whar he settin' at, an' here he come, swingin' his gol'-head cane, an' sa'nt'in' 'long like he gwine on a promenade.

"I know'd by dat, suh, dat Marse Bolivar been watchin' Marse Tumlin's motions, an' he seed dat trouble er some kind wuz on han'. He walk up, he did, an' atter he cut his eye at Marse Tumlin, he turn ter me an' laugh ter hisse'f—he had de purtiest front teef you mos' ever is see, suh–an' he 'low, 'Well, dang my buttons, ef here ain't ol' Minervy Ann, de warhoss fum Wauhoo! Wharsomever dey's trouble, dar's de ol' warhoss fum Wauhoo.' Wid dat, he lock arms wid Marse Tumlin, an' dey march off down de street, me a-follerin'. You ain't kin fin' two men like dem anywhar an' eve'ywhar. Dey wa'n't no blood-kin—dey married sisters—but dey wuz lot closer dan br'ers. Hit one an' you'd hurt de yuther, an' den ef you wa'n't ready ter git in a scuffle wid two wil'-cats, you better leave town twel dey cool off.

"Well, suh, dey ain't took many steps 'fo' dey wuz laughin' an' jokin' des like two boys. Ez we went up de street Marse Tumlin drapt in a sto' er two an' tol' um dat ol' Joshaway Gossett vow'd dat he ain't got fifty cash dollars in de bank. Dish yer money news is de kin' what spreads, an' don't you fergit it. It spread dat day des like powder ketchin' fire an' 'twa'n't no time 'fo' you could see folks runnin' 'cross de squar' des like dey er rabbit-huntin', an' by dinner-time dey wa'n't no bank dar no mo' dan a rabbit. Folks say dat ol' Joshaway try mighty hard ter 'splain matters, but dem what had der money in dar say dey'd take de spondulix fus' an' listen ter de 'splainin' atterwards. 'Long to'rds de noon-hour ol' Joshaway hatter fling up his han's. All de ready money done gone, an' folks at de do' hollin' fer dat what dey put in dar. I dunner how he ever got 'way fum dar, 'kaze dey wuz men in dat crowd ripe ter kill 'im; but he sneaked out an' went home, an' lef' some un else fer ter win' up de shebang.

"De bank wuz des ez good ez any bank, an' folks got back all dey put in dar des ez soon ez dey'd let ol' Joshaway show his head in town; but he drapt dat kinder bizness an' went back ter farmin' an' note-shavin'. An' all bekaze he want skyority fer Marse Tumlin, which his word des ez good ez his bon'. He mought not er had de money when de clock struck de minit, but what diffunce do dat make when you know a man's des ez good ez gol'? Huh! no wonder dey broke ol' Joshaway down!"

Aunt Minervy Ann's indignation was a fine thing to behold. Her scorn of the man who wanted Major Perdue to put up security for his note was as keen and as bitter as it had been the day the episode occurred. She paused at this point as if her narrative had come to an end. Therefore, I put in a suggestion.

"Was this what you call frailing out the Gossett boys?"

"No, suh," she protested, with a laugh; "all deze yer gwines-on 'bout dat ar bank wuz des de 'casion un it. You bleeze ter know dem Gossett boys, suh. Dey had sorter cool down by de time you come here, but dey wuz still ripe fer any devilment dat come 'long. Dar wuz Rube an' Sam an' John Henry, an' a'er one un um wuz big ez a hoss. Dey use ter come ter town eve'y Chuseday an' Sat'day, an' by dinner-time dey'd be a-whoopin' an' hollin' in de streets, an' a-struttin' 'roun' mashin' folks' hats down on der eyes. Not all de folks, but some un um. An' all fer fun; dat what dey say.

"Tooby sho', dey had a spite ag'in Marse Tumlin and Marse Bolivar atter de bank busted. Dey show'd it by gwine des so fur; dey'd fling out der hints; but dey kep' on de safe side, 'kaze Marse Tumlin wa'n't de man fer ter go 'roun' huntin' a fuss, ner needer wuz Marse Bolivar; but fetch a fuss an' lay it in der laps, ez you may say, an' dey'd play wid it an' dandle it, an' keep it fum ketchin' col.' Dey sho' would, suh. When dem Gossett boys'd come ter town, Marse Tumlin an' Marse Bolivar would des set' 'roun' watchin' um, des waitin' twel dey cross de dead-line. But it seem like dey know des how fur ter go, an' right whar ter stop.

"Well, suh, it went on dis away fer I dunner how long, but bimeby, one day, our ol' cow got out, an' 'stidder hangin' 'roun' an' eatin' de grass in de streets like any yuther cow would 'a' done, she made a straight shoot fer de plantation whar she come fum.

"Miss Vallie tol' Marse Tumlin 'bout it, an' he say he gwine atter her. Den some er de niggers in de nex' lot tol' me dat de cow wuz out an' gone, an' I put out atter her, too, not knowin' dat Marse Tumlin wuz gwine. He went de front street an' I went de back way. Ef de town wuz big ez de streets is long, we'd have a mighty city down here; you know dat yo'se'f, suh. De place whar de back street jines in wid de big road is mighty nigh a mile fum de tempunce hall, an' when I got dar, dar wuz Marse Tumlin polin' 'long. I holler an' ax 'im whar he gwine. He say he gwine atter a glass er milk. Den he ax me whar I gwine. I say I'm gwine atter dat ol' frame dat nigh-sighted folks call a cow. He 'low dat he'd be mighty thankful ef de nex' time I tuck a notion fer ter turn de cow out I'd tell 'im befo'han' so he kin run 'roun' an' head 'er off an' drive 'er back. He wuz constant a-runnin' on dat away. He'd crack his joke, suh, ef he dyin'.

"We went trudgin' 'long twel we come 'pon de big hill dat leads down ter de town branch. You know de place, suh. De hill mighty steep, an' on bofe sides er de road der's a hedge er Cherrykee roses; some folks calls um Chickasaw; but Chicky er Cherry, dar dey wuz, growin' so thick a rabbit can't hardly squeeze thoo um. On one side dey wuz growin' right on de aidge uv a big gully, an' at one place de groun' wuz kinder caved in, an' de briar vines wuz swayin' over it.

"Well, suh, des ez we got on de hill-top, I hear a buggy rattlin' an' den I hear laughin' an' cussin'. I lookt 'roun', I did, an' dar wuz de Gossett boys, two in de buggy an' one ridin' hossback; an' all un um full er dram. I could tell dat by de way dey wuz gwine on. You could hear um a mile, cussin' one an'er fer eve'ything dey kin think un an' den laughin' 'bout it. Sump'n tol' me dey wuz gwine ter be a rumpus, bekaze three ter one wuz too good a chance for de Gossett boys ter let go by. I dunner what make me do it, but when we got down de hill a little piece, I stoop down, I did, an' got me a good size rock.

"Terreckly here dey come. Dey kinder quiet down when dey see me an' Marse Tumlin. Dey driv up, dey did, an' driv on by, an' dis make me b'lieve dat dey wuz gwine on 'bout der bizness an' let we-all go on 'bout our'n, but dat idee wa'n't in der head. Dey driv by, dey did, an' den dey pulled up. We walkt on, an' Marse Tumlin lookt at um mighty hard. Rube, he was drivin', an' ez we come up even wid um, he 'low, 'Major Perdue, I hear tell dat you slap my pa's face not so mighty long ago.' Marse Tumlin say, 'I did, an' my han' ain't clean yit.' He helt it out so dey kin see fer deyse'f. 'I b'lieve,' sez Rube, 'I'll take a closer look at it.' Wid dat he lipt out er de buggy, an' by de time he hit de groun', Marse Tumlin had knockt 'im a-windin' wid his curly-hick'ry walkin'-cane. By dat time, John Henry had jumpt out'n de buggy, an' he went at Marse Tumlin wid a dirk-knife. He kep' de cane off'n his head by dodgin', but Marse Tumlin hit a back lick an' knock de knife out'n his han' an' den dey clincht. Den Rube got up, an' start to'rds um on de run.

"Well, suh, I wuz skeer'd an' mad bofe. I seed sump'n had ter be done, an' dat mighty quick; so I tuck atter Rube, cotch 'm by de ellybows, shoved 'im ahead faster dan he wuz gwine, an' steer'd 'im right to'rds de caved-in place in de brier-bushes. He tried mighty hard ter stop, but he wuz gwine down hill, an' I had de Ol' Boy in me. I got 'im close ter de place, suh, an' den I gi' 'm a shove, an' inter de briers he went, head over heels. All dis time I had de rock in my han'. By de time I turn 'roun' I see Sam a-comin'. When de rumpus start up, his hoss shied an' made a break down de hill wid 'im, but he slew'd 'im 'roun', an' jumped off, an' here he come back, his face red, his hat off, an' ol' Nick hisse'f lookin' out'n his eyes. I know'd mighty well I can't steer him inter no brier-bush, an' so when he run by me I let 'im have de rock in de burr er de year. 'Twa'n't no light lick, suh; I wuz plum venomous by den; an' he went down des like a beef does when you knock 'im in de head wid a ax."

Aunt Minervy Ann, all unconscious of her attitudes and gestures, had risen from the floor, and now stood in the middle of the room, tall, towering, and defiant.

"Den I run ter whar Marse Tumlin an' John Henry Gossett had been scufflin'; but by de time I got dar John Henry squalled out dat he had 'nuff; an' he wa'n't tellin' no lie, suh, fer Marse Tumlin had ketched his cane up short, an' he used it on dat man's face des like you see folks do wid ice-picks. He like to 'a' ruint 'im. But when he holla dat he got 'nuff, Marse Tumlin let 'im up. He let 'im up, he did, an' sorter step back. By dat time Rube wuz a-climbin' out'n de briers, an' Sam wuz makin' motions like he comin'-to. Marse Tumlin say, 'Lemme tell you cowardly rascals one thing. De nex' time a'er one un you bat his eye at me, I'm gwine ter put a hole right spang th'oo you. Ef you don't b'lieve it, you kin start ter battin' um right now.' Wid dat, he draw'd out his ervolver an' kinder played wid it. Rube say, 'We'll drap it, Major; we des had a little too much licker. But I'll not drap it wid dat nigger dar. I'll pay her fer dis day's work, an' I'll pay 'er well.'

"Well, suh, de way he say it set me on fire. I stept out in de middle er de road, an' 'low, *Blast yo' rotten heart, ef you'll des walk out here I'll whip you in a fa'r fight. Fight me wid yo' naked han's an' I'll eat you up, ef I hatter pizen myse'f ter do it.*'"

Once more Aunt Minervy Ann brought the whole scene mysteriously before me. Her eyes gleamed ferociously, her body swayed, and her out-stretched arm trembled with the emotion she had resummoned from the past. We were on the spot. The red hill-side, the hedges of Cherokee roses, Major Perdue grim and erect, Sam Gossett struggling to his feet, John Henry wiping his beaten face, Rube astounded at the unwonted violence of a negro woman, the buggy swerved to one side by the horse searching for grass—all these things came into view and slowly faded away. Aunt Minervy Ann, suddenly recollecting herself, laughed sheepishly.

"I ain't tellin' you no lie, suh, dat ar Rube Gossett stood dar like de little boy dat de calf run over. He mought er had sump'n ugly ter say, but Marse Tumlin put in. He 'low, 'Don't you fool yo'se'f 'bout dis nigger 'oman.

When you hit her you hits me. Befo' you put yo' han' on 'er you come an' spit in my face. You'll fin' dat lots de cheapes' way er gittin' de dose what I got fer dem what hurts Minervy Ann.'

"Well, suh, dis make me feel so funny dat a little mo' an' I'd a got ter whimperin', but I happen ter look 'roun', an' dar wuz our ol' cow lookin' at me over a low place in de briers. She done got in de fiel' by a gap back up de road, an' dar she wuz a-lookin' at us like she sorry. Wid me, suh, de diffunce 'twixt laughin' an' cryin' ain't thicker dan a fly's wing, an' when I see dat ol' cow lookin' like she ready ter cry, I wuz bleeze to laugh. Marse Tumlin look at me right hard, but I say, 'Marse Tumlin, ol' June lis'nin' at us,' an' den *he* laughed.

"Dem Gossett boys brush deyse'f off good ez dey kin an' den dey put out fer home. Soon ez dey git out er sight, Marse Tumlin started in ter projickin'. He walk all 'roun' me a time er two, an' den he blow out his breff like folks does when dey er kinder tired. He look at me, an' say, *'Well, I be dam!'* 'Dat would 'a' been de word,' sez I, 'ef ol' Minervy Ann hadn't 'a' been here dis day an' hour.' He shuck his head slow. 'You hit de mark dat time,' sez he; 'ef you hadn't 'a' been here, Minervy Ann, dem boys would sholy 'a' smasht me; but ef I hadn't 'a' been here, I reely b'lieve you'd 'a' frailed out de whole gang. You had two whipt, Minervy Ann, an' you wuz hankerin' fer de yuther one. I'll hatter sw'ar ter de facts 'fo' anybody'll b'lieve um.' I 'low, ' 'Tain't no use ter tell nobody, Marse Tumlin. Folks think I'm bad 'nuff now.'

"But, *shoo!* Marse Tumlin would 'a' mighty nigh died ef he couldn't tell 'bout dat day's work. I ain't min' dat so much, but it got so dat when de Gossetts come ter town an' start ter prankin', de town boys 'ud call um by name, an' holla an' say 'You better watch out dar! Minervy Ann Perdue comin' 'roun' de cornder!' Dat wuz so errytatin', suh, dat it kyo'd um. Dey drapt der dram-drinkin' an' spreein', an' now dey er high in Horeb Church. Dey don't like me, suh, an' no wonder; but ef dey kin git ter hev'm widout likin' me, I'd be glad ter see um go.

"Well, suh, I call de ol' cow, an' she foller long on 'er side er de briers, an' when she got whar de gap wuz, she curl 'er tail over 'er back an' put out fer home, des for all de worl' like she glad 'kaze me an' Marse Tumlin frailed out de Gossett boys.

"I say, 'Marse Tumlin, I'm a member er de church an' I don't b'lieve in fightin', but ef we hadn't er fit wid dem Gossetts we'd 'a' never foun' dat ol' cow in de roun' worl'.' He 'low, 'An' ef we hadn't er fit wid um, Minervy

Ann, I'd 'a' never know'd who ter take wid me fer ter keep de boogerman fum gittin' me.'

"Dat night, suh, Marse Bolivar Blasengame come rappin' at my do'. Hamp wuz done gone ter bed, an' I wuz fixin' ter go. Marse Bolivar come in, he did, an' shuck han's wid me like he ain't seed me sence de big war. Den he sot down over ag'in' me an' look at me, an' make me tell 'im all 'bout de rumpus. Well, suh, he got ter laughin', an' he laughed twel he can't hardly set in de cheer. He say, 'Minervy Ann, ef dem folks say a word ter hurt yo' feelin's, don't tell Tumlin. Des come a-runnin' ter me. He done had his han's on um, an' now I want ter git mine on um.'

"Dat 'uz de way wid Marse Bolivar. He wa'n't no great han' ter git in a row, but he wuz mighty hard ter git out'n one when he got in. When he start out he stop on de step an' say, 'Minervy Ann, I didn't know you wuz sech a rank fighter.' 'I'm a Perdue,' sez I. Wid dat he got ter laughin', an' fur ez I kin hear 'im he wuz still a-laughin.' He b'longed ter a mighty fine fambly, suh; you know dat yo'se'f."

Major Perdue's Bargain

WHEN NEXT I had an opportunity to talk with Aunt Minervy Ann, she indulged in a hearty laugh before saying a word, and it was some time before she found her voice.

"What is so funny to-day?" I inquired.

"Me, suh—nothin' tall 'bout me, an' 'tain't only ter-day, nudder. Hit's eve'y day sence I been big 'nuff fer to see myse'f in de spring branch. I laughed den, an' I laugh now eve'y time I see myse'f in my min'—ef I' got any min'. I wuz talkin' ter Hamp las' night an' tellin' 'im how I start in ter tell you sump'n 'bout Marse Paul Conant' shoulder, an' den eend up by tellin' you eve'ything else I know but dat.

"Hamp 'low, he did, 'Dat ain't nothin', bekaze when I ax you ter marry me, you start in an' tell me 'bout a nigger gal' 'cross dar in Jasper County which she make promise fer ter marry a man an' she crossed her heart; an' den when de time come she stood up an' marry 'im an' fin' out 'tain't de same man, but somebody what she ain't never see' befo'.'

"I speck' dat's so, suh, bekaze dey wuz sump'n like dat happen in Jasper County. You know de Waters fambly—dey kep' race-hosses. Well, suh, 'twuz right on der plantation. Warren Waters tol' me 'bout dat hisse'f. He wuz de hoss-trainer, an' he 'uz right dar on de groun'. When de gal done married, she look up an' holler, 'You ain't my husban', bekaze I ain't make no promise fer ter marry you.' De man he laugh, an' say, 'Don't need no promise atter you done married.'

"Well, suh, dey say dat gal wuz skeer'd—skeer'd fer true. She sot an' look in de fire. De man sot an' look at 'er. She try ter slip out de do', an' he slipped wid 'er. She walked to'rds de big house, an' he walkt wid 'er. She come back, an' he come wid 'er. She run an' he run wid 'er. She cry an' he laugh at 'er. She dunner what to do. Bimeby she tuck a notion dat de man mought be de

205

Ol' Boy hisse'f, an' she drapped down on her knees an' 'gun ter pray. Dis make de man restless; look like he frettin'. Den he 'gun ter shake like he havin' chill. Den he slip down out'n de cheer. Den he got on his all-fours. Den his cloze drapped off, an' bless gracious! dar he wuz, a great big black shaggy dog wid a short chain roun' his neck. Some un um flung a chunk of fire at 'im, an' he run out howlin'.

"Dat wuz de last dey seed un 'im, suh. Dey flung his cloze in de fire, an' dey make a blaze dat come plum out'n de top er de chimbley stack. Dat what make me tell Hamp 'bout it, suh. He ax me fer ter marry 'im, an' I wan't so mighty sho' dat he wan't de Ol' Boy."

"Well, that is queer, if true," said I, "but how about Mr. Conant's crippled shoulder?"

"Oh, it's de trufe, suh. Warren Waters tol' me dat out'n his own mouf, an' he wuz right dar. I dunno but what de gal wuz some er his kinnery. I don't min' tellin' you dat 'bout Marse Paul, suh, but you mustn't let on 'bout it, bekaze Marse Tumlin an' Miss Vallie des' ez tetchous 'bout dat ez dey kin be. I'd never git der fergivunce ef dey know'd I was settin' down here tellin' 'bout dat.

"You know how 'twuz in dem days. De folks what wuz de richest wuz de wussest off when de army come home from battlin'. I done tol' you 'bout Marse Tumlin. He ain't had nothin' in de roun' worl' but a whole passel er lan', an' me an' Miss Vallie. I don't count Hamp, bekaze Hamp 'fuse ter b'lieve he's free twel he ramble 'roun' an' fin' out de patterollers ain't gwine ter take 'im up. Dat how come I had ter sell ginger-cakes an' chicken-pies dat time. De money I made at dat ain't last long, bekaze Marse Tumlin he been use' ter rich vittles, an' he went right down-town an' got a bottle er chow-chow, an' some olives, an' some sardines, an' some cheese, an' you know yo'se'f, suh, dat money ain't gwine ter las' when you buy dat kin' er doin's.

"Well, suh, we done mighty well whiles de money helt out, but 'tain't court-week all de time, an' when dat de case, money got ter come fum some'rs else 'sides sellin' cakes an' pies. Bimeby, Hamp he got work at de liberty stable, whar dey hire out hosses an' board um. I call it a hoss tavern, suh, but Hamp, he 'low its a liberty stable. Anyhow, he got work dar, an' dat sorter he'p out. Sometimes he'd growl bekaze I tuck his money fer ter he'p out my white folks, but when he got right mad I'd gi' Miss Vallie de wink, an' she'd say: 'Hampton, how'd you like ter have a little dram ter-night? You look like youer tired.' I could a-hugged 'er fer de way she done it, she 'uz dat cute. An' den Hamp, he'd grin an' 'low, 'I ain't honin' fer it, Miss Vallie, but 'twon't do me no harm, an' it may do me good.'

"An' den, suh, he'd set down, an' atter he got sorter warmed up wid de dram, he'd kinder roll his eye and 'low, 'Miss Vallie, she is a fine white 'oman!' Well, suh, 'tain't long 'fo' we had dat nigger man trained—done trained, bless yo' soul! One day Miss Vallie had ter go 'cross town, an' she went by de liberty stable whar Hamp wuz at, leastways, he seed 'er some'rs; an' he come home dat night lookin' like he wuz feelin' bad. He 'fuse ter talk. Bimeby, atter he had his supper, he say, 'I seed Miss Vallie downtown ter-day. She wuz wid Miss Irene, an' dat 'ar frock she had on look mighty shabby.' I 'low, 'Well, it de bes' she got. She ain't got money like de Chippendales, an' Miss Irene don't keer how folks' cloze look. She too much quality fer dat.' Hamp say, 'Whyn't you take some er yo' money an' make Miss Vallie git er nice frock?' I 'low, 'Whar I got any money?' Hamp he hit his pocket an' say, 'You got it right here.'

"An' sho' 'nuff, suh, dat nigger man had a roll er money—mos' twenty dollars. Some hoss drovers had come 'long an' Hamp made dat money by trimmin' up de ol' mules dey had an' makin' um look young. He's got de art er dat, suh, an' dey paid 'im well. Dar wuz de money, but how wuz I gwine ter git it in Miss Vallie's han'? I kin buy vittles an' she not know whar dey come fum, but when it come ter buyin' frocks—well, suh, hit stumped me. Dey wan't but one way ter do it, an' I done it. I make like I wuz mad. I tuck de money an' went in de house dar whar Miss Vallie wuz sewin' an' mendin'. I went stompin' in, I did, an' when I got in I started my tune.

"I 'low, 'Ef de Perdues gwine ter go scandalizin' deyse'f by trottin' down town in broad daylight wid all kinder frocks on der back, I'm gwine 'way fum here; an' I dun'ner but what I'll go anyhow. 'Tain't bekaze dey's any lack er money, fer here de money right here.' Wid dat I slammed it down on de table. 'Dar! take dat an' git you a frock dat'll make you look like sump'n when you git outside er dis house. An' whiles you er gittin', git sump'n for ter put on yo' head!' "

Whether it was by reason of a certain dramatic faculty inherent in her race that she was able to summon emotions at will, or whether it was mere unconscious reproduction, I am not prepared to say. But certain it is that, in voice and gesture, in tone and attitude, and in a certain passionate earnestness of expression, Aunt Minervy Ann built up the whole scene before my eyes with such power that I seemed to have been present when it occurred. I felt as if she had conveyed me bodily into the room to become a witness of the episode. She went on, still with a frown on her face and a certain violence of tone and manner:

"I whipped 'roun' de room a time er two, pickin' up de cheers an' slammin' um down ag'in, an' knockin' things 'roun' like I wuz mad. Miss Vallie put her sewin' down an' lay her han' on de money. She 'low, 'What's dis, Aunt Minervy Ann?' I say, 'Hit's money, dat what 'tis—nothin' but nasty, stinkin' money! I wish dey wan't none in de worl' less'n I had a bairlful.' She sorter fumble at de money wid 'er fingers. You dunno, suh, how white an' purty an' weak her han' look ter me dat night. She 'low, 'Aunt Minervy Ann, I can't take dis.' I blaze' out at 'er, 'You don't haf'ter take it; you done got it! An' ef you don't keep it, I'll rake up eve'y rag an' scrap I got an' leave dis place. Now, you des' try me!' '"

Again Aunt Minervy Ann summoned to her aid the passion of a moment that had passed away, and again I had the queer experience of seeming to witness the whole scene. She continued:

"Wid dat, I whipt out er de room an' out er de house an' went an' sot down out dar in my house whar Hamp was at. Hamp, he 'low, 'What she say?' I say, 'She ain't had time ter say nothin'—I come 'way fum dar.' He 'low, 'You ain't brung dat money back, is you?' I say: 'Does you think I'm a start naked fool?' He 'low: 'Kaze ef you is, I'll put it right spang in de fire here.'

"Well, suh, I sot dar some little time, but eve'ything wuz so still in de house, bein's Marse Tumlin done gone down town, dat I crope back an' crope in fer ter see what Miss Vallie doin'. Well, suh, she wuz cryin'—settin' dar cryin'. I 'low, 'Honey, is I say anything fer ter hurt yo' feelin's?' She blubber' out, 'You know you ain't!' an' den she cry good-fashion.

"Des 'bout dat time, who should come in but Marse Tumlin. He look at Miss Vallie an' den he look at me. He say, 'Valentine, what de matter?' I say, 'It's me! I'm de one! I made 'er cry. I done sump'n ter hurt 'er feelin's.' She 'low, ' 'Tain't so, an' you know it. I'm des cryin' bekaze you too good ter me.'

"Well, suh, I had ter git out er dar fer ter keep fum chokin'. Marse Tumlin foller me out, an' right here on de porch, he 'low, 'Minervy Ann, nex' time don't be so dam good to 'er.' I wuz doin' some snifflin' myse'f 'bout dat time, an' I ain't keerin' what I say, so I stop an' flung back at 'im, *I'll be des ez dam good ter 'er ez I please—I'm free!* Well, suh, stidder hittin' me, Marse Tumlin bust out laughin', an' long atter dat he'd laugh eve'y time he look at me, des like sump'n wuz ticklin' 'im mighty nigh ter death.

"I 'speck he must er tol' 'bout dat cussin' part bekaze folks 'roun' here done got de idee dat I'm a sassy an' bad-tempered 'oman. Ef I had ter work fer my livin', suh, I boun' you I'd be a long time findin' a place. Atter dat, Hamp, he got in de Legislatur', an' it sho wuz a money-makin' place. Den we had eve'ything we wanted, an' mo' too, but bimeby de Legislatur' gun out, an' den dar we wuz, flat ez flounders, an' de white folks don't want ter hire Hamp des kaze he been ter de Legislatur'; but he got back in de liberty stable atter so long a time. Yit 'twan't what you may call livin.'

"All dat time, I hear Marse Tumlin talkin' ter Miss Vallie, 'bout what he call his wil' lan'. He say he got two thousan' acres down dar in de wire-grass, an' ef he kin sell it, he be mighty glad ter do so. Well, suh, one day long to'rds night, a two-hoss waggin driv' in at de side gate an' come in de back-yard. Ol' Ben Sadler wuz drivin', an' he 'low, 'Heyo, Minervy Ann, whar you want deze goods drapped at?' I say, 'Hello yo'se'f, ef you wanter hello. What you got dar, an' who do it 'blong ter?' He 'low, 'Hit's goods fer Major Tumlin Perdue, an' whar does you want um drapped at?' Well, suh, I ain't know what ter say, but I run'd an' ax'd Miss Vallie, an' she say put um out anywheres 'roun' dar, kaze she dunner nothin' 'bout um. So ol' Ben Sadler, he put um out, an' when I come ter look at um, dey wuz a bairl er sump'n, an' a kaig er sump'n, an' a box er sump'n. De bairl shuck like it mought be 'lasses, an' de kaig shuck like it mought be dram, an' de box hefted like it mought be terbarker. An', sho' 'nuff, dat what dey wuz— a bairl er sorghum syr'p, an' a kaig er peach brandy, an' a box er plug terbarker.

"I say right den, an' Miss Vallie'll tell you de same, dat Marse Tumlin done gone an' swap off all his wil' lan', but Miss Vallie, she say no; he won't never think er sech a thing; but, bless yo' soul, suh, she wan't nothin' but a school-gal, you may say, an' she ain't know no mo' 'bout men folks dan what a weasel do. An den, right 'pon top er dat, here come a nigger boy leadin' a bob-tail hoss. When I see dat, I dez good ez know'd dat de wil' lan' done been swap off, bekaze Marse Tumlin ain't got nothin' fer ter buy all dem things wid, an' I tell you right now, suh, I wuz rank mad, kaze what we want wid any ol' bob-tail hoss? De sorghum mought do an' de dram kin be put up wid, an' de terbarker got some comfort in it, but what de name er goodness we gwine ter do wid dat ol' hoss, when we ain't got hardly 'nuff vittles fer ter feed ourse'f wid? Dat what I ax Miss Vallie, an' she say right pine-blank she dunno.

"Well, suh, it's de Lord's trufe, I wuz dat mad I dunner what I say, an' I want keerin' nudder, bekaze I know how we had ter pinch an' squeeze fer ter git 'long in dis house. But I went 'bout gittin' supper, an' bimeby, Hamp, he come, an' I tol' 'im 'bout de ol' bob-tail hoss, an' he went out an' look at 'im. Atter while, here he come back laughin'. I say, 'You well ter laugh at dat ol' hoss.' He 'low, 'I ain't laughin' at de hoss. I'm laughin' at you. Gal, dat de finest hoss what ever put foot on de groun' in dis town. Dat's Marse Paul Conant's trottin' hoss. He'll fetch fi' hunder'd dollars any day. What he doin' here?' I up an' tol' 'im all I know'd, an' he shuck his head; he 'low, 'Gal, you lay low. Dey's sump'n n'er behime all dat.'

"What Hamp say sorter make me put on my studyin'-cap; but when you come ter look at it, suh, dey wan't nothin' 'tall fer me ter study 'bout. All I had ter do wuz ter try ter fin' out what wuz behime it, an' let it go at dat. When Marse Tumlin come home ter supper, I know'd sump'n wuz de matter wid 'im. I know'd it by his looks, suh. It's sorter wid folks like 'tis wid chillun. Ef you keer sump'n 'bout um you'll watch der motions, and ef you watch der motions dey don't hatter tell you when sump'n de matter. He come in so easy, suh, dat Miss Vallie ain't hear 'im, but I hear de do' screak, an' I know'd 'twuz him. We wuz talkin' an' gwine on at a mighty rate, an' I know'd he done stop ter lis'n'.

"Miss Vallie, she 'low she 'speck somebody made 'im a present er dem ar things. I say, 'Uh-uh, honey! don't you fool yo'se'f. Nobody ain't gwine ter do dat. Our folks ain't no mo' like dey useter wuz, dan crabapples is like plums. Dey done come ter dat pass dat whatsomever dey gits der han's on dey 'fuse ter turn it loose. All un um, 'cep' Marse Tumlin Perdue. Dey ain't no tellin' what he gun fer all dat trash. *Trash!* Hit's wuss'n trash! I wish you'd go out dar an' look at dat ol' bob-tail hoss. Why dat ol' hoss wuz stove up long 'fo' de war. By rights he ought ter be in de bone-yard dis ve'y minnit. He won't be here two whole days 'fo' you'll see de buzzards lined up out dar on de back fence waitin', an' dey won't hatter wait long nudder. Ef dey sen' any corn here fer ter feed dat bag er bones wid, I'll parch it an' eat it myse'f 'fo he shill have it. Ef anybody 'speck I'm gwine ter 'ten' ter dat ol' frame, deyer 'speckin' wid de wrong specks. I tell you dat right now.'

"All dis time Marse Tumlin wuz stan'in' out in de hall lis'nin'. Miss Vallie talk mighty sweet 'bout it. She say, 'Ef dey ain't nobody else ter 'ten' de hoss, reckin I kin do it.' I 'low, 'My life er me, honey! de nex' news you know you'll be hirin' out ter de liberty stable.'

"Well, suh, my talk 'gun ter git so hot dat Marse Tumlin des had ter make a fuss. He fumbled wid de do' knob, an' den come walkin' down de hall, an' by dat time I wuz in de dinin'-room. I walk mighty light, bekaze ef he say anything I want ter hear it. You can't call it eave-drappin', suh; hit look ter me dat 'twuz ez much my business ez 'twuz dern, an' I ain't never got dat idee out'n my head down ter dis day.

"But Marse Tumlin ain't say nothin,' 'cep' fer ter ax Miss Vallie ef she feelin' well, an' how eve'y thing wuz, but de minnit I hear 'im open his mouf I know'd he had trouble on his min'. I can't tell you how I know'd it, suh, but dar 'twuz. Look like he tried to hide it, bekaze he tol' a whole lot of funny tales 'bout folks, an' 'twan't long befo' he had Miss Vallie laughin' fit ter kill. But he ain't fool me, suh.

"Bimeby, Miss Vallie, she come in de dinin'-room fer ter look atter settin' de table, bekaze fum a little gal she allers like ter have de dishes fix des so. She wuz sorter hummin' a chune, like she ain't want' ter talk, but I ain't let dat stan' in my way.

"I 'low, 'I wish eve'body wuz like dat Mr. Paul Conant. I bet you right now he been down town dar all day makin' money han' over fist, des ez fast ez he can rake it in. I know it, kaze I does his washin' and cleans up his room fer 'im.'

"Miss Vallie say, 'Well, what uv it? Money don't make 'im no better'n anybody else.' I 'low, 'Hit don't make 'im no wuss; an' den, 'sides dat, he ain't gwine ter let nobody swindle 'im.'

"By dat time, I hatter go out an' fetch supper in, an' 'tain't take me no time, bekaze I wuz des' achin' fer ter hear how Marse Tumlin come by dem ar contraptions an' contrivances. An' I stayed in dar ter wait on de table, which it ain't need no waitin' on.

"Atter while, I 'low, 'Marse Tumlin, I like ter forgot ter tell you—yo' things done come.' He say, 'What things, Minervy Ann?' I 'low, 'Dem ar contraptions, an' dat ar bob-tail hoss. He look mighty lean an' hongry, de hoss do, but Hamp he say dat's bekaze he's a high-bred hoss. He say dem ar high-bred hosses won't take on no fat, no matter how much you feed um.'

"Marse Tumlin sorter drum on de table. Atter while he 'low, 'Dey done come, is dey, Minervy Ann?' I say, 'Yasser, dey er here right now. Hamp puts it down dat dat ar hoss one er de gayliest creatur's what ever make a track in dis town.'

"Well, suh, 'tain't no use ter tell you what else wuz said, kaze 'twan't much. I seed dat Marse Tumlin wa'nt gwine ter talk 'bout it, on account er bein' 'fear'd he'd hurt Miss Vallie's feelin's ef he tol' 'er dat he done swap off all dat wil' lan' fer dem ar things an' dat ar bob-tail hoss. Dat what he done.

Yasser! I hear 'im sesso atterwards. He swap it off ter Marse Paul Conant.

"I thank my Lord it come out all right, but it come mighty nigh bein' de ruination er de fambly."

"How was that?" I inquired.

"Dat what I'm gwine ter tell you, suh. Right atter supper dat night, Marse Tumlin say he got ter go down fer ter see a man on some business, an' he ax me ef I won't stay in de house dar wid Miss Vallie. 'Twa'n't no trouble ter me, bekaze I'd 'a' been on de place anyhow, an' so when I got de kitchen cleaned up an' de things put away, I went back in de house whar Miss Vallie wuz at. Marse Tumlin wuz done gone.

"Miss Vallie, she sot at de table doin' some kind er rufflin', an' I sot back ag'in de wall in one er dem ar high-back cheers. What we said I'll never tell you, suh, bekaze I'm one er deze kinder folks what ain't no sooner set down an' git still dan dey goes ter noddin'. Dat's me. Set me down in a cheer, high-back er low-back, an' I'm done gone! I kin set here on de step an' keep des ez wide-'wake ez a skeer'd rabbit, but set me down in a cheer—well, suh, I'd like ter see anybody keep me 'wake when dat's de case.

"Dar I sot in dat ar high-back cheer, Miss Vallie rufflin' an' flutin' sump'n, an' tryin' ter make me talk, an' my head rollin' 'roun' like my neck done broke. Bimeby, *blam! blam!* come on de do'. We got one er dem ar jinglin' bells now, suh, but in dem times we had a knocker, an' it soun' like de roof fallin' in. I like ter jumped out'n my skin. Miss Vallie drapped her conflutements an' 'low, 'What in de worl'! Aunt Minervy Ann, go ter de do'.'

"Well, suh, I went, but I ain't had no heart in it, bekaze I ain't know who it mought be, an' whar dey come fum, an' what dey want. But I went. 'Twuz me er Miss Vallie, an' I want gwine ter let dat chile go, not dat time er night, dough 'twa'n't so mighty late.

"I open de do' on de crack, I did, an' 'low, 'Who dat?' Somebody make answer, 'Is de Major in, Aunt Minervy Ann?' an' I know'd right den it wuz Marse Paul Conant. An' it come over me dat he had sump'n ter do wid sendin' er dem contraptions, mo' 'speshually dat ar bob-tail hoss. An' den, too, suh, lots quicker'n I kin tell it, hit come over me dat he been axin' me lots 'bout Miss Vallie. All come 'cross my min', suh, whiles I pullin' de do' open.

"I 'low, I did, 'No, suh; Marse Tumlin gone down town fer ter look atter some business, but he sho ter come back terreckly. Won't you come in, suh, an' wait fer 'im?' He sorter flung his head back an' laugh, soft like, an' say, 'I don't keer ef I do, Aunt Minervy Ann.'

"I 'low, 'Walk right in de parlor, suh, an' I'll make a light mos' 'fo' you

212

kin turn 'roun'. He come in, he did, an' I lit de lamp, an' time I lit 'er she 'gun ter smoke. Well, suh, he tuck dat lamp, run de wick up an' down a time er two, an' dar she wuz, bright ez day.

"When I went back in de room whar Miss Vallie wuz at, she wuz stan'in' dar lookin' skeer'd. She say, 'Who dat?' I 'low, 'Hit's Marse Paul Conant, dat's who 'tis. She say, 'What he want?' I 'low, 'Nothin' much; he does come a-courtin'. Better jump up an' not keep 'im waitin'.'

"Well, suh, you could 'a' knock'd 'er down wid a fedder. She stood dar wid 'er han' on 'er th'oat takin' short breffs, des like a little bird does when it flies in de winder an' dunner how ter fly out ag'in.

"Bimeby, she say, 'Aunt Minervy Ann, you ought ter be 'shame or yo'se'f! I know dat man when I see 'im, an' dat's all.' I 'low, 'Honey, you know mighty well he ain't come callin'. But he wanter see Marse Tumlin, an' dey ain't nothin' fer ter hender you fum gwine in dar an' makin' 'im feel at home while's he waitin'.' She sorter study awhile, an' den she blush up. She say, 'I dunno whedder I ought ter.'

"Well, suh, dat settled it. I know'd by de way she look an' talk dat she don't need no mo' 'swadin'. I say, 'All right, honey, do ez you please; but it's yo' house; you er de mist'iss; an' it'll look mighty funny ef dat young man got ter set in dar by hisse'f an' look at de wall whiles he waitin' fer Marse Tumlin. I dunner what he'll say, kaze I ain't never hear 'im talk 'bout no-body; but I know mighty well he'll do a heap er thinkin'.'

"Des like I tell you, suh—she skipped 'roun' dar, an' flung on 'er Sunday frock, shuck out 'er curls, an' sorter fumble' 'roun' wid some ribbons, an' dar she wuz, lookin' des ez fine ez a fiddle, ef not finer. Den she swep' inter de parlor, an', you mayn't b'lieve it, suh, but she mighty nigh tuck de man's breff 'way. Mon, she wuz purty, an' she ain't do no mo' like deze eve'y-day gals dan nothin'. When she start 'way fum me, she wuz a gal. By de time she walk up de hall an' sweep in dat parlor, she wuz a grown 'oman. De blush what she had on at fust stayed wid 'er an' look like 't wuz er natchual color, an' her eyes shine, suh, like she had fire in um. I peeped at 'er, suh, fum behime de curtains in de settin'-room, an' I know what I'm talkin' 'bout. It's de Lord's trufe, suh, ef de men folks could tote derse'f like de wimmen, an' do one way whiles dey feelin' annuder way, dey wouldn't be no livin' in de worl'. You take a school gal, suh, an' she kin fool de smartest man what ever trod shoe leather. He may talk wid 'er all day an' half de night, an' he never is ter fin' out what she thinkin' 'bout. Sometimes de gals fools deyse'f, suh, but dat's mighty seldom.

213

"I dunner what all dey say, kaze I ain't been in dar so mighty long 'fo' I wuz noddin', but I did hear Marse Paul say he des drapt in fer 'pollygize 'bout a little joke he played on Marse Tumlin. Miss Vallie ax what wuz de joke, an' he 'low dat Marse Tumlin wuz banterin' folks fer ter buy his wil' lan'; an' Marse Paul ax 'im what he take fer it, an' Marse Tumlin 'low he'll take anything what he can chaw, sop, er drink. Dem wuz de words—chaw, sop, er drink. Wid dat, Marse Paul say he'd gi' 'im a box er terbarker, a bairl er syr'p, an' a kaig er peach brandy an' th'ow in his buggy-hoss fer good medjer. Marse Tumlin say 'done' an' dey shuck han's on it. Dat what Marse Paul tol' Miss Vallie, an he 'low he des done it fer fun, kaze he done looked inter dat wil' lan', an' he 'low she's wuff a pile er money.

"Well, suh, 'bout dat time, I 'gun ter nod, an' de fus news I know'd Miss Vallie wuz whackin' 'way on de peanner, an' it look like ter me she wuz des tryin' 'erse'f. By dat time, dey wuz gettin' right chummy an' so I des curl up on de flo', an' dream dat de peanner chunes wuz comin' out'n a bairl des like 'lasses.

"When I waked up, Marse Paul Conant done gone, an' Marse Tumlin ain't come, an' Miss Vallie wuz settin' dar in de parlor lookin' up at de ceilin' like she got some mighty long thoughts. Her color wuz still up. I look at 'er an' laugh, an' she made a mouf at me, an' I say ter myse'f, 'Hey! sump'n de matter here, sho,' but I say out loud, 'Marse Paul Conant sho gwine ter ax me ef you ain't had a dram.' She laugh an' say, 'What answer you gwine ter make?' I 'low, 'I'll bow an' say, "No, suh; I'm de one dat drinks all de dram fer de fambly."'

"Well, suh, dat chile sot in ter laughin', an' she laugh an' laugh twel she went inter highsterics. She wuz keyed up too high, ez you mought say, an' dat's de way she come down ag'in. Bimeby, Marse Tumlin come, an' Miss Vallie, she tol' 'm 'bout how Marse Paul done been dar; an' he sot dar, he did, an' hummed an' haw'd, an' done so funny dat, bimeby, I 'low, 'Well, folks, I'll hatter tell you good-night,' an' wid dat I went out."

At this point Aunt Minervy leaned forward, clasped her hands over her knees, and shook her head. When she took up the thread of her narrative, if it can be called such, the tone of her voice was more subdued, almost confidential, in fact.

"Nex' mornin' wuz my wash-day, suh, an' 'bout ten o'clock, when I got ready, dey want no bluin' in de house an' mighty little soap. I hunted high an' I hunted low, but no bluin' kin I fin'. An' dat make me mad, bekaze ef I

214

hatter go down town atter de bluin', my wash-day'll be broke inter. But 'tain't no good fer ter git mad, bekaze I wuz bleeze ter go atter de bluin'. So I tighten up my head-hankcher, an' flung a cape on my shoulders an' put out.

"I 'speck you know how 'tis, suh. You can't go down town but what you'll see nigger wimmen stan'in' out in de front yards lookin' over de palin's. Dey all know'd me an' I know'd dem, an' de las' blessed one un um hatter hail me ez I go by, an' I hatter stop an' pass de time er day, kaze ef I'd 'a' whipt on by, dey'd 'a' said I wuz gwine back bofe on my church an' on my color. I dunner how long dey kep' me but time I got ter Proctor's sto', I know'd I'd been on de way too long.

"I notice a crowd er men out dar, some settin' an' some stan'in', but I run'd in, I did, an' de young man what do de clerkin', he foller me in an' ax what I want. I say I want a dime's wuff er bluin', an' fer ter please, suh, wrop it up des ez quick ez he kin. I tuck notice dat while he wuz gittin' it out'n de box, he sorter stop like he lis'nin' an' den ag'in, whiles he had it in de scoop des ready fer ter drap it in de scales, he helt his han' an' wait. Den I know'd he wuz lis'nin'.

"Dat makes me lis'n, an' den I hear Marse Tumlin talkin', an' time I hear 'im I know'd he wuz errytated. Twa'n't bekaze he wuz talkin' loud, suh, but 'twuz bekaze he wuz talkin' level. When he talk loud, he feelin' good. When he talk low, an' one word soun' same ez anudder, den somebody better git out'n his way. I lef' de counter an' step ter de do' fer ter see what de matter wuz betwix' um.

"Well, suh, dar wuz Marse Tumlin stan'in' dar close ter Tom Perryman. Marse Tumlin, 'low, 'Maybe de law done 'pinted you my gyardeen. How you know I been swindled?' Tom Perryman say, 'Bekaze I hear you say he bought yo' wil' lan' fer a little er nothin'. He'll swindle you ef you trade wid 'im, an' you done trade wid 'im.' Marse Tumlin, 'low, 'Is Paul Conant ever swindle *you?*' Tom Perryman say, 'No, he ain't, an' ef he wuz ter I'd give 'im a kickin'.' Marse Tumlin 'low, 'Well, you know you is a swindler, an' nobody ain't kick you. How come dat?' Tom Perryman say, 'Ef you say I'm a swindler, you're a liar.'

"Well, suh, de man ain't no sooner say dat dan *bang!* went Marse Tumlin's pistol, an' des ez it banged Marse Paul Conant run 'twix' um, an' de ball went right spang th'oo de collar-bone an' sorter sideways th'oo de p'int er de shoulder-blade. Marse Tumlin drapt his pistol an' cotch 'im ez he fell an' knelt down dar by 'im, an' all de time dat ar Tom Perryman wuz stan'in' right over um wid his pistol in his han'. I squall out, I did, 'Whyn't some er you white men take dat man pistol 'way fum 'im? Don't you see what he fixin' ter do?'

"I run'd at 'im, an' he sorter flung back wid his arm, an' when he done dat somebody grab 'im fum behime. All dat time Marse Tumlin wuz axin' Marse Paul Conant ef he hurt much. I hear 'im say, 'I wouldn't 'a' done it fer de worl', Conant—not fer de worl'.' Den de doctor, he come up, an' Marse Tumlin, he pester de man twel he hear 'im say, 'Don't worry, Major; dis boy'll live ter be a older man dan you ever will.' Den Marse Tumlin got his pistol an' hunt up an' down fer dat ar Tom Perryman, but he done gone. I seed 'im when he got on his hoss.

"I say to Marse Tumlin, 'Ain't you des ez well ter fetch Marse Paul Conant home whar we all kin take keer uv 'im?' He 'low, 'Dat's a *fack*. Go home an' tell yo' Miss Vallie fer ter have de big room fixed up time we git dar wid 'im.' I say, 'Humph! I'll fix it myse'f; I know'd I ain't gwine ter let Miss Vallie do it.'

"Well, suh, 'tain't no use fer ter tell yer de rest. Dar's dat ar baby in dar, an' what mo' sign does you want ter show you dat it all turned out des like one er dem ol'-time tales?"

Mingo

In 1876, CIRCUMSTANCES, partly accidental and partly sentimental, led me to revisit Crooked Creek Church, near the little village of Rockville, in Middle Georgia. I was amazed at the changes which a few brief years had wrought. The ancient oaks ranged roundabout remained the same, but upon everything else time had laid its hand right heavily. Even the building seemed to have shrunk; the pulpit was less massive and imposing, the darkness beyond the rafters less mysterious. The preacher had grown gray, and feebleness had taken the place of that physical vigor which was formerly the distinguishing feature of his interpretations of the larger problems of theology. People I had never seen sat in the places of those I had known so well. There were only traces here and there of the old congregation, whose austere simplicity had made so deep an impression upon my youthful mind. The blooming girls of 1860 had grown into careworn matrons, and the young men had developed in their features the strenuous uncertainty and misery of the period of desolation and disaster through which they had passed. Anxiety had so ground itself into their lives that a stranger to the manner might well have been pardoned for giving a sinister interpretation to these pitiable manifestations of hopelessness and unsuccess.

I had known the venerable preacher intimately in the past; but his eyes, wandering vaguely over the congregation, and resting curiously upon me, betrayed no recognition. Age, which had whitened his hair and enfeebled his voice, seemed also to have given him the privilege of ignoring everything but the grave and the mysteries beyond.

These swift processes of change and decay were calculated to make a profound impression, but my attention was called away from all such reflections. Upon a bench near the pulpit, in the section reserved for the colored members, sat an old negro man whose face was perfectly familiar. I had known

217

him in my boyhood as Mingo, the carriage-driver and body-servant of Judge Junius Wornum. He had changed but little. His head was whiter than when I saw him last; but his attitude was as firm and as erect, and the evidences of his wonderful physical strength as apparent, as ever. He sat with his right hand to his chin, his strong serious face turned contemplatively toward the rafters. When his eye chanced to meet mine, a smile of recognition lit up his features, his head and body drooped forward, and his hand fell away from his face, completing a salutation at once graceful, picturesque, and imposing.

I have said that few evidences of change manifested themselves in Mingo; and so it seemed at first, but a closer inspection showed one remarkable change. I had known him when his chief purpose in life seemed to be to enjoy himself. He was a slave, to be sure, but his condition was no restraint upon his spirits. He was known far and wide as "Laughing Mingo," and upon hundreds of occasions he was the boon companion of the young men about Rockville in their wild escapades. Many who read this will remember the " 'possum suppers" which it was Mingo's delight to prepare for these young men, and he counted among his friends and patrons many who afterward became distinguished both in war and in the civil professions. At these gatherings Mingo, bustling around and serving his guests, would keep the table in a roar with his quaint sayings and local satires in the shape of impromptu doggerel; and he would also repeat snatches of orations which he had heard in Washington when Judge Wornum was a member of Congress. But his chief accomplishments lay in the wonderful ease and fluency with which he imitated the eloquent appeals of certain ambitious members of the Rockville bar, and in his travesties of the bombastic flights of the stump-speakers of that day.

It appeared, however, as he sat in the church, gazing thoughtfully and earnestly at the preacher, that the old-time spirit of fun and humor had been utterly washed out of his face. There was no sign of grief, no mark of distress, but he had the air of settled anxiety belonging to those who are tortured by an overpowering responsibility. Apparently here was an interesting study. If the responsibilities of life are problems to those who have been trained to solve them, how much more formidable must they be to this poor negro but lately lifted to his feet! Thus my reflections took note of the pathetic associations and suggestions clustering around this dignified representative of an unfortunate race.

Upon this particular occasion church services were to extend into the afternoon, and there was an interval of rest after the morning sermon, covering the hour of noon. This interval was devoted by both old and young to the discussion of matters seriously practical. The members of the congregation had brought their dinner baskets, and the contents thereof were spread around under the trees in true pastoral style. Those who came unprovided were, in pursuance of an immemorial custom of the section and the occasion, taken in charge by the simple and hearty hospitality of the members.

Somehow I was interested in watching Mingo. As he passed from the church with the congregation, and moved slowly along under the trees, he presented quite a contrast to the other negroes who were present. These, with the results of their rural surroundings superadded to the natural shyness of their race, hung upon the outskirts of the assembly, as though their presence was merely casual, while Mingo passed along from group to group of his white friends and acquaintances with that familiar and confident air of meritorious humility and unpretentious dignity which is associated with good-breeding and gentility the world over. When he lifted his hat in salutation, there was no servility in the gesture; when he bent his head, and dropped his eyes upon the ground, his dignity was strengthened and fortified rather than compromised. Both his manners and his dress retained the flavor of a social system the exceptional features of which were too often, by both friend and foe, made to stand for the system itself. His tall beaver, with its curled brim, and his blue broadcloth dress-coat, faded and frayed, with its brass buttons, bore unmistakable evidence of their age and origin; but they seemed to be a reasonable and necessary contribution to his individuality.

Passing slowly through the crowd, Mingo made his way to a double-seated buggy shielded from all contingencies of sun and rain by an immense umbrella. From beneath the seat he drew forth a large hamper, and proceeded to arrange its contents upon a wide bench which stood near.

While this was going on, I observed a tall, angular woman, accompanied by a bright-looking little girl, making her way toward Mingo's buggy. The woman was plainly, even shabbily, dressed, so that the gay ribbons and flowers worn by the child were gaudy by contrast. The woman pressed forward with decision, her movements betraying a total absence of that undulatory grace characteristic of the gentler sex, while the little girl dancing about her showed not only the grace and beauty of youth, but a certain refinement of pose and gesture calculated to attract attention.

Mingo made way for these with ready deference, and after a little I saw him coming toward me. He came forward, shook hands, and remarked that he had brought me an invitation to dine with Mrs. Feratia Bivins.

"Miss F'raishy 'members you, boss," he said, bowing and smiling, "en she up 'n' say she be mighty glad er yo' comp'ny ef you kin put up wid cole vittles an' po' far'; en ef you come," he added on his own account, "we like it mighty well."

Accepting the invitation, I presently found myself dining with Mrs. Bivins, and listening to her remarkable flow of small talk, while Mingo hovered around, the embodiment of active hospitality.

"Mingo 'lowed he'd ast you up," said Mrs. Bivins, "an' I says, says I, 'Don't you be a-pesterin' the gentulmun, when you know thar's plenty er the new-issue quality ready an' a-waitin' to pull an' haul at 'im,' says I. Not that I begrudges the vittles,—not by no means; I hope I hain't got to that yit. But somehow er 'nother folks what hain't got no great shakes to brag 'bout gener'ly feels sorter skittish when strange folks draps in on 'em. Goodness knows, I hain't come to that pass wher' I begrudges the vittles that folks eats, bekaze anybody betweenst this an' Clinton, Jones County, Georgy, 'll tell you the Sanderses wa'n't the set to stint the'r stomachs. I was a Sanders 'fore I married, an' when I come 'way frum pa's house hit was thes like turnin' my back on a barbecue. Not by no means was I begrudgin' of the vittles. Says I, 'Mingo,' says I, 'ef the gentulmun is a teetotal stranger, an' nobody else hain't got the common perliteness to ast 'im, shorely you mus' ast 'im,' says I; 'but don't go an' make no great to-do,' says I, 'bekaze the little we got mightent be satisfactual to the gentulmun,' says I. What we got may be little enough, an' it may be too much, but hit's welcome."

It would be impossible to convey an idea of the emphasis which Mrs. Bivins imposed upon her conversation. She talked rapidly, and yet with a certain deliberation of manner which gave a quaint interest to everything she said. She had thin gray hair, a prominent nose, firm thin lips, and eyes that gave a keen and sparkling individuality to sharp and homely features. She had evidently seen sorrow and defied it. There was no suggestion of compromise in manner or expression. Even her hospitality was uncompromising. I endeavored to murmur my thanks to Mrs. Bivins for Mingo's thoughtfulness, but her persistent conversation drowned out such poor phrases as I could hastily frame.

"Come 'ere, Pud Hon," continued Mrs. Bivins, calling the child, and trimming the demonstrative terms of "Pudding" and "Honey" to suit all exigencies of affection,—"come 'ere, Pud Hon, an' tell the gentulmun howdy. Gracious me! don't be so *countrified*. He ain't a-gwine to *bite* you. No, sir, you won't fine no begrudgers mixed up with the *Sanderses*. Hit useter be a *common* sayin' in Jones, an' cle'r 'cross into Jasper, that pa would 'a' bin a rich man an' 'a' owned *niggers* if it hadn't but 'a' bin bekase he sot his head ag'in stintin' of his stomach. That's what they useter say,—use n't they, Mingo?"

"Dat w'at I year tell, Miss F'raishy—sho'," Mingo assented, with great heartiness. But Mrs. Bivins's volubility would hardly wait for this perfunctory endorsement. She talked as she arranged the dishes, and occasionally she would hold a piece of crockery suspended in the air as she emphasized her words. She dropped into a mortuary strain:

"Poor pa! I don't never have nothin' extry an' I don't never see a dish er fried chicken but what pa pops in my mind. A better man hain't never draw'd the breath of life,—that they hain't. An' he was thes as gayly as a kitten. When we gals'd have comp'ny to dinner, pore pa he'd cut his eye at me, an' up an' say, says he, 'Gals, this 'ere turkey's mighty nice, yit I'm reely afeared you put too much inguns in the dressin'. Maybe the young men don't like 'em as good as you all does;' an' then pore pa'd drap his knife an' fork, an' laugh tell the tears come in his eyes. Sister Prue she useter run off an' have a cry, but I let you know I was one er the kind what wa'n't so easy sot back.

"I'd 'a' bin mighty glad if Pud yer had er took airter pa's famerly, but frum the tip eend er her toe nails to the toppermust ha'r of her head she's a Wornum. Hit ain't on'y thes a streak yer an' a stripe thar,—hit's the whole bolt. I reckon maybe you know'd ole Jedge June Wornum; well, Jedge June he was Pud's gran'pa, an' Deely Wornum was her ma. Maybe you might 'a' seed Deely when she was a school-gal."

Cordelia Wornum! No doubt my astonishment made itself apparent, for Mrs. Bivins bridled up promptly, and there was a clearly perceptible note of defiance in her tone as she proceeded.

"Yes, sir-ree! *An' make no mistake!* Deely Wornum married my son, an' Henry Clay Bivins made 'er a good husbun', if I do have to give it out myse'f. Yes, 'ndeed! An' yit if you'd 'a' heern the rippit them Wornums kicked up, you'd 'a' thought the pore chile'd done took 'n' run off 'long of a whole passel er high pirates frum somewheres er 'nother. In about that time the ole Jedge he got sorter fibbled up, some say in his feet, an' some say in his head; but his wife, that Em'ly Wornum, she taken on awful. I never seen her a-gwine on myse'f; not that they was any hidin' out 'mongst the Bivinses er the Sanderses,—bless you, no! bekaze here's what wa'n't afeared er all the Wornums in the continental State er Georgy, not if they'd 'a' mustered out under the lead er ole Nick hisse'f, which I have my doubts if he wa'n't somewheres aroun'. I never seen 'er, but I heern tell er how she was a-cuttin' up. You mayn't think it, but that 'oman taken it on herse'f to call up all the niggers on the place an' give 'em her forbiddance to go an' see the'r young mistiss."

"Yit I lay dey tuck'n' sneak 'roun' en come anyhow, ain't dey, Miss F'raishy?" inquired Mingo, rubbing his hands together and smiling blandly.

"*That* they did,—*that* they did!" was Mrs. Bivins's emphatic response. "Niggers is niggers, but them Wornum niggers was a cut er two 'bove the common run. I'll say that, an' I'll say it on the witness stan'. Freedom might 'a' turned the'r heads when it come to t'other folks, but hit didn't never turn the'r heads 'bout the'r young mistiss. An' if Mingo here hain't done his juty 'cordin' to his lights, then I dunner what juty is. I'll say that open an' aboveboard, high an' low."

The curious air of condescension which Mrs. Bivins assumed as she said this, the tone of apology which she employed in paying this tribute to Mingo and the Wornum negroes, formed a remarkable study. Evidently she desired me distinctly to understand that in applauding these worthy colored people she was in no wise compromising her own dignity.

Thus Mrs. Bivins rattled away, pausing only long enough now and then to deplore my lack of appetite. Meanwhile Mingo officiated around the improvised board with gentle affability; and the little girl, bearing strong traces of her lineage in her features,—a resemblance which was confirmed by a pretty little petulance of temper,—made it convenient now and again to convey a number of tea cakes into Mingo's hat, which happened to be sitting near, the conveyance taking place in spite of laughable pantomimic protests on the part of the old man ranging from appealing nods and grimaces to indignant gestures and frowns.

"When Deely died," Mrs. Bivins went on, waving a towel over a tempting jar of preserves, "they wa'n't nobody but what was afeared to break it to Emily Wornum, an' the pore chile'd done been buried too long to talk about before her ma heern tell of it, an' then she drapped like a clap er thunder had hit 'er. Airter so long a time, Mingo thar he taken it 'pun hisse'f to tell 'er, an' she flopped right down in 'er tracks, an' Mingo he hepped 'er into the house, an', bless your life, when he come to he'p 'er out'n it, she was a changed 'oman. 'T wa'n't long 'fore she taken a notion to come to my house, an' one mornin' when I was a-washin' up dishes, I heern some un holler at the gate, an' thar sot Mingo peerched up on the Wornum carry-all, an' of all livin' flesh, who should be in thar but ole Emily Wornum!

"Hit's a sin to say it," continued Mrs. Bivins, smiling a dubious little smile that was not without its serious suggestions, "but I tightened up my apern strings, an' flung my glance aroun' tell hit drapped on the battlin'-stick, bekaze I flared up the minnit I seen 'er, an' I says to myse'f, says I, 'If hit's a fracas you er huntin', my lady, I lay you won't hafter put on your specs to fine it.' An' then I says to Pud, says I,

" 'Pud Hon, go in the shed-room thar, chile, an' if you hear anybody a-hollerin' an' a-squallin' ther', shet your eyeleds an' grit your teeth, bekaze hit'll be your pore ole granny a-tryin' to git even with some er your kin.'

"An' then I taken a cheer an' sot down by the winder. D'reckly in come Emily Wornum, an' I wish I may die if I'd 'a' know'd 'er if I'd saw 'er anywheres else on the face er the yeth. She had this 'ere kinder dazzled look what wimmen has airter they bin baptized in the water. I helt my head high, but I kep' my eye on the battlin'-stick, an' if she'd 'a' made fight, I'd be boun' they'd 'a' bin some ole sco'es settled then an' thar if ole sco'es ken be settled by a frailin'. But, bless your heart, they wa'n't never no cammer 'oman than what Emily Wornum was; an' if you'd 'a' know'd 'er, an' Mingo wa'n't here to b'ar me out, I wish I may die if I wouldn't be afeared to tell you how ca'm an' supjued that 'oman was, which in her young days she was a tarrifier. She up an' says, says she,

" 'Is Mizzers Bivins in?'

" 'Yessum,' says I, 'she is that-away. An' more'n that, nobody don't hafter come on this hill an' holler more'n twicet 'thout gittin' some kinder answer back. *Yessum!* An' what's more, Mizzers Bivins is come to that time er life when she's mighty proud to git calls from the big-bugs. If I had as much perliteness, ma'am, as I is cheers, I'd ast you to set down,' says I.

"She stood thar, she did, thes as cool as a cowcumber; but d'reckly she ups an' says, says she,

" 'Might I see my little gran'chile?' says she.

" 'Oho, ma'am!' says I; 'things is come to a mighty purty pass when quality folks has to go frum house to house a-huntin' up pore white trash, an' a-astin' airter the'r kin. Tooby shore! tooby shore! Yessum, a mighty purty pass,' says I."

I cannot hope to give even a faint intimation of the remarkable dramatic fervor and earnestness of this recital, nor shall I attempt to describe the rude eloquence of attitude and expression; but they seemed to represent the real or fancied wrongs of a class, and to spring from the pent-up rage of a century.

"I wa'n't lookin' fer no compermise, nuther," Mrs. Bivins continued. "I fully spected 'er to flar' up an' fly at me; but 'stedder that, she kep' a-stan'in' thar lookin' thes like folks does when they er runnin' over sump'n in the'r min'. Then her eye lit on some er the pictur's what Deely had hung up on the side er the house, an' in pertic'lar one what some er the Wornum niggers had fetched 'er, whar a great big dog was a-watchin' by a little bit er baby. When she seen that, bless your soul, she thes sunk right down on the floor, an' clincht 'er han's, an' brung a gasp what looked like it might er bin the last, an' d'reckly she ast, in a whisper, says she,

" 'Was this my dear daughter's room?'

"Maybe you think," said Mrs. Bivins, regarding me coldly and critically, and pressing her thin lips more firmly together, if that could be,—"maybe you think I oughter wrung my han's, an' pitied that 'oman kneelin' thar in that room whar all my trouble was born an' bred. Some folks would 'a' flopped down by 'er, an I won't deny but what hit come over me; but the nex' minnit hit flashed acrost me as quick an' hot as powder how she'd 'a' bin a-houndin' airter me an' my son, an' a-treatin' us like as we'd 'a' bin the offscourin's er creation, an' how she cast off her own daughter, which Deely was as good a gal as ever draw'd the breath er life,—when all this come over me, hit seem like to me that I couldn't keep my paws off'n 'er. I hope the Lord'll forgive me,—that I do,—but if hit hadn't but 'a' bin for my raisin', I'd 'a' jumped at Emily Wornum an' 'a' spit in 'er face an' 'a' clawed 'er eyes out'n 'er. An' yit, with ole Nick a-tuggin' at me, I was a Christun 'nuff to thank the Lord that they was a tender place in that pore mizerbul creetur's soul-case.

"When I seen her a-kneelin' thar, with 'er year-rings a-danglin' an' 'er fine feathers a-tossin' an' a-trimblin', leetle more an' my thoughts would 'a' sot me afire. I riz an' I stood over her, an' I says, says I,

" 'Emily Wornum, whar you er huntin' the dead you oughter hunted the livin'. What's betwix' you an' your Maker *I* can't tell,' says I, 'but if you git down on your face an' lick the dirt what Deely Bivins walked on, still you won't be humble enough for to go whar *she's* gone, nor good enough nuther. She died right yer while you was a-trapisin' an' a-trollopin' 'roun' frum pos' to pillar a-upholdin' your quality idees. These arms helt 'er,' says I, 'an' ef hit hadn't but 'a' bin for *her*, Emily Wornum,' says I, 'I'd 'a' strangled the life out'n you time your shadder darkened my door. An' what's more,' says I, 'ef you er come to bother airter Pud, *thes make the trial of it. Thes so much as lay the weight er your little finger on 'er*', says I, '*an I'll grab you by the goozle an' t'ar your haslet out*,' says I."

Oh, mystery of humanity! It was merely Mrs. Feratia Bivins who had been speaking, but the voice was the voice of Tragedy. Its eyes shone; its fangs glistened and gleamed; its hands clutched the air; its tone was husky with suppressed fury; its rage would have stormed the barriers of the grave. In another moment Mrs. Bivins was brushing the crumbs from her lap, and exchanging salutations with her neighbors and acquaintances; and a little later, leading her grandchild by the hand, she was making her way back to the church, where the congregation had begun to gather.

For my own part, I preferred to remain under the trees, and I soon found that this was the preference of Mingo. The old man had finished his dinner, and sat at the foot of a gigantic oak, gazing dreamily at the fleecy clouds that sailed across the sky. His hands were clasped above his head, and his attitude was one of reflection. The hymn with which the afternoon services were opened came through the woods with a distinctness that was not without a remote and curious suggestion of pathos. As it died away, Mingo raised himself slightly, and said, in a tone that was intended to be explanatory, if not apologetic,

"Miss F'raishy, ef she ain't one sight, den I ain't never seed none. I s'pec' it seem sorter funny ter you, boss, but dat w'ite 'oman done had lots er trouble; she done had bunnunce er trouble—she sholy is! Look mighty cu'us dat some folks can't git useter yuther folks w'at got Ferginny ways, but dat's Miss F'raishy up en down. Dat's her, sho'! Ole Miss en ole Marster dey had Ferginny ways, en Miss F'raishy she wouldn't 'a' stayed in a ten-acre fiel' wid um,—dat she wouldn't. Folks w'at got Ferginny ways, Miss F'raishy she call um big-bugs, en she git ho*stile* w'en she year dem name call. Hit's de same way wid niggers. Miss F'raishy she hate de common run er niggers like dey wuz pizen. Yit I ain't makin' no complaints, kaze she mighty good ter me. I goes en I suns myse'f in Miss F'raishy back peazzer all day Sundays, w'en dey ain't no meetin's gwine on, en all endurin' er de week I hangs 'roun' en ploughs a little yer, en hoes a little dar, en scratches a little yander, en looks arter ole Miss' gran'chile. But des let 'n'er nigger so much ez stick der chin cross de yard palin's, en, bless yo' soul, you'll year Miss F'raishy blaze out like de woods done cotch afire."

Mingo paused here to chuckle over the discomfiture and alarm of the imaginary negro who had had the temerity to stick his supposititious chin over the fence. Then he went on:

"I dunner whar Miss F'raishy git de notion 'bout dat chile a-faverin' er de Wornums, kaze she de ve'y spit en image er ole Miss, en ole Miss wuz a full-blood Bushrod. De Bushrods is de fambly what I cum fum myse'f, kaze w'en ole Miss marry Marster, my mammy fell ter her, en w'en I got big 'nuff, dey tuck me in de house fer ter wait on de table en do er'n's, en dar I bin twel freedom come out. She 'uz mighty highstrung, ole Miss wuz, yit I sees folks dese days put on mo' a'rs dan w'at ole Miss ever is. I ain't 'sputin' but w'at she hilt 'er head high, en I year ma mammy say dat all the Bushrods in Ferginny done zactly dat a way.

"High-strung yer, headstrong yander," continued Mingo, closing one eye, and gazing at the sun with a confidential air. "Ef it hadn't er bin fer de high-strungity-head-strongityness er de Bushrod blood, Miss Deely wouldn't 'a' never runned off wid Clay Bivins in de roun' worril, dough he 'uz des one er de nicest w'ite mens w'at you 'mos' ever laid yo' eyes on. Soon ez she done dat, wud went 'roun' fum de big house dat de nigger w'at call Miss Deely name on dat plantation would be clap on de cote-house block, en ole Miss she shot 'erse'f up, she did, en arter dat mighty few folks got a glimpse un 'er, 'ceppin' hit 'uz some er de kin, en bless yo' soul, *dey* hatter look mighty prim w'en dey come whar she wuz. Ole Marster he ain't say nothin', but he tuck a fresh grip on de jimmy-john, en it got so dat, go whar you would, dey wa'n't no mo' lonesomer place on de face er de yeth dan dat Wornum plantation, en hit look like ruination done sot in. En den, on top er dat, yer come de war, en Clay Bivins he went off en got kilt, en den freedom come out, en des 'bout dat time Miss Deely she tuck 'n' die.

"I 'clar' ter gracious," exclaimed Mingo, closing his eyes and frowning heavily, "we'n I looks back over my shoulder at dem times, hit seem like it mighty funny dat any un us pull thoo. Some did en some didn't, en dem w'at did, dey look like deyer mighty fergitful. W'en de smash come, ole Marster he call us niggers up, he did, an 'low dat we 'uz all free. Some er de boys 'low dat dey wuz a-gwineter see ef dey wuz free sho' nuff, en wid dat dey put out fer town, en some say ef dey wuz free dey wuz free ter stay. Some talk one way en some talk 'n'er. I let you know I kep' my mouf shot, yit my min' 'uz brim-ful er trouble.

"Bimeby soon one mornin' I make a break. I wrop up my little han'ful er duds in a hankcher, en I tie de hankcher on my walkin'-cane, en I put out

226

arter de army. I walk en I walk, en 'bout nine dat night I come ter Ingram Ferry. De flat wuz on t'er side er de river, en de man w'at run it look like he gone off some'r's. I holler en I whoop, en I whoop en I holler, but ef dey wuz any man 'roun', he wuz hidin' out fum me. Arter so long I got tired er whoopin' en hollerin', en I went ter de nighest house en borrer'd a chunk, en built me a fier by de side er de road, en I set dar en nod twel I git sleepy, en den I pull my blanket 'cross my head en quile up—en when I do dat, it's good-by, Mingo!

"Boss," said Mingo, after a little pause, "you don't b'leeve in no ghos'es en ha'nts en sperrits, does you?"

An apparently irrelevant inquiry, suddenly put, is sometimes confusing, and I fear I did not succeed in convincing Mingo of my unbelief.

"Some does en some don't," he continued, "but ez fer me, you kin des put me sorter 'twix' en 'tween. Dey mout be ghos'es en den ag'in dey moutent. Ole nigger like me ain't got no bizness takin' sides, en dat w'at make I say w'at I does. I ain't mo'n kivver my head wid dat blanket en shot my eyes, 'fo' I year somebody a-callin' un me. Fus' hit soun' way off yander.

" 'Mingo!—O Mingo!' en den hit got nigher—'Mingo!—O Mingo!'

"I ain't 'spon' ter dat, but I lay dar, I did, en I say ter myse'f,

" 'Bless gracious! de man on t'er side done come; but how in de name er goodness is he know Mingo?'

"I lay dar, en I study en I lissen, en I lissen en I study; en den I doze off like, en fus' news I know yer come de call,

" Mingo!—O Mingo!'

"Hit soun' nigher, yit hit seem like it come fum a mighty fur ways, en den wiles I wundin' en studyin', yer she come mo' plainer dan befo',

" 'O Mingo!'

"I snatch de blanket off'n my head, en sot up en lissen, I did, en den I make answer,

" 'Who dat callin' Mingo 'way out yer?'

"I lissen en I lissen, but nobody ain't callin'. I year de water sneakin' 'long under de bank, en I year de win' squeezin' en shufflin' 'long thoo de trees, en I year de squinch-owl shiver'n' like he cole, but I ain' year no callin'. Dis make me feel sorter jubous like, but I lay down en wrop up my head.

"I ain't bin dar long 'fo' bimeby yer come de call, en it soun' right at me. Hit rise en it fall, en de wud wuz,

" 'Mingo!—O Mingo! Whar my little baby? My little baby, Mingo! Whar my little baby?'

"En den, boss, hit seem like I year sump'n like a 'oman cryin' in de dark like 'er heart gwineter break. You kin laff ef you mineter, but I ain't dast ter take dat blanket off'n my head, kaze I know my young mistiss done come back, en mo'n dat, I know she uz stannin' dar right over me.

"Tooby sho', I wuz skeer'd; but I wa'n't so skeer'd dat I dunner w'at she mean, en I des broke inter de bigges' kinder boo-hoo, en I say, sez I,

" 'Make yo' peace, Miss Deely! make yo' peace, honey! kaze I gwine right back ter dat baby ef de Lord spar' me. I gwine back, Miss Deely! I gwine back!'

"Bless yo' soul, boss, right den en dar I know'd w'at bin a-pester'n' un me, kaze des time I make up my min' fer ter come back ter dat baby, hit look like I see my way mo' cle'r dan w'at it bin befo'. Arter dat I lay dar, I did, en I lissen en I lissen, but I ain't year no mo' callin' en no mo' cryin'; en bimeby I tuck de blanket fum off'n my head, en lo en beholes, de stars done fade out, en day done come, en dey wa'n't no fuss nowhars. De squinch-owl done hush, en de win' done gone, en it look like de water done stop sneakin' en crawlin' und' de bank.

"I riz up, I did, en shuck de stiffness out'n my bones, en I look 'way 'cross de river ter de top er de hill whar de road lead. I look en I say, sez I,

" 'Maybe you leads ter freedom, but, bless God! I gwine back.'

"Des 'bout dat time I see de fe'ymun come down ter de flat en onloose de chain, en make ez he wuz comin' 'cross arter me. Wid dat I raise up my hat en tip 'im a bow, en dat's de las' I seed un 'im.

"I come back, I did," continued Mingo, reflectively, "en yer I is, en yer I bin; en I ain't come none too soon, en I ain't stay none too close, n'er, kaze I dunner w'at mout er happin. Miss F'raishy been mighty good, too, sho'. She ain't useter niggers like some w'ite folks, en she can't git 'long wid um, but she puts up wid me mighty well. I tuck holt er de little piece er groun' w'at she had, en by de he'p er de Lord we bin gittin' on better dan lots er folks. It bin nip en tuck, but ole tuck come out ahead, en it done got so now dat Miss F'raishy kin put by some er de cotton money fer ter give de little gal a chance w'en she git bigger. 'T won't b'ar tellin' how smart dat chile is. She got Miss Deely peanner, en, little ez she is, she kin pick mos' all de chunes w'at 'er mammy useter pick. She sets at de peanner by de hour, en whar she larnt it I be bless ef *I* kin tell you,—dat I can't!"

The little girl had grown tired of the services in the church, and ran out just as the old man had put my horse to the buggy. Mingo knew a shorter road to Rockville than that by which I had come, and, taking the child by the hand, he walked on ahead to show me the way. In a little while we came to the brow of a hill, and here I bade the old man and his charge good-by, and the two stood watching me as I drove away. Presently a cloud of dust rose between us, and I saw them no more; but I brought away a very pretty picture in my mind,—Mingo with his hat raised in farewell, the sunshine falling gently upon his gray hairs, and the little girl clinging to his hand and daintily throwing kisses after me.

Selected Bibliography

COULTER, E. Merton. *Georgia: A Short History*. Chapel Hill: Univ. of North Carolina Press, 1960.

HARRIS, Joel Chandler. *Balaam and His Master and Other Sketches and Stories*. Boston and New York: Houghton Mifflin and Company, 1891.

———. *The Bishop and the Boogerman*. New York: Doubleday, Page and Company, 1909.

———. *The Chronicles of Aunt Minervy Ann*. New York: Charles Scribner's Sons, 1899.

———. *Daddy Jake the Runaway and Short Stories Told After Dark*. New York: The Century Company, 1889.

———. *Free Joe and Other Georgian Sketches*. New York: Charles Scribner's Sons, 1887.

———. *Gabriel Tolliver: A Story of Reconstruction*. New York: McClure, Phillips and Company, 1902.

———. "Literature in the South," *Atlanta Constitution*, 30 November 1879, p. 2, cols. 2–3.

———. *Little Mr. Thimblefinger and His Queer Country: What the Children Saw and Heard There*. Boston and New York: Houghton Mifflin and Company, 1894.

———. *The Making of a Statesman and Other Stories*. New York: McClure, Phillips and Company, 1902.

———. *Mingo and Other Sketches in Black and White*. Boston: Ticknor and Company, 1884.

———. *On the Wing of Occasions*. New York: Doubleday, Page and Company, 1900.

———. "Provinciality in Literature—A Defense of Boston," *Atlanta Constitution,* 29 January 1880, p. 2, cols. 2–3.

———. *Qua: A Romance of the Revolution,* ed. Thomas H. English. Emory University Publications, Sources and Reprints, Ser. 3. Atlanta: Emory University, 1948.

———. *The Shadow Between His Shoulder-Blades.* Boston: Small, Maynard and Company, 1909.

———. *Sister Jane: Her Friends and Acquaintances.* Boston and New York: Houghton Mifflin and Company, 1896.

———. *Stories of Georgia.* New York: American Book Company, 1896.

———. *Tales of the Home Folks in Peace and War.* Boston and New York: Houghton Mifflin and Company, 1898.

JONES, LeRoi. *Blues People: Negro Music in White America.* New York: William Morrow and Company, 1963.

John Tumlin has taught English at New Mexico State University, Emory University, and Southern Technical Institute. These stories have been selected from first editions of Joel Chandler Harris volumes at the Emory library: *Mingo and Other Sketches in Black and White* (1884), *Free Joe and Other Georgian Sketches* (1887), *Daddy Jake the Runaway* (1889), *Balaam and His Master and Other Sketches and Stories* (1891), *Tales of the Home Folks in Peace and War* (1898), *The Chronicles of Aunt Minervy Ann* (1899), and *On the Wing of Occasions* (1900). This book was planned and produced by The Beehive Press, which publishes books about Georgia and the South. Its pressmark, which appears above and pictures bees busy at their hive, expresses the enthusiasm of this work; the source of the pressmark—an early colonial pamphlet entitled *An Impartial Enquiry into the State and Utility of the Province of Georgia* (London, 1741)—suggests a spirit of free intellectual endeavor. This book was printed at The Stinehour Press, Lunenburg, Vermont.

THE BEEHIVE PRESS
321 Barnard Street
Savannah · Georgia 31401